About the

USA Today bestselling author **Anderson** writes emotional contemporary romance full of sparkling banter, sizzling heat and uplifting endings – perfect for readers who love to escape with empowered heroines and arrogant alphas who are too sexy for their own good. When not writing you'll find her wrangling her four children, three cats, two goldish and one dog...and snuggled in a heap on the sofa with her husband at the end of the day. Follow her at: natalie-anderson.com

Pippa Roscoe lives in Norfolk near her family and makes daily promises that this is the day she will leave the computer and take a long walk in the countryside. She can't remember a time when she wasn't dreaming of gorgeous alpha males and misunderstood heroines. Totally her mother's fault of course – she gave Pippa her first romance at the age of seven! She is inconceivably happy that she gets to share those daydreams with you! Find out more at: @PippaRoscoe, pipparoscoe.com

Abby Green spent her teens reading Mills & Boon romances. She then spent many years working in the Film and TV industry as an Assistant Director. One day while standing outside an actor's trailer in the rain, she thought: there has to be more than this. So she sent off a partial to Mills & Boon. After many rewrites, they accepted her first book and an author was born. She lives in Dublin, Ireland and you can find out more here: abby-green.com

European Escapes

July 2023
Madrid

August 2023
Sicily

September 2023
Sweden

January 2024
Paris

February 2024
Prague

March 2024
Athens

April 2024
London

May 2024
Berlin

European Escapes: Athens

NATALIE ANDERSON

PIPPA ROSCOE

ABBY GREEN

MILLS & BOON

First Published in Great Britain 2024
by Mills & Boon, an imprint of HarperCollins*Publishers* Ltd,
1 London Bridge Street, London, SE1 9GF

www.harpercollins.co.uk

HarperCollins*Publishers*
Macken House, 39/40 Mayor Street Upper,
Dublin 1, D01 C9W8, Ireland

ISBN: 978-0-263-32308-5

This book contains FSC™ certified paper and other controlled sources to ensure responsible forest management.

For more information visit: www.harpercollins.co.uk/green

Printed and Bound in the UK using 100% Renewable Electricity
at CPI Group (UK) Ltd, Croydon, CR0 4YY

THE GREEK'S ONE-NIGHT HEIR

NATALIE ANDERSON

For Evelyn the Awesome,

I could say it was because you asked so nicely,
but really it's because you're amazing.

CHAPTER ONE

'YOU SHOULD BE resting, not worrying about me.' Theo Savas paced across the theatre foyer, working to keep his concern inaudible. He'd lived with his grandfather since he was ten and this was the first time in the last twenty years the old man had directly referenced something so personal. Revoking this rule wasn't just unsettling, it was unsafe. 'You've just come through a major operation—'

'And that's given me the opportunity to think. It's time, Theodoros. Your birthday is only a few weeks away.'

The lights above Theo flickered, signalling it was time for guests to take their seats, but he couldn't end this call without steering Dimitri back to unconcerned calm.

'Are you suggesting I'm getting old?' His joke was weak but he'd try anything to defuse his grandfather's escalating anxiety. Except anxiety was infectious and the vibes coming through the phone were making Theo's own muscles tense. That was in addition to the latent strain of the actual topic. 'There's plenty of time—'

'At this rate I'll never meet my great-grandchildren—'

'You're not about to die,' Theo interrupted. He'd ensured Dimitri had been seen by the best specialists and they'd insisted that with quality rest Dimitri should recover well. 'You've years left in you.'

'I'm serious. You need to settle down…'

'And I will,' Theo reassured him softly and rolled his shoulders.

He ached to resist Dimitri's attempt to add yet another burden of responsibility, yet he couldn't brush him off.

Distantly he watched the ushers guide the last arriving theatregoers towards the doors. He needed to move if he was going to make it in there. He stepped forward but a whirlwind of a woman swept in front of him, cutting him off. The tall, slender tornado didn't stop to say sorry, indeed she didn't even see him screech to a halt to stop himself smacking into her. She just kept searching her cavernous handbag while racing towards the usher.

'How about Eleni Doukas? She's beautiful.'

Theo inwardly shuddered. Was Dimitri suggesting a woman for him?

'Don't you like very beautiful women?' Dimitri added.

Theo bit back a grimace. Sure, he liked women—beauty being only one of their attractions. But most women he met wanted vastly more than what he was prepared to give.

'Or Angelica.' His grandfather offered another contender for his consideration. 'She would be suitable. You've not seen her in years.'

Theo had reasons for that. Ironically they were the exact reasons his grandfather would probably welcome. Cultured, well-educated, perfectly connected Angelica had made it clear she'd accept marriage and produce four children while turning a blind eye to extra-marital affairs. But Theo would never be unfaithful and he'd never accept infidelity from his wife either. He knew too well the blisters, welts and scars that such affairs inflicted. The fact was that while Angelica had offered herself as the ultimate convenient wife, while it was the sort of arrangement Theo ought to accept, and while it was certainly what those in his milieu expected him to accept, the prospect of any matrimonial arrangement at all appalled him.

But Dimitri didn't need to know that.

'It has been a while…' Theo murmured, agreeing in order to soothe.

His gaze locked on the scene unfolding outside the theatre door. The blind-haste brunette was still rummaging in her bag. Unlike most of the women present, she wasn't wearing a shimmering gown. Instead black slim trousers encased her long, long legs. He focused on her feet and saw black flats—so, unaided by towering heels, that striking height was all her own? Interest rippled through him like the faintest breeze bringing relief on a hot summer's noon. She wore a black wool cardigan beneath which a grey blouse was buttoned to the neck. The dull combination gave nothing away of her figure, other than that she was slender. But it was her expression that pushed him closer.

She was still searching through her bag while casting desperate glances at the unmoved usher and as Theo neared he heard her talking endlessly in a hushed, frantic whisper. Was she trying to buy time? Faking her way in? She was doing a good job because she tugged something even in Theo's safely entombed heart. Her eyes glimmered with suspicious brightness and her cheeks paled as the doors further along from hers were shut.

'If not Angelica—'

'Arrange it,' Theo decisively interrupted Dimitri. The thought of some possible bride parade was crazy, but he'd consent just to give Dimitri something to look forward to.

He walked towards the pair standing at the last open door to the theatre. The woman had whitened beyond pale and interesting. Any more loss of blood and she'd faint. The honest entreaty in her expression lanced through him. Not faking. Mortified.

'Introduce me to your three top picks,' he authorised his grandfather.

'You're serious?' Dimitri wheezed.

'Yes.' Theo sighed, serious about meeting them, but not about marrying any. 'You're tired and worrying.' And the old man was bored with being bedridden. At the very least this would give him something satisfactory to think about for the rest of the evening. 'Make the arrangements.'

If it would settle the old man's pulse, then he'd handle a couple of weekends being polite to houseguests. The nurse had warned his grandfather might experience a period of feeling low—apparently it sometimes followed lifesaving surgery. Theo would do almost anything to lift his spirits.

'I'm flying home first thing so I'll see you tomorrow afternoon,' he said. 'We'll talk more about it then, I promise. I need to work now.'

'Good, Theodoros,' his grandfather muttered huskily. 'Thank you.'

Theo paused, an arrow of discomfort silencing him. Usually Dimitri was all steel—unblemished and immoveable, capably tolerating the burning heat of business, but today, in revealing his wishes for Theo to find a wife? Dimitri discussing *any* kind of relationship rang Theo's warning bell, reminding him that Dimitri was more vulnerable than he appeared. And his grandfather didn't need to thank him, Theo was the one who owed. Everything.

'It's all right.' He cleared his own husky throat. 'Sleep well.'

He ended the call and walked the last few paces of the foyer. As the main financial backer for this ballet production, he'd been given the best seat in the house. Which, if he wasn't mistaken, he'd just forfeited because the usher had closed the door with brutal finality.

If he'd walked a little faster, he might've made it but he was still distracted by that trouble in the form of a tall brunette. And he badly needed a moment of distraction.

'I'm so sorry.' She pleaded with the usher as she swept back behind her ear a tendril that had loosened from the long braid that hung down her back. Her eyes were very large and very worried and she desperately ransacked her bag yet again. 'I had it, I promise I had it—'

'I'm sorry, ma'am.' The usher stood, an impenetrable force, in front of the shut door. 'But without your ticket...'

Leggy Brunette's slender shoulders slumped. 'Yes, of course. It's just that...it was in here.' She searched her trouser pockets, then glanced around the floor as if somehow her ticket would materialise. 'I promise I had it…'

'Unfortunately it's too late.' The usher brusquely ended the conversation.

Hunching as if to hide, Leggy Brunette turned away, the curve of her pretty mouth dropping.

'Problem?' Theo stepped sideways, into her path.

She glanced up at him absently, then stopped dead. Her eyes widened and her second glance turned into a shocked stare. Theo happily stared back.

Her eyes were more than blue, they had a hint of pale purple, and he took another step closer on auto. 'You couldn't find your ticket?'

She shook her head and kept staring.

Theo couldn't hold back a small smile. Apparently she couldn't find her voice either. He was used to getting a reaction from women, but rendering one speechless?

At least some colour was flooding back into her face. But suddenly she swallowed and turned away. He couldn't resist following. She stopped at the nearest table and, amused, he watched as yet again she fruitlessly searched her bag. He caught a glimpse of something bulky in its depths, surely not a blanket?

'You know, they'll never let anyone in late,' he said softly to let her down gently. 'They won't interrupt the performance once it's begun.'

She dropped her hands and darted another glance at him. 'I know.' Her voice was adorably husky with her English accent soft and clear. 'It's just that I *had* it.'

And she *really* wanted to watch the ballet? Her ticket loss was definitely genuine. Her sharp disappointment nicked his skin and the absurd desire to see her smile slid into his blood.

'Oh, Mr Savas.' The theatre usher suddenly appeared

at his side, looking flustered. 'I can sneak you in if you'd like to follow me quickly…'

For a split second his eyes met those lavender-blues and he watched the consternation bloom within them.

'I wouldn't want to interrupt the rest of the audience,' he dismissed the usher's invitation smoothly. 'But thank you anyway.'

The usher beat a hasty retreat and Theo faced Leggy Brunette.

'No one gets in late unless they're ridiculously rich?' she muttered, soft reproach in her expression.

Uh… Yeah. 'I have a spare ticket you can use for the second half,' he murmured impulsively.

She looked away again as if the sight of him somehow hurt her unusual eyes. 'Um…' She fiddled with the strap of her insanely huge bag. 'That's really kind of you, but I couldn't.'

'Why not?' he asked. He wanted her to say yes and Theo was pretty used to getting what he wanted these days. 'It's a spare ticket,' he reiterated. 'You can still see the entire second half.'

Her hand twisted in the strap while more colour rose in her cheeks. He knew she was tempted, but wary.

'There's no trick,' he reassured softly. 'Just a ticket.'

She drew her lower lip between her teeth and bit down on it. 'Really?'

'Yes, really.' He chuckled. People didn't usually dilly-dally about taking things from him. 'It's not a big deal.'

That colour swarmed more deeply and she quickly glanced past him. 'You…don't have a date you're here with?'

Was *that* the reason for her incredulous expression? He suppressed another smile. 'No. Do you?'

'No.' She shook her head quickly.

Satisfaction surged with surprising force. 'Then I guess it's meant to be, right?'

'I…' She paused. 'Right.'

'And now we might as well have a drink while we wait, don't you think?' He nodded towards the gleaming theatre bar, his body thrumming with anticipation.

She turned to face him, her lavender eyes gazed directly into his and her chin lifted with a little pride. 'May I get you a drink, to say thank you?'

For a second Theo was bereft of speech. The women he dated never offered to pay. They knew him, knew how wealthy he was and they were happy to meld into his lifestyle. But his brunette in distress had no idea who he was and apparently had no desire to just take whatever she could from him.

'Please,' she added. 'I wouldn't want to feel indebted to you.'

Indebted by a mere ballet ticket? That thread of sensual awareness tightened. Was she worried he'd ask her to pay him back in some nefarious way? Well, she could remain calm, Theo had never needed to coerce a woman in his life. He might have money, but he wasn't spoiled and he'd never presume.

'Okay,' he said equably, but then couldn't resist teasing her prim dignity. 'But are you sure you have your wallet on you? You wouldn't want to make offers you can't fulfil.'

'Very funny.' Sparks lit her lavender eyes, but then her expression wrinkled. 'Damn it, you've made me need to check now.' She rummaged in her bag again—were those chopsticks in there? But then she extracted a small coin purse with a flourish. No sleek leather wallet filled with elite credit cards for her.

'I knew I had it,' she said victoriously. 'But I swear I had the ticket too.' She groaned ruefully. 'What an idiot.' A sudden little giggle bubbled out.

To his astonishment, his whole world narrowed until he saw only her—sparkling eyes and pretty lips and delight—

and he found himself smiling back at her. Frankly it was the most he'd smiled in months.

'How about you go ahead and order?' he suggested huskily. 'I need a second to arrange the seat with the staff.'

'What would you like to drink?'

'You choose.' He shrugged. 'I'll have whatever you're having.'

'Are you sure you want to risk that?' she asked, her expression wrinkled again.

'Why?' He was surprised into another smile. 'Now I'm intrigued. Quick, go decide for the both of us.'

He couldn't resist watching her walk towards the bar. He really was intrigued—she was a contrary mix of shy and awkward and assured. Tall, slender, feminine and acutely refreshing. Just the tonic given the last two months of stress, isolation and uncertainty. But she was definitely cautious and perhaps she was right to be, given his inner temptation was to skip the ballet altogether and carry her back to his bed for the night. He'd worship those long limbs and work very hard to put a smile on her pillowy pout…

So not appropriate. Or normal. Not for him. He'd never followed in the footsteps of his playboy father and he never wanted to. He shook off that outrageous whisper of sin and strode towards the theatre staff. One drink, then it was back to duty.

When he walked back to the bar she was sitting all alone with two tall glasses in front of her and quite obviously trying not to appear self-conscious.

He placed the ticket on the bar beside the two drinks and lifted one. 'All arranged.'

He needed the drink. But on swallowing he quickly stifled his immediate grimace and subsequent smile. This sour fiery stuff wasn't quite the champagne he'd been expecting. At first glance he'd guessed she'd be a sweet romantic—sensitivity and shy awkwardness were obvious in her eyes.

But then she came out with a line of soft-spoken sarcasm, a penchant for rocket fuel as an aperitif and a self-deprecating giggle that stole a rare smile from him.

'Thanks,' she said to him earnestly. 'That's so kind of you.'

Oddly he didn't want her to think he was *kind.* He wanted a bit more of a reaction than that. He wanted… he paused to battle the full force of what he wanted…but, yeah, it was pretty much everything he shouldn't want. It was everything illicit.

Leah Turner sipped her drink, stifling the urge to surreptitiously pinch herself. This kind of thing *never* happened to her. Somehow the most gorgeous guy had intercepted her during her most humiliating moment and gallantly turned her disappointment into something else altogether. And, man, he was gorgeous. Tall, lean, muscular, powerful, he exuded a sensual magnetism that was beyond normal. *She'd* most certainly never felt sexual attraction from one look. He was so dazzling it was hard to think and she wasn't sure what she was more rapt about—not missing the entire ballet, or stealing a few minutes of this man's time.

Because those eyes of his? Green eyes were usually a mix of colours—green mixed with blue or hazel, or bronze. But his were pure forest green. So rare, so startling, she had to constantly tell herself not to stare at him. She tried to stare at her glass instead, but only lasted a mere second before lapsing and gawping at him again. 'You're important around here?'

'No.'

She didn't believe him. She'd watched him speak with the theatre manager and that woman had been all deferential smiles and soothing words. He held more than charm. He held power. Hell, he'd made Leah feel as if she'd done *him* a favour by saying yes to taking the ticket.

He smiled and there was something a little dangerous in it. 'Why are you here alone?'

His accent curled her toes and made her an appalling cliché. She had no idea what the mix was, but it melted her like a lonely snowflake on a sunny windowsill.

'I'm not.' She lifted her chin. 'My friend is already here, but she's onstage.'

'She's a dancer?'

'Yes. She sent me the ticket but I was running late because I'd stopped to help Maeve with something.'

'Maeve?'

'One of the residents at the care home I work at. She's lovely and we bond over—' Leah paused, realising she was prattling. 'Over stuff,' she finished. He didn't need to know about her new job and the people she'd already fallen for. 'Why were you running late?'

'I was on a call.'

'Girlfriend problems?' she guessed, cheekily personal but it just had to be the case. 'Is that why you're alone? Did she stand you up?'

His eyebrows lifted in a quizzical look.

'What—you're never stood up?' she asked before thinking, *of course, he wasn't.*

'No girlfriend.' That gorgeous smile crept across his face as if he were pleased to be able to correct her. '*That's* the real problem. According to my grandfather anyway.'

'You were talking to your *grandfather*?' She was surprised. 'He wants you to settle down?'

He nodded mock seriously. 'And provide heirs to the family fortune.'

For certain there *was* a family fortune. His suit was so beautifully fitting it had to be tailor-made and the gleaming watch on his wrist screamed luxury style. 'You don't want to do that?'

'Not yet,' he said, obviously and unashamedly repelled by the idea.

'Yet?' she queried doubtfully because that wicked light in his eyes made her laugh. There was too much fun to be had first, clearly. How could he not be a playboy? All the women who'd want him, it'd be too easy. But she played along. 'Because you have too much to do? Too busy with work? Too many other options?'

'None of the above.' He chose another answer altogether. 'Hence no date to the ballet…'

'I don't believe you're out of options,' she said. 'You've *chosen* not to bring a date.' She cocked her head. 'Because you don't want to settle down at all?'

He met her gaze with knowing amusement.

She shook her head sadly. 'Why do I get the feeling your poor grandfather is going to be waiting a while…'

He rolled his shoulders and his amusement faded as something far more serious flickered in his eyes. 'He's been unwell—this is preying on him. Hence the lecture.'

Leah watched him blink away that sliver of pain. That he'd not ended the call soon enough to get into the theatre showed he had patience and loyalty and respect for his relative.

'Family expectations can be hard,' she offered with soft honesty. 'I'm an eternal disappointment to mine.'

He looked back into her eyes and they were held for a moment—silent scrutiny, total awareness—and she was struck by the conviction there was much more buried beneath his perfect surface.

'I don't believe you'd ever be a disappointment,' he finally muttered—so low and so serious that she couldn't smile and shake it off.

Instead a heated flush swept over her skin and she swallowed back the hard lump that had formed in her throat. 'Well, you'd be wrong.'

He gazed at her for another moment of that unspoken communication—the deeply guarded truth, not the superficial denial that there was anything wrong.

Then he blinked and his lips twitched. 'Your family want you to marry too?'

Laughter burst out, breaking that intensity. She shook her head.

'Quite right, it's a dreadful idea,' he teased.

'No,' she said firmly. 'It isn't—'

'You're wrong.' He saluted her with his drink again. 'All marriages end up miserable.'

'Wow…is that what happened to you?'

He almost choked on his drink and then laughed. 'Not married. Never married. Never will marry.'

Yes, the only ring in his world was the ring of finality.

'Because…' She inhaled deeply as she studied him thoughtfully. 'Parents?'

He flashed a look at her—pure pain, pure denial, pure promise of retribution.

'Yeah,' she murmured meekly. 'Poor grandfather.'

'You think I'm that predictable.' He took another sip.

'I think that everyone feels pain, sometimes,' she said. 'And often the people who inflict the most pain are the people we're meant to be closest to.'

'I'm not close to them,' he said softly, then forced another smile. 'So, tell me about your dancer friend. Is it her debut?'

'No, it's just that I've only recently moved to London so I haven't been able to see her perform until tonight.' She shifted guiltily on her chair as she remembered. 'And now I've missed her.'

'Only the first half. And she doesn't need to know you've missed that.'

'You think I should lie to her?'

He smiled at her as if she were a timid little lamb. 'You're omitting a little of the truth. That's not a lie.'

'Of course it's a lie,' she corrected him flatly. 'It's not completely honest.'

'And we should always be completely honest?' He shook his head and laughed openly.

'You think I'm wrong?'

'Naïve, perhaps.' He leaned closer. 'Sometimes telling the truth serves no purpose. When it can only hurt the person who has to hear it, why would you?' He broke off with a sharp breath.

She had the feeling he wasn't thinking of her little 'missing the first half' mistake any more.

'So you'd omit the truth, or tell a lie, to protect someone?' she asked.

'Of course.'

He said it with such quiet certainty, she knew he had and did. She thought of the grandfather all over again and wondered what it was he protected him from.

That quizzical look lit his eyes again. 'What would hurt your friend more? Knowing you missed the first half, or never knowing you missed it?'

'If she ever found out I *lied*, that would hurt her the most. But if I tell her the truth, she'll just laugh at me.'

He stilled, his gaze keen on her. 'And that doesn't hurt you?'

She shrugged. 'My crime isn't that critical and I'm already laughing at myself.' She eyed him. 'We can laugh together. Sharing pain takes some of the sting out of it, doesn't it?'

'Not always.'

'Hmmm.' She pondered it. 'The problem is, one omission inevitably leads to more lies—she'll ask what I thought of something in the first half and I'd have to lie then.'

'Or you could just not talk about it at all.'

She laughed. 'So your solution is to just bury everything and live in total denial? Pretend nothing bad ever happened?' She leaned closer. 'It'll only come back to haunt you.'

'Don't tell me you believe in ghosts.'

'Well, I believe some things—feelings mostly—can't stay buried. They rise like zombies and eat your brain to the point where you can't think clearly any more.' It happened to her frequently.

'So you always act on your emotions?' he queried. 'Act on gut feelings rather than with rational thought?'

She sighed. 'I'm human. I try to be a good one and not hurt others.'

'So honesty it is?'

'Ideally, yes.'

'Ideally.' He sent her an indulgent smile. 'So how, ideally, will your friend react?'

'I know she'll laugh. It's not the first time I've messed up.'

'You've known her a while?'

'We grew up in the same town and were in ballet class together.'

'But you don't dance any more?'

'My passion outweighed my talent.'

'Surely passion's the most important ingredient?' His eyes gleamed. 'Talent without passion is nothing. Skills can be learned, passion can't.'

'Well, that may be so, but I'm already taller than average.' She shrugged, long skilled at masking her self-consciousness about it. 'Put me in pointe shoes and I tower over most men.'

It wasn't the only reason she'd quit, but he didn't need to know anything more about her constant inability to meet her parents' expectations.

'Is that why you wear flat shoes now? So you're not taller than your men?'

Her *men*? She choked back a laugh at the thought. 'I

wear them because they're comfortable. I dress to please myself, not some man.'

He grinned appreciatively. 'Sure. But you're not taller than me. You could wear high heels when we go out.'

'I'm not going out with you.'

'Aren't we out right now?' he teased.

She shook her head. 'By accident, not design.'

'So wouldn't you go out with me if I asked?'

'Would you ask?'

That smile hovered around his mouth and he took another sip. 'Perhaps it's better if I omit to answer—the truth might terrify you. It mildly terrifies me.' His gaze clung to her lips and radiated a flash of heat that rippled over her. 'What is it you like about ballet? The costumes? Because it's romantic?'

'There's nothing romantic about ballet,' she scoffed, covering that moment of awareness. 'It's ruthless.'

'You mean bloody blisters and sprained muscles?'

'I mean more than that. Did you know in this ballet the girl goes mad and dies of a broken heart because the man she loved *lied* to her,' she said with a pointed look. 'Because he *omits* to tell her he's betrothed to another woman. I don't think that's *romantic*.'

He chuckled but then leaned forward to tease. 'It was the prospect of marriage, see? It caused all the problems.'

She rolled her eyes even as she laughed. Just then theatre doors opened and the audience spilled out, shattering the sense of intimacy that had built between them. Somehow that time had sped by and she was sorry it had gone so quickly.

'It's probably time to take your seat.' He gestured behind her. 'You don't want to leave it too late…'

'Okay.' But the flutters in her stomach wouldn't cease. That she was going to spend the rest of the evening with him? Even though she knew he was just amusing himself, it was still unbelievable.

Leah followed the waiting usher, her pulse quickening as the woman guided her to the best seat in the theatre. Overcome with appreciation she turned to thank him, but he wasn't with them. Somehow he'd disappeared in the crowd. Too late she realised the truth. He wasn't sitting with her because it wasn't a *spare* ticket he'd given her. It was his own.

Disappointment hit as that unusual bubble of happiness and hope popped. She hadn't had the chance to thank him or even say goodbye. Instinctively she knew she wasn't going to see him again. Who said chivalry was dead?

But to think that for a second she'd thought he'd actually been attracted to her. She was mortified at the memory and glad he'd now gone, given he'd clearly just been filling in time.

As the lights dimmed it took a few minutes for her to appreciate the ballet but then Zoe appeared onstage and she was swamped with pleasure and pride for her friend.

After the final curtain call Leah walked to the artists' entrance at the back of the theatre to meet her and give her friend the gift she'd made. Her lost ticket confession resulted in them both giggling and then Zoe insisted Leah accompany her to the opening night company party to make it up to her. Secretly she wanted to escape home alone so she could remember her handsome stranger. Instead she smiled and said yes, ruefully thinking of him again as she omitted honesty to save her own embarrassment.

Theo Savas stalked out of the theatre, determined to resist the tempting whisper telling him to seek out that slender brunette with the hopelessly soft eyes. He forced himself to make the mandatory appearance at the ballet's opening night celebration. He couldn't skip it, given the party was at the hotel he was staying in. But he could escape early and have some space and privacy before his early flight home to Athens. He had little desire to socialise beyond the cursory showing of his face.

His mind teased, replaying the light conversation he'd had with the tall, ticketless sylph. He'd watched her from the distance during the ballet, happy in the back-row seat off to the side management had found for him. She'd sat motionless through the performance, apparently entranced, and she'd applauded energetically. But he'd seen a hint of sadness on her mouth when she'd turned to leave. Theo had pressed back into the crowd as competing instincts had warred within him. He had affairs only rarely—always discreet, always without strings, always unencumbered by emotion or the weight of baggage. There were no *hearts* involved in his dalliances. Physical pleasure was just a freely given gift—very simple, very satisfying. The suggestion of anything more was not. He'd seen the hurt it caused when it mattered too much.

And he didn't think the leggy brunette was the no-strings, no-hearts type.

As he walked into the reception room the nearest group of women turned to stare, then smile. One peeled off and walked over.

'You're Theo Savas.'

'I am.'

Invitation shone in the pretty dancer's eyes but he turned away from it as he invariably did. Yet he still couldn't shake the recollection of that brunette's lavender-blue gaze or the awkward interest that had shone from it. Regret curled.

'I'm—'

'I'm sorry,' he interrupted the woman briefly. 'I can't stop to chat.'

He'd check in with the company director and get out of here. But as he turned to seek out the director he spotted a tall figure on the other side of the room. His second glance morphed into a stare. And he smiled. Every sense sharpened. She was in shadow, but her silhouette was unmistakable. Triumph allowed temptation to burst free. His ticketless damsel must have been invited to the after-party by her dancer friend.

'Hey.' He caught her arm to get her attention in the crowd, barely quelling the impulse to pull her close.

'Oh…' Her pupils dilated as she stared up at him. There was no hiding the sensuality that sparkled in her eyes. 'What are you doing here?'

'I could ask you the same question.' He couldn't drag his hungry gaze from her face. It was as if he'd not seen her in months, not mere minutes. 'Where's your friend?' He didn't really care. All that mattered was that they had a second chance and he wasn't letting her slip away again. Not yet.

She glanced around then pointed to a petite woman animatedly talking to a group of dancers. 'Zoe's over there.' As she watched her that sparkle in her eyes dimmed. 'She's… busy at the moment.'

'She's left you alone.'

'You left me alone too.'

He stilled, silenced by that hint of reproach.

'She's having a good time' she added quickly, failing to mask her awkwardness in the sudden pregnant moment. 'She deserves to.'

'And you don't?'

'I did have a good time. But you gave me *your* ticket.' She looked up at him. 'Why did you do that? You missed the whole thing.'

He could omit a couple of little facts and bask in her gratitude, but he didn't want to lie to her. Not after that oddly intimate little conversation they'd had before the ballet. 'Actually, they gave me another seat, so like you I didn't miss the second half.'

That seat at the very side of the theatre had been perfect, because while it had given him an obstructed view of the stage, it had also given him an angled view of her…though that little fact he *was* going to omit.

'Oh, good. I'm so glad.' A faint wash of colour bloomed over her face. 'It was still very kind of you.'

'Mmm…' He still didn't feel very kind right now. He felt achy. 'It was my pleasure.' He'd enjoyed watching the emotions flit across her face. 'I get to go to the ballet a lot. The theatre, opera, sports fixtures…it comes with my job.'

'You don't enjoy it?'

'Sure. Mostly.' But when he had other issues pressing on his mind, not so much. And right now he had too much on his mind. It had been a miserable few months. He just wanted to forget it all for a while. Temptation beckoned. Maybe his method was standing right in front of him. And maybe, he just couldn't resist.

He held his hand out to her. 'Theo Savas.'

Leah didn't want to keep staring but she couldn't seem to tear her gaze away from him. 'Leah Turner.'

A premonition warned her, but the urge for the slightest touch was irresistible and she put her hand in his. For a second they were locked together in a moment of physical intimacy that felt much more powerful than a mere handshake should.

As she stared into his eyes her thoughts jumbled. He'd just been kind earlier—hadn't expected to see her again, hadn't known she was going to be at this party. His gift had been just that, a simple gift with no strings—just a thoughtful, generous moment between strangers.

But the banked fire in his gaze now? The sizzle shooting up her arm? The electricity short-circuited her brain. She couldn't look away from him. She couldn't release him any more than he could seem to release her.

'I should get going,' she mumbled.

'Why?'

She swallowed. 'I have work tomorrow.'

'So? I have a flight first thing.'

She couldn't help smiling. 'Is it a competition?'

'You tell me.'

She shook her head. 'I'm not a fan of competition.'

'No?' He nodded. 'No one likes losing.'

So true but she doubted he'd ever lost much.

'How about collaboration, then?' He was somehow closer. 'We'd work together to achieve a common goal…'

Her mouth was so dry she had to lick her lips before she could answer. 'And that goal would be?'

His eyes were serious even as his mouth curved into a wicked smile. Intensity beneath the charm. 'The best night of our lives.'

'Wow. Setting a big goal.'

'Always. If you don't aim high…' His smile faded as he studied her. 'I didn't expect to see you again.'

'Are you sorry you have?'

'I was sorry I didn't stay earlier. I was sorry I let you go.'

Her heart trembled. So why had he? She couldn't bring herself to ask. She still couldn't move either. Someone pushed past behind her, jostling her in the throng. He released her hand only to wrap his arm around her shoulder and draw her closer against his side. Just like that the rest of the world faded.

'You want to go somewhere quieter?' he asked.

Leah had never gone 'somewhere quieter' with anyone ever. But she knew what it meant. 'You barely know me.'

'And I'm not going to.' He smiled ruefully. 'I go back to Greece tomorrow.'

He was in town for only the one night. Was he letting her know this would only be a one-time thing? Was she right in thinking there might even be a one time? She opted for diversion so she could process all the signals she was too inexperienced to be certain of. 'You're from Greece? Whereabouts?'

'Athens.' His gaze didn't waver—it was as if he knew she needed a moment to process. 'But I have a holiday home on an island.'

Of course he did. He probably had homes everywhere.

'Have you ever been there?' he asked, seeming to reach for the same delaying diversion she was.

She shook her head.

'No interest?' He looked aghast.

She laughed. 'I'd love to go there one day.'

'Sail around the islands, right?' He smiled as if it was what everybody wanted.

'I'm sure that would be amazing, but I'd really like to go to Delphi.'

'You studied Classics? The Antiquities?'

She shook her head. 'No, it's silly, but one of my favourite books was set in Delphi.'

'What book?'

'You probably haven't read it…'

'I'm actually quite well read—what's the title?'

She shook her head. 'It's an old paperback, you won't know it…' She'd found it in the reception of the doctor's one time and smuggled it home and hidden it from her parents. A romantic suspense wasn't on the prescribed list her parents had drawn up for her.

He smiled, guessing that she didn't want to tell him. 'You'll have to travel there then, to see if it lives up to its literary imagining.'

'I've only just moved to London.' She shrugged. 'Greece might have to wait a while.'

'So you're new to town and I'm just passing through… yet fate has made it so we meet twice in the one night.'

'And you want me to…'

'Yes.' Something smouldered in his eyes. 'You know what I want you to do,' he said. 'I want you to come with me. And yes, I mean exactly what you're thinking.'

Yes, he'd changed. In the theatre, he'd held back for some reason. Now, he'd decided and he wasn't holding back at all.

'You're…not shy.' She bit her lip.

'But you are. Don't be afraid to go for what you want.'

She hovered—not indecisive, but insecure. 'I'm not good at this,' she confessed.

He didn't laugh at her. His expression was both encouraging and strained. He lifted a hand and cupped her jaw, the soft touch silencing her.

'I'm not going to give you a report card, Leah,' he breathed, closer still. 'Anyway, there's no "good", only amazing. And for the record—so as not to omit any important details—I have no intention of either of us being hurt.'

There was a tension within him—a cause of worry or concern. For her?

'Want me to give you an example?' he asked in a husky whisper.

Her pulse thundered. She should pull back and say no. But she didn't want to and her body decided for her. She rose a half-inch on her toes and met his descending mouth.

Who knew a kiss could be so careful? It began as little more than a soft slide of his lips over hers. His fingers weaved into her hair at the nape of her neck as he held her loose but close. But then his other hand lifted to her waist, pulling her against his body, and the pressure of his mouth on hers increased, the intimacy intensified as he teased her with his tongue. With slow, devastating skill he inexorably pulled a deep response. Not just acquiescence and acceptance but action in return. He unsealed a vast yearning within her and something in her soul leapt—reaching for connection, commanding her to slide her hands up his firm chest to his broad shoulders…to *hold* him to her every bit as much as he was holding her.

But he stirred more than the heated blood and the sudden slick restlessness of her hips.

A burst of emotion burned careful right the way down to ruthless. Raw hunger was unleashed within—forced into revealing itself by the increasingly demanding counterpart within him. This wasn't just want, this was *craving.* She arched, opening for him—seeking more with her own touch, her own tongue and hands and press of her body. And he more than let her. His feet spread as he braced to take more of her in his hold and kissed her thoroughly—his strokes designed to soothe and torment at the same time. She knew it was crazy—that it didn't make sense—but there was something more than this delicious, uncontrollable lust between them. And it was this something more that made this undeniable.

She shook, violently trembling from head to foot, as sensation rampaged through her like a river released from a decades-locked dam.

At her shudder he ripped his mouth from hers. 'What do you think?' His breathing was so roughened his speech sounded slightly slurred.

Thought had very little to do with it. She gazed up, relieved he'd not released his hold on her because she felt dizzy. She drank in the light flush on his skin and the glittering depths of his eyes—basking in the possessive focus he bestowed on her. Still pressed tightly against him, she felt not only his physical desire, but his restraint. She knew he'd walk away from her if she wished.

But that other ache welded her to him, that hidden, true, tender need. His reasons were no doubt different from hers, but she felt his loneliness ran as deep. For the first time she was compelled to both give and take of something unequivocally intimate.

Her answer was so simple, so easy. She couldn't let this rare moment go. She couldn't let *him* go.

'I think I'm coming with you.'

CHAPTER TWO

His smile was a blazing mix of triumph and sensual determination and barely hidden relief. She realised he was as delighted and as dazed as she was and somehow that multiplied the myriad want and need and hot mess of yes within her.

'I can't leave without saying goodbye to Zoe,' she muttered.

'Of course.' He escorted her through the crowd, stepping back when they came up to her friend.

'Sorry, Zoe.' Leah caught her attention. 'I'm going to call it a night—'

'Since when do you know Theo Savas?' Zoe interrupted her, managing to screech and whisper at the same time. 'Since when does Theo Savas kiss anyone in public like that?'

'You saw…just then?' Leah's body smoked with embarrassment.

'OMG, yes, go.' Zoe laughed and pulled her into a quick, tight hug. 'You must, just, *go*. Do everything I would and more,' her friend whispered in her ear. 'For heaven's sake, have some fun for once!'

Leah's pulse hammered as Theo firmly grasped her hand and led her through the crowded function room and into the sudden silence of the hotel corridor. She was floating, not walking, right? In the elevator he glanced down at her and smiled but she saw the question in his eyes and tension in his body.

She felt the question too—since when did *she* wander off with a complete stranger? Before tonight she'd never considered it, would never have thought she *would*… Yet he didn't feel like a stranger, more of a kindred spirit—as complicated and careful, those layers of responsibility and obligation hiding other needs and wants. She'd do all she could for someone she cared about; that he did too struck a chord—as if they were vibrating in harmony even though there could be nothing more than this one night between them. And then there was that sheer physical response that she just couldn't release herself from.

She'd never done anything adventurous, nothing reckless or fun either. She'd spent so long trying to please her parents and fit in with their impossible standards and it was past time to have one night just for her. She wanted to share it only with him.

He unlocked the door of his hotel suite and she stepped inside. The drapes didn't cover the tinted windows and the London skyline was like fairy lights. She turned and took in the rich interior—pure luxurious space and decadence. But then Theo stood in the centre of it and the sumptuous background faded away. He was like a sun god—casting everything else in shadow.

She couldn't be the first woman to fall completely beneath his spell but she was quite calm about that. She felt too pleased to have seen him again and realise that he was—amazingly—attracted to her too.

'Do you do this all the time?' she asked, too fascinated to think before asking.

'Not as often as you're thinking.'

She wasn't sure she *was* thinking any more—she was still floating on that gravitational pull right towards him. 'I don't do this, ever.'

'Never ever?'

She shrugged as embarrassment heated her skin. She wasn't going to tell him he was with a woman no other man had ever chased. A woman crippled by an inferiority complex bigger than Jupiter. What did it matter what she'd done or not done before? Right now there was this and it was too powerful to ignore. She wanted more of his touch—of that connection and elation when he'd kissed her. More than seduction, more than madness, it was an ache unlike anything she'd known burning low in her belly. Its searing intensity rapidly escalating until it seemed to singe her inside and out, leaving her breathless because of this urgent, unstoppable need to touch.

'I should offer you a drink or something.' He ran his hand through his hair and huffed out a breath as if he too were struggling to recover.

It seemed imperative to feel again that need that mirrored her own. 'I'm happy with just the "or something",' she mumbled shyly.

He looked startled for a second, then smiled. He moved towards her—graceful, powerful, careful. 'I wanted this from the moment I saw you.'

She jerked her head, negating the compliment because she was unable to believe him. 'You don't have to tell me… nice things.'

Something flickered in his expression. 'You're not used to people telling you the truth? You're beautiful, Leah. Robbed me of my self-control in seconds.'

She closed her eyes. She didn't want to listen—didn't want words to destroy her belief in this moment. But then she sensed he was close. She could feel his heat and his tension.

'If I don't have to tell you,' he whispered softly right in her ear, 'then I'll *show* you.'

A paralysing desire took hold at the sound of his determined promise. She half expected a furious onslaught of passion—she would have welcomed that too. But it wasn't.

It was slow, delicious torture. Another slow kiss—easing her back into his arms. Every touch not only a tease, but a celebration of her. Making her breathless, making her move closer, making her want something she couldn't articulate. As she trembled, he picked her up and carried her through to the bedroom and set her down on the big bed.

She shrugged out of the cardigan and then he took over, unbuttoning then peeling the blouse from her body. He paused to gaze at the white bra beneath, then undid it, pulling away the little lace cups that covered her small breasts, and he groaned. Not judging her but enjoying her. Not disappointed, but delighted. There was nothing to be had here but pleasure. She felt a reckless safety in his arms. No one had kissed her like this. His touch silenced anxious thought and she let herself be carried away by the basic instinct of her body—caving in to the demand to shift closer, to move with him and torment him back. He unzipped her trousers and slid them down, lifting her feet to slip her shoes from them at the same time.

'Scarlet silk.' His hot laugh tickled against her skin as he roved back up her body, lingering over her hips. 'That I didn't expect.'

'What did you expect? White cotton granny pants and a chastity belt or something?'

He laughed again and bent to kiss her upper thigh, nibbling on the edge of the silk as he went.

Leah moaned. Truth was, this was the first pair of sexy undies she'd bought herself. Even then she couldn't get it right and wear a matching bra. But she hadn't wanted her bra to be visible beneath her blouse, so she'd gone with white.

'It confirms a theory I've been developing about you,' he murmured.

'And what's that?' She could hardly string the words together.

'That you're more sensual than you appear…you've been hiding your true scarlet self.'

'You're reading too much into it—they were the first I grabbed from the drawer.'

'Because you have a drawer *full* of scarlet silk?'

She couldn't reply. *Where* was he kissing her…slowly inching along the waistband of those scarlet panties? Secrets and desire swamped her and she was shy about the fact that he'd discovered something she'd barely recognised within herself. She'd bought the one pair because it had been all she could afford. It had taken so long to choose which one; she'd wanted them all. Her secret enjoyment of them wasn't so secret now. She shivered.

'You "don't do this, ever", Leah?' He paused and looked back up to her eyes.

She didn't want to lie to him. She didn't want to hold anything back, but it was hard to push the answer past the lump in her throat. 'No.'

As he nodded it occurred to her that he already knew the answer. He'd been able to *tell*?

A slither of mortification chilled her skin. 'Does that bother you?'

'No.' He lifted himself up to lie beside her and searched her features. 'But are you sure you want me to be your first one-night stand?'

The reminder that that was all he was offering didn't bother her. But his blunt question revealed he hadn't realised the entire truth about her. Where he meant one night, she meant ever at *all*.

She nodded, her voice stolen by shyness and the fear that if she told the truth he'd stop. The last thing she wanted was for him to stop.

He kissed her mouth. His hand teased one breast, then the other, then rubbed firmly down her stomach, slipping beneath the waistband of those scarlet panties. At her shocked gasp, his kisses deepened. But he didn't stop his hot exploration—his fingers delving lower, stroking where she was most sensitive, discovering for himself her most secret place.

With every lash of his tongue, of his fingertips, the last of those knots holding her in reserve loosened until she was totally undone. Reduced to nothing but heat and light, pliable in his hands, she didn't just let him touch all he liked, she hungered for it—writhing like an animal. She arched, seeking more caresses, parting her lips to invite another deep kiss—her tongue tangling with his, her hand clawing his shoulder in an aching invitation to come closer.

'Yes,' he praised her in a gravelly voice as she moaned in desperation.

His fingers slid, his thumb strummed and his mouth sealed over hers again—stoking her until she went beyond burning and tumbled into total meltdown.

Time stopped as her hips bucked and she rode his hand. In those lost moments, there was nothing else in her world but him, in the escalating rhythm and depth of plundering touch. She tautened for one last infinite moment of torment and then his attention finally tore her apart. She screamed as ecstasy hit in a wave that smashed her to pieces.

Theo rubbed his forefinger back and forth along the waistband of her panties, lightly toying with her while she recovered from the most beautiful orgasm he'd had the pleasure of giving. He ached to strip her free of them and plunge into her hot, tight body. But her comment that her panties ought to be white replayed in his mind. White was the colour of innocence. And she'd joked about a chastity belt? He'd been too far gone for that to register properly. He glanced up at her face and recognised the gleam of resurging desire in her eyes. But there was shyness as well and the slight wariness—of a novice?

A weight of warning pressed low on his spine. He levered up from the bed and didn't break free of her gaze as he shucked his tie and swiftly unbuttoned his shirt. Her lips parted as she stared, avidly watching as he stripped.

As his hands went to his belt buckle she stilled. Impatient, he shoved both his trousers and boxers down, revealing his bulging erection and watching intently for her reaction. She couldn't resist looking—couldn't take her eyes off him—but they widened in shock and he saw her swallow. And as he stepped back to the bed her breathing quickened.

'This isn't just your first one-night stand, is it?' he asked, his voice harsher than he could control.

Her eyes widened more and he knew he had to ask the follow-up.

'Are you a virgin, Leah? Is the "never ever", actually never *anything*?'

She bit her lip and insecurity flashed.

'How could you not tell me?' He knew he was right—her reaction to his nudity said it all.

Her face filled with a fiery sweet warmth that scorched his soul—he couldn't turn away from her even when he probably should.

'How could you tell?' she asked.

'It was your comment that these ought to be white. And the chastity belt?' He stroked the scrap of scarlet silk that would now be the only barrier between them.

That rosy bloom of embarrassment spread over every inch of her pale skin. 'Do you want me to leave?' She was very still but her hands formed into fists at her sides.

'No.' Raw hunger clawed more savagely within him, but he was determined to resist—to do what was right here. 'Why didn't you want to tell me?'

'I didn't want you to stop.'

The hint of wounded look in her eyes smote what had been—until tonight—an impenetrable heart. 'I won't stop if you don't want me to.'

She gazed into his eyes. He saw the trust. He saw the need. He vowed not to let her down.

'Let's just play, okay?' he clarified. 'We don't have to...'

'Do everything?' She swallowed. The glimmer of disappointment was so obvious in her lavender eyes.

'Decide right now.' He bent and kissed her, unable to stand the droop of disappointment on her full, lush mouth. And at first touch he sank back onto the bed, unable to resist getting as close as he could to her. He'd make her come again, he'd taste her, there was so much they could still do; there were so many other ways to fulfil the need savaging its way through his limbs.

She was revelation all over again. He lost himself in the sensation, the warmth and pleasure of touching her. He removed her silky scarlet panties so slowly, tormenting them both. And then he kissed her, tasting her there, teasing her with his tongue until he had to grip her hips hard to hold her still as she succumbed to her next orgasm.

Her screams suspended time. Bewitched, he let her push him onto his back. He pulled her above him. But with every slow second that he savoured as she blanketed him with her soft slender body, the yearning to have her completely deepened. Recklessness rose within him because she wasn't holding back at all. Untutored but unashamed, her hips circled against his, the tight, delicious rub of her nipples scored his chest so degree by degree his, oh, so noble desire to hold back lessened.

It was as if he'd unlocked a simple, small box only to discover it opened into myriad compartments...each like a room full of willingness and warmth. The depths of her response, her abandon, became unreserved. He stilled at the smoky curiosity in her gaze and the unconscious seeking sweep of her hands over him. She wanted touch. She wanted to explore her sensuality, through him. How could he deny her?

She tracked her fingertips down his abs. Unable to stay relaxed, every muscle tensed with desire as she tracked lower. He ached for her to cup him. His erection strained higher, he felt the searing tightening in his balls, the urge to thrust against her palm rushed. He licked his lips because his mouth was parched and holding back now was almost killing him.

'Do you want me to kiss you?' she asked softly.

He wanted anything. Everything. He blinked.

She smiled, a burst of pleasure in her eyes. 'Want me to help you find your tongue?'

Heat strained his body. That playful whisper knocked once more on his well-entombed heart. 'You don't have to…'

'Did you feel you had to for me?' She looked up at him, shyness glimmering in her eyes as she whispered huskily.

'No,' he sighed, unable to form complete sentences. 'Wanted to.'

'I can't want to?'

He swallowed and gave in. 'Go right ahead.' With a groan he closed his eyes, desperate to summon self-control as he felt her breath on him.

She cupped him and it was sweet torture.

'Oh.' She looked at him as he flinched. 'Can I—?'

'Do anything. Anything you want. Just don't stop.' His breathing roughened.

She didn't stop. He watched, all his senses sharpened and arrowed on her. She was stunning—her long hair had loosened, tumbled about her shoulders, her long, lean, pale limbs unfolded around him. Her mouth was on him. Her mouth—

'Stop. *Stop.*' He dragged in a harsh breath.

She froze and pulled back with a worried expression. 'I'm sorry—'

'No.' He rubbed his forehead with a hard hand and groaned. 'It's just… I'm going to come.'

'Don't you want to?'

His shout of laughter hurt. His whole body ached. 'I wanted to warn you—'

'I don't want to stop,' she whispered.

The desire in her eyes stiffened him impossibly more. He growled his assent, unable to form another word, his want was too great. And then she sucked him dry.

His heart pounded so loud he thought it was going to burst. When he could finally open his eyes, he saw her smiling down at him—pride and amusement gleaming in her gaze. She was energised and so beautiful. She wasn't just insatiable, but capable of experiencing an intensity he knew was rare. And of sharing it with that gorgeous little laugh of hers.

'You okay?' He didn't know why he was asking her when he was so light-headed he wasn't sure he'd ever be able to sit up again. But then adrenalin fired him anew. Because he realised she was incredibly aroused. She'd liked touching him, tasting him. Getting and giving pleasure was always a great way to spend a night, but this was something else. This felt sweeter and sexier than anything.

'I still don't want to stop,' she said in the softest whisper. 'I still don't want you to stop.'

Her confession just demolished him. He was unable to resist and desperately aching to please her—wanting her to be more than sated, more than thrilled. He didn't want to deny her anything. So when he should've been spent, he was hard again and filled with an arrogant, outrageous determination. Who was he to tell her what she should or shouldn't do anyway? She knew he was leaving in the morning. She knew there was only this between them, only now. And she'd given them both permission to make the most of it. All he wanted now was to make it the best he could for her. Which meant keeping himself in check for a while yet. And being certain.

'I've never slept with a virgin before, Leah,' he said hoarsely, still catching his breath.

Her lashes veiled her eyes. 'Not even when you were a virgin?'

'No, I wasn't the first for my first. Do you really want to talk about—?'

'Did she make it good for you?'

A wry smile curved his lips. 'She did.'

'Then maybe think of this as paying it forward?' She looked as if she was braced for rejection.

He just couldn't deny her. 'You know you can change your mind. I'll—'

'Theo—'

'I don't want to hurt you,' he confessed rawly. It was incredibly true. Somehow, this woman he'd met only a few hours ago was precious to him. She mattered.

Her expression softened. 'If it hurts, maybe you can kiss it better...' She trailed off, suddenly shy.

That wave of protectiveness welled in him. He turned, swiftly searching the bedside table drawers. Relieved, he tossed the small box he'd found onto the bed. He'd leave nothing to chance.

Leah moaned as he pressed kisses across her collarbones and down her décolletage. He was so patient—too patient really. When he finally braced above her, anticipation heightened to a new level. He was big and heavy and wonderful. The slick hot reality impinged as she saw his muscles bunch. He braced as he held back. She knew he was being careful; she could tell in the way he watched her so closely. His concern melted her all the more.

'Please,' she murmured, knowing he needed to hear her wish again.

His expression tensed and he moved. Leah gasped as his big body invaded hers—tearing that last tiny barrier to bury deep inside her. He caught her sharp cry in a quick kiss.

'Sorry,' he muttered. His gaze was filled with searching concern for her. Of course that compassion was there—because if it wasn't she never would have sought this with him.

'Are you okay?' He framed her face and kissed her again and again—so gentle and lush.

He was pressed so deeply into her. So incredibly close. And it was so overwhelming she could only nod, as she adjusted to his possession and to the millions of nerve endings that had sparked to life within her—that suddenly sought so much more.

He held firm, slowly kissing her until the stillness was too much for her—she needed him to move. Warmth overflowed. She'd not expected it would be this intimate and yet of course it was. She revelled in the tender passion of his kisses and her body relaxed until she was no longer just accepting his invasion, but welcoming it—slickening, heating, until she instinctively rocked her hips to help. He kissed her again and his groan reverberated into her chest. He moved then too, taking control, making it magic, and she completely forgot that first moment of pain in her building delight. She followed his rhythm, learning this dance until instinct urged her to hold him closer still. She wrapped her arms and legs around him, clinging close with every part of her as the spasms of delight snuck up on her so swiftly.

'Don't stop,' she breathed desperately. 'Please, don't stop.'

But as she curved more tightly around him, so close to completion, he growled and suddenly froze.

'Theo?' she asked.

'Trying…' he gulped a breath '…not to be too rough.'

But she needed *all* of him.

'Finish me,' she begged.

At her broken plea she felt his restraint unravel and

power surged in his body. He lost it—thrusting harder and faster and it was so dizzying, so intense, so unbearably good. She could only try and hold on, but her restraint had fled too. She clawed his skin, grasping him as tight as she could in her grip as her body and mind locked on him. But he didn't stop, he pounded closer and fiercer, pushing them higher, further and faster until everything exploded in a flash of heat and light and utter, utter ecstasy.

Hours later Leah blinked, wishing she'd eaten more carrots as a kid so her night vision was better. Instead, she tripped over her shoe and muffled her squawk of pain as she hopped and tried to see well enough to find her other one. Her clothes had been scattered on the floor around the bed and, while she'd found most of them, she just needed this one last thing.

'Why are you trying to sneak out?' The lazy tease in his voice made her shiver.

'Sorry.' She stifled her nervous laughter.

As he switched on the lamp she glanced at him, embarrassment curling her spine. 'I didn't mean to wake you.'

His eyebrows lifted. 'Because you didn't want to talk to me?'

She swallowed. 'I just…'

His low chuckle filled the void. 'Relax. This doesn't have to be awkward.'

'No?' But she needed to escape now because the temptation to fling herself back into bed, wrap herself around him and never let him go was just a little too strong.

He leaned out of bed and reached for his phone. 'Give me your number.'

She stilled; the crowd of clamouring emotions shaking her up needed to settle. 'I don't think that's a good idea,' she said bravely. The night was over, the magic gone—wasn't it? 'We don't even live in the same country.' She drew in a breath. 'So…there's no point, is there?'

She wanted him to argue with her and say he wanted to see her again. But she had the feeling she'd spend the rest of eternity hoping he'd call. And if he did? Would she end up his booty call when he was in London? He didn't want a relationship, and never marriage, remember? And she did want those things. So this needed to stay as a finite dream night.

'No point?' he echoed quietly.

She turned away as he got out of bed and scooped his trousers up from the floor. She couldn't see his body again, couldn't stop to talk more. If only she'd not fallen over her shoe she'd be out of here by now. It had been great sex, that was all. Other people experienced this all the time. She couldn't be all inexperienced and needy now.

'At least let me get you home safely.'

She couldn't resist glancing back at him. 'I'll be fine on the—'

'I'm only going to phone down to the porter and order you a cab.' He sombrely studied her with those intense eyes. 'I wasn't going to drive you myself. I have to get to the airport, remember?'

'Okay, thanks.'

But her heart pounded appallingly quick and hard as he strolled towards her and made it impossible to think.

She couldn't look away. He was extraordinarily beautiful. Bronzed skin, strong, sleek muscle. She couldn't believe she'd had the privilege of touching him *everywhere*. She swallowed, clawing back the desire to do it again right now.

She couldn't possibly kiss him goodbye but just walking away seemed rude. For lack of a better idea she held out her hand for him to shake before he got too close. He paused, as if debating whether to take her hand or do something else entirely.

'No regrets, Leah?' he asked softly, finally clasping her hand in his in a handshake like no other. Could he feel her thundering pulse through her skin?

'None.' She couldn't get her voice above a whisper. 'But it's done.'

'Okay. Then, bye, beautiful Leah.' He glanced down at their linked hands for a brief moment and then released her. 'Thank you for a wonderful night.'

'Thank you too,' she echoed awkwardly and quickly turned away. 'Bye.'

On the way down to the ground floor she squared her shoulders and refused to feel any sadness. *Refused.* She'd had an amazing night—the best night of her life, just as he'd promised. As she acknowledged that, a surprising shot of confidence lifted her. So what if she had bed hair? So what if the porter waiting to escort her into the taxi could tell she'd spent the night barely sleeping because one man—one *amazing* man—had wanted her and she'd wanted him and together they'd done all kinds of wonderful?

Things were looking up. She'd moved to London, she had her own place, a new job she actually wanted and she was going to make such a go of it.

Finally, her life was only going to get better.

CHAPTER THREE

'WHAT DO YOU think of this pattern, Leah?'

Smiling, Leah paused by the open doorway of her favourite resident's room. She loved her job as receptionist in the private care facility in North London—mainly because she loved the residents. They were interesting and she enjoyed, not only being able to help them and their families, but just talking to them too. She'd been here coming up five months and as her confidence had increased, her bond with them all had built.

Now she went into Maeve's room to study the paper the old woman was holding up to her. They'd discovered a kindred fondness for knitting early in Leah's employment. It was a favourite way of relaxing, aside from reading, for them both. So Leah looked at the picture with interest. It was a pattern for a baby jacket. She'd thought Maeve's grandchildren were all older. Perhaps there was going to be a great-grandchild?

'I thought I'd better get started for you, but wasn't sure which colour you're going to need. Have you found out? Should I do pink or blue?' The elderly woman's eyes twinkled with curiosity.

Startled, Leah let out a stunned little laugh. Maeve wanted to knit this for *her*? *Why?* 'I'm not pregnant, Maeve.'

'You're just the right age to be pregnant,' Maeve said. 'I was about your age when I had my first.'

Leah laughed again—was this a sweet case of wishful thinking? 'I'm sorry, Maeve, but—'

'You can't fool me, you know. I know it's the norm these days not to say anything until you're a few months gone, but you can't hide how radiant you are now. You have so much more colour and sparkle than when you first started.'

Leah's breathing quickened. Did she? That was because when she'd started, she'd only just moved away from her parents. It had taken a while to bounce back from the pressure they'd put on her for so long and to accept that what she wanted to do with her life wasn't anything they'd ever approve of.

'I'm on a health kick,' Leah explained, because that was true. She'd been eating well and exercising…it wasn't anything else. It couldn't be.

'You don't drink coffee any more,' Maeve pointed out, looking very pleased with herself. 'Because you're blooming.'

Leah stared at the older woman and slowly shook her head again. But inside she was beginning to panic. She *had* become sensitive to certain smells and tastes, but that was because she'd chosen to eat so well—wasn't it? It was impossible for her to be pregnant because she was single and she'd never—

'Leah?'

'I think the pattern looks beautiful.' She forced a quick smile. 'I just need to…um…' Her brain wouldn't compute. She couldn't think of a reason to leave—she just threw another smile at Maeve and dashed from the room.

Oh. Leaning against the wall in the corridor outside, she breathed hard. For the first time in for ever she thought of that magical night. She'd been trying to forget it—to move on and not judge every man she passed by the impossible standard that was Theo Savas. Of course, no one compared. That night had been part of the reason her confidence had grown too. But for her to have got *pregnant*? She couldn't have. He'd used protection each time—she'd seen him. And that night had been months ago and she'd had her period since, right?

Oh, no. She put her hand to her mouth as she frantically tried to think, but the panic zombies had eaten her brain.

She'd always had an irregular cycle and she'd been so busy she hadn't been paying attention to that much because she'd thrown herself into her work in part to help herself forget *him* and now she couldn't remember…

Oh, no, no, no. Cold horror curdled her blood. What Maeve had noticed was true. She suddenly loathed the smell of coffee. And her skin was kind of amazing in a way it had never been before. And now she remembered other things she'd not realised before—that tiredness that had leached her for a while a few weeks ago? She'd attributed it to getting used to life in London with all the commuting and everything, but what if it had been symptomatic of something else?

Impossible. It just had to be impossible. Please could it be impossible?

But what if…? The appalling possibility took hold. She was so terrified she couldn't concentrate at all on her work. For the first time she left the second her shift was over, and stopped by a pharmacy on her way home. Once she was alone in her tiny apartment, her hands trembled as she opened the pregnancy test.

Even doing this was ridiculous, right? In a few minutes she'd be giggling about wasting her money. There was no way she could be pregnant. The idea was just a farrago of fact and fantasy planted by a confused elderly woman and taken on by her because she had some random make-your-skin-glow fever…right?

Two minutes later bright blue stripes appeared on the white background.

No, no, no, no, no.

Leah stared stupidly at the positive result. It couldn't be correct. It just couldn't. *How* could she be pregnant?

Her zombie mind now zinged with endless unanswerable questions. Where had the morning sickness been? Or all the other symptoms? More importantly, what was she going to do? And most terrifyingly, how was she going to tell *him*?

All these months she'd been trying not to obsess over him like some loser stalker. Now she had to make contact. How was she going to do that? And how on earth was he going to react?

Please, no.

With shaking hands she used the second test in the box. And cried when she got the same result. She picked up her phone and begged her way into a last-minute appointment with an after-hours doctor who was able to give her a scan to check on the baby's development. Leah stared at the grey whirls of motion on the screen as they formed into an image that made her eyes smart. Tiny and perfect. And *terrifying.*

Apparently everything was just as it should be for just over four months gestation. Everything appeared healthy and normal and all she had to do was keep eating well and taking care of herself.

'Would you like me to phone someone for you?' The attending nurse smiled at her as the doctor left the room. 'You've gone very pale.'

'No, thank you,' Leah murmured, standing up to leave. 'I'm fine. I'm often pale.'

'If you're sure…?' The concern didn't leave the nurse's eyes.

'Yes,' she said, aching to get out of there. 'Thank you anyway.'

Back alone in her apartment, she folded her legs beneath her on the sofa and tried to come up with a plan, except all she could do was hunch in a disbelieving ball.

She had to tell him.

Truthfully she'd searched for him online months ago in a moment of weakness just after their one night together. She'd even avoided seeing Zoe much because she couldn't bring herself to share a moment of that night with anyone.

She'd discovered Theo Savas was regarded as Greece's most eligible bachelor. Heir to a business banking empire that had branches around the world—he was now CEO and game-changer of that enterprise and apparently he could do no wrong because he'd broadened the family holdings, buying diverse companies and creating a conglomerate of success. There wasn't a hint of scandal about him—he wasn't known for partying ways, no rolling parade of beautiful girlfriends in the media, no salacious rumours of his endless succession of one-night stands.

But he had them. He was just discreet and courteous and too clever to leave a woman dissatisfied…

He was going to be horrified. But as much as she really didn't want to, she had to tell him. The question was *how.* Not for the first time she regretted not taking his phone number. Until today those regrets had been tempered by the knowledge she'd saved herself from making a complete idiot of herself by begging him for another night. That wasn't how Theo Savas rolled. He was too busy being the banking CEO, the charitable gift-giver, the employer of many, sponsor of the arts… He was too busy being perfect.

Would he even remember who she was?

She searched him again on her phone. His company's main headquarters were in Athens and there was another office in London, more in other cities around the world. But there was no email address for him—only a public contact address. She couldn't put something this personal into an email that would be read by an administrative assistant. She'd have to phone.

She tried the Athens branch first.

'I'm sorry, do you speak English?' Leah asked the woman who answered in rapid Greek.

'Of course.' The woman's reply was professional and immediate. 'How may I help you?'

'I'd like to speak to Theo Savas, please.' Leah tried to

sound confident and assertive but her nerves were fluttering so hard they rendered her breathless.

'May I ask who is calling?'

'Leah.' She cleared her throat, wincing at her own rushed answer. 'It's important I speak with him.'

There was a pause. 'Mr Savas is very busy. May I ask what it is in regards to?'

'I…' Leah braced as a wave of hot embarrassment swarmed over her skin. 'It's a personal matter.'

There was an even longer pause. 'If it is a personal matter, then you will know Mr Savas's personal number on which to contact him.' The woman's tone was cruelly cool.

Mortified, Leah hung up in a flash.

Why did he need such a dragon-led first line of defence? Did he have women trying to get in touch with him all the time?

Probably, she realised morosely. And the brutal fact was her pregnancy would appal him. He wasn't ready to settle, even if his grandfather wanted him to. And neither he nor his grandfather would want him to have a child with some random one-night stand. He moved in exalted circles—his clients were CEOs, royals, celebrities—he'd be expected to marry and have a family with someone from the same social strata. That wasn't her. She was utterly unsuitable—not educated, not successful, not glamorous or gorgeous… She faced the reality. She wasn't anything he'd either need or want. And she couldn't bear to think of her child knowing it was an unwanted disappointment to its father.

She was that to her parents.

Nor could she contact her parents and ask for their help. She gently held her lower abdomen as she briefly considered, then dismissed, the possibility. This precious baby deserved protection. It deserved to be loved and secure and never to face the judgment of her impossible-to-please parents. She wanted her child never to experience that inferior feeling she'd had all her life. She might not have much else, but she had unlimited love and support to offer her child. And she had to do the right thing for it.

She had to get in touch with Theo to at least give him the chance to consider how, or if, he wanted to be involved in their baby's life.

She glanced down at the website she'd pulled up with its list of addresses and phone numbers. What if she went to his London office and spoke with someone there? If she could convince them how important it was that she speak with Theo directly? But how could she convince them? She shrivelled with embarrassment at the thought of telling a stranger anything of that intimate night, but she had no choice.

The next morning Leah stood on the other side of the street from his London office and watched the people come and go from the building. All were smartly attired—exactly the opposite of her in her old wool coat with her homemade cardigan and her patched black jeans beneath. Her legs trembled and she pulled her coat more tightly around her and made herself step inside the lobby.

The place was beyond intimidating with its sleek interior. She looked at the perfectly coiffed women at the counter and just knew she'd get the same response as she'd got from the Athens receptionist. She'd be exposed in front of all these smooth professionals who were giving her sideways looks as it was. She didn't fit in here—she knew it, they knew it. She didn't have the money, looks or status.

Why had she refused to give Theo her number? Why had she refused to take his? Why had that contraception failed?

She felt too fragile to cope with public scrutiny and rejection. But as she glanced around, she realised her hesitation had caught the attention of the security guard.

He was staring at her, unsmiling. All those old feelings of insecurity and inferiority burned. She was so out of place—*again*. She wasn't good enough—she was *never* good enough. Humiliated, hurting, scared, Leah pushed forward and went up to the counter. This wasn't about her. This was about her baby.

'I'd like to get in touch with Theo Savas, please,' she said quietly to the receptionist.

Leah liked working on reception. She liked greeting people with a smile and being able to help them with their enquiries or to help them find the person they'd come to visit. This woman didn't look as though she enjoyed her job. There was no welcoming smile.

'Is he expecting you?'

'No, but I need to—'

'Mr Savas has no immediate plans to visit the London office at this time,' the receptionist informed her with precise finality.

'If I could just get a phone number—'

'I'm not authorised to give his private number out.'

'I understand, but if I could leave my number…' Leah was shaking with humiliation and embarrassment at the lack of courteous help.

The woman typed something on her screen. 'Your name and number?'

'Leah Turner,' she mumbled and then gave her phone number. 'You'll make sure he gets that message?'

'Certainly,' the woman answered with frosty dismissiveness. 'Was there anything else?'

'No. Thank you.'

It was too awful.

Leah watched her phone for days. But there was no call, no message and she could think of no other way to get in contact with him. She couldn't phone or email or scrape together the money to get to Athens…and even if she did get there, it wasn't as if she could knock on his door because she had no idea where he lived. And doubtless he'd have security staff there too—protecting him from random women.

She sighed. As much as she dreaded it, she was going to have to go back to his wretched bank.

CHAPTER FOUR

'DO YOU HAVE a moment, Theo?'

Theo glanced up as his security chief, Philip, paused in his doorway, an ominous-looking red file in his hands.

'Of course.' Theo sat back in his chair, eyes narrowing as Philip entered and closed the door behind him. 'What is it?'

'A woman visited the London office last week,' Philip said without preamble. 'The guard on the ground noticed her before she went up to Reception. There was also a call to the Greek office the day before.'

A woman? Theo raised his brows at Philip's ferociously serious expression. 'You think she's a threat?'

Philip extracted a photo from the folder. 'We pulled this from the security footage. It's the woman you asked for that summary report on a few months ago. Leah Turner.'

Theo stilled as every muscle in his body tensed. Leah? His Leah-of-the-Lost-Ticket?

He stared at the glossy image Philip had put on his desk and tried to breathe but it was as if a monster had grabbed his guts in a giant fist and squeezed hard. Because it was her—all legs and pale skin. In this picture she wore a wool jacket and a worried look. Why?

'What did she want?' His voice was so gravelly he barely recognised it as his own.

'To speak with you on a personal matter.'

She'd tried to contact him? Why now? Why months later? A surge of triumph ripped through him, swiftly followed by anger. 'Why wasn't she put through?'

He sighed and held up his hand. 'Never mind.' His staff would never interrupt him for, or give out his personal details to, a woman who'd just called in. 'Did she leave her number?'

'Unfortunately the details she left at Reception were mislaid.' Philip frowned. 'I've just interviewed the staff member—'

'How long ago was this?' Theo snapped.

'It didn't cross my desk until this morning.' Philip sounded apologetic. 'I'm sorry for the delay.'

Theo drew a steadying breath as he stared at her picture, but it didn't stop the roar of his blood as feral *want* blazed. But that want mixed with a deeper delight. He'd *missed* her. A flat-out desperate need to know ached.

'Would you like me to—?'

'Leave it with me,' Theo dismissed him brusquely, needing privacy to process. 'And close the door on your way out.'

He needed to be alone to breathe and think and dampen down the fire arcing through his body.

'Philip,' he relented just as his man reached the door. 'Thank you.'

He hadn't opened the report on the lovely Leah Turner. He'd ordered it after that night they'd shared because he'd found himself unable to stop thinking about her. He'd half hoped to discover something in the report that would kill his constant interest in her. But it had got so bad that when the report had arrived he'd decided to exercise restraint and not even read the thing—to prove his self-control to himself and not make that intolerable yearning worse. Usually he was very good at self-control. So that report sat in a file on his home screen. Mocking him. Tempting him.

Every night since the ballet, he'd dreamed of being with her again and again. His imagination had inevitably returned to her dark hair, her pale skin, her long, long limbs… But it was the loss of something more ephemeral that had kept him awake—the sparkle in her eyes when she'd made one of her surprisingly astute comments or inadvertent slips of the tongue, the shy playfulness that had emerged with only a little encouragement and most of all that soft laugh and the emotional expressiveness that he'd found both a welcome and a warning…the thing he'd been most unable to resist responding to.

She'd not wanted to see him again. She'd not wanted his number. She'd avoided his touch in the morning. He'd taken that to be a kind of self-preservation instinct, because he too knew finality was for the best.

Circumstance had then buried Theo in a gamut of responsibility. On his return to Athens that day, Dimitri had taken a turn for the worse, forcing Theo to cancel all upcoming travel. For months he'd stayed home to oversee Dimitri's care while working around the clock to keep the business on track. The old man was finally better now and he'd even revived that inconvenient idea to find Theo a suitable wife. But, for all his comments to placate Dimitri, Theo still had zero intention of following through on the idea.

Now he stared at the still of Leah—wrapped in that bulky wool jacket despite the spring weather—and it was her worried expression that struck him most. Why had she wanted to see him? Why now—all these months later?

He shoved his chair back and stood, rapidly assessing the pros and cons of immediate departure. But the decision was already made. He needed to see her in person.

He'd needed that for months.

CHAPTER FIVE

THE IMPERIOUS KNOCKING on her door startled Leah so much she dropped a stitch. She scrambled to her feet, heart thudding as she crossed the room. She didn't get visitors at this time of night.

'Hello?' she called through her door.

'Open up, Leah.'

Her knees actually buckled. She braced both hands on the door—whether to keep herself upright or hold the door secure she wasn't sure, as raw elation flared a split second before fear exploded. A welter of emotions cascaded through her body. Was that really—?

'Leah? It's Theo.'

He was so arrogant he didn't give his surname. He didn't need to.

'Open up, Leah.'

She was so thrown she obeyed almost without thinking, somehow distanced from reality. She saw dark blue jeans first, and then glanced up to take in the white tee stretched snug across a masculine chest that looked so powerful a rush of something illicit pooled low in her belly. She snapped her attention further north, only to be ensnared by his gorgeously rare green gaze.

Time simply stopped.

She had to tell him.

'Theo.' She dragged in a decent breath, trying to clear her head.

The casual clothing didn't make him any less powerful or less intimidating than when he'd been in his perfect suit. If anything he seemed more dangerous. He looked literally edgier, as if a little loss of weight had sharpened his features, making them more starkly apparent. He was more sensational than she remembered. Her body hummed and all she wanted was to move closer.

'What are you doing here?' she asked vacantly, still unable to stop staring.

He didn't answer. He was too busy staring back at her. His gaze trawled over every inch of her face, then her body. Her self-consciousness grew as the silence thickened. Her leggings were so faded they were more grey than black, with a hole at the knee, and her oldest pair of lurid leg warmers were barely clutching her calves. Her tee was old too. But happily it was loose. She curled her toes into the thin rug beneath her feet, almost squirming through his undeniably sensual inspection. Everything—her thoughts, senses, wants—heightened. It was as if she'd only been half alive these last few months and the second he'd crossed her threshold she'd been plugged back into the mains power supply. Energy and excitement thrummed through her veins.

She had to tell him.

'I heard you were trying to get in touch with me.' He smiled but his eyes were sharp as he watched her jerkily step away from him.

She couldn't smile back. She wasn't sure she could even speak. But now was the time. Horribly short of breath but trying to hide it, she leaned against the wall for support as he closed her door and walked into the middle of her too-small flat.

'How did you hear that?' she asked.

'You called into the London branch.'

'So you got my message.'

'Unfortunately the message was lost or I'd have got here sooner.'

He hadn't got the message? 'If you didn't get the message then how—?'

'There were cameras, security guards.'

'And I looked suspicious?' She'd laugh if she weren't so terrified about telling him. 'How did you get my address?'

'My security team is very good.'

At what? Protecting him from the unwanted attentions of women? Did they have to do that often?

His gaze didn't waver from her. 'All of this is irrelevant. Why did you want to see me, Leah?'

She felt as if she were standing on the edge of a very high precipice and had no choice but to jump off. 'I'm pregnant.'

He didn't move. In fact he remained so still she wondered if she'd actually said it. Had her words even been audible? She swallowed hard.

'I'm pregnant.' She made herself repeat it, only now her throat had tightened so much it came out on a husky breath.

'Congratulations,' he said mechanically.

She stared, waiting for more of a response. But he still didn't move. She realised he didn't fully understand. She made herself breathe again and pushed on. 'I'm pregnant by you.'

'No.' He was uncompromising in stance and in denial. 'It's not mine. We slept together months ago.'

'Yes. I'm four months pregnant.'

His mouth compressed and his searing gaze skimmed over her body again. 'You don't look four months pregnant. You'd be larger.'

'And you're an expert?' Anger suddenly bubbled within her—she wasn't an idiot and she wasn't going to let him treat her like one. 'Because I'm so tall, there's room for the baby to hide,' she muttered. 'But the doctor said everything's developing okay.'

He stared at her fixedly. 'It's not possible. I used condoms.'

'Well, apparently one of them failed.' Her heart clogged her throat, choking her.

He remained rigid in the centre of the small room. 'And you've known all this time?'

'No, of course not.' She frowned. 'I only found out last week.'

An almost vicious brightness lit his eyes, slicing through her. 'Well, I'm no expert,' he drawled, 'but how is *that* possible?'

'I…um…' She swallowed. 'I've been so busy, I just didn't realise—'

'You didn't realise?' He stepped forward before stopping himself with a jerk. Tension streamed from his body.

She winced at the flare of fury in his eyes. 'I went to the doctor last week. She confirmed it. Then I tried to contact you.'

'You tried?' he echoed sarcastically.

A horrible hot feeling slithered inside as she nodded.

'You phoned my office but didn't leave your number. You walked into the London office once. You gave up pretty quickly.'

His scathing assessment flayed. He was right. She'd not done enough.

He shook his head. 'Am I the only possible father?'

His question stabbed—how could he think otherwise? She paused; had he had other lovers since her? Of course, he probably had. That reality hurt more than it should. But he'd known she'd been a virgin—hadn't he realised how rare it was for her?

'You think I started having casual sex every other night?' She glared at him. 'We can get a DNA test if you don't believe me.'

His eyes blazed before he abruptly turned away, rolling his shoulders. 'No. It's okay. I believe you.' His voice sounded flat and hard. He drew in a deep breath and swung back to face her. 'What's the plan?'

'Plan?' she echoed.

'You're four months pregnant. You'd failed to contact me, so what were you going to do?'

'I was going to…' She swallowed. She'd been trying to get over her panic enough to make progress. She'd been failing on that so far.

'Were you going to go home to your parents?' He watched her closely.

'No,' she muttered. She wasn't ready to face the recriminations and rolled eyes, the sighs of impatience because she'd failed to meet their standards again. She couldn't even move to another city and make a success of it.

'You haven't told them either?'

'They're very busy and they live too far away.' She'd never want her baby in that cold intellectual environment where normal people couldn't perform highly enough.

'I live even further away.' He stepped towards her. 'Have you thought about that?'

She hadn't thought about it at all. She'd not been able to get past worrying about telling him. Frankly she'd been too paralysed to predict his reaction. But it was bad. Bitter betrayal burned in his eyes and he was coldly furious, the antithesis of the man she'd trusted so completely that night. There was no softening in his reserve now.

'You travel a lot.' She tried to reason a way out of the mess. 'If you want, you can visit…a lot.'

'If I want?' He looked astounded. 'You think I'll settle for seeing my child every other week at best?' The lethal way he fired his words made goosebumps lift—let alone the impact of what he'd actually said.

He loomed closer, even angrier. 'Not going to happen, Leah. *Never* going to happen. Have you talked to *anyone* about this?'

'Only the doctor.' She hated how pathetically breathy her answer sounded.

She'd not told anyone at work. She'd avoided Maeve. She'd not returned Zoe's last call… She'd been in denial.

'Good. That means we can work out our story more effectively.'

'Our story?'

'We're getting married.'

'What?' Her jaw dropped.

'You're pregnant. It's my baby. I'm not having my child born illegitimate.'

'And I don't get any choice in this?'

'So explain your choice to me, then. What are you going to do? Stay in this tiny bedsit? Are you going to head straight back to work the second you've given birth and leave my baby in a nursery all day? How did you think you were going to make ends meet, Leah?'

He was asking too many questions. Making too many judgments. A barrage of tests designed to trip her up—like those dreaded pop quizzes her parents inflicted on her randomly and repeatedly so she never had any chance of relaxing. Not when she failed them every time because their required pass mark was one hundred per cent correct. That old performance anxiety reared, rendering her unable to think at all. Instead she lashed out. 'I'm *not* going to marry you.'

'Why not? You know you'll never have to work another day in your life,' he exploded.

As if that were relevant? 'I didn't even know who you were. I wasn't the one who provided the condoms. Or the one who put them on. I'm not the one who didn't bother to check they'd…' She trailed off.

'Survived the event?' he interpolated with dry precision.

'No. And guess what? I like my life. I like my home here. I like the people I help in my job. I want to work. I certainly don't want to leave it all to live a life of intolerable boredom in a foreign country with a husband who resents me.'

His face whitened. 'Too bad,' he choked. 'Because here we are. It isn't what you want? It's not what I want either. But it's what's *right*. Pack your things.'

She stared at the stranger he'd become. Or perhaps he always was this ruthless and she'd just not seen it that night because she'd stupidly given him everything he'd wanted? She couldn't reconcile that suave, amusing man with the cold authoritarian before her now.

'I don't want to fight, Leah.' He ran a hand through his hair roughly.

'You just want me to do everything you want.'

'Yeah.' He actually threw a smile in her direction. Well, a tight, determined baring of the teeth that a more generous person might mistake for a smile. 'I'm good at fixing problems and you have to agree this is a problem.'

It was a huge problem. 'What's your plan, then?'

He ruffled his hair again and then sighed. 'In the long term, we won't have to impact on each other's lives much.'

Chills swept over her skin. This was no romance. No rescue. He wasn't suggesting marriage because he *liked* her. This was only about securing their child's future. But the details were too scarce. 'What do you mean?'

'I mean we can come up with an arrangement that suits us both.'

Still not enough. 'What kind of arrangement?'

He had a distant look in his eyes. 'We'll marry, we'll raise this child. But you and I will live largely separate lives. I have several properties.'

'Separate.' She swallowed the sting of his cool rejection. She couldn't let it bother her. He clearly didn't feel any of the attraction to her that she still felt for him. Not even just physical. 'Theo, we had a really nice night, but it was supposed to end there,' she said stoutly.

'Well, there's no ending it now,' he muttered. 'We're stuck with each other for a lifetime.'

'We don't have to be.'

'What does that mean?' he asked pointedly. 'Are you prepared to give me full custody?'

All the air whooshed from her lungs. 'What? No!'

'Because I'll not step back from my responsibility, Leah. If you're having my baby, I'm going to provide for it. Always.'

His vehemence shocked her. He'd said he didn't want to marry. She'd thought that meant he'd not want children either…but now he was all 'instant family'—why?

'Don't make this more difficult than it needs to be,' he added, watching her closely, his expression shutting down as if he could read the questions burning inside her. 'We can work it out.'

'Yes,' she agreed. 'But it doesn't have to mean marriage.' She struggled to drag in a calming breath. 'You said you'd never marry.'

Theo's jaw locked so hard it hurt. 'You're pregnant.'

Nothing but regret filled him. History was repeating in the worst of ways. He'd failed her, his grandfather, himself. He knew accidents happened. He was one himself. And he had to do a better job of fixing this than his parents had. And as much as he didn't want it, there was only one way to do that. But he could hardly compute what she'd told him. Truthfully he was still recovering from being in the same airspace as her again—still battling the urge to haul her close and kiss her. He needed calm and logic to create a cool-headed contract with her.

Yet as he stared, as she stiffened in defensiveness, a primal possessiveness stole his reason, its fierceness shocking his self-control from him. He'd claim what was his. He'd *protect* it. Always. He'd even protect it from himself.

'I won't have an illegitimate child, Leah,' he said roughly. 'He or she deserves my name and all the privileges that come with it.'

'You mean money?'

'I mean many things, but, yes, that's one of them. My child also needs the proper protection… You do too.' He glanced at her. 'You have no idea what comes with wealth like ours.'

'Is it a terrible burden?' Her eyes glinted as she lobbed the acerbic little taunt.

He refused to react to her bite. 'The child also needs more than physical security. A sense of belonging.' Theo closed his mind to his own old memories of insecurity and betrayal. 'I'm sorry if that's too old-fashioned for you, but…' Bitterness almost overwhelmed him. Surely he could give more than he'd received? Except he really couldn't bear the thought of caring for a tiny, vulnerable baby. He didn't have what it took.

'It's not old-fashioned. It's honourable.' She sighed. 'It's just—'

'We're talking about a baby, Leah,' he interrupted, unable to stand the argument, let alone the actual reality. 'It doesn't get more life-changing than that. I'll take my share of the responsibility.'

Her lips compressed. 'But you're taking *all* the responsibility and becoming a dictator in the process.'

Her flash of temper tested his determination not to lose his again. But if he reacted now the way he really wanted, then this wouldn't become the safe, serviceable arrangement they both needed. Her earlier words haunted him—*a life of intolerable boredom with a husband who resented her*? She'd encapsulated his mother's life in one sentence. And look at the mess of betrayal and hurt that had led to.

He refused to excavate the past now. All that mattered was that he ensured Leah had everything she needed. Except he didn't really know how—not beyond the basics of providing four walls, a roof and food. He paced across the tiny room, rapidly working out the only way they could forge a viable future. She'd hardly have to see him. They simply had to agree to the arrangement.

Right now she wouldn't look at him. She was scared and angry. Frankly so was he. 'Pack your things. It's getting late.'

She kept staring at the floor. 'I'm not leaving with you.'

'I'm not leaving without you.' Her persistence tore his temper. 'You might have only recently found out about this pregnancy, but you didn't exactly try hard to get in touch with me. How do I know you're not going to skip town in the middle of the night?'

'You don't trust me.'

He braced inwardly at the hurt he heard in that soft sentence and just reiterated the fact. 'I'm not leaving without you.'

'Well, I'm not leaving here tonight. Good luck on my tiny sofa.'

'I'm not sleeping on the sofa, Leah.'

'You're not welcome in my bed,' she declared huskily.

'Is that right?' He stepped closer and felt the frisson of sensual awareness. Her words were pure challenge—a denial of the electricity sparking between them. It was still there—he'd seen it the second they'd laid eyes on each other again. But it was in both their interests to let her deny it. 'Then it's my hotel suite.'

'I'm not—'

'It has more than one bedroom,' he growled. 'Will that appease your outraged virtue?' He whirled away so he wasn't tempted to prove how hollow her words were. But the room wasn't anywhere near large enough for him to get the distance he needed. 'It's that or we stand here arguing all night.'

She folded her arms. 'I can't just pack up everything tonight.'

He glanced about. 'Why not? It won't take long.'

She shook her head. 'You're a jerk, you know that?'

'Leah.' He struggled for control—so close to throwing her over his shoulder and carting her down to the waiting car himself. He never let his emotions get the better of him, but it was almost impossible now. 'It's getting late.'

'I could join you later. In a week or so.'

It was unacceptable to him. 'We're sticking together until we're married.'

She looked aghast. 'We can't just get married.'

True. He nodded. 'It'll take about a week to get the paperwork processed.'

'A *week*?'

Yeah, he was moving fast but he'd make no apology for it. He could only try a little joke. 'That'll give you time to find something to wear.'

'Because that's the most important thing I have to consider?'

He bit back his smile as she slammed her retort at him. Backed into a corner, she could still hold her own.

'Stop stalling for time and go pack or we'll go without any of your clothes.' He was right about this. She just needed to admit it.

'Fine. Your suite. Separate rooms.' She marched all of five feet through to the bedroom.

Theo paced around the small lounge again. It was small and drab, the carpet worn and the walls in desperate need of a fresh lick of paint. But he noticed the few decorations she'd added to personalise the place—the warm-looking throws draped over the sofa, the knitted cushion covers. Then he spotted the pinboard. There was a photo of Leah with that ballet friend of hers, the menu of a Thai take-away around the corner, a couple of hand-drawn designs on grid paper, a theatre ticket. He peered closer.

'This is your ticket to the ballet?' he asked as she returned with a rucksack and that ginormous ugly handbag.

A rush of memory loosened his restraint and he smiled.

'It turns out I'd left it here all along.' She looked embarrassed. 'That night, that's why I couldn't find it in my bag. Pretty useless, I know.' She actually smiled.

He couldn't hold back his little laugh and studied the ticket again. 'You had quite a good seat.'

'I told you, Zoe is my friend.' She glanced at him. 'Or do you not believe me about that now?' Soft hurt flickered in her eyes, fading out that smile. 'I've never given you reason *not* to trust me, Theo.'

She didn't realise that, for him, trust wasn't freely given and then lost. It had to be earned. 'I guess we don't know each other very well, Leah.'

Her expression became a little pinched. 'I guess getting married will change that.'

Leah swallowed hard when he didn't reply. She'd thought she had known him. That they'd connected more than physically that night. And *she* had most certainly trusted him. For him not to trust her hurt. Now she was mortified he'd seen she'd kept that ballet ticket as a keepsake of the night they'd spent together.

She picked up her rucksack again. 'I'll need to come back to get everything else.'

As wary as she was of going with him, how could she argue? He was right—what alternative could she suggest? She didn't have his kind of money, power, experience or authority. And not only would her family be mortified and unwilling to help, they were actually *unable* to offer the emotional support she really wanted for her child. If Theo had a warm relationship with his grandfather, and he seemed to, then that might be better. At the very least she had to give him the chance. She owed him that.

'You have a current passport?' he checked.

'Yes. Why?'

'Because we need to get home quickly.'

'You expect me to go to *Greece*? When? Tomorrow?'

'Exactly.'

It was happening too fast. Get married in a week? Go to Greece tomorrow? Leave with him tonight?

He watched her solemnly. 'We need to work this out and I can't leave my family for long.'

'But you think I can leave mine?'

'You haven't told your parents the good news. I guess that says a lot about your relationship with them.' He took the bags from her. 'We'll fly to Athens first thing in the morning.'

'I can't just not turn up to my work.' She couldn't believe his arrogance. 'I need to work out my notice. I need to say goodbye to my residents. Or do you think that because I'm just a receptionist I can ditch everything and leap to your beck and call?'

He stared at her fixedly, rather as if he was inwardly counting to ten. 'Okay.' He released a slow sigh. 'We'll figure it out in the morning. For now, let's get to my hotel and get some rest.'

Leah stared stonily out of the passenger window at the darkening sky and said nothing. It wasn't the same hotel as that night at the ballet. This one was polite discretion with no big logos—secret luxury in the heart of Mayfair. She followed Theo to the suite on the top floor. The lounge alone was almost three times the size of her little flat.

'Take whichever room you want,' he muttered.

'You've not taken one already?'

'I came straight from the airport to your apartment.'

The atmosphere thickened. He'd not known her news but he'd come straight to see her? Just because she'd appeared in his London office?

She couldn't turn away from his gaze. It was as if she were pinned in place by that intense scrutiny. Somehow this place felt more intimate than her apartment despite it being so much bigger. Maybe it was the mood lighting or the luxuriousness of the furnishings, but suddenly she was too aware of sensation, the temptation of intimacy and touch. Smoky memories curled. She gritted her teeth, wanting to regain control of herself. He didn't want *that.* He wanted them to live separate lives, together in name only for the sake of their baby.

'I'll come with you to talk to your boss tomorrow before we leave for the airport,' he said huskily.

'Because I'm incapable of talking to them on my own?' She couldn't hold back her defensiveness. 'Are you afraid I'll say something I shouldn't?'

'No.' He stepped closer. 'Because I'm afraid they won't let you go. One of those oldies will ask you to make them a pot of tea and we'll never get you out of there.' He gazed at her intently. 'You're a pushover, Leah. A tug on the heartstrings is all it takes.'

A tug on the heartstrings? Was that what he'd done with her that night? Had that connection she'd thought they'd forged just been a ploy? She shook her head, not able to believe that. 'There's nothing wrong with being kind to people.'

'Nothing at all.' He gazed at her for another moment, then rolled his shoulders. 'We'll go see your parents after we've been to your work in the morning. What are they like?'

'You don't need to—' She couldn't tell him about her parents and she certainly didn't want him to meet them. 'Just forget I mentioned it. I don't need to go see them.'

'You're going to leave the country and not even see them to say goodbye? You don't want to invite them to the wedding?'

'They won't come.'

He blinked. 'Now I can't wait to meet them.'

'Too bad,' she echoed his earlier dismissal. 'You're not.'

'Leah,' he sighed. 'I'm trying to meet you halfway. I'm trying *not* to be a dictator.'

'So by simply informing me of tomorrow's itinerary, you're *not* being a dictator?' she asked.

He took her shoulders in a firm grip. 'I'm going to be their son-in-law, you don't think they'd want to meet me—vet me first?' A quizzical look lit his eyes. 'There's no need for me to pass any parental approval?'

They'd probably love to meet him. But they wouldn't believe for a second that he was in love with her. They'd see the situation for what it was—a hoax. A mortifying necessity because she'd stuffed up. For them to know that? She wanted to shrivel into a ball and hide. She didn't need them to witness yet another of her failures. Because they expected nothing less, right?

'Tell me about them.' He cocked his head, watching her as if he were trying to solve a cryptic puzzle. 'What do they do? It can't be that bad.'

'It's not that I'm ashamed of them, more the other way round.' She huffed a sigh. 'They're academics. My younger brother too. They've lived near the university all my life.'

'Academics?' His eyebrows lifted.

'Professors, in fact. And my younger brother, Oliver, is so gifted he's already a senior lecturer.' While she was a receptionist at a care home. 'Their careers are everything to them.'

He looked thoughtful. 'What do they think of your career choice?'

'You mean you can't guess?'

He gave her shoulders a gentle squeeze. 'What's their specialisation?'

'Other than criticism?' she half joked. 'Chemistry.'

'Chemistry?' His eyes widened and he couldn't suppress his smile.

She couldn't resist a small smile back, but then she had a flash of how awkward it was going to be. 'My parents are very—' She broke off, unable to explain just how laser-precise their perceptions were. 'They'll see in a second that we're not…'

'Not what?' He waited. 'You're having my baby so we've obviously had sex. We find each other attractive.'

'We *found* each other attractive. *Once*.'

That intensity deepened in his expression. His vivid green eyes were backlit with remnants of that magic night and the phantom delight he'd showered upon her. 'I thought you always opted for the truth, Leah,' he said quietly.

'Well.' She sucked in a steadying breath. 'Maybe you were right. Sometimes it might be better not to say anything.'

'Denial?' His smile faded as he gazed down at her. 'For protection.'

That heat spiralled like a whisper of smoke within her. More memories teased—of sizzling touch and sweet torment. But she had to ignore the urge to lean closer, and pull back instead. Because he didn't want her. He wanted separate lives.

'It's late,' she muttered. 'I should get some rest.'

'Yes. Go. Sleep.' He released her, that remote, reserved man once more. 'It seems we have a big day tomorrow.'

CHAPTER SIX

'Of course, you must leave right away, Leah,' Seth said quietly. 'But we're really going to miss you.'

Leah nodded; her throat had tightened too much to answer.

Her boss sent her a smile that was both encouraging and sad before he turned to Theo. 'There really was no need for you to give us such a generous donation…'

'Leah was concerned about leaving you so quickly without a replacement organised,' Theo said. 'But with my grandfather the way he is…'

'Of course. We understand.' Seth glanced back to Leah. 'But we are sad to see you go.'

Leah looked to the floor to hide her emotion. This was the first job she'd loved and the first job she'd totally nailed. There'd been no massive list of qualifications required, just the ability to put people at ease. Her life had blossomed here—she was going to miss it too.

'I need a quick moment,' she murmured to Theo and walked down the corridor before he had a chance to respond.

She stopped at Maeve's open door and lightly rapped her fingers on the frame.

'You're leaving us.' Maeve pushed out of her plush armchair and held her arms out.

'Yes.' Leah stepped in and gave the tiny woman a tight hug. 'But I have something I wanted to give you.' She stepped back, blinking quickly and pulling out the small knee blanket she'd put in her handbag.

'It's the purple, with that rib I can't manage with my arthritic old hands.' Maeve took it from her with a smile.

'Yes.' Leah smiled past the lump in her throat. 'I thought

it would help keep those draughts out.' Maeve couldn't knit the complex patterns she used to, and Leah knew she felt the cold.

'I have something for you too.' Maeve picked up a clear bag from her table and held it out to Leah. 'I decided on white, seeing you weren't sure…'

Leah's heart melted as she lifted out a tiny woollen baby jacket. 'Maeve, it's just beautiful. Thank you so much.' Her throat closed. It would have taken a lot of effort for Maeve to get it finished in time and Leah would treasure it always.

Maeve clasped Leah's fingers with her shaking hands. 'You're going to be a wonderful mother, Leah.'

Leah blinked, warmth flooding her. This relationship was so precious to her. 'I'll come and visit you when I'm in town again.' Her throat tightened. She didn't want to say goodbye. She was going to miss her. She was going to miss all the people she'd been working with.

'Leah,' Theo called quietly from the doorway. 'I'm sorry. We need to go.'

'Is that him?' Maeve asked.

'Yes.' Leah half chuckled as she saw the shrewd assessment in Maeve's eyes as she craned her neck to take stock of Theo.

'You'll take care of her, won't you?' Maeve questioned him pointedly.

As embarrassed as she was, warm amusement and appreciation trickled through Leah. It touched her that Maeve cared. She cared about her too.

Theo smiled his most charming smile. 'Yes.'

Ten minutes later Leah stared out of the window as the car sped out of central London, her pulse accelerating at the same pace. The driver had closed the partition, giving them a level of privacy she didn't really want. When she was alone with Theo, her thoughts went a little wild.

'I can't believe you used your money and your grandfather to get me out of my contract,' she muttered.

'I wasn't using my grandfather. I told the truth,' Theo answered calmly.

'Well, you certainly used your money,' she murmured, submitting to the niggling need to provoke him.

'Leah.' He reached out and covered her clenched fist with his hand.

His touch stilled her antagonism but she couldn't rid herself of all her anxiety. She knew they would resolve this situation and, while he was annoyingly decisive, he was at least trying. She should do the same.

'Your grandfather is really that unwell?' she asked.

'He had heart surgery recently.' Theo's tone grew reserved. 'But he's getting better.'

She wondered why he was reticent about him. 'How's he going to feel about this?'

His expression hardened and he released her hand. 'It'll be fine.'

Leah watched him closely. 'He's just going to be okay with you turning up engaged to a woman you barely know, who's four months along already?'

'Dimitri doesn't need to know every detail—or lack thereof—of our relationship.'

'You're going to lie to him?'

'I'll tell him the important facts and that's enough. His well-being is paramount.'

Would he be upset by some of the 'less important' facts?

She paused, sensing his reluctance to talk, but she was unable to resist probing further. He'd asked about her family—couldn't she do the same? 'You're close?'

His hesitation made her senses even more acute.

'I've lived with him since I was ten.' His voice was so low it was hard to hear over the purr of the engine. 'I owe him everything.'

'Why did you go to live with him?'

'My father passed away.'

'I'm sorry.' She gazed at him. His emotionless countenance was unsettling.

'I went to live with Dimitri. That is why I'm not going to abandon my child now.' He drew in a sharp breath. 'We can do better…'

Because *he'd* felt abandoned? Leah swallowed back the deeply personal questions that sprang to mind. He'd not mentioned his mother and she was wary of asking more because there was pain in his expressionlessness. Her heart ached as her apprehension rose. 'What's your grandfather—Dimitri—like?'

He sighed, but the faintest smile softened his mouth. 'Authoritarian, old and unwell. I won't let him be upset by anything or anyone.'

'Do you think he'll be upset by me?' She bit her lip, anxious about the answer.

He glanced at her, his eyes flaring with something before his lashes lowered. 'No one could be upset by you.'

Somehow it wasn't the answer she'd wanted. Somehow it skittled the little emotional self-control she'd restored. 'Because I'm just a harmless little thing who couldn't possibly hurt anyone?' she asked.

Because she was powerless and inconsequential? As useless as her parents had made her feel? The parents she was about to face and confess her life-changing mistake to?

'Because you're a kind person who'd never be deliberately rude to anyone.' He held her gaze solemnly. 'But you shouldn't have to put up with him either. You won't see him much.'

She blinked. 'I don't have to put up with him? Is he scary?'

'He used to be.' A whisker of a smile flashed on his

face. 'But then I grew up. He only wants what he thinks is best for me.'

'He was tough on you when you were younger?'

Another hesitation made her lean closer to listen.

'He had exacting standards and I needed to prove myself to him. But I'm grateful for them. We get on well. As I said, I owe him everything.'

Leah knew all about exacting standards but, unlike her, Theo would have surpassed them all.

The car ate up the miles to Cambridge and her nerves ratcheted. The research institute was so familiar—the white walls and bright lights beneath which she'd faded, invisible and insignificant. She'd eventually realised that restocking the chemicals cupboard wasn't the job for her. She needed a job where she was around people more. And she'd needed to get away from the triple eclipse of her family.

Drawing a deep breath, she knocked on the door of her parents' office. They'd both be there. They always were.

'Leah?' Her father looked up from his desk. 'This is a surprise. Is everything all right?'

Of course he'd immediately assume things might not be all right. Leah tried not to let that bitterness rise. It wasn't their fault that, for super-smart people, they couldn't understand her.

'Everything is…' she drew breath '…really great. Is Mum here too?'

'Of course.' It was her mother who replied.

Leah took satisfaction at the swiftly concealed surprise on Theo's face as her mother appeared from the next room. While her father was like her—tall, thin and dark-haired—her mother was the absolute opposite. Short, blonde, beautiful and brilliant enough to earn her double PhD in half the time it normally took, Leah's mum adored challenging stereotypes—insisting women didn't need to meet societal expectations of beauty or brilliance. She'd rejected make-up, dresses, high heels and insisted Leah never wear them either. Only her mother wasn't angular and un-pretty like Leah—she had no idea what it was like not to be wildly attractive naturally.

'What brings you here?' Her mother looked at her. 'And your friend?'

'This is Theo Savas,' Leah began. 'Theo, these are my parents, Jocelyn Franks and James Turner.' Her nerves tightened.

Theo extended a hand. For a moment her father just stared at it before giving it a weak response. She should have told Theo her parents weren't physically demonstrative people.

'We're here because…um…actually, you're going to be grandparents.' She just blurted it out.

'Pardon?' Anger—and that old impatience—built on her mother's face, mottling her flawless skin.

'I'm pregnant.' Leah tried to stay calm but her brain was malfunctioning the way it always did when her mother was about to test her on one of her many impossible quizzes.

'You're responsible for this?' Her mother turned to Theo. 'Did you take advantage of her?'

Leah gaped. Couldn't *she* be responsible? Was she invisible all over again? She refused to be that—not in front of Theo. Not when she now knew some people believed in her. People like Seth and Maeve. 'Maybe I took advantage of him?'

'Oh, Leah.'

That withering dismissal, that disappointment?

Leah pasted on her smile, determined not to let this happen in front of Theo. 'We're getting married in Greece next week—'

'I should think so.' Her father turned with low fury to Theo. 'You're going to take care of her?'

It was the same question Maeve had asked but it sprang

from something so different. He wasn't asking Theo this because he thought she was a treasure, worthy of only the best treatment. But because he thought she was the opposite—helpless and hopeless.

'I knew it was a mistake to let you go to London on your own—'

'I might not have your PhDs, but I'm not stupid—'

'You've just told us you're *pregnant*.'

'And that makes me stupid?' She gazed at her mother sadly. Because having a child was a bad thing? That was her mother's attitude, wasn't it? Or, at least, having a child who was an eternal disappointment was.

'You've got no qualifications, Leah.' Her mother shredded her. 'We've been looking after you for years, since you dropped out. We got you that job in the lab—'

'I've been looking after you,' Leah pointed out in a choked voice. 'Who cooked all the meals? Who arranged everything you were too busy for?'

'That was to give you something to do.' Her mother glared at her. 'You think we can't cook, Leah?'

'You never did.'

'You know it's not the best use of our time,' her father said.

Leah gaped. Because her parents' time was more precious than hers? Their 'real' work—all those intellectual achievements—were too important to be interrupted with anything like parenting or maintaining a normal house? They'd paid for a cleaner and now it seemed they'd just 'allowed' Leah to do the cooking. How marvellously kind of them. Hadn't they thought she might have plans and dreams of her own that she'd rather be fulfilling?

She'd realised how desperately she'd needed to start over and live her own life. And she'd been succeeding. And she'd continue to succeed without them.

'Well.' She cleared her throat. 'Thanks for keeping an

eye out for me all this time but you no longer need trouble yourselves. We're leaving for Greece today.'

'Leah.' Her father frowned, his tone patronising. 'You can't just—'

'I'm sorry if you can't make it to the wedding, given it's such short notice.' Theo stepped forward. 'But we can't delay our happy occasion a day longer than necessary.' He wrapped his arm around her and drew her too close. 'Leah is so special to me. I'll take care of her and our baby.' He gazed into her eyes as if he were love-struck. 'You don't need to worry about her.'

She wanted to point out that she didn't need *any* of them to 'take care of her'. But there was a glimmer of something more than amusement in his expression and it hurt. She didn't want his sympathy. But as he looked at her that expression deepened to devastatingly serious. 'Anyway, you've never needed to worry about her. She can look after herself—'

'Leah? I didn't know you were here for a visit.'

She turned, pulling out of Theo's hold as her brother, Oliver, walked into the office.

'I'm just leaving.' She braced because her emotions were almost beyond control and she'd not expected Oliver to be away from his lab. 'I'm moving to Greece. Getting married. Having a baby. You should come to the wedding,' she summarised as swiftly as she could. 'No joke.'

'What?' Oliver pulled the beanie off and gaped at her. 'When? I have my—'

'Research, I know. It's okay. I'll send you a photo.' She just wanted to get out of there as quickly as possible because she loved her little brother. 'We need to leave now.'

She walked, not even checking to see if Theo was with her. She knew he would be. Just as she knew her parents wouldn't stop her. But as she crossed the threshold her brother called her name. She couldn't not glance back.

'You'll phone?' He was still gaping.

'Of course.' Because she knew he couldn't say it as well, but he did care.

He saluted her and realised he held the beanie. He suddenly smiled. 'Thanks for this. It's the best one yet.'

She nodded and left. She was going to miss Oliver the most—she'd cared for her younger brother, even when he'd been too buried in books to realise he needed it.

She couldn't trust herself to speak as they got back into the car. Theo apparently had a few things to digest too, because the first fifteen minutes of the drive back were in complete silence. But then she felt him turn towards her.

'Your family are—'

'Amazing, I know.' She smiled brightly because it was that or burst into tears.

'That wasn't the word I was going to use.'

'But they are,' she argued lightly. 'Bona fide geniuses, the three of them. With just a normal IQ, I'm the odd one out.' She shook her head but was unable to stop the words tumbling. 'You didn't need to step in. You didn't need to act as if…'

'As if what?' His eyes glinted. 'I actually *want* to marry you?'

'I don't need you to say that to them. Or take care of me now.' She couldn't hold back. Her parents' words had stung. Just because she didn't have three degrees didn't mean she was incapable of looking after herself. 'I'm not incompetent. I could have made it work. Women do, you know, raise kids on their own.'

He reached out and covered her tight fist with his big hand. 'I know you could handle this alone, Leah. You're amazing. You just handled the hell out of *them*,' he added. 'But the point is you don't have to be alone now. You're not solely responsible for this situation.'

She desperately wished she could escape the emotion overwhelming her at his words.

'Why does your brother wear a beanie in summer?' he asked with a wry smile.

She shot him a sideways look, startled by the change in topic. 'He gets cold in the lab. And he has sensitive ears and it's better if they're warm.'

'So you gave it to him?'

'Knitting is the new black, didn't you know?'

'You made it?'

'Yes, I made it. You don't think I'm capable of that?'

'Easy, tiger.' He laughed gently. 'I'm not like them, Leah. I thought you'd bought it for him because, yes, it looked good enough quality to have been bought. You gave that little rug to that old lady at the home as well. But I get the impression your parents had very high standards.'

'I was never going to get the grades they expected from me.' She'd tried so very hard but they'd expected brilliance and perfection.

'That's why you stopped dancing?'

'They said it interfered with my schoolwork too much.' She shrugged in a helpless gesture. 'They couldn't understand why I wasn't like them and they tried so hard to make me like them—honestly, the books, the tests, the tutoring… And you see what they think of me now.' She looked at him. 'Only good for the cooking and cleaning, right? They actually think you took advantage of me. I must be rescued. I can't take care of myself. I must get walked all over…all because I don't have the same skill set or dreams they do.'

'It wasn't your fault you couldn't live up to their expectations,' he said quietly. 'But you gave up your dream.'

'They wouldn't pay for my classes any more and I couldn't get my marks high enough to get them to resume them.'

'You didn't fight in other ways? Didn't clean the dance studio in exchange for free lessons?'

She gazed at him. Just like that he'd worked up an independent solution. That was what he would have done, or something else inventive to get what he wanted. She had no doubt he'd be defiant in the face of denial or rejection. That was why he was the CEO of a massively successful bank now. He'd have done anything to prove them wrong, wouldn't he? He had that kind of strength and self-belief. She didn't.

'I wanted to *please* them,' she whispered, that little truth torn from her. She'd wanted their love. She'd seen the warmth in their eyes when Oliver had done well—every time he'd surpassed her. She didn't begrudge his achievements—she'd only wanted a little of the adoration they'd shown him. 'I wanted their approval. I've always wanted that and I've never got it and I tried so hard for so long.' And now she was tired of trying to live up to everyone else's expectations. 'I couldn't do what they wanted. Then I couldn't do what *I* wanted because they stopped me. So then I grew a spine. I moved to London. I got my job.' She'd left and she'd had that magic night with Theo and things really had turned around. Her confidence had grown. She sniffed. 'But now I get to do what *you* want me to do.'

'Don't be sad,' he murmured, a sparkle lighting his eyes. 'I think you're going to like the island.'

'Island?'

'Your new home.'

'You mean Athens?'

'Athens initially.' He nodded. 'Then the island.'

An island that was different from Athens? 'But you work in Athens?' she clarified.

'Yes.'

So he'd be in Athens and she'd be on some other island?

Was this what he'd meant about space—that she'd not actually live with him?

'You're sending me to my own kind of Alcatraz?'

He laughed. 'You don't want to know anything about it?'

'I don't need to. I'm sure its unspeakably beautiful. There'll be a pool and an amazing house and probably some billion-dollar view…but it's still a prison.' She couldn't get her head around it, couldn't consider it in any kind of positive light. 'What am I supposed to do all day?'

'You'll have assistants. Nannies. A cook.'

Was that what he'd meant when he'd said she didn't need to be alone now? He was going to arrange a massive coterie of staff for her? But *he* wasn't going to be there?

He leaned forward. 'Don't you want a break, Leah? You'll want for nothing—'

Except friends, or a partner, or a *lover*. She shivered. 'I spent too long buried away in a laboratory not talking to real people. I *like* people. I like meeting them, talking to them—'

'You'll have a tiny little person all of your own to take care of soon enough.'

'Who won't be able to talk back to me for months…'

'And as I said, you'll have staff.'

'Wonderful. People who are *paid* to spend time with me.'

He laughed. 'And, believe it or not, other people live on the island. Nice people.'

The prospect of being apart from *him* really wasn't what she wanted. But for him?

He sobered and a perplexed frown creased his forehead. 'The last thing I want is for you to be unhappy. I thought you'd want to live in a place where you can relax.' He shook his head. 'Just wait till you see it, Leah.'

She sat in silent contemplation. All her life she'd wanted someone to love her, just for her. And she wasn't about to get it. But she couldn't help wondering why Theo didn't want that too. Didn't he feel bereft at the prospect of an emotionless marriage? She was sure she hadn't imagined that flare of heat in his eyes when he'd seen her again. Didn't he even want to try to use that as a basis for something more? Obviously not.

Her heart sank all over again as she realised he truly didn't want any of it at all.

CHAPTER SEVEN

THEY WERE DRIVEN to the airport where a discreet crew were waiting for them. A tall, serious-looking man handed Theo a briefcase and murmured in his ear before he left to board ahead of them.

'I don't always use the private jet, but I thought we needed the privacy for this trip,' Theo explained as he led her up the staircase into the sleek jet.

Privacy? For what? Her pulse skipped.

'I don't want everyone watching us and wondering who you are.' He pulled a pale blue bag out of the briefcase and handed it to her as she sat in the wide luxurious leather armchair. 'We'll present you when we're ready.'

Present her? 'What's this?' She peered into the bag and saw a small jewel box nestled in tissue paper. A wave of cold trepidation washed over her but she was aware of him watching, so she faked calm. Her fingers trembled only the slightest as she opened the box and stared at the ring. 'Is it real?' she choked.

'Considering the price, I hope so.'

She gazed at the enormous diamond. Of course it was real. He was too rich to need to fake it. 'When did you get it?'

'I didn't. One of my assistants picked it up on the way to the airport. I apologise if you don't like it—apparently there was a limited selection.'

Massive solitaires were always in style, weren't they? The box blared the luxurious branding. But she couldn't quite believe he'd got someone else to buy it.

'Try it on and see if it fits.'

Because that was all that mattered—she didn't need to like it. It didn't mean anything. They just needed to make it fit and off they went as fiancés. She pushed the platinum band onto her cold finger. 'Lucky guess.'

He nodded and pulled a laptop from his briefcase. 'You can shop in Athens, get whatever else you need.'

'I don't need anything else.' She didn't need this giant lump of ice on her finger either.

'You're going to need a little more than the black tee shirts and trousers you've stuffed in that small bag. At some point that baby is going to make its presence known.'

'I'll get some bigger black tees and trousers when I need to,' she muttered obstinately. She did *not* want his wealth showered upon her. In fact, she wanted to take as little as possible from him—after all, he wanted little from her too.

But he'd glanced up from his laptop and now a small smile was flitting around his mouth. 'Why black?'

'Why not?'

'You make me think of a shadow…like you're trying not to stand out.'

'Women my height always stand out,' she pointed out grimly.

'For all the right reasons. You should make the most of your attributes.'

She gaped, momentarily unable to answer.

'And don't forget to get some more of those little scarlet silk things,' he murmured wickedly, and then looked back at his screen.

Leah stared hard at him for a while longer but apparently he was going to spend the rest of the flight working on his laptop. He'd just been amusing himself with a flippant moment. She shook her head. He was a conundrum—so often reserved and serious, and then there were flashes of fun and humour and, right this second, she really didn't like him for it.

As they landed hours later, a wave of nervous anticipation scurried along her veins. She'd never thought she'd visit Greece any time soon and she had to confess she was excited at the prospect of discovering its ancient culture and history, tasting the beautiful food, experiencing the lifestyle…although she rapidly discovered Theo's wasn't a normal lifestyle. It was almost obscene. She had only a moment to breathe in the warmer, vibrant atmosphere before more security guys in tailored suits and silence escorted them from the plane to a powerful black car with tinted windows. She glimpsed a bustling city filled with people, traffic, buildings, but they drove for quite a while and eventually the landscape changed. The properties became bigger with green spaces between them. Off a side street she saw palm trees forming a guard of honour the length of an esplanade.

'You live in the suburbs?' Somehow it wasn't quite what she'd expected.

'We have a compound on the coastline now known as the Athenian Rivera,' he said solemnly. 'The land has been in the family for decades.'

A compound? On a riviera? Leah had only seen such things in music videos.

'Will I meet Dimitri tonight?' she asked.

'Tomorrow would be better. He should be resting for the night by now.'

He'd gone all remote again—she felt the tension in his silence and the loss of his smile. All earlier easiness was now omitted from his demeanour. She focused on what she could see, catching glimpses of a beautiful mansion-lined beach just before they turned into a driveway. Large gates automatically swung back to allow the car through. They rounded a corner and a building came into view—not old and traditional but sleek and modern, extremely opulent and stylish. As she gaped at the perfect landscaping and the subtle exterior lighting showing off the architecture, the front door opened and a stunning woman strolled out.

A gorgeous blue dress clung to her voluptuous body and a pleased smile curved her full lips.

'Who's that?' She gasped involuntarily.

She heard the muttered oath beneath Theo's breath and he swiftly got out of the car. The rhythm of the stunning woman's high-heeled shoes bumped unevenly when she saw Leah emerge and stand just behind Theo.

'Angelica.' Theo bestowed kisses on the woman's cheeks. 'I'm sorry I wasn't here to greet you properly—'

The woman purred something in Greek.

'Leah.' Theo turned, still speaking in English to include her. 'May I introduce you to our good family friend, Angelica Galanis?'

Family friend? Was that what she was?

'Angelica, this is Leah.'

But Theo didn't give Angelica any additional explanation of Leah.

A low cough made all three of them turn. An elderly man with a cane was in the open doorway. Leah froze. This just had to be Dimitri. While he was shorter than Theo and frail, he had a familiar steely look in his gaze. Leah surreptitiously wiped her hands on her jeans. She felt crumpled and stale and never more out of place. And she'd been out of place a lot.

'Theodoros?' The older man looked from Theo to Leah.

'Dimitri.' Theo clamped Leah's hand in his and walked towards the waiting man. 'I wanted to introduce you formally tomorrow, but this is wonderful. I am pleased to introduce you to Leah.'

Dimitri simply stared.

'Leah is my fiancée.'

She heard the muffled gasp of surprise from the woman just behind them. Dimitri said nothing to her directly but whispered a short comment to Theo. Theo wrapped his arm around Leah's waist and pulled her close. The old man's breathing became ragged and Theo spoke to him in reassuring tones before lifting his voice to call something in Greek.

An older woman immediately appeared behind Dimitri. Given her deferential manner, Leah guessed she was on the staff. Theo quietly spoke to the woman and a moment later she escorted Dimitri down a long corridor lined with large portraits. Even through the thick walls Leah could sense the older man's emotion—it was strong enough to reverberate all the way through her own ribcage.

'My grandfather is still recovering from his operation,' Theo said smoothly and guided her into the polished foyer. He smiled at her as if there were nothing at all awkward about the situation—as if they were truly intimate. 'We'll spend time with him properly tomorrow.'

'Theo, it's very late and obviously not the right time for you to have a house guest.' Angelica's face was flushed and her English was heavily accented. 'I should probably go…' She trailed off.

'It's late, please stay tonight and we'll make travel arrangements for you in the morning,' Theo replied smoothly.

Despite his charming exterior, Leah could sense his underlying tension too. The 'welcome home' committee seemed to have exacerbated it.

'I apologise again for not being here to welcome you properly,' he said to Angelica. 'But thank you for understanding this is a personal time for us.'

Theo stiffened as Angelica's gaze lingered on the glittering ring on Leah's finger. He stepped between the two women, protecting Leah from Angelica's scrutiny. She was paler than usual and she'd half turned away; defensiveness seeped from her hunched shoulders. It was as if she was trying to be that shadow as he'd suggested on the plane. She'd been hurt before. Having met her parents, he understood more. But she ought to stand tall. He didn't want her to feel any fear, any inferiority here. 'Are you hungry, Leah?' he asked gently.

She shook her head.

He held out his hand to her. 'Come, I'll take you to our quarters.'

She put her hand in his and he turned and bowed to Angelica. He'd clean forgotten the woman was coming to visit and of course Dimitri would have stayed up to welcome him with his guest. Instead now Dimitri was tired and shocked. Theo couldn't blame him. Tomorrow he'd ensure the old man believed he and Leah were happy. While he hated lying, he didn't want Dimitri to know he'd messed up.

And now there was Leah. He knew he had to give her some space and a chance to take all this in. She hadn't wanted to stay in touch after that night at the hotel. She hadn't even wanted to kiss him goodbye. Now he'd dragged her to a foreign country where she didn't speak the language and she'd been given an awkward welcome. He'd almost done to her what had been done to him all those years ago and he was furious with himself.

That large diamond dug into his palm as he clasped her fingers and led her to the stairs. He felt a heel about the blunt way he'd just handed that to her too. But he refused to lie to her. It was imperative he maintain distance between them. He'd start as he meant to go on.

Except all he wanted to do was kiss away the sad tilt to her mouth and restore that passionate warmth in her eyes. He wanted to hear her husky little laugh again.

'This is my suite.' He opened the door to his private wing and waited for her to walk in.

'Angelica is an old family friend?' There was no missing the suspicious curiosity in her eyes.

'I forgot Dimitri had invited her to stay this weekend. If I'd remembered I would have cancelled the invitation.' He gritted his teeth.

'Is it a special occasion?'

'Not that I'm aware of.'

'Why had he invited her?'

He closed the door behind them. 'Why do you think?'

'Your grandfather invited her to stay with you as a prospective what—bride?' She frowned. 'He doesn't trust you to pick a woman on your own?'

'He doesn't trust that I'll ever make a *permanent* pick,' Theo said tightly. 'I was keeping him happy while he recovers.'

'Keeping him happy?' she echoed. 'Because you never wanted to get married.'

'Actually now I do. To you.' He made himself walk forward and open the door to her bedroom.

She came to an abrupt halt and spun to face him. 'You expect me to sleep in the same bed as you?'

He glanced and saw the big bed behind her. Her tone pushed him that last notch over the edge. Now he was alone with her again at last desire washed over him, loosening the bonds of self-control he'd been straining against for hours. In truth, for months. He'd wanted her the second he'd seen her again. He'd never stopped wanting her since that night. The whole 'I'm pregnant' thing ought to have shut it down. It hadn't.

'Is this for the look of it, Theo?' She jerked her head towards the bed. 'Because there are other people here?'

He couldn't control himself enough to reply. It was a mistake, because in the face of his silence, he felt her emotions fire.

'I can play that part if you want.' She flicked back her hair and stepped up to him, her lavender eyes deepening with almost liquid intensity. 'I'll jump up and down on that bed and scream with ecstasy all through the house so everyone in the neighbourhood hears. I'll—'

'Be amazing?' he challenged, his body almost bursting with the feral energy he'd held leashed for so long. 'Bring it on.'

She jerked her chin at him defiantly. 'You think you can just order me around? That I'll do *anything* you ask me to?'

He breathed hard but those knots were slipping. He *did* want her to do anything and her loss of temper was oddly welcome. It had been a long, trying day and both of them needed to vent. But he was *not* the villain here.

'My grandfather's rooms are in another building on the other side of the tennis court. Angelica is in the guest house on the other side of the pool. You can be as loud as you like.'

He'd jump her on the bed with him if she wanted. And he'd happily make her scream.

'If they're that far away, then why do I need to be in your room?'

'You don't,' he snapped. 'This is my *wing*, Leah. There's more than one bedroom in here.'

She gaped and then a flush swept up her face. 'Why? For your secret harem?'

He laughed roughly at her temper and inwardly revelled at the way the colour made her radiance return. She looked so much more alive than the cautious woman of only moments earlier.

'Stop being so poisonous.' He stepped closer, unable to keep any distance at all. 'We slept in separate rooms last night, remember? I'm not about to insist that change. Or is it that you want to be back in my bed?'

Was that what it was? Now they had privacy, she could voice her thoughts. And now that she was beyond provoked, she'd revealed what was uppermost in her mind.

'What? *No!*' But her mouth formed a full-lipped pout and her purple-tinged eyes shimmered with passion.

Sizzling sexual tension pulled him closer still. They'd have separate lives, yes, but maybe clearing this heated fog might be the best thing for them both. He didn't want to fight. Didn't want anything else from her... But *this*? The pull was undeniable.

'You want to be back there every bit as much as I want you there,' he muttered.

'If you think I want you—'

'You're not a good liar, sweetheart. You've told me that yourself.' He couldn't resist a second longer. Reaching out, he cupped her jaw.

'Theo...'

Satisfaction merged with desire at her soft whisper of submission and the gentle lean into his touch. His need had such power, he was driven to kiss, not her mouth, but that delicate, sensitive skin of her neck. He'd take more, touch more, do everything unexpected and delightful. She shivered, her hands lifted, not to push him away but to clutch his shirt and pull him closer still. This was what he wanted. Her embrace, her smile, her playfulness.

Her soft moan made him giddy with triumph and the diabolical desire to tease her overpowered him.

'Oh, no,' he said as he nibbled his way down. He wanted her as tortured as he'd been these last weeks and then he wanted to assuage it. 'No screaming your ecstasy,' he softly echoed her taunt. 'You've got to be quiet. If you're not quiet, I'm going to stop.'

'You're not going to start,' she muttered breathlessly.

'I already have and you're already ahead of me.'

'You arrogant...'

But she trailed off as his fingers traced the neckline of her loose tee.

'I might be arrogant but I'm not wrong.' He pulled her fully into his embrace. 'Be quiet, Leah. Or I stop.'

Leah knew she could say no and he'd stop. She could say anything and he'd stop. But the last thing she wanted was for him to stop. So, instead, she smiled.

He kissed along her cheekbones, then her eyelids so

she closed her eyes. His fingertips teased and she moaned again. Her skin was so sensitive to his touch. She heard his muttered oath, a mumble of something hot and ferocious, and then his hands lifted her. He swiftly crossed the floor to the bed and tumbled down onto it with her. She cried out with the powerful pleasure of being with him like this again. Of having him above her, caressing her, pinning her with his magnificent body.

'You don't want me to stop, do you?' he whispered hotly against her mouth.

She kept silent but arched her hips to meet his—uncaring about the layers of clothes between them. She just needed to feel him. She sought him the one way she could—with her body, closing her mind to any more repercussions. His laugh was smothered on her skin as he kissed down her torso, lifting her tee out of his way with his teeth. But he wouldn't let her touch him back. He kept her too busy squirming, seeking more of his wicked mouth. She shook with need. He traced his hand carefully over her, making her quiver. She gasped as his hand easily slipped beneath the loose waistband of her jeans, then deeper to where she was slick and hot. She heard his harshly drawn breath as he discovered just how much she wanted him. She didn't care how much she was feeding his ego with her response right now. She didn't care that he now knew he could do whatever he wanted, whenever he wanted, if he wanted. She was too needy.

'Theo—' She shivered, desperately biting her lip. She didn't want him to stop but she couldn't hold back her cry.

He looked into her eyes. His were filled with tender heat as he stroked her with a firm but gentle touch. 'Let it out, sweetheart,' he muttered roughly. 'I want to hear you, want to see you, want to feel you.' His groan was soul-filled. 'I have missed you.'

Any game was forgotten, burned to cinders by the honesty in that scorching whisper. An outpouring of warmth and want flooded her. He didn't give her a chance to answer, or himself an opportunity to say anything more, because he kissed her—so thoroughly, so passionately, while his fingers teased her to the point of no return. She arched—high and taut, straining for the release only he could bring.

'Leah.' He broke free and breathed.

'Yes!' She convulsed, her cry echoing as her whole world was obliterated.

She drowned in the tumultuous sensations, utterly, utterly undone. She couldn't find the energy to open her eyes and she didn't want to. She wanted to stay in this half-dream-state of delight.

I have missed you.

That whispered secret had felled her. She'd missed him too. She'd missed this closeness. This easiness. But now total exhaustion scrubbed her ability to do anything—to speak, move, think. She wanted to open her eyes but she couldn't. She felt him brush her hair from her face, then he gently repeated the motion again, then again. Until Leah discovered she couldn't resist anything any more—not him. Nor the pull of a profound sleep.

CHAPTER EIGHT

LEAH FURIOUSLY SCRUBBED her body, rejecting the lingering warmth from last night and trying not to appreciate the stunning luxury of the gleaming marble bathroom. Despite that wide blue sky and brilliant sunshine outside, her mood was bad because when she'd woken she'd discovered he wasn't there. It wasn't the fact that he wasn't there that made her disgruntled. It was that she'd *wanted* him to be there. If he'd really missed her, why had he left so early? Or was it just that he'd missed *sex*?

Had he only touched her because she'd provoked him? Because he was venting the frustrations of a very long day? Except he'd not asked for anything for himself after her release. He'd merely proved his power over her and then he'd stayed and stroked her hair and that was mortifying. She had no idea when he'd left her, only that he had. She'd woken, still half dressed, not even in the bed but on top of it and covered by a light blanket that he must have put over her.

She swiftly towelled dry, pulled on a fresh tee and jeans and then glanced out of the window at that incredible view again. There was a gorgeous lap pool with guest houses on both sides and, beyond that, the crystalline sea stretched for miles. It was the bluest water she'd ever seen.

But now she could see Theo and Angelica seated at a big table on the terrace. Theo was in trousers and white shirt, his sleeves rolled back enough to show off his tanned forearms. She clamped down on that restless ache.

Angelica wore another stunning summery dress, her hair and make-up immaculate. She was clearly at ease with having staff serve breakfast, felt no awkwardness in wondering what to say or how to say it. The fact was, they looked good together. Leah was nothing like that woman. She wasn't Greek. Or beautiful. Or from the 'right society'. She was a pregnant nobody, with no qualifications, no real achievements to date. Her black jeans and black tee were too old, loose and casual—they didn't fit the scene. And nor did the rest of her. She froze, not wanting to go down and join them. She didn't think she could fake it.

Pull it together.

She had to get over herself. He'd taken her by the hand, he'd introduced her as his fiancée. If she chose not to go down there now, then wasn't *she* choosing to be invisible again? For so long she'd wanted to escape that doormat role; she couldn't revert to it just because she was scared. She had to do better for her baby and make this work.

By the time Leah made it down to the ground floor Angelica was standing ready for departure. 'It was fascinating to meet you, Leah,' she said. 'I'm sure we'll see each other again.'

Despite that polite farewell, there was no mistaking Angelica's sharp curiosity. Leah fought the instinct to cover her belly. She turned towards the terrace as Theo guided Angelica to the car. She'd fuel up, ready to face his family.

Theo watched the car head down the drive, taking Angelica away. No doubt she'd tell everyone about the woman he'd brought back with him. His instinctive need to protect Leah built, but he'd face Dimitri first. Their meetings usually didn't go much beyond balance sheets and brainstorming business expansions. They lived and breathed the banking business and their unspoken agreement had cemented over the years—they never discussed the past. But while Theo had protected the old man for so long, he couldn't have him hate Leah.

'Tell me about her,' Dimitri said quietly when Theo went to the old man's study to explain.

Theo thought about the way she supported her ballet friend, her brother, those elderly residents at that home. 'She's very caring.' But he braced—there was no point prevaricating. 'She's pregnant.'

Dimitri didn't move.

'You'll make her welcome,' he added, wondering if that man had even heard what he'd said. 'I am responsible for her.'

To his total astonishment and total discomfort, Dimitri's eyes filled.

'She's having your child?' the old man clarified.

'Yes.' He still had to steel himself to admit it aloud, let alone prepare for the reaction he was about to get.

'I didn't think…' The old man breathed out. 'Good, Theo.'

Good? Theo blinked, gobsmacked by the old man's obvious emotion. *Good?*

'She will have my great-grandson.' Pride lit the old man's face.

Theo still couldn't stand to imagine an actual baby, but at Dimitri's satisfied certainty he couldn't help a small tease. 'Or great-granddaughter.'

'Wonderful.' Dimitri actually beamed at the prospect. 'Then you'd better go take care of her.'

No more questions? No desire to know more? No judgment? Theo couldn't believe it.

Hurting more somehow, he pushed away the previously unimaginable mental picture of Dimitri hovering over a bundle in Leah's arms. He felt as if he were skating on the thinnest of ice. With one wrong move, it would crack and they'd be dragged down to drown in frigid waters. But if he kept his steps careful, they could all stay safe.

She was standing by the pool. How could such a slender silhouette be such a distraction? Such temptation. His pulse quickened at the memory of late last night. But as he registered her pale façade, regret rose. She'd been tired last night and she'd misunderstood about the bedroom and he shouldn't have taken advantage of her innocence and anger and emotional vulnerability to satisfy his own needs. He'd lost control, no longer able to resist the desire to touch her. All he'd wanted was to lose himself with her again. He'd only hauled his control back when she'd all but fainted away in an exhausted heap after her orgasm had hit. A fact that had made him feel all the more guilty.

They had to focus on getting their marriage arranged and to provide security for the child. The paperwork for the wedding was in hand so it was simply a matter of getting through the next few days. Once they were married, they could take a breath and figure out the future more gently. Until then, *he* needed to regain control.

'How did you sleep?' he asked, even though it was obvious in her expression.

'Very well, thank you.' She lifted her chin. 'I realise now that you were just helping me to…relax.' She breathed in. 'Thank you for that. It was thoughtful.' She glanced at the table. 'But I'll manage with just a glass of warm milk from now on.'

A glass of milk? He stared. She couldn't be serious. And as for him helping her to relax? As if there'd been any thought that had gone before what had happened?

Her coolness sparked his desire to prove her a liar all over again. His desire simply to touch her again. He was appalled at the realisation he had zero control. *Zero.* All he wanted was to get close again and know that starburst of heat. But he rejected the want winding him tight. He'd go to the office in Athens. Bury himself in the work he'd missed while he was London collecting her. He'd regain focus and get ahead. When in doubt, achieve.

At that thought, a great wave of resistance rose. How

much he wanted to stay scared him. He never wanted to skip work. It was always his escape. But now?

'I need to go into the office,' he said brusquely before he could change his mind.

'Today?'

'I had an extra day in the UK. I need to catch up.' He was good at doing what was necessary and *this* was necessary.

'Because you're so behind from one extra day away?' Her lashes hid the glittering sharpness of her eyes.

'I'll be back in time for dinner.' He needed distance. She was already paying too steep a price for his reckless behaviour and he couldn't trust himself not to repeat it.

'And what do you want me to do while you're gone?' she asked softly.

'Rest, Leah. You need it.' He'd go to work. After their wedding he'd take her to the island and show her that life wasn't going to be a total disaster.

'I need it?'

There was only a lone ember of provocation in her soft echo, but he couldn't resist throwing one last little retaliation as he forced his feet to take him away. 'Go have that hot milk and relax.'

Leah stomped back into the mansion. How was she supposed to 'relax'? What was she supposed to do with her time? She knew no one but Theo and she didn't know him at all well. His grandfather hadn't appeared since last night. She wasn't sure he even spoke much English and she certainly couldn't speak Greek. She had no transport options, no map of the city anyway and no money. Sure, she could swim in that pool, but she had no swimsuit and she wasn't sure skinny dipping would be a good idea. Worse, she realised Theo might've been right: her jeans collection wasn't going to cut it. She needed clothing appropriate enough to mix with the Angelicas of Athens. Not dresses though. Leah didn't wear dresses…

She could eat from the platters of nibbles that constantly appeared on the nearest occasional table but she was too wound up to have any appetite. She could sleep up in that gorgeous bedroom but she only needed to set foot in there and all the memories of his touch tormented her. She could definitely read because she'd discovered there were books everywhere, not just in the stunning library. There was a home movie theatre too and a ballroom that was beautiful but wistfully empty. It was a grand home for a large family and she ought to feel amazing. Instead she literally walked away from it all. But as she reached a path that she guessed led to the beach, a security guy materialised in front of her. She stopped and smiled at him warily.

'If you would like to walk along the beach, I will escort you,' he said briskly in heavily accented English.

'Oh, no, thank you.' She backed up a pace. 'Sorry if I bothered you.'

There was no return smile. 'I'm here to ensure your safety.'

'Oh, okay. Thank you.'

So there were boundaries to this world? She marched back inside feeling odd about not being able to come and go alone as she pleased. She'd get her knitting. It seemed ridiculous to be working with wool in such warm weather but it always relaxed her. And she really needed to relax. She walked along the corridor and glanced again at the collection of formal portraits that hung so prominently positioned. There was a wedding portrait of Dimitri and his wife, and another of that woman alone, looking a little older. Then there was a portrait of a younger man Leah suspected was Theo's father. He looked no older than about fifteen. There was no portrait from his wedding, indeed there was no image at all of Theo's mother. And then there was the one of Theo and Dimitri together. Theo looked about eighteen. Both he and Dimitri were in suits, formally posed. There was no smile and man-hug. They stood separate, angled in front of a large desk. It looked as if it had been taken at an office. Theo's first day at work? Had he been groomed to be the head of the Savas empire from the start? What about his father? Because there was no equivalent 'line of succession' photo of him. Her curiosity deepened. Theo hadn't mentioned his mother at all in his brief explanation of why he'd come to live with Dimitri. And it had been a *very* brief explanation.

She gathered her bag from her room and returned poolside to lose herself in the blissfully soothing repetition of stitch after stitch. She wasn't interrupted—other than with trays of food—but slowly, inexorably, her nerves tightened. When would he return home? They had to talk some more, surely. She couldn't spend all her days like this.

He phoned her late in the afternoon.

'I won't be back until after dinner tonight,' he said brusquely as soon as she answered. 'Don't wait up.'

The businesslike way he delivered the minimal message was chilling. And that disappointment? She didn't want to admit to that at all.

The early evening stretched out—slow and painful. She saw Dimitri in the distance but he didn't come near her and frankly now she was too intimidated and heartsore to face someone else's disappointment or judgment. She asked the housekeeper if she could dine alone in her bedroom. Of course it was no problem.

In safe, private misery she flicked on the television in the small lounge simply because she had nothing better to do. She scrolled through the channels, pausing on what she guessed was the local news channel. They were showing a live feed from the waterfront just up the coast. Intrigued, she watched for a while; it looked like the cream of Athens society—all the gorgeous Angelicas. But then she stared harder at the screen. Was that *Theo*?

She blinked. It *was*. She'd recognise his height and imposing presence from fifty feet and he was dressed to disturb in dinner jacket and white tie. And there were women near him—beautiful, designer-clad beauties. Was this what he considered *work*? Quaffing champagne down at some fancy marina?

She stilled, unsure what to do, quelling the urge to phone him. She waited for his return but in the end fell asleep before she heard his car. In the morning she expected to see him at breakfast, but there was still no sign. It was the housekeeper who informed her with a slightly confused air that he was already at work. That was when Leah realised he'd not returned home all night. Hurt burgeoned—built by his lack of consideration, of contact. Was this what it was going to be like? How could he go from concerned and courteous to simply…absent?

She wanted him to see her as she'd thought he once had. She didn't want to be invisible and taken for granted again.

As the day passed in isolation, her hurt festered, morphing into fury. By the time he finally returned, *after* dinner, she was practically shaking with pent-up rage. She'd hidden away in her room again, not wanting anyone to witness their 'reunion'.

She heard his footsteps as he climbed the stairs—she'd left her door ajar so she'd be forewarned. Now he nudged her door further open with his fingers.

'Nice of you to call in,' she said acidly, loathing her shrewish tone but unable to hold it back.

'I told you I had to work late yesterday.' He leaned against the doorjamb and regarded her carefully. 'It got so late it was best for me to stay in town.'

'You really think I'm stupid, don't you?' She was so hurt.

'Why do you say that?'

'You weren't at "work" last night. You were at a party.' He was avoiding her. He'd been avoiding her for the last couple of days.

'Actually, it wasn't a party. It was the launch of a new yacht.'

'Is this what it's going to be like? You're just going to lie by omission…or semantics? Like how you treat your grandfather? You let him think the best through half-truths, to kid yourself you're keeping him happy? Is that what you're planning to do with me?'

He straightened and came into the room, closing the door behind him. 'I'm not lying at all to you.' He gazed at her steadily and walked slowly towards her. 'I've never lied to you.'

'No, you're just planning to send me away so you can pretend I don't exist most of the time.' She sprang up and stepped away, putting the armchair safely between him and her. 'That's why you're not involving me in any of your life here. Lock me in the attic, why don't you?'

'Leah—'

'Don't patronise me or act like you're trying to protect me. Why not just tell me the truth?' She shook her head.

'It was work. I'm the CEO of one of the largest private banks in the world and we have several subsidiaries in a variety of industries. Patronage, sponsorship, networking are all part of the remit. We're powerful, we need to contribute to society. So it's part of my job to maintain the profile and reputation at a certain level. To develop the goodwill and trust of investors and clients.'

'Is that why you didn't want me there? Because I'm not going to maintain the reputation of you or your family or your precious business?'

'Would you really want to go?' He looked surprised. 'You're in no state to be out there yet—you're exhausted. You don't speak the language or—'

'Look the part?'

'Or have the knowledge to deal with these people. *Yet.*' He put his hands on his hips and gazed at her. 'Give us some time, Leah.'

The injustice of that comment made her flare. 'You're the one not giving us any *time*, Theo. You're using work to avoid me. And your grandfather. I might not be able to negotiate billion-dollar deals but attending a *party* hardly requires a master's in rocket science. It's not hard to talk to people.' She glared at him. 'Yet it seems that, for you, talking is really hard. Why didn't you ask me?'

'Perhaps I should have.'

'Perhaps? You just want to hide me away on your prison island.'

'It's *not* a prison.' He actually laughed.

'You don't want me to be seen.' She tossed her head, refusing to let his humour placate her. 'But I'm used to people looking at me and judging. I can ignore them.'

A frown formed on his face. 'What do you think they see?'

She didn't want to think about this. 'I can't care about what they see or think. I won't be hidden away like something to be ashamed of. Not by the man I'm going to marry.'

She couldn't be treated as if she were inferior or an embarrassment. She'd had enough of that in her life already.

'Is that what you thought I was doing?' He took in a deep breath. 'Leah, while we're married, I'll never humiliate you. I'll never cheat on you. I will be loyal.'

But she wanted more than integrity. She wanted so much more that she dared not think about. 'How many properties do you have?' she asked desperately.

'Does it matter?'

'Where are they? Perhaps there's a destination that might suit me better. Paris? New York? I'd quite like to live in Manhattan.'

'You'll be within a thirty-minute flight distance from me,' he said grimly.

'Thirty minutes?'

'I just want to protect you,' he said. 'And the child,' he added belatedly.

'From what? What's so awful about Athens that we have to be locked away on Prison Island?'

He folded his arms. 'I just want you to have the privacy and space to be happy.'

'You mean *you* want privacy and space away from us most of the time. You'll just swoop in on the weekends and be the fun guy and then leave.'

'The fun guy?' He looked stunned for a second, then sobered again. 'That's not what it's about. Dimitri needs to believe that we're happy. For as long as he's alive, you and I are happy.'

'He's not stupid. If we're living apart most of the time, he'll suspect we're not happy.'

'But if we're together all the time he'll be *certain* we're unhappy. Always having to show a happy façade is impossible.'

A happy *façade*? Was it beyond the realms of possibility that they could actually *be* happy? Couldn't this feeling become something else? Something more? Or was she really totally alone in thinking there *was* this feeling? There was something linking them together.

'I'll visit you on the weekends but we'd have space and privacy there and wouldn't have to carry on an act in front of him. You can rest.'

'Do I want to rest?' She exploded. Had he been carrying on an act when he'd touched her so intimately last night? When he'd told her he missed her? 'Maybe I want to live life.'

'And you will.' He paced away from her. 'I'm not trying to hide you away.'

'No? Then why have you brought me here and left me alone?'

'I...' He flexed his hands. 'I'm trying to get my head around everything.'

'And I'm not? Can't we do this *together*, Theo?' She tried to break through his barriers. 'I don't want someone making all the decisions as if I have nothing of value to contribute.'

'That wasn't my intention.' He shifted and pivoted to face her again. 'You want more from me.'

'Some communication,' she muttered. 'Some discussion.'

'All right.' He sighed and reached out as if he could no longer resist, gently rubbing his fingertip along her jaw. 'Leah...'

She turned helplessly into his touch, hating herself as she did. 'Don't use my weakness to distract me.'

His eyebrows lifted. '*Your* weakness?'

She closed her eyes. 'This wasn't what I meant when I said I wanted more from you.'

He drew an audible breath. 'Do you think it's only you who wants...this?' He sounded almost choked. 'But I can't be the kind of husband you should have.'

She opened her eyes and gazed straight into his. 'Why would you think that?'

He froze, a rigid expression masked his thoughts. Again she realised he was battling something deep inside—something painful.

'You're kind, Theo. I know you'll support me. You've said you'll be faithful and I believe you. What else do you think a husband needs to do?'

He was so rigid she grew wary of his answer.

'I can't love you, Leah.'

She stilled, shocked by his quiet, so calm confession.

'I can't love anyone,' he added huskily.

His eyes flashed with sorry sincerity and seemed to ask for her forgiveness. But why would he say that?

'You love your grandfather,' she whispered. She'd seen it. Almost everything he did, he did with that man in mind.

'I *owe* my grandfather,' he corrected softly and stepped back. 'I'm sorry, Leah.'

CHAPTER NINE

RETURNING FROM A lonely breakfast the next day, Leah paused on the threshold of her room. The housekeeper was in there, carefully folding Leah's cardigan.

'Thank you,' Leah said shyly, aware there wasn't a lot of warmth in the woman's face. 'We haven't properly met—my name is Leah.'

She hadn't been introduced to anyone properly yet. Theo had been in too much of a rush to deal with his work crisis and it seemed none of his staff were overly friendly.

'Amalia.'

Leah offered her a smile and saw the way she was looking at the ribbed pattern on her cardigan. 'Do you knit?'

Amalia glanced, her expression softening. 'I make lace.'

'Oh.' Leah stepped closer, her interest flaring. 'I'd love to watch you some time…' She trailed off awkwardly. Perhaps it wasn't the done thing to chat?

But then Amalia smiled and gestured at the cardigan. 'Did you make this?'

'I did, yes.' Leah smiled. 'I knit a lot—it relaxes me. Though I probably won't need to as much. It's very warm here…'

She trailed off again. She was babbling—nervous and awkward and too eager to engage in desperately needed social contact.

But Amalia finally smiled. 'It can get cold here in winter.'

'Does it?'

'It even snows in Athens—'

'No.' She'd had no idea.

Amalia laughed and nodded.

Encouraged, Leah nibbled her lip but then smiled. 'Actually, I need to buy some clothes,' she said. She needed to look the part as best she could. She needed to make an effort to embrace the country and culture her child was going to be born into. 'Would you be able to help me? Come with me?'

'Shopping?' Amalia looked startled.

'Yes.' Leah nodded hopefully. 'I have no idea where to go.' Or what to get.

Amalia looked pleased. 'Of course—'

'Oh, thank you,' she breathed out with a rush of relief. 'And I need a wedding dress…'

'You wouldn't make one?' Amalia gestured at Leah's bag. 'You could knit with silk.'

Leah's smile blossomed. 'I've love to.' She'd been working on a pattern for a while—a dress of her own design she *would* wear. 'But I don't have enough time before the wedding.'

'What if I helped you? I have lace…'

'You'd do that?' Leah was stunned.

Amalia straightened. 'You're marrying Theodoros.'

Of course, this was about Theo. Did Amalia care for him? Theo worked so hard, he was a dutiful grandson and a good boss…maybe Amalia and the other staff weren't only wary while they decided whether she was good enough for him? Were they protective of him? Why? Because they loved him? She had the feeling he was very easy to love.

'You know him well?' she asked gently, hoping she was hiding how curious she was about him. Why did he have this huge sense of duty but total denial of love? Why did he think he was incapable of it? She didn't believe him. She couldn't when his actions said so much otherwise. She was sure he always tried to do what was best for those he was close to. He'd do that for their baby too, wouldn't he? She *had* to believe that.

'I've worked for Dimitri for years,' Amalia said. 'My husband too.'

'Really?'

Amalia smiled. 'And my sons did too, before they went away to study.'

'So you were here when Theo arrived?' Leah asked cautiously.

'Yes.' Amalia glanced at her, as if she knew there were a million more questions on Leah's tongue. 'He was very quiet when he first arrived.'

Leah held her breath, not wanting to interrupt Amalia and stop her, wondering why Theo had been so quiet. Had he been afraid?

'He had little Greek, of course,' Amalia said. 'But he studied very hard. He has always worked very hard.'

Always? Hadn't he got up to mischief like most teenagers? Hadn't he ever rebelled?

I owe my grandfather.

Perhaps not. Had he always been so determined to pay him back? Why? Wasn't it natural for a grandfather to take in a grandson when his parents had gone? But where had his mother gone?

'I'll arrange the driver if you would like to go shopping now,' Amalia said, interrupting Leah's thoughts. 'Ten minutes, okay?'

'Perfect. *Thank you.*'

The plan put a lift in Leah's step, but when she came downstairs a few minutes later to find Amalia, Dimitri was sitting in the living room.

'Amalia is taking you shopping,' he said without preamble.

'Yes.' She automatically moved to adjust the cushion that was awkwardly positioned behind him.

'You want to spend money?' he asked warily when she'd fixed it and stepped back.

'Yes.' She smiled, battling hard not to be afraid of him. It was their first proper conversation and he was openly questioning her motives.

But she didn't blame him for not trusting her yet.

'I need something suitable when I meet Theo's business colleagues. I don't want to let him down.' And that was the truth. She wanted to please both Theo and his grandfather.

But Dimitri's demeanour didn't thaw.

Leah worried her lip and made herself ask the honest question. 'Do you think I'm after his money?'

'Aren't you?'

She paused. So much for Theo convincing him that their engagement was a love match.

'No,' she said firmly. 'I'm here because he insisted on it.' She swallowed and sat in the chair opposite his. 'I don't know Athens at all, in fact this is my first time to Greece. And I'm sorry if my arrival is a surprise to you. But I think we both want the best for Theo. I'm having his baby and I most definitely want the best for my child. But to be honest, I need some help.'

His expression finally softened.

'I don't speak any Greek,' she confessed in a relieved rush. 'Do you think Amalia can help me find a tutor?'

'You want to learn Greek?'

'Of course.' She was going to be living here for the foreseeable future, she didn't want to feel isolated from everyone for ever and she wanted her baby to enjoy its dual heritage. 'It might take me a while though,' she admitted with a sudden laugh. 'I'm not very academic.'

'I will help you.' He nodded slowly.

'You will?' She beamed at him. 'Thank you.'

He shot her a look. 'Thank you. *Efharisto.*' He then waited, looking at her expectantly.

'You mean *you'll* help me?' she asked. Dimitri himself?

'Thank you. *Efharisto,*' he repeated.

'Efharisto?'

'Yes. *Ne.*' He suddenly clapped his hands and called to Amalia. 'Come, you will speak to her only in Greek. Greek all the time.'

'*Ne*, Dimitri.' Amalia smiled and gestured for Leah to follow her.

Fortunately, Amalia disregarded Dimitri's order while they shopped. But *unfortunately* Amalia simply smiled and said yes to everything Leah tried on in the high-end boutiques of Athens. It was sweet and supportive, but truly not that helpful.

Theo had said she'd hidden behind her black clothing and perhaps he was right. She'd tried to avoid that backlash because of her height and slenderness. But maybe she should enjoy all the colours she loved and had always turned away from? Not just scarlet panties…

Not for him. For herself, right?

Except really, she realised it was *because* of him. He'd *seen* her that night and he'd liked what he'd seen. And she'd liked the person he'd made her feel free to be. The person confident enough to speak up for what she wanted with him. Confident to speak up to her parents for once. The person confident to call *him* to account too… She glanced again at the racks of clothing and turned her back on the black.

Three hours into the reinvigorated shopping marathon, her phone rang.

'Will you accompany me to an exhibition tonight?' Theo said.

'Pardon?'

'A driver will collect you at seven.' He paused. 'If you would like, that is.' She heard his smile. 'I am trying to ask, not dictate.'

'Okay,' she agreed cautiously, yet her heart raced because he'd listened and he was trying to include her. A fragile bubble bloomed—if he could try like this, maybe he could open up even more? Maybe he might even develop deeper feelings? She shivered, pushing away that wisp of a wish—*one day at a time.*

'I'm busy with meetings until late and I'll get changed at the office,' he said.

She glanced at the silky fabric hanging in front of her. 'I don't wear dresses, Theo.'

'Nor do I.' He laughed. 'Will you be ready?'

'Yes.'

Hours later she avidly stared out of the window, drinking in the sights as she was driven into the centre of Athens. Theo was waiting outside the gallery. Bowled over by the sight of him in that black tuxedo, she braced, slamming back her nerves. She was *not* concerned by his silent scrutiny.

'We need to—' He broke off and cleared his throat.

'To?'

'Walk inside.'

'I believe I'm capable of that,' she said with a shy laugh. 'Are you?'

He cleared his throat again. 'Scarlet, Leah?'

'Is it okay?'

'Does it need to be?' He finally smiled. 'You don't need my approval.'

'Maybe I would like it.'

He took her hand and drew her close to his side. 'It's not my approval you have, Leah. It's something else. Something raw. Something I can't deny. Something I can't turn off.' He breathed out. 'Who did your make-up?'

'I did.'

'You have skills.'

'I didn't let my mother stop me doing everything I was interested in. I just did it in secret. Sometimes.'

'What else did you do in secret?'

She just smiled at him and shrugged.

'I'm glad you're not doing it in secret now,' he admitted. 'I'm glad you're here letting the world see you.'

'They're seeing all right,' she noted with a wry grimace and her nerves mushroomed. 'They're staring.'

He cocked his head and blinked at her with teasing arrogance. 'What makes you think they're staring at you? I'm the one they're interested in.'

She choked on a giggle. 'Good point.'

'No.' He shook his head. 'They're staring because you look stunning.'

Heat travelled all over her body and he wrapped his arm around her to draw her closer.

'What are you doing?' she half gasped.

'You're the one who wanted to be treated like my fiancée.' He brushed a kiss against her cheek. 'This is how I'd do that. I'd stay close and kiss her often.'

'No, you wouldn't,' she breathed. 'That's not dignified enough for your grandfather.'

'You think I'm too uptight for displays of affection?'

'I think you're conscious of your position and you modify your behaviour depending on who's around.'

'Doesn't everyone?' He laughed. 'Isn't that just good manners?'

'But people still do what they want. They put themselves first. I don't know that you do.'

'Haven't I done that with you once already?' He stilled and faced her. 'You want me to put my desires first and damn who's watching? Damn the consequences?'

'Can you?'

He cupped the nape of her neck, pulled her to him and kissed her. It was a long, luscious kiss.

He lifted his head and laughed down at her dazed expression. 'You dared me to.'

She shook her head. 'That was just part of your PR plan. You weren't taking me seriously.'

'If I did what I really wanted right now, we'd both be arrested.'

She felt his hard heat digging into her pelvis.

'So now we have a problem,' he muttered hotly. 'I need you right here to preserve my blushes in front of all these people, but if you stay there, my little problem isn't going to go away.'

'*Little* problem?' she echoed archly.

'It's a good thing you're wearing trousers. If it was a skirt I'd have flipped it up and bent you over that piano already.' He grinned at her gasp. 'Sorry. Too honest?' His smile faded. 'I want you too much.'

'You've got some of my lipstick.' She gestured to her mouth, mirroring the placement of the smudge.

'So help me.' His slightly strangled-sounding request was oddly serious.

'Theo Savas.' A man interrupted them loudly and Theo instantly straightened, his expression smoothing back to reserved.

'You can't return to Athens and hide in the corner all evening.' The stranger's gaze skimmed over Leah, his eyes widening. 'And you are?'

'Leah Turner, my fiancée,' Theo answered for her.

'So the crazy rumours are correct?' The man stared back at Theo.

'They're not crazy,' Theo said coldly.

Rather rudely the man switched to Greek but frankly Leah was glad she didn't have to listen. She extracted herself from Theo's hold and with a small smile at him stepped aside to view the nearest painting.

As soon as she did, a designer-clad, stunningly polished woman swept over to her. 'You're Leah, aren't you? Theo Savas' fiancée.'

'That's correct.' She smiled. 'And you are?'

'Phoebe, a friend of Theo's. We're delighted and intrigued that you could join us. We know nothing about you.'

Leah couldn't help her little laugh. Not hiding the curiosity, was she? 'What did you want to know?'

'Everything, of course.' The woman smiled back. 'Where did you meet Theo?'

'In London, a few months ago. It's been a whirlwind.'

The woman nodded. 'I'm not going to lie, we're all stunned. I never imagined he'd settle down. Certainly not so soon.'

Leah recognised the sharp questions in the woman's eyes but she gently shrugged and didn't reply. Theo was right: sometimes it was better to remain silent.

'Will you have lunch some time?' the woman invited.

'I'd like that very much, thank you.' Leah answered honestly, even though she knew the woman really just wanted to mine her for information. But she also knew the way to get people to soften up was to get them speaking. 'It's important to me to get to know Theo's world here in Athens and I'd love to see more of the city. What are some of your favourite spots?'

Having despatched his overly curious business acquaintance, Theo remained at a slight distance so he could watch her. Frankly he was still getting his head—and his libido—around her outfit. Her black trousers were nothing like her usual baggy jeans. These were silk and sleek, they sat ultra-low on her narrow waist and showed off the slim length of her legs. The scarlet blouse she had on top was almost sheer at the back, revealing a sweep of gleaming skin all the way down to the small of her back. The shirt hid that slight curve of her belly and he was glad people wouldn't realise she was pregnant. Not yet. He was still getting used to that idea himself.

Her hair was entwined somehow into a low twist at the nape of her neck. She had a touch of make-up on—something to make her eyes seem even bigger, brighter, and a slash of red lipstick that made her mouth irresistibly kissable.

He shouldn't have kissed her. Not because the world was watching, but because he wanted more. He wanted to *know* more too—what other secret dreams did she have? What other secret bold action did she want to take? This was the woman who'd thrown all caution to the wind that night with him. He'd been so privileged. He wanted her to feel that freedom with him again. He didn't know why the desire was this strong but he was sure they needed to get rid of it. He'd hoped it would dissipate, that he could ignore it…but he couldn't and he knew she couldn't either. It would be better to exhaust it. Then they could move forward with a calm, easy plan for the future. It didn't need to be a big deal.

And people *were* staring at her. She was so tall, so striking. So sexy. But also that mandatory engagement notice had run in the newspaper and everyone was agog. He'd laughed off the swirling rumours about his grandfather's quest to find him a suitable fiancée, but that he'd come back from London with a woman?

He couldn't help moving closer again—that protective urge rising even when he knew Leah didn't want it, or need it, given the apparent ease with which she was talking to Phoebe Mikos. But *he* needed it. He stood alongside her, listening as she asked more questions than she answered. She politely asked about places to see, things to do, intuitively making the most of these people's pride in their city, but she did it with an artless charm that made everyone around her smile.

'Do you mind if we leave, Leah?' he asked her eventually.

She turned to him and he saw the relief in her eyes. He drew her out and quietly directed his driver to take them to the Athens villa.

'You enjoyed yourself?' he asked as she stifled a yawn.

'It wasn't too bad,' she murmured. 'Your friends aren't so scary.'

'They're not all friends,' he couldn't help warning despite having seen her at ease there. The worry within him bloomed again.

'Competitors? Rivals? Threats?' She chuckled. 'None of those people could hurt you.'

'No?' Her certainty burned somehow. 'Do you think I don't feel anything?' he asked—even when he'd been the one trying to convince himself that he didn't. 'That I'm inhuman somehow?'

It was stupid to even ask. He'd been the one to tell her he couldn't love anyone—and that was true, wasn't it? It had to be.

She turned to face him. Her eyes were like deep pools and he just wanted to dive in.

'No. I know you've been hurt,' she breathed. 'I just don't know how.'

He rejected her words. But her vulnerability shone through—all that soft emotion pierced his own defence. He should say nothing but when she looked at him like that he couldn't help himself.

'They could hurt you,' he muttered.

'So it's me you're worried about?' She shook her head. 'I can let it wash over me.' Her frown formed as he said nothing. 'You don't believe me?'

'My mother struggled to break in here,' he confided huskily. 'Like you she wasn't Greek, she was American. They met on one of his trips away.' There'd been many trips away. 'She didn't speak the language. I didn't either until I came to live with Dimitri.' His father hadn't seen any need to teach him and his mother had been too absorbed with her own problems to bother to find him a tutor. 'He didn't bring either of us back to Greece. When he finally did, she came home most nights without him.'

He'd been ten years old when he'd discovered her drinking alone late at night, drowning that humiliation and loneliness from leaving his father at one of his all-night parties with all those other women. She'd screamed at Theo for disturbing her and sent him from the room. But he couldn't go back to bed. How could he sleep when the sound of her bitter sobs rang through the door she'd neglected to slam?

'They were miserable.' Leah sat very still. 'Did Dimitri know?'

'Dimitri lost his only child.' Theo too was frozen, his heart encased in the ice that had formed there so long ago. 'And he blamed my mother for everything.'

CHAPTER TEN

THEO SUDDENLY MOVED and Leah glanced out of the window, only just realising that the car had stopped outside a stunning building on the corner of an obviously exclusive part of downtown Athens. 'We're not going back to the compound?'

His eyes glittered in the darkness as he held the door for her. 'This is my city villa.'

Taken aback, Leah tried—and failed—not to be completely floored by the perfect façade of the historic villa.

'Is this where you slept the other night?' When she stepped inside, her heart stopped. Hard oak floors, and a marble staircase led up to more luxuriously styled furnishings. But here on the ground floor there was an internal decorative pool, of all things. The villa encapsulated a sense of peace that ought to have been impossible in the centre of such a vibrant city. She walked away from him, just to catch her breath. From this room there were incredible panoramic views of the Acropolis. Right now it was lit up, a beacon of ancient romantics. It was beyond beautiful but, inexplicably, anger welled within her.

'This is where you bring your women, so your grandfather doesn't see them,' she said with a laugh, but a curl of bitterness spiralled even as she tried to stop it. This was the scene of his secret seductions. All those beautiful women she'd seen tonight? Had any been his lover?

He had a whisker of a smile on his face. 'I don't wish to be disrespectful and—'

'You don't want to get his hopes up.'

His eyes were intent upon her as she gazed about the beautiful place.

'And you thought I'd want to stay here with you?'

'Leah,' he said softly. 'You're going to be my wife.' He crossed the small space between them. 'There hasn't been anyone in my bed since that night with you. I'm not and never have been promiscuous.'

The awful thing was, the nearer he got to her, the less she cared about those other women, whether they existed or not. They no longer mattered—she knew they'd meant little to him anyway. Because that was how he survived, wasn't it? With an impenetrable heart. Because he had been hurt. And it sounded as if his mother had been hurt too.

'Are you okay?' He frowned at her.

'I just…have a bit of a headache,' she muttered, stalling so she could try to think.

'Then let's get you a drink of water, shall we?'

She followed him into the kitchen. He leaned back against the counter, watching enigmatically as she sipped the iced water and briefly held the cold glass against her burning face.

'You should have been a model,' he suddenly said, his voice husky. 'You could have made millions.'

She laughed and put her glass down, her fingers stupidly shaky. 'Use my quirky features?'

'You must have considered it. Surely all tall, ultra-thin girls are approached at some point?'

'My parents forbade it.'

'Oh.' He grimaced. 'Of course they did.'

'I was supposed to make something of my brain, not my body.'

'So they wouldn't let you make the most of one of your assets.' He cocked his head. 'In fact, they made you feel… what? Ashamed of it somehow?'

She hated his insightfulness.

'And the other girls at school gave you grief?'

'They called me anorexic, of course. Then they saw how

much I ate and assumed I must be bulimic. I'm just bony. It's the way I am.'

'I know.' He watched her. 'So your mother didn't like you wearing make-up or anything?'

'She refused to give money to an industry that thrives on insecurities.' She shrugged her shoulders. 'But you've seen her, she's the epitome of normal beauty ideals, right?'

He shook his head. 'We all like different things—'

'Don't be cute. You know what I mean. She's beautiful by anyone's standards. She doesn't need make-up or nice clothes to look amazing.'

'Nor do you. Nor does anyone.'

'But that doesn't mean they can't be fun. That doesn't mean you can't play with them and express yourself in all kinds of ways.' She'd just wanted to have a little fun.

'Usually you wear almost nothing but black—that's your self-expression?'

She shrugged. 'I gave in and just wore what's acceptable.'

'It doesn't matter how loose or dark you keep your clothing, you can't actually hide, Leah. You're not and never will be invisible.'

Yet almost all her life she'd wanted to be. Ironically, the only time she'd felt free of performance pressure was when she was onstage.

'Not tonight at least, no.' She smiled down at her blouse. 'Is this your way of saying you like it?'

'You should wear whatever you want to wear. Be the shadow, be the sunlight, be whatever you want. Just be yourself in that moment. There is no right or wrong.'

She smiled at him.

Something unfathomable flickered in his eyes. 'Why did you say yes to me that night?'

'Why?' She was stunned he'd need to ask. 'Your ego needs a stroke?'

'No, I really want to understand. Why me? Why that one night? Why not some other guy, some other time?'

'There was no other guy. No other time.'

'I don't believe you.'

She stared at him. 'Um…have you forgotten you were my first?'

'Oh, I'll never forget that,' he purred. 'But I think you had other chances before me. Maybe you just didn't notice them.'

'That's very kind of you. But no.' She shook her head.

'Liar.'

She stared at him, then glanced away. 'Okay, there was one guy who asked me out. But he didn't want *me*, he wanted to get on my mother's research team.'

'He tried to use you to get close to your parents?'

She nodded. 'I was working in their laboratory as an assistant. Because I didn't finish my degree.' Because she'd failed in their eyes.

'Because you never wanted to actually *do* the degree.'

'The things we try to do to please our parents, right?' she murmured. 'Like you marrying me to please your grandfather.'

'That's not the same,' he scoffed.

'Isn't it?'

'Nobody held a gun to my head to make me take you to bed,' he said. 'That desire is very real. It's *still* very real.'

She didn't reply; she couldn't.

'So did you date him?' he prompted her.

She shuddered to even think of it. 'We went out for about a month.'

'And you didn't sleep with him?' His eyebrows arched.

'One month isn't that long—'

'You weren't into him.'

Shocked, she laughed. 'No, he wasn't really into me.'

'No, he would have been. *You* didn't let him close.'

She paused.

'If you'd really been attracted to him you would have. You slept with me, a total stranger you met that very night.'

Um, that had been *so* different.

He chuckled. 'Come on, Leah. Aren't I just a little bit right? That other guy didn't turn you on and there was no other chance because you never let there be one. You buried yourself away in a laboratory with a bunch of guys too shy to see past their microscopes.'

'Don't stereotype them.' She mock-punched him.

'I bet it's true. And then you go work with a bunch of old people? You say you don't want to be invisible but you have been hiding, Leah.' He stepped closer. 'Maybe you only picked me because you found out I was leaving the very next day. In that way, I was safe.'

'You were a total stranger—how safe was that? It was an insane risk to go off with you.'

'Is that why you said yes to me, Leah?' He leaned closer. 'Because you thought I couldn't hurt you?'

She hadn't thought anything of the sort. She hadn't thought at all. 'I said yes because I couldn't say no to you. You're irresistible, okay?' She folded her arms across her chest.

'So are you.'

She shook her head.

'They killed your self-confidence.' He reached for her. 'That shouldn't have happened—'

'How was I supposed to stop them?' she flung back, broken. 'All my life, Theo…my grades weren't good enough. I'm too tall. Too angular. Too different… Nobody wants to get hurt, Theo. You don't either.' She pushed back. 'In fact, you work stupidly hard to protect people *you* feel responsible for. Not only do you not want to get hurt, you don't want anyone around you to get hurt either.'

He lifted his chin, his gaze sharpening.

'What developed that over-protectiveness, Theo? Who did you see get hurt?' She waited but then continued boldly. 'It's not your grandfather. He's strong. He's a powerful man who's only recently become vulnerable. This goes back further than that. Who *couldn't* you help? Was it your mum?'

'I'm not over-protective. The truth is I have no desire to have to protect anyone.'

'Not even people you care about? Or is it that you don't want to care about people *because* you were hurt?' She paused. 'Why did you go to live with Dimitri? What happened to her?'

Theo sighed and turned away from her. This evening was not going the way he'd envisaged. He'd rather hoped they'd be on to round two by now; but somehow he'd ended up bringing up things he shouldn't have in the car on the drive back and now she wanted to know more.

'Just tell me, Theo,' she muttered. 'You can tell me anything. I won't judge.'

He never talked to anyone about this. And there was such a risk if he told her the truth. But he didn't want to brush off her concern. He knew he had to explain even just a little of it—so she'd understand why it was he couldn't give her everything she ought to have. He owed her that. 'They had a blazing affair that led to a shotgun marriage.'

Shock, then consternation pinched her face. 'Your mother got pregnant?'

'With me. Yes.'

She swallowed. 'And you're an only child.'

'Correct.'

Her colour receded. He knew she was picturing their future, drawing the parallels to his past. He didn't blame her—he'd done the same.

'They were miserable.' He forced himself to continue with the sorry story and finish it as briefly as he could. He didn't want her taking it on board or reading anything into it. He never talked about it because it didn't matter, it didn't mean anything. It was in the past and could stay there. She never needed to know the whole of it. 'The sizzle fizzled pretty quickly. It became a mess of fights and infidelity.' He didn't go deeper into details. 'After my father died in a car accident my mother decided she couldn't give me the best life so she sent me to live with Dimitri.' He breathed out. 'I'm not going to repeat those past mistakes, Leah. We won't be unhappy like that.'

She was silent for a long moment. 'This is why you came up with your prison island plan?'

'It seemed like a good idea,' he muttered. She didn't realise what that island meant to him but, of course, what was a heaven to him might be a hell for her. He couldn't make assumptions on her behalf any more. 'But we'll work something else out if you'd prefer.'

Her eyes widened. 'You're not going to send me away the second we're married?'

'No.'

Relief unfurled at his words, tempered by the sad history he'd just told her. No wonder he'd thought separation from the start was for the best. It sounded as though his parents' marriage had been a mess. Leah's heart ached. She desperately wanted to know more, but his expression had shuttered and she knew he'd hated having even this brief discussion about it. He was reserved—as private as he was protective—and she could respect that even though really she just wanted to reach out and touch him and tell him she was sorry for what he'd been through. Maybe she had to handle this with the same emotional restraint that he was. Because this 'sizzle would fizzle', wouldn't it?

Her heart puckered at the prospect. She couldn't imagine not wanting to be near to him. But at least she knew he wasn't going to be unfaithful—not when he'd been this scarred. She tried to push past it, to get them both back on an easier track. She'd focus on the practicalities of their immediate future.

'Do we have to marry at the town hall or something?' Would there be a bunch of strangers staring at them as they waited in a crowded hall outside before their five-minute service?

He shook his head. 'I've secured permission for us to marry on the compound.'

'So there won't be many people?'

'Dimitri will be there. My security team…' He paused, as if realising how impersonal it all sounded. 'I'm sorry your family are unable to attend.'

'I'm sorry Oliver can't make it, but it'll be more fun without my parents.' Honestly, she was brightened by the news she wasn't going to have to parade in front of people she didn't know. 'We could get married in our pyjamas before breakfast,' she said, shooting him a kittenish smile to ease the tension.

'Dimitri wouldn't approve.'

'Well, we mustn't disappoint him.' She chuckled. 'After all, this is only about pleasing your grandfather.'

'Oh, snarky Leah is back, your headache must be better.' But a rueful smile had lightened his features as she'd laughed. 'Do you have something to wear?'

'You just said there aren't going to be many people there,' she said limpidly.

'*I'm* going to be there,' he gasped, mock-wounded.

'That's good, I guess,' she pondered with thoughtful pretence, enjoying this turn back towards the easy banter with that bite of desire beneath. She loved it when he eased up on his solemnity and she wanted to wipe away the remnants of that old hurt in his eyes. In this very immediate future, she could touch him on this most literal of levels. 'It's the only time you'll ever see me in a dress.'

'Do you hate your legs or something?' His smile turned

sly and he stepped forward to tug at her scarlet blouse. 'You have no idea how good they feel locked around me.'

The awkwardness melted inside her. Why did it take only this? Only a smile and a look and a touch and she was cast back towards him, happily seeking more of his caresses. 'Theo—'

'They're gorgeously long and stronger than they look.' He glanced down and then swiftly lifted his lashes to imprison her in his heated green gaze. 'I get so turned on when you have me in your grip.'

'Like I'm some spider?' She playfully ducked his reach for her, but was breathless beneath it.

He laughed. 'Stop trying to avoid my compliments.'

'Oh, you were complimenting me? I thought you were telling me my legs are like…tweezers or something while trying to maul me at the same time.'

'Maul you?' His laugh morphed into a sexy growl and he planted firm hands on her hips, keeping her right where she wanted to be. 'You want me to show you again?'

'Show me what?' She couldn't resist leaning into him, giving up on any idea of escape.

'What we're really good at.'

She'd wanted this again so much, for so long. She couldn't possibly say no.

He drew her closer and that look in his eyes intensified. 'Let me touch you.'

She loved that he asked, even when he knew her answer. And even when she knew he meant only this, only now, she lifted her chin. He met her parted mouth with his in a kiss so hot, so desperately needed she moaned helplessly. Her eyes closed as she was thrown instantly back into that delicious firestorm of delight and desire.

'Your legs are the perfect length for me too…' he teased between kisses. 'If only you had some heels on, even just a couple of inches.'

'I can't wear heels,' she gasped, on one last joke. 'I'd trip over.'

He caught her laugh with a kiss. 'You're graceful as hell and you know it. Anyway, you wouldn't need to walk, you could just brace against the wall. You'd be the perfect height for me. Otherwise I'd have to bend and get muscle burn.'

She huffed another breathless laugh. 'Always thinking of the practicalities?'

'We'd be able to sustain it for longer.'

She couldn't sustain herself for long at all around him, and the prospect of hot sex against the wall made her knees buckle.

His laugh was an exultant sexy sound but she didn't care. All that mattered was that he'd slid his arm beneath her and scooped her up. He climbed the stairs, effortlessly carrying her to a vast bedroom. She couldn't look away from him as he set her in the centre of the bed. His eyes glazed as his focus dropped and he looked down her body. That rapt, fixated look made her toes curl. And then it began. Pure attraction, pure pleasure flowed as he stripped them both bare with lingering caresses. But her desire was underpinned by that other ache—that need for touch that was more than physical—and that made her feel everything so very much more. She sobbed, her emotion unstoppable in that moment when he thrust within her again. At last.

'Theo—' she cried out at the culmination of relief and craving.

'I'm here.'

Yes.

CHAPTER ELEVEN

'THEO HAS LEFT for work already.' Leah smiled apologetically as she poured Dimitri a cup of tea as he joined her at the table on the terrace. Since that conversation when she'd asked him to help her, Dimitri had thawed—coaching her in beginner Greek phrases and instructing Amalia to do the same. The week had passed with increasing ease and speed. Theo had returned her to the compound early the morning after the exhibition and Amalia had swung into action to help her with preparations. She'd enlisted her cousin and aunt as well because they were so low on time.

This morning the sun warmed Leah's back as she resumed knitting the white silk as quickly and as neatly as she could. Amalia was already working on her section too. Theo had left well over an hour ago.

'He works too hard.' Dimitri stirred his tea. 'Perhaps he will work less now there is a child coming.'

'Perhaps.' Leah didn't hold out much hope but she'd heard the wistful tinge to the older man's words and she didn't want to lie to him.

Dimitri studied her with his faded version of Theo's bright green eyes. His held more blue and weren't as vivid yet he still seemed to see right through her.

'He's not perfect,' Dimitri said.

'No one is.' She smiled, unsure where he was going with this but she wasn't going to say a word against Theo to his grandfather.

'I was too hard on him.'

For a moment she held Dimitri's gaze, recognising that hint of arrogance in the way he held his head. But then he dropped his chin and his shoulders sagged.

'I didn't want him to become like his father, but Theo

was always different…' The old man coughed. 'He's loyal. He cares deeply…'

Leah stared at him, realising how hard it was for him to say any of this.

'He loves you very much. He doesn't want to let you down,' she said.

'I know. Because of that, he works too hard.' He gazed across the pool. 'Perhaps now he has you, that will change.'

Dimitri had been a workaholic as well. The discipline in his daily routine proved that. While routine could provide a safe structure and enable achievement, it could also reinforce bad habits. Strengths were also weaknesses, sometimes, and working too hard for too long could definitely become a weakness.

She smiled to hide her thoughts. 'Theo and I understand each other. We respect each other.'

'But you don't love each other.'

Her skin cindered with embarrassment. She respected Theo. She'd be loyal to him and she was insanely attracted to him. Anything more than that, she couldn't bear to consider.

'Perhaps that is good.' He picked up his coffee. 'Marrying for suitability rather than love works better in the long term.' He nodded. 'He is different from his father.'

So his father had married for love? Or what he'd thought at the time had been love. Theo had called it a 'blazing affair' that had led to an unplanned pregnancy. She and he hadn't had the affair. They'd had only the one night. Though they'd had a couple more since.

'Is he different from you?' Leah asked, curious enough to push past her nerves. 'Did you marry for love or was it merely a suitable arrangement?'

'It began as one and became another. That is what happens.'

'A suitable arrangement grew into love?' she asked.

'As it will for you.'

Of course he wanted to believe that. He loved Theo and he didn't want what had happened to his son to happen to his grandson.

'You don't think the same can happen in reverse?' she asked warily. 'An unsuitable love match can't become suitable?'

Dimitri's expression shut down. 'No.'

Wild love—wild *lust*—didn't last. She suspected Theo thought they were burning out the lust between them, then it would become a convenient arrangement somehow. But for her, the intensity hadn't lessened. It was worsening.

Because it's not just lust.

She closed her mind to that awful whisper and poured both herself and Dimitri some fresh orange juice. She'd focus on finishing her dress and learning Greek.

Theo returned every night to the riviera compound, unable to spend another night away from her. He'd carve out their new normal after the wedding, but right now the temptation to return to her was extreme. And he couldn't resist it. He couldn't resist the need to touch her. But his discomfort was growing. He couldn't seem to think as clearly. He found himself distracted at work—wondering what she was doing. It was unacceptable.

He knew some distance was required.

Tonight he roved through the house but knew she'd be on the terrace. She liked the sunset. He heard her laughter as he neared. He walked faster but quietly, surprised by the sound of other voices, others laughing.

He paused in the open doorway. Leah sat at the table, her back to him. She looked vibrant in loose white linen trousers and a clingy blue shirt. Amalia was with her and so was Dimitri. They were laughing together. He didn't think he'd ever seen Dimitri laugh like that. She didn't notice him for a while. They were sampling a selection of traditional sweet cakes.

'Leah likes the lemon.' Dimitri noticed him first and sat back with a satisfied twinkle in his eye as he called to him. 'She has good taste.'

Theo stared as Leah smiled and coyly thanked Dimitri in Greek. She had a private joke going with his grandfather? Since when did they begin talking like this? Since when did his grandfather joke?

Theo shook his head and pulled out a chair to join them, trying to shift the uneasy weight pressing down on his chest. 'Preferring the lemon over the plum?'

Her eyes sparkled as she smiled again at his grandfather. His gut tightened and his appetite vanished. He didn't want dinner. He didn't want to sit here and watch them all laughing together. He wanted her alone, in his bed, her attention all on him.

He stilled, stunned at his own rabid—*jealousy*?

He should have known what damn sweet she liked. *He* should have sought it out for her. His grandfather seemed to know more about her than he did. His staff too…

And whose fault is that?

He'd been determined to work as much as he could this week. Determined to do this right so he didn't ruin her life completely. He refused to let her become miserable. But suddenly he wasn't sure what was right any more.

His island idea had definitely been wrong. He'd not understood her need for companionship or to feel valued, visible in her role as his fiancée. And now, he didn't like the thought of her being so far away. Even a thirty-minute flight time felt too long.

He couldn't understand why he couldn't keep this simple. Why did he suddenly want things he'd never wanted before in his life? Never had he ached to leave work early the way he did now knowing she was here.

He somehow got through supper, listening to them talking and laughing, watching Leah at ease—chatting, funny, kind. It was late when Amalia walked Dimitri back to his building, leaving Theo alone with Leah at last.

'You came home earlier tonight.' She broke the silence with her soft voice.

He nodded, unable to take his eyes off her.

'Are you going to work tomorrow morning?' Her chin lifted.

'Yes.' He leaned back in his seat and tried to ignore the slight pout of her lower lip. 'I figured it gives me something to fill in the time before the ceremony.'

She put down her spoon. 'What happens after? You go back to work?'

'No,' he answered mildly, despite the tension stringing him out. 'We go on our honeymoon.'

'To prison island?' Her lashes lowered, hiding her eyes.

'It's a surprise.' To his astonishment he actually felt a little nervous about it.

The feeling compelled him to silence her next question in the best way possible. He couldn't resist any longer anyway. He stalked around the table and kissed her till she was breathless. He ached to pull her to her feet and hustle her inside so he could have her in his bed. Restraint was imperative yet apparently impossible. Rebellion at his self-imposed restrictions bubbled his blood. He couldn't stand the need and the want clawing within him. Since when did he want anything with this intensity?

'I'm not sleeping with you tonight,' he said huskily. 'It's the eve of our wedding, it'd be bad luck.'

'Well, we wouldn't want any more of *that*.' Something flashed in her eyes.

His breath stalled in his lungs. 'That's how you feel? That this was unlucky?'

She put her hand on her belly. 'No,' she whispered. 'I

don't think that about this. It's a miracle in a way…coming into being…against all odds, right?'

He still didn't want to think about the child. Instead he kissed her again until every nerve tingled.

'No,' he muttered with a low groan as he pulled away from her. 'Not tonight.'

He watched the dazedness in her eyes dissipate as disappointment loomed. His gut ached. He hated disappointing her. Which was exactly why he needed to prove his restraint now and build distance back again over the coming days.

'I'll see you tomorrow, Leah,' he said huskily.

When she'd become his wife.

He went to work in the morning purely to put himself beyond temptation. But he got no actual work achieved. He spent a couple of hours pacing while talking on the phone, finalising the arrangements for their travel later in the day. The idea had come to him when he'd been unable to sleep a couple of nights ago and he'd been unable to resist putting it in play.

He returned to the compound in time to shower. His tailor had delivered the new suit and shirt. His shoes were new too. Everything was new. Except him. He was still the same—with the same failings. She had no idea really. Tension tightened his muscles as he dressed. He'd consider this a contractual meeting like any other, right? Just another merger.

But he'd never wanted to make promises like this to someone. Not these deeply personal promises he knew he could never keep.

Fidelity—fine. Honour—fine. To love?

Leah was sweet. And she was having a *child*. He breathed out, refusing to undo the top button of the stiff shirt that suddenly strangled him.

He turned his back on his reflection and strode outside.

Dimitri was sitting out on the terrace. Amalia was also there with her husband and their son. Leah had insisted they attend as guests, not staff. He was glad she'd charmed them. It shouldn't have surprised him; when anyone got to know Leah, they discovered her sweet generosity.

They'd had a shade put over the pergola to protect them from the stunning blue sky and the heat of the sun. Tendrils of white flowers and greenery had been wound around the pillars and made the compound even more picturesque than usual. His security team had swept the beach and ensured there was no one with any cameras and long-range lenses hiding out. They had complete privacy. He'd called in Philip, his security chief, as his witness. The official from the city arrived and briefly ran over the paperwork with him. All that remained was for his bride to appear. He stared down at his watch. Would she keep him waiting? His breathing shallowed. Suddenly it seemed imperative—he *needed* to see her right now.

The official coughed discreetly and Theo looked up.

His throat tightened. She was a column of white and silver—gleaming like a pale angel with a smile that was both pure and a little playful. The tiny sparkle of confidence felled him. She walked towards him. The white flowers that she held low covered that gentle curve of her belly. A lace shawl covered her shoulders. A white bodice—was it knitted?—hugged her hips and flared from there in a cloud of soft tulle—a subtle reminder of the softness to be found in her straight slenderness. It was all he could do to hold himself upright. He couldn't wait to slip her out of it. He couldn't look at her but he couldn't tear his gaze away. It was like being strung on a medieval torture device. The official stood in front of them, alternately speaking in Greek, then English, so his bride understood. Theo braced, forcing himself to stop staring at her like a crazy man—to take in the ceremony and actually speak when required.

A quick glance behind her showed his grandfather sitting in a chair, leaning forward on his walking stick. A week ago Theo would've expected the old man would be prune-faced, given she wasn't one of his picks, but he was actually smiling and relaxed. He genuinely liked her.

Theo looked at Leah again. Something ached within him. He didn't want to hurt her and he would. It was in his DNA.

The official was beaming and looking at him expectantly. She was looking at him too—too trusting, too wary, too wanting. That panic—to protect her—surged within him. But he was supposed to kiss her now. He bent forward and brushed his lips over hers in the briefest of touches. He couldn't allow himself anything more or he'd lose all control.

At last it was over. They were married.

'Are you sorry your family isn't here?' His voice was hoarse as he walked with her to pose for a photo.

She shook her head. 'No.'

But there was a yearning look within her eyes that smote his heart. He steeled himself against it.

'Your dress…' He struggled to push the words past the tightening in his throat. 'You made it.'

She bit her lip, glancing down. 'Yes.'

'How did you have the time?' He couldn't fathom it. It was so intricate and beautiful, it had to have taken hours.

'Amalia and her family helped. They knitted around the clock once they saw the design.'

His heart seemed to stop. 'Who designed it?'

'I did. I adapted an idea I'd been working on.'

He nodded and looked down and that was when he saw her shoes. His mouth felt as if wads of cotton wool had been stuffed into it. He couldn't swallow or speak. He could only stare and then try like hell to control the desire coursing through his body—but it was as if the sluices at an ancient dam had been unlocked.

They were silver shoes, dainty, with delicious little high heels.

And they were for him. He appreciated the gesture more than he'd imagined he could appreciate anything. Touched a part of him so deeply buried he'd not known it was there. All he wanted to do was touch her.

He ached to rid himself of this desperate need. Why hadn't it eased over these past few days? Why wasn't it settling now that he had her safety and security ensured? He had everything working in play just as he wanted it. Yet his tension was now worse than ever.

Leah stared up at Theo, watching the storminess build in his emerald eyes. He was so silent, so inscrutable. She swallowed. 'You don't like it?'

'Like what?' he muttered, blinking as if he'd lost track of the conversation.

Embarrassment curled within her. 'My dress.'

She shouldn't have made it. Should have just bought one of those amazing designer numbers in central Athens. It had taken so many hours, so much planning. She'd had so much companionship with Amalia.

Theo's expression sharpened and he opened his mouth.

'Theo, Leah,' Amalia called to them, breaking the spell.

Leah glanced; the photographer wanted another photo. Theo put his arm around her waist and pulled her closer. He did it with such speed, she was almost tipped off balance. Leah glanced up at him to read his expression, given the tension she could feel within him. But he'd looked to the lens. He wasn't smiling.

'Perfect,' the man said.

Theo released her waist but immediately took her hand in his and led her to the table. It was laden with a selection of delicacies—a celebratory feast Leah could barely touch. Theo didn't each much either.

'Traditions are important,' Dimitri said stiffly. 'It might be a small wedding but it is important to do things properly.'

She felt Theo's tension magnify as they were called to cut the beautiful cake.

They sliced into the cake together and, once everyone had a small piece, Dimitri made a toast to them.

Leah nibbled at the cake, stupidly nervous, which was crazy given she was no wedding-night virgin. She *knew* Theo. Yet at the same time she didn't. Right now she couldn't figure out what he was thinking, only that it was apparently unpleasant. Her heart sank; he really hadn't wanted to do this. The intimacy she'd thought they'd built over the last few days was nothing.

'Leah and I need to get going now,' he said to Dimitri.

The old man replied in Greek. Theo smiled and Dimitri, Amalia and the others melted away with teasing smiles.

But Theo dropped his polite smile as he walked towards her.

'Should I go get changed?' she asked him anxiously. She didn't know what he had planned.

'No,' he snapped grimly. 'We need to leave right away.'

CHAPTER TWELVE

SHE WAS ALMOST afraid to speak, his expression was that severe as he led her to the helipad. But she refused to be afraid of her husband. 'So it's not prison island?' she attempted a joke.

'No.' He waited for her to climb into the helicopter ahead of him.

So now they were en route to who knew where. He helped her with the headset and she then watched out of the window as they took off. The view over the mainland was just stunning—she drank in the blue waters and stunning settlements. Then they seemed to lower and slow a little. She leaned forward, gazing intently as ancient ruins came more sharply into view. Ruins she recognised because she'd studied them online a few thousand times years ago when caught up in the romance of the novel she'd loved.

'Is that Delphi?' She turned to him, her heart thudding because she knew it was. 'You *remembered*.' And she was so touched.

'I remember everything about that night,' he muttered—all soft, serious intensity.

She couldn't turn away from him—he was so still, as if he was struggling to contain something. The tension between them tightened. 'Thank you.'

'Go on,' he ordered roughly. 'Look.'

She turned towards the window again as they circled the site. The setting sun cast a burning glow on the ancient hewn stone. It was majestic and so moving. She knew Theo had timed their trip to perfection so she had this magical view—this was why he'd insisted they leave the compound so suddenly. Her vision misted at his thoughtfulness.

They circled the ancient ruins one last time and then

headed away from the mountains, passing over the terracotta roofs of a village below. It was so picturesque, with narrow cobbled streets that she could see even from this height. Eventually the chopper lowered to a secluded property on the far outskirts of the village.

As she stood back on the ground Leah paused, conscious of her appearance as the helicopter lifted up and away. She glanced about anxiously, expecting an assistant to appear to carry their luggage in, but no one emerged from the magnificent building.

'The staff left about five minutes ago,' Theo said, lifting the two overnight bags himself. 'So we're alone.'

She followed him from the helipad along the pathway until they turned a hedged corner into the private heart of the property. She paused near the edge of the pool and took in the inviting atmosphere. There was soft music playing from discreet speakers. Candles burned in glass jars placed in carefully chosen spots. The small circles of flickering light cast a warm glow around the terrace, almost creating a semi-circular stage.

'The American half of me wants my first dance.' Theo dropped the bags and faced her. That rough edge to his voice was even grittier.

She swallowed, realising that he was holding something fierce back. 'Theo—'

'I apologise for the lack of a live band.' He slowly paced towards her. 'But I wanted us to be alone.'

'Why?'

'I'm a terrible dancer.' He held out his hand and his smile was tight.

'I don't believe you.'

He wasn't terrible at anything. But she put her hand in his and he drew her into that little lit space on the terrace.

'I don't know how I've resisted touching you all day.'

He pulled her into his arms. 'I can't resist any more. You look beautiful.' He stared into her eyes.

That warmth within trickled more quickly, more deeply—becoming a heat that needed release.

'And you're wearing heels,' he noted.

'I figured it wouldn't matter if I fell over when it was only you watching.'

'Only me?' He cocked his head and finally his smile appeared.

It was unfair of him to flirt with her when he didn't really mean it. And the truth was she was likely to tumble *because* it was him. He put her so on edge, so aware of every movement, every breath when she was with him, yet not with him. Now she simply ached for his touch.

'This lace thing is pretty, but I'm afraid I'm going to tear it if I hold you closer.'

'I wore it to cover my shoulders…' she muttered breathlessly. 'And to hide the fact that…'

'That what?'

'I'm not wearing anything beneath the dress.' She swallowed. 'I tried but you could see the lines…'

He inhaled deeply. 'So you're telling me that beneath this angelic surface, there's a temptress. I think I knew that.' He pulled her hips against his and she felt just how much he liked how she looked. 'I remember those scarlet panties,' he whispered.

'Good thing there's no audience,' she said with a chuckle.

'Right now I wouldn't give a damn if there was.' His breathing roughened. 'I can't wait any more, Leah.'

That twisting serpent of heat bit her too. She threw herself into the gorgeous escape of this—their touch, in the magic they created together. Hot and dream-like, the searing need enveloped her. They were moving, but not really dancing. Somehow she was back against the wall of the building and she gasped as he plundered, kissing his way down her neck. She threw her head back to let him and glimpsed the darkening sky above and saw the stars emerging. His fingers moved and the silver strap slipped off her shoulder in the haste and the front of her dress dropped enough to bare her breast.

He stared, savage hunger etched on his face. 'Leah.'

She shivered as his fingers teased in gentle swirling motions that only made her fire flare. She needed him. Now.

'I don't know how to get you out of this dress fast enough without damaging it,' he groaned.

She'd laugh if she weren't so desperate. 'Then don't.'

Looking into her eyes, he moved, freeing himself with the simple slide of a zip, and then he lifted the skirt of her dress and pressed close, nudging her legs further apart with his.

'You wore the shoes for me,' he muttered roughly, 'so we could do this.'

She felt a flash of vulnerability—a sudden fear that the effort she'd gone to revealed something more, something she hadn't wanted him to see. But there was no time to fret as he took her hands in his, palm to palm, and laced their fingers. She gasped, anticipation soaring as he braced them on the wall either side of her head.

There was this between them. *This*. Powerful. Primitive. Unsophisticated. Undeniable. The simplest, most basic of needs. The drive to get closer to him pushed her to arch her hips forward as her shoulders pressed against the wall. But not only were her hands locked in his, her gaze was locked in the fierceness of his focus too. Neither smiled; it was impossible in this supreme intensity. She felt him, close and hard and almost hers. Hunger and passion forced her to rock, sliding closer still. And he was right there.

'See?' he gritted, almost smiled, but the tension was too strong. 'Perfect.'

He watched her as he thrust. Her scream echoed through

the night. But he didn't stop. He possessed her—physically and beyond as his gaze seared through to her soul and she met him arch for thrust, in a frantic, fast ride that was so explosive, so powerful it could end only one way. In an almost instant eruption of blinding, white-hot pleasure.

And then there was silence. They were still completely dressed. Still desperately entwined—their fine clothes tangled. But her emotions were torn—because that had been so much more than *simple*. The sheer desperation, the total annihilation stunned her. As did the deeper, complex yearning it revealed.

'What a first dance,' she mumbled, seeking a way to claw some lightness back into the atmosphere because it was so intense that she couldn't breathe.

She carried her pretty, heeled shoes in one hand while her husband held her other hand tightly, leading her through the silent villa up the stairs to the moonlit room. She faced him and felt that desire ricochet back. Because they were so far from done.

'Slower this time, Leah.' He carefully slipped the wrap and the dress from her body and placed them over a chair reverently.

He glanced at her, then practically tore his trousers and shirt off with such fierce speed she chuckled. But then he stepped forward and she couldn't laugh any more and he made true on his promise. It was slow. It was thorough. And it destroyed her.

Long fingers of sunlight slid up the bed, slowly warming and waking her. She felt Theo's arms around her and smiled secretly. He must have sensed her waken because he began gently tracing patterns on her back.

'You're not leaving right away to go to work?' she asked sleepily.

'Leah,' he admonished piously. 'It's our honeymoon.'

'As if that minor fact would stop you.' She smiled and kept her eyes closed.

'Did you wake up on the wrong side of the bed? Or just not get enough sleep last night, darling?' He pressed a kiss to her shoulder and slid out of bed.

She didn't want to get out of bed ever. She wanted him to get back into it. And he knew. But he didn't come back to her; instead he picked up her dress from where he'd placed it and carefully put it on a hanger. 'Thank you.'

'It's stunning.' He picked up the accompanying lace, which had fallen by her side of the bed. 'Did Amalia loan you this?'

Surprised, she reached out and ran her fingertip over the delicate lace. 'No, Dimitri gave that to me. You didn't realise?'

'Realise what?'

'He said his wife made it. She wore it on their wedding day.'

He stared at the lacework in his hands. 'And he gave it to you?' His lips twisted into a rueful smile. 'You've won him over completely.'

'It's because I'm carrying the next Savas.'

'No, it's because he likes you. You're patient with him—I've seen you pouring his tea and plumping his pillows.'

'He's an old man, Theo. Of course I'm patient and it's not hard to be kind.'

'You're patient with everyone. You do things for people.' He drew in a deep breath. 'And you're talented. You made the blanket you gave that woman at the home. Your cardigan you wore that night at the ballet…'

She nodded.

'I saw the drawings in your apartment. They were on graph paper.'

'I work up the patterns, yes.'

'You learned some maths then, back with your parents' insistence.' He grinned.

'I wasn't bad at it, I just wasn't good enough by their impossible standards. I'd be sent to my room to study and end up knitting to help me relax,' she acknowledged. 'I made leg warmers for my ballet class. Awful stripes from ugly leftover balls of wool that were cheap. Zoe wore hers to company class the other week and a friend wanted some.'

'You could sell them.'

'They take a while for me to knit. They can buy machine-made ones for cheaper.'

'So you've thought about it.' He sat beside her. 'Yours are artisan creations. Hand-crafted, beautiful wool—a premium product.'

She shook her head and giggled at the flattery. 'Hardly. I make mistakes. I can't put a massive price tag on imperfect pieces.'

'Handmade doesn't have to mean perfect.' He looked thoughtful. 'You could sell the patterns. People would then knit them themselves.'

She hesitated, half tempted by his idea. 'You think they're that good?'

'Don't you?' He turned her face up when she glanced down. 'Don't you believe in yourself, Leah?'

She swallowed again.

'Because you should. Just because you didn't get top in every damn math or physics class doesn't mean you're not capable of amazing things. It's just different.'

'I know that. I know.'

'There's a difference between knowing and *believing*.'

He stole her breath with his words. Then he kissed her and stole everything else she had to give.

A blissful hour later he nudged her with a smile. 'Let's go exploring.'

She wasn't sure she'd ever be able to move again. But she let him tug her to her feet and followed him into the shower. Theo drove them to Delphi, where they spent the afternoon exploring the ruins.

'This is incredible.' The beauty of her surroundings amazed her but at the same time she was keenly aware of the strong man walking beside her. 'Thank you.' She glanced towards him, only her gaze ensnared with his. 'You're supposed to be seeing the sights.'

'I am.'

She rolled her eyes, but when she swallowed it was hard to push past the lump that had formed there. This was so lovely, it scared her. He took the lead, turning into the most knowledgeable tour guide ever, telling her anecdotes about the area, pointing out all kinds of features.

'I read up yesterday morning,' he explained as she looked at him in disbelief over one obscure fact.

'I thought you were working.'

'I couldn't concentrate.'

Theo couldn't resist holding her hand as they turned to walk back down the hillside. When he'd watched her at the ballet she'd been like this—the expressive emotions flickering on her face. There was nothing better than seeing her entranced. Smiling. Moved. He liked it best of all when she was moved by him—by his touch. In bed—vulnerable and exposed.

'Do you need to check in with Dimitri?' she asked as they walked back towards the car.

She really cared for the old man. He glanced at her and knew she was genuine. She was good at building relationships—she had an easier relationship with Dimitri than Theo had ever had. Which was remarkable given her own family dynamics. 'What about you checking in with your family?'

'I did. My brother sent a message back yesterday morning,' she said happily. 'He actually remembered.'

Smiling, Theo phoned Dimitri, who immediately asked

to speak to Leah. With dutiful mockery, he passed his phone to her and watched as she shyly said hello in Greek. It was only a couple of moments before she ended the call.

'I think he likes you more than me,' Theo teased as he drove them back to the private villa.

She grinned and looked at him. 'You're the CEO of his business, Theo. That's after adding to the conglomerate. You've done everything he's ever asked of you. More than everything.'

'He expected nothing but the best.' He stilled.

'And you've always delivered.' She angled her head. 'But what do you want for yourself, Theo? I have my outlet—what's yours?' She leaned close. 'Please don't say it's having one-night stands with women in London…'

He couldn't smile. 'I have my work. I like my work.'

'Is that enough?'

What else was there? He got into the car and waited for her to fasten her seat belt before driving off. 'I was young when I went to live with Dimitri,' he said. 'He was a tough taskmaster, but it was a good distraction.'

'And that's it? You just work? I thought the adage was work hard, *play* hard…'

'I don't feel my life is boring, Leah.' It certainly wasn't any more. Not with her in it.

But he felt her gaze on him, too searching, too soft.

'You take it upon yourself to ensure Dimitri's happiness—by pleasing him.'

'Like you've never tried to please anyone?' He forced a laugh. 'You make that your life's work.'

'We both had expectations placed on us—the difference is I failed all mine. But you surpassed them—awards, accolades, grades, prizes, acquisitions, business acumen… and you've been perfect ever since,' she muttered.

'I have been so far from perfect, Leah.' He grimaced.

He didn't want her feeling sorry for him; it was preposterous. 'No one is perfect.'

'Were you afraid he'd send you away too?'

Suddenly it was as if all the oxygen had been sucked from the car.

'Is that what happened?' she asked softly. 'Did your mother send you away?'

He kept his eyes on the road and pressed harder on the accelerator. He didn't talk about that—ever.

'Why did she let you go?' Leah was so calm and soft and insistent and somehow…safe.

It was the question he'd spent most of his life asking and he still didn't know the answer. All he knew was that it hurt. It would always hurt. He just never admitted it. He never let it get this personal with anyone. But Leah disarmed him with her self-deprecating lovely laugh that made him smile. She was so gorgeously human and he truly couldn't resist confessing it to her.

'She said it would be better for me to be with the Savas family. That she couldn't look after me properly any more.' He sighed. 'She'd started drinking and only drank more as their marriage fell apart.' He cleared his throat. 'Don't think badly of her.'

Leah shook her head slightly.

'My father was Dimitri's golden boy. He was their only child and I guess he had a lot of pressure on him. But he was also spoilt and selfish and partied hard. And I guess it was partly rebellion that made him marry the girl he'd got pregnant and move to the States with her.' He tensed. 'He was unfaithful from the start. My mother kept me informed—justifying her own indiscretions, her own addictions. But I didn't need her to tell me. He brought them to our house.'

As a kid he'd walked in on his father kissing another woman when he'd had no clue what he was seeing. Only that it felt wrong to witness. He'd never wanted to know any of it. He'd been a kid.

'She drowned her hurt in drinking and they fought all the time while maintaining this…supposedly glamorous lifestyle. My dad visited Greece often—keeping up with his friends here, supposedly satisfying Dimitri with his efforts to learn some of the business…but he didn't really care. He brought my mother and me here only the once for my tenth birthday. My mother hated it here. When he got back late one night they had another big fight and he stormed out again. He shouldn't have been driving. The crash killed him instantly. It was lucky there was no one else involved.' He still felt furious with his father for that. 'Dimitri blamed my mother for everything. In his opinion she was why they'd never lived in Greece—because she wasn't Greek. She was the one burning through the money, being unfaithful… Dimitri thought it was all her fault because my father was miserable with her—of course he was going to play up a bit. And then there was me, the reason they'd had to marry in the first place.'

He parked the car outside the villa but sat still, staring through the windscreen, lost in his drive down nightmare lane. 'Dimitri was so angry with her. I overheard him telling her he'd have insisted on a DNA test to prove she hadn't trapped my father with another man's bastard, if it weren't for the fact that I was the spitting image of him. I couldn't stand to hear him talk to her like that when I knew what my father had really been like…'

He'd been torn between defending his mother while burying all the details she'd shared with him. The affairs, the misery and heartache and the rage she'd felt towards his father. Her attempts to make him jealous. All Theo had wanted to do was make her feel better. But he'd failed in that.

'And then, after the funeral, it was time to go home.

But my mother said she didn't want me. That she'd never wanted me and that it was best for me to stay with Dimitri.'

'She left you in Greece and returned home to the States?'

He'd begged her to take him with her. Instead she'd signed over all parental rights to Dimitri. A man he'd barely known at the time.

'You must have been heartbroken. You were a *child*.'

He'd been terrified.

'You'd just lost your father, and then your mother too?'

He didn't want her sympathy. He didn't know why he'd told her any of this but now he'd started he couldn't seem to stop. 'The one time I fought Dimitri was when he said something back about her to me. I lost it so badly I thought he was going to…' He breathed in. 'But he didn't. He just never mentioned her name again. I didn't either. We never talk about her or my father. We discuss the business, politics…anything that isn't personal. And it's good. It works.'

That had only changed slightly since Dimitri had got sick and he'd started in on Theo finding a wife.

'Where's your mother now? Are you in contact with her at all?'

He already felt as if he'd been carved open and this memory was like pouring scalding acid on the bleeding wounds, but he couldn't stop the pain—the truth—flowing out. 'A few years ago… I wanted to know where she was, if she was okay…' He'd been a fool to think that, just because he'd made a success of himself, anything would have changed. That she'd want to know him. 'She didn't welcome my visit, didn't want to know. She didn't even want any of my money. She just wanted me to leave her alone. She said her life was better without me. And mine was better without her.'

'Theo—'

'It is better.' He didn't want to hear any different—how could he?

'Is it?'

'Why would I want to revisit it, Leah? My mother was humiliated and hurt and she lashed out. She drowned her sorrows so much that she couldn't stop. My father was beyond miserable too. I can't let anyone else feel that—not Dimitri, not you. I can't let it happen again.'

'Dimitri said he was too hard on you,' she said.

'He told you that?' Shocked, he finally looked at her. 'He's never told me that.'

She looked so serious and concerned. 'Maybe you should talk to him.' She leaned forward to get nearer. 'You should talk to him about what really happened between your parents. Dimitri told me you're different from your father. Maybe he already knows some of it, Theo. You know he's a smart man.'

A smart *business*man, but a blind old fool when it came to his son. Why would Theo ruin that memory for him?

'I wouldn't ever do that.' He rejected the idea immediately, pushing back into his seat. 'He was so hurt by Dad's death. I watched him struggle with grief for so long. Isn't it kinder to leave him believing the good in his son?'

Theo had never wanted to let Dimitri down either. He'd never wanted to do anything that might hurt him—that might make Dimitri push him away.

'He gave me everything I needed—a home, an education, structure and discipline… I owe him, Leah. I can't hurt him.'

'But holding all that in hurts you.'

Now he was looking at her he couldn't seem to look away and that was bad because everything was rising now—all those feelings he'd blocked for years.

'You must have been so lonely.'

And she was right there, looking at him with those compassionate, velvety eyes as everything just slipped from him—the things he'd never said aloud to anyone—and his heart was racing so fast he felt dizzy. 'After a month or so, we went on a boat to Dimitri's holiday home for a weekend. It wasn't like any place I'd ever been to before—I don't mean beautiful buildings, but a place that was a total escape. I was free to roam and swim. It was vast and private and the sea so blue, so warm.' He shook his head as he confessed his last little secret. 'You might have thought it sounded like a prison, but it's always been paradise to me.'

'Oh, Theo—'

At the catch in her whisper he blinked and forced himself to break the connection. He unfastened his belt and got out of the car.

'I should get some food,' he said briskly. 'You must be hungry.' He headed straight into the kitchen.

Anything to change the topic and keep him busy so he wouldn't have to look at her, so he wouldn't give way to that yearning inside compelling him to seek solace in her hold. He couldn't stand to see the empathy in her eyes, or bear the ache it caused.

'You can cook too?' Her laugh sounded strained. 'I don't know why I'm surprised.'

'Actually…' he breathed out, seemingly unable to stop being honest now '… I only have a couple of dishes in my repertoire and they're not great. I just didn't want us to be disturbed.'

He didn't want to have to pretend in front of people.

Maybe that had been a mistake. Maybe having staff around right now might help him reclaim his distance. And perspective. Because the one person he couldn't seem to pretend anything in front of was Leah.

He wasn't even hungry. He didn't know why he was even in the damn kitchen. But she'd opened the fridge and was absently staring at the contents as if she hoped a three-course meal would magically appear if she looked for long enough.

'Don't,' he muttered. He didn't want her waiting on him, helping him, being that kind person who did things for other people all the time. He didn't want her to care for him in the same way she cared for her oldies or in doing nice things for her friends. That wasn't what he wanted. He didn't want anything from her, right? 'You don't have to—'

'Maybe we could just make do,' she interrupted him. 'Pull together a few things picnic style?'

He nodded, unable to argue any more. They briefly worked in silence, but their bodies brushed too close despite the spaciousness of the kitchen. The air almost hummed as his tension built. He sensed hers rising too and that only escalated his. Confusion swirled, twisting into a tornado that he didn't know how to safely release. The silence thickened to the point where he couldn't stand it any more. He stopped what he was doing and stared at her.

She'd stopped too, the moment he had. Her eyes reflected everything—the turmoil, the vulnerable hunger that couldn't be hidden. He couldn't seem to hold anything back from her any more. 'Leah…'

He felt her shudder as he pulled her into his arms. His heart slammed against the palm she placed on his chest and his brain was fried by the look in her eyes as she rose on tiptoe to bring herself closer.

'Maybe we just make do with what we have?' he muttered.

What they had was *this*. With one kiss they ignited. Desperate to assuage the aching energy that had coiled so unbearably in the course of that conversation, they were wordless now. Swiftly pushing clothes aside, seeking skin, seeking complete contact. He lifted her back onto the big table and with almost no preamble pushed close and hard and deep and it still wasn't enough. She instantly tightened her legs around his waist in response, forming the hottest, tightest vice, and it was as if she were never going to release him. He ground harder, faster, pushing as powerfully as he could, but he still couldn't get close enough. The shocking thing was *this* didn't feel enough any more. That aching hole in his chest hurt—that place where other people had a heart. He growled in agony, in absolute frustration.

But she grabbed his burning face in her hands and kissed him. The passion in her deep caress destroyed that ache in an arc of pure lightning. It wasn't just pleasure branding through his skin and flesh and blood to bone. It was peace and tumultuous contentment and it was perfect. Now it was fiercer than ever. Better than ever.

But now he needed it more than ever.

CHAPTER THIRTEEN

THE FULL MOON bathed the room with pale light even at three in the morning. Still wide awake, Theo tried not to fidget and disturb Leah's sleep but he couldn't rest. He felt flayed, old wounds oozed. That physical bliss had ebbed and allowed cool, biting air—and anxiety—in.

Beside him Leah shifted position, then shifted again. A moment later she left their bed and went into the bathroom.

Theo waited, but the longer she was gone, the more his concern grew. He followed her to knock on the door. 'Leah? You okay?'

She opened the door. She held one hand pressed below her belly button. His senses hit full alert. 'What's wrong?'

She shook her head and rubbed her stomach slightly. 'Nothing.'

It didn't look like nothing. He gazed at her. The soft swell of her belly was bigger now, the secret within her starting to show. Bared like this she was so beautiful, but so very vulnerable.

'You're sore?' He carefully placed his palm just below hers and caressed the curve of her belly. Her skin was so soft and warm he went all the more gently. But mid-sweep he felt a jab against his palm. He stilled and held his palm firm and felt it again—the smallest of punches. It hit him with stupefying power. He glanced up and intercepted her wide-eyed gaze.

'You can feel that?' she breathed.

His throat completely constricted, so he merely nodded mutely.

'It's like this at this time. I think it's got day and night mixed up.' She still whispered, as if afraid speaking would silence the tiny communication.

It? Their baby? Another punch felled those walls that had barely begun their rebuild within him. He was feeling their baby. It was here. Alive and kicking.

He licked his lips and struggled to get his brain back. 'Does it hurt?'

'Not at all.'

'It's…' He didn't know what it was. He didn't know what to say. He didn't know what he was feeling.

'Like something out of a sci-fi movie,' she whispered with a chuckle.

She jolted a smile from him—he could never hold back a smile when she laughed.

'It doesn't seem real, does it?' she whispered.

He shook his head. But it was. *Real.*

He pulled his hand away and motioned for her to get back into bed with him. He held her gently and listened to her breathing, hearing the change as she relaxed and drifted back to sleep. No such bliss for him. Adrenalin coursed through his body. There was a baby on its way. Stupid, but while he'd *known* that, he'd not really *believed* it. He'd not felt it—not literally, like just now. But not inside himself either. Now the fact hit him as if he were being buried in a box by a load of wet cement—he was going to be a father.

And he had no idea how he was going to do that. All he knew was that he didn't want to be like his father. Or even his grandfather—unable to communicate. He never wanted his child to hold in a bottomless well of hurt the way he had.

He wasn't ready. He'd *never* be ready. In fact, he didn't want this at all.

He didn't want the responsibility of his child's happiness weighing on him. He couldn't handle Leah's either. She had her own loves and passions and she should fulfil her own dreams. He couldn't bear it if she ended up *resenting* him…he never should have tied her to him. Yet he couldn't fight that need curling within him to claim them both, protect them both—

Panic pushed his 'problem-solve' button, but the only possible option he could come up with was his original plan. They shouldn't live together. He could ensure their safety and financial security best if he was away from them. He couldn't live with them both and let them down. He couldn't live with *himself* if he did that—especially not now he knew her so well. She deserved better than the little he could provide emotionally and he couldn't stand to see disappointment or disillusionment build in her eyes because of what he lacked. He'd never be able to meet their greatest, deepest needs.

Distance simply had to be restored. Except, at the thought, regret like nothing he'd ever known rose within him.

But Theo was used to holding himself together and doing what was necessary. And this was necessary.

Leah woke and found herself alone again. Her heart dropped—she hated waking without him. The yearning inside was for more than his touch now; she wanted him to open up to her more. To share more of himself. The hurt he'd faced broke her heart. She'd hardly been able to breathe as he'd told her. And all she'd been able to do was listen, then to hold him. He didn't realise what he gave. Or how much more she wanted.

She found him pacing out by the pool. Her steps slowed as she saw he was already dressed. He looked too smart in his suit and with a remote expression in his eyes. A shard of glass pierced her heart. She knew what he was about to say.

'We need to go back to Athens.'

And there it was. She looked at him and then back at the view towards the mountain behind him. 'Okay.'

Disappointment bloomed within her chest.

'It's work—'

'It's okay,' she repeated.

She didn't want him to explain or try to make excuses. This was the reality and she shouldn't expect more from him. But the last few days had been so lovely—not just their time in Delphi, but leading up to the wedding. She'd had snatches of a future—of dreams and hope for happiness with him.

'I need to work, Leah.'

'Why?' Anger took over the hurt. 'You're supposed to be on your honeymoon.'

'I'm responsible for a lot of people. I can't let them down.'

'Of course.' It was that loyalty and sense of duty again. The relentless drive to do what was right for everyone but himself. 'And you tell me I seek approval too much.' She couldn't hold back the bitter twist to her lips.

'This isn't about seeking anyone's approval—this is about other people's livelihoods.'

'It's always about other people, isn't it, Theo?' She looked at him. 'What about *you*?'

He looked at her. 'You don't need to worry about me.'

'No, you wouldn't want that, would you?' she said. 'Someone to worry about you. Someone to care.'

'I can look after myself, Leah.'

And that was the way he liked it?

He felt duty to many people and for her no more than any other. But she rebelled at that thought. There was more between them than mere sex now and she was sure he felt it too. Yesterday had been the most magical day. She wanted that Theo back—the one who'd let her in. But he'd shut down when he'd felt the baby move. He'd tried to hide it, but he couldn't. He'd not touched her properly since and not talked to her either. Fatherhood was a duty that he was determined to fulfil, but that was all. He didn't actually want it.

* * *

'You're back sooner than I thought,' Dimitri greeted them when they landed back at the compound. 'I have a present for you.' He led the way inside, clapping his hands together in almost childlike excitement.

Leah stared. A huge photo of Theo and her from their wedding now hung in pride of place in the centre of that collection of Savas portraits. Leah was aghast.

It was an arty shot, filtered with black and white, but somehow they'd coloured in the silver of her dress…the techniques made her look ethereal and so staggeringly glamorous she couldn't quite believe it was her. And with his sharp suit and solemn visage, Theo looked like a fallen angel. But the appalling thing was their pose—while Theo was staring straight into the camera, her face was turned towards him. She was smiling at him and there was heavenly adoration in her eyes and there was no hiding it from anyone who bothered to look. She didn't want to see Theo's reaction yet she couldn't stop herself staring as he studied the picture. He didn't break that remote countenance and he didn't say a word.

Disconcerted, she glanced at Dimitri and saw the satisfaction in his eyes as he surveyed the portrait. This was what the old man had wanted, wasn't it? Someone to love his grandson. What he didn't realise was that it wasn't enough. Theo had to *want* that love. And he didn't.

She hated disappointing Dimitri almost as much as Theo did. She could understand why he worked so hard to keep the man happy. But the same was true in reverse. Dimitri would do anything for Theo. He was desperate to see him happy and content. They loved each other but they were too lacking in communication skills to admit it. And Theo lacked the trust to be vulnerable enough to share the truth of the past.

So she forced on a smile and faced Dimitri. 'It's beautiful, Dimitri. Thank you.'

He patted her arm and walked through to the lounge, leaving them alone.

'I need to get to the office,' Theo muttered.

'Theo?' It was that huskiness that compelled her to follow him. She followed him out to his car, pushed past the embarrassment of that portrait. 'Don't go.'

He stopped walking. His broad shoulders tensed as he pivoted to face her. He didn't want to have this conversation? Nor did she. But suddenly it was imperative. Somehow she had the courage. She was done hiding.

'Leah—'

'You don't have to go today. You're choosing to. Don't avoid me, Theo.' It was so obvious he was. Just as he avoided Dimitri.

'It's not you, Leah.'

Of course it was. Yes, they had some issues but they could handle them, couldn't they? But not if he left. Not if he chose to shut her out again. She'd thought they'd really communicated, that he'd really felt something for her...but then he'd felt the baby and she was scared it had all become too real for him.

'You know what?' She drew in a breath of determination. 'I'm not the same woman you met that night in London. I've got more confident. I'm not afraid to wear the colours I like. To say what I really think. To do whatever it is I want. You know why? Because just that once, *you* picked me. And that made me realise other people might like me too...and that it actually doesn't matter if they don't. It's okay not to please everyone.' She stepped closer to him. 'You saw me, Theo, and you've believed in me ever since. You've listened to me up till now—please keep listening.'

'Leah—'

'You can't hide that hurt in there for ever.'

An impatient expression flashed in his eyes. 'I knew I shouldn't have—'

'What? Talked to me? What's wrong with opening up to someone? Is it really that awful?' For him, that rejection had run so deep. 'I know you never wanted to marry anyone. I know you were just keeping Dimitri happy when you said you'd meet those women. You weren't intending on going through with any seriously. I know you think you don't want children. You only married me because it was the right thing to do.'

'You claim to know so much, yet you won't accept what I'm incapable of,' he growled at her. 'You need to understand that I cannot be anything more than what I am.' His hands shook at his sides before he clenched them into fists. 'I'm an emotional failure. I couldn't give my mother what she needed. I couldn't meet Dimitri's requirements. I can't meet yours.'

'What requirements do you think I have?' she asked him, desperately trying to understand what he thought she wanted of him. 'I'm in love with *you*, Theo. And *you* know that. That's why you're shutting me out now.'

'No.' He tensed and backed away from her, shaking his head in pure denial. 'You might think you're in love with me. But you're not.'

He didn't believe her? His doubt slammed her momentum to a halt.

'I shouldn't have slept with you again.' Turning away, he shakily ruffled a hand through his hair.

She was appalled. 'You think you've been trifling with my emotions?' Did he not accept how *real* this was?

'Of course I have. You've not had…'

'Any other lovers?' she finished for him. 'No, I haven't. But that doesn't make me an idiot, Theo. Don't treat me like someone who doesn't know her own mind, her own body, her own feelings.'

He closed his eyes momentarily. 'Even if you mean them, I can't carry that burden.'

'It's a *gift*,' she pleaded with him to understand. 'Not a life sentence. It's light. Love, laughter, support.'

'No, it's not. You cannot deny there's a responsibility on me. On my actions. I need to be careful because you're vulnerable.'

'All you have to do is act like a *human*. Not be cruel. You don't have to love me back.'

'Good, because I can't return those feelings. Not ever.'

She flinched. His words hit her heart like burning-hot bullets. Was it only her? Or was it anybody who tried to get close who he pushed away?

'I know you don't want to be hurt,' she said to him again, softly—more hesitant now. 'I'm so sorry your parents were unhappy, but that wasn't your fault.'

'How can you say that?' he roared. 'They were only together because of me. They fought because of me. He died because of me.'

'They were adults. They made choices. It was never *you*.'

'Of course it was me.' He rolled his shoulders. 'She never wanted me.' He glanced at her. 'And that's okay. Look at me properly, Leah—do I look like someone who's struggling? I'm *fine*. I'm happy. I like my life as it is and I don't need you—' He broke off, his breathing sharp.

She shook her head, refusing to believe his rejection. 'You told me it wasn't my fault I couldn't live up to my parents' expectations. Why isn't it the same for you? Why take the blame for their incompatibility? You were the innocent. You're not responsible for everyone and everything. It's not down to you to protect us all—not this baby, not Dimitri, not me.' She gazed at him. 'Maybe it's just fate? Maybe we just lucked out with the parent thing. But you know what? We can't change it—we can only accept it. And we have to appreciate what's really good. *We're* good, Theo. You and me. And I'm not going to raise this baby the way my mother raised me. We're not them, Theo.'

'No. And I know you'll be a wonderful mother. But I'm still not capable of being what *you* want, Leah.'

'You already *are* what I want. Just as you are.'

He jerked his head and his gaze dropped. 'I can't give your baby—'

His voice cracked.

'*Our* baby,' she whispered.

'Stop,' he snapped, fury unleashed. 'Just stop. I have *tried,* Leah. But this? It's never going to happen. You ask too much.'

She stared at him. He meant it, he really meant it. And she suddenly knew there was nothing she could say to change his mind. He didn't think he could be enough for her.

'I get that you don't want this from me.' She breathed carefully so she could still speak. 'But you should talk to Dimitri, Theo. You should be as honest with him. Because you *do* love him.'

She might've been wrong to read anything more into their relationship, but she was certain about that.

'I can't.' His chest rapidly rose and fell and he spun away from her, yanking open the car door. 'I have to go.'

Leah stood still as his car roared off into the distance, shocked by the rejection buffeting her soul. She'd pushed him too far—asked for things he'd never wanted to give. Or at least, not to her. Should she just have done as he wanted, without saying anything? Should she have stayed silent and kept it all in?

No. That was what he did and look how well that worked.

Her invisibility was ended and the bittersweet irony was because that was thanks to *him*. He'd turned her life upside down all those months ago. But those changes had begun from that one magical night. He'd injected a confidence within her and she'd held that memory close. It had been like a bubble inflating her heart. And while he'd just stomped on it, it wasn't going anywhere. She wouldn't let his rejection destroy her; she wouldn't revert to the person she'd been before meeting him.

She'd come too far. And what she'd asked for hadn't been too much. It hadn't been anything more than she deserved. It was what everyone deserved—to be loved, wholly and completely and unconditionally. For a few magical moments he'd made her feel as if she could have it all. They were good together in so many ways. But he was under no obligation to give her anything more than what he'd originally offered…if he didn't care for her. He didn't. But her heart ached, her whole body ached…because she so badly wanted to believe he did.

She desperately wanted to run away, but she refused to. She wasn't doing that to her baby. Nor to Dimitri. Not even to Theo. None of them deserved that. They all—including her—deserved a family. And they'd make one—though it might not end up being particularly conventional. She'd do everything she could to ensure her child received love from both its parents. Because he would love this baby, she knew he would, even if he couldn't yet believe that of himself.

But she had to cope with her own heartbreak too. She had to get away from him to do that. The only solution she could see was for her to go to his island holiday home as he'd suggested from the start. Theo could work in Athens, keep an eye on Dimitri and whatever else he needed and she could avoid him.

It wasn't his fault he hadn't fallen in love with her the way she had with him. But she couldn't stand to stay another night with him. She certainly couldn't sleep with him again. *That* would destroy her. And she couldn't trust herself around him. He couldn't have absolutely everything from her because she *did* deserve more.

To preserve herself, she had to leave now.

CHAPTER FOURTEEN

THEO ROLLED HIS shoulders as he walked across the terrace. Dimitri was sitting by the pool, with a pile of reading material on the table beside him and one of Leah's blankets draped over his knees. He looked tired and his eyes held only a shadow of the warmth that had been there this morning when Theo had returned with Leah.

'You've been doing too much again.' Theo frowned as he saw the tinge of greyness in the old man's face. 'You're still supposed to take it easy.'

He looked towards the house, his chest tightening at the prospect of seeing Leah. The words she'd so passionately declared had echoed in his mind all day. Going to work had been pointless other than to simply escape her. But he couldn't even do that—his mind had replayed the moment over and over. She'd stood there with such dignity like a tall, slender tree. And he'd cut her down.

He wanted to kick himself. He'd been such a fool to think he could have any kind of relationship with her. He'd known, hadn't he, right from the start that she was gentler than most? She'd been a virgin, for heaven's sake. No one had made her feel special or wanted before—of course she thought she'd developed feelings for him. He braced, holding off seeing her. Was she still hiding upstairs? Still crying? Was she too upset to sit with Dimitri and stumble over a few Greek words while working on a new pattern? He hated the thought of her being distraught.

It finally dawned on him that the place felt too silent.

'You worked late,' Dimitri muttered.

'There was a lot of work that needed doing,' he replied. And it had taken him three times as long because his concentration was shot.

I'm in love with you.

He shook off the memory. Again.

'You've been married less than a week,' Dimitri commented.

Theo didn't answer.

The reality of last night had given him every reason to keep his distance. But the desire to see her, just to see, was too strong. It wasn't sexual desire, it was concern. Just concern. He needed a glimpse to ensure she was okay. Then he'd retreat.

'Leah?' he called out as he entered the house, holding back the desire to run.

She didn't reply.

Unease scraped down his spine. He gave up on his restraint and ran up the stairs, taking two at a time. 'Leah?'

He walked into their room. It felt emptier. He suddenly realised the whole house felt emptier. Suspicion ballooned and he glanced in the wardrobe. Her eveningwear was still there, but those pairs of jeans, those tees, were gone. He pulled open the first of the drawers in her stand. Her silky, scarlet smalls were gone.

She was gone.

He froze, trying to process it. Then panic hit. Where had she gone? Was she okay? Why?

But he knew why. He knew exactly why. He'd hurt her.

He raced back downstairs just as Dimitri came into the house.

'What's wrong?' The old man watched him.

'I think she's left me.' He could hardly breathe as he strode past Dimitri to double-check the lounge.

'Pardon?'

'Leah. She's gone.' His anger leaked.

'Pardon?' Dimitri glowered at him.

'What part of "left me" don't you understand?' he stormed back as rage blew him apart.

'You're the one who doesn't understand,' Dimitri growled. 'You think she's left you? Is that what Leah would really do?'

Theo froze, then whirled to glare at his grandfather. 'Do you know where she is? Why didn't you tell me?'

'Why didn't you ask?'

'I don't have time for games, Dimitri. Where is she?' He needed to know she was okay.

'Why leave her alone all day? Bored and lonely with no one but an old man for company.'

'You're not that old and this place isn't boring.' He drew in a breath. 'I don't have time for this. I'll get Philip to help find her. She can't have gone far.'

'Philip is with her.'

'What?'

'She's gone to the island.'

Theo reached out and pressed his fingers to the wall to balance himself as he gaped at Dimitri. 'She what?'

'She said that was what you wanted.'

She hadn't run away? She wasn't alone out there in Athens, checking herself into some boarding house or something? She wasn't on a plane back to England?

Relief was like a blissfully cool balm soothing the rawness inside but then that very balm began to heat, burning his wounds worse. He'd thought she'd chosen to vanish—to run and hide from him completely because she'd been hurt. But she hadn't—she'd simply done as he'd originally asked.

He slumped against the wall, his legs empty of all strength. 'Okay. Okay, good.'

It was good, wasn't it? It was what he'd wanted. It would make things simple. So why did he feel worse than he had when he'd thought she was missing?

'You're not going there now?' Dimitri looked confused.

'No.' He drew a breath. 'I'll check in with Philip on the phone. There's no need for me to go.'

'I sent Amalia with her.' Dimitri's mouth thinned. 'To care for her.'

The unspoken criticism hung heavy. Theo rejected it. 'Thank you,' he said curtly.

He turned his back to avoid his grandfather's colossal disapproval. Flashes of memory tortured him as he climbed the stairs towards terrible privacy—her laughter that night in the theatre foyer, her latent playfulness, her humour and kindness. But all that warmth was lost to him. Because Theo *couldn't* care for her. He couldn't give what she needed. He'd always known she'd be better off away from him. And so would his child.

But he wasn't better off. Three long, hellish days and nights later he was nothing but worse. Nothing but angry. Nothing but poison. He missed her. And he hated that he missed her. He hated that she had got to him in a way no one ever had. That she'd made him want things. Things he was so afraid of losing that it was easier not to have had them in the first place.

'You need to rest.' He watched Dimitri silently push his dinner around his plate. The old man looked frailer than ever.

'How's Leah?' Dimitri asked.

He couldn't answer. He didn't know.

'I don't like to see you like this,' Dimitri added with a belligerent edge.

Like what? He wasn't the one who looked as if he was about to keel over.

Theo shovelled a bite of food into his mouth and chewed, tasting nothing.

'I didn't think you'd do this.'

Theo looked sharply at Dimitri. He recognised that low throb of anger. He just knew the rarely voiced criticism that was coming—Dimitri was about to blame his mother.

'That you'd be like—'

'I'm nothing like *him*,' he snapped. 'I'd never treat Leah the way my *father* treated my *mother*.' He instantly sucked in a breath but it was too late to pull the words back.

Dimitri flinched and turned ashen.

'I'm sorry,' Theo muttered, dropping his fork with a clatter. 'I didn't—'

'Don't be sorry,' Dimitri interrupted firmly, despite his complexion. 'Tell me.'

Conflicted, Theo froze. But he remembered Leah's entreaty for him to speak honestly with Dimitri. And he remembered that easing inside when he'd talked to *her*. He ached to talk to her like that again and, thanks to her, he finally realised he ought to with his grandfather too. 'I don't want to hurt you.'

'I know my son was not a saint,' Dimitri said. 'I know they both suffered.'

'I think maybe they brought the worst out in each other.'

'And you were caught between them.'

'No,' Theo sighed. 'They just didn't care, Papou.'

The pet name for his grandfather slipped out. And then all the secrets slipped—snatches of truth and hurt tumbled free, the memories that had cut most deeply. Dimitri put his hand on his shoulder and just listened and somehow Theo told him even more—even about that awful trip to see his mother. All the things he'd held back for so long because he hadn't wanted to hurt him. But Dimitri's low growl wasn't an expression of pain for himself, but empathy for Theo. There was no changing any of it, Theo understood that. But in sharing there was acknowledgement and acceptance and finally forgiveness—of those parents who just hadn't had it in them to be there for him. And it was, he finally believed, something lacking in *them*, rather than something missing in him.

'I'm proud of you, Theo.' Gruff and awkward, Dimitri

shook him in a fumbling hug. 'I want to see you happy. I want to see Leah happy.'

'So do I.' Theo buried his face in his hands. 'But I…'

'What's worse?' his grandfather asked simply. 'The thought of life with her? Or without?'

CHAPTER FIFTEEN

FIVE DAYS.

No contact.

He'd not called, not left any messages, not visited. There'd been nothing. And that was a good thing. Because Leah was getting on with it.

Amalia was staying with her in the main villa while a security guard stayed in the gatehouse at the edge of the property. Leah knew the older woman was worried about her. But she needn't be. Things were fine. How could they not be when she now lived in this breathtaking place with its crisply white, curved buildings and stunning clear blue waters? The view was unbelievable—all sea, all sky. Every day she watched the sun rise and then later set, a beautiful blinding blaze set against that backdrop of brilliant blue. It was gorgeously warm, sweet and spicy wild herbs scented the air and she'd never known a place as perfect could exist. Theo had been right.

But the beauty broke her heart all the more, because it was something that screamed to be shared.

But there'd be no wallowing in bed and weeping. During the day, her determination held. She swam in the pool or at the private beach, then walked to the nearby village. Initially she'd greeted the locals with only a smile and a smattering of her appalling Greek but already a few of the women now stopped to talk for longer. Theo had been right about that too.

When she returned to the villa, she worked on plans. At first it had been purely for distraction. But as she'd thought about it more, a tiny spark had flared and now she was all in. Theo had been right to get her thinking more about that was well. Why shouldn't she create some kind of business with her knitting and pattern designs? Some kind of community? Her enthusiasm for that consumed the daylight hours.

But the tears came in the small hours when she was too tired and sleepless and sad to stop them. The loneliness was like nothing she'd experienced because she'd had a glimpse of what could've been. She missed him on so many levels. He'd made more than just her body come alive; he'd made her laugh. He'd been fun, intelligent, attentive and so caring, even though he couldn't see that in himself.

But he'd not been effortlessly falling into love the way she had. And she was not going to lie—that *hurt*. She couldn't want love from someone unable—and unwilling—to give it. She couldn't stay, knowing she wasn't enough for the person she wanted that unconditional love from. It had been hard enough being a disappointment to her parents.

At least Theo hadn't *lied*. And who was she to try to change him?

Every time a helicopter swept overhead she stiffened with nerves. Would he ever come see her or was he going to ignore her for ever? There'd been no helicopters at all today. The sun was high and she'd got too hot even in the shade outside, so she'd gone to her bedroom to try to catch up on some of the sleep that had been eluding her.

So far, no sleep.

At a movement in the doorway, she glanced up, expecting it to be Amalia, with one of the delicious treat trays she regularly brought her. But it wasn't Amalia.

Theo stepped into her room—tall, serious, *devastating*.

Her heart whacked so hard and fast against her ribcage she put her fist to her chest to hold it inside.

'What are you doing here?' She scrambled off the bed.

She'd thought she was getting on top of her feelings, but in a flash they were all back, all-consuming. Elation. Desolation. It was far too soon to see him. It was always going to be too soon. And her bedroom was too intimate a space.

'Leah.'

How could she collapse so completely when all he did was look at her like that and say her name? She clenched her teeth, willing herself to stay strong and in control.

'What do you want?' she asked defensively as he stood watching her every move.

'I can't visit you?'

'Not unannounced, no.' She squared her shoulders. It was time to set the rules she needed in place to survive this.

His gaze didn't waver and that green deepened. 'But we're married.'

'We're not a normal married couple.' To her horror her voice weakened.

Because they were never going to be that. He didn't want that.

He still didn't move, yet somehow he seemed nearer. 'How are you finding prison island?'

She wanted to scream her heartache at him. She wanted to hate him for it. But she was so unprepared for seeing him again and the last thing she felt was hate. 'It's beautiful,' she said.

To her surprise something that looked like anger flared in his eyes.

'Really?' His soft query was laced with a lethal edge. 'So you're going to be happy here?'

She stared in disbelief that he'd asked that. Her anger burned closer to the surface. 'Don't you want me to be happy?'

Another expression flickered across his face but he swiftly stiffened and she couldn't even try to read it.

'It's better for us to live apart,' she said firmly. He'd been right.

But he didn't say anything, he just kept looking at her as

if he couldn't believe she was in front of him, as if he were afraid that if he so much as blinked she might disappear. And it wasn't fair of him to look at her like *that.*

'What do you want from me, Theo?' she flared. She was trying to give him what he'd wanted. '*Why* are you here? The baby's not due for a few months. Can't you just leave me alone and let me deal with—?'

She broke off, not wanting to name the blistering emotions steamrollering through her.

'After you first left…' His voice was so croaky it faded away.

She watched as he visibly fought for control.

'I thought I'd come and tell you it was all okay, that you should go back to Britain if you wanted. I'd set you up and pay for everything and come visit you and the baby when it suits you…but I don't want you to do that.'

Pain welled inside her. 'I wouldn't want to. The baby needs you. You need the baby too.' Because that was true. He might not think he had anything more to offer their child than financial security, but he did. 'That's why I'm here.'

But she pressed her lips together, not admitting her own need of him. He didn't want that.

He watched her, waiting, as if he knew there was more she wanted to say but couldn't.

'It's not the baby I need, Leah,' he muttered jerkily. 'It's you.'

Painful tears blinded her and she shook her head.

'Leah?'

'No.' She turned away, because she couldn't believe him. 'No, Theo.'

Somehow he was right there, his hands on her shoulders, pressing with firm but gentle pressure to get her to turn back to face him.

She ached to resist. But she still didn't have the strength. 'Please…' She broke off and closed her eyes to hold back those burning tears. But they slipped free anyway, tracking down her cheeks.

'Leah.' His thread of a voice broke. 'I'm so sorry.'

She sucked in a shaky breath. 'You don't need to be sorry. It's okay. I'm okay.' This was going to be fine. 'You just need to stay away and let me get on with it for a while.'

'You really meant it.' A whisper—of disbelief, of regret, of sorrow.

That she loved him? 'Of course I did.'

He was gazing into her eyes and she couldn't look away now because he was looking at her with such anguish. 'I'm sorry I didn't know how to accept that gift, Leah. I'm so sorry. No one's given me that before. And that it was you?' He shook his head. 'It meant too much. You'd given me something so fragile—like burning, just-blown glass—and I was too scared to take hold of it in case I warped it somehow. In case it really was nothing more than a bubble that would burst if I even breathed. I just didn't know how to handle it.'

She stilled, unsure she could believe what she thought he was trying to say.

'I'm mucking this up.' He groaned and moved closer still. 'I'm not okay, Leah. I'm not fine. I miss you.'

'But this is what you wanted.' There was a lump in her chest as if she'd swallowed a giant jagged piece of ice.

'I think I've been afraid for so long that I forgot I even was. It's just normal. I didn't even recognise I'd put defences in place. That afternoon when I came home and found out you'd gone I didn't realise you'd come here. I thought you'd left for good.'

'I could never do that to you. I couldn't hide your child from you. Not knowing you the way I—'

'I know, sweetheart. I know and I'm sorry. It was so stupid of me. I'm not great at understanding love, Leah.' He nodded. 'And I know you're used to feeling hurt by those who should show you the greatest care. But you shouldn't be. You deserve so much more than that.'

She swallowed.

'I used my parents as an excuse to keep you away. I didn't want to care. I didn't think I actually could. But, Leah, I've fallen for you. From that very first night, I just couldn't let myself recognise it.'

She shook her head. 'No.'

He tensed, his eyes widening. 'No?'

'Not from that first night,' she muttered. 'It's all…circumstance. If it weren't for this baby, we wouldn't have seen each other again.'

'I don't think that's true.'

'Of course it is—'

'How did I know where to find you?' he interrupted. 'When I came to London after you walked into the bank, how did I find you?'

'You…used your magical too-much-money powers to track down my address.'

'Yes, that's exactly what I did. But do you know *when* I did that?'

'After I called into the office…'

'No. I had my team put together a report on you the day I returned to Greece. The day after we spent the night together.'

She stared at him. Right after that? 'But you didn't do anything with it.'

He swallowed. 'I dreamed of you. But I thought I was doing the right thing for both of us.'

'Because I'm not—'

'Because I have this stupid terror inside that I couldn't get past. Not until you came back and lit up my world. Until you then left and I realised how horrendous life is without you. How much I want and need you in it because I love you. I'm so sorry I've hurt you and that I let you go.

I never should have done that. Have I ruined this completely, Leah?'

She was reeling inside. She had to take this chance; she had to have a playful moment. 'Not completely.'

He suddenly smiled.

'Keep talking.' Her heart pounded but she couldn't stop a little laugh of disbelief and delight escaping. 'Just keep talking.'

'Come home with me.' That old assurance sounded in his voice again.

'Why?' She needed more, she needed to hear it again and again. But she cupped his face in her hands as he asked.

'Because I love you. I miss you. I want you. I need you,' he confessed, leaning closer as he too struggled to breathe. 'Everything I never thought I'd say. Never thought I'd feel. I want it all with you, Leah.'

His gaze blazed with such intimate intensity and truth she almost couldn't bear it.

'Theo—'

He kissed her—as if he couldn't resist any more. As if he'd run out of words and only action was left to convince her, as if he couldn't get enough of her, as if she were the most precious thing in the world, breathlessly, brokenly. His whole body shook against hers, as if he was trying to go gently, but the strength of his need kept slipping through resulting in a soul-breaking, star-bursting kiss that she wanted never to end.

'Don't let go of me.' Tears sprang to her eyes again. 'Please don't ever let go of me.'

'Never. Never again. I'm so sorry.'

She was home in his arms. His grip on her tightened and he kissed her again. Everything was unleashed now—uncontrollable, unstoppable—the need to touch, to possess, to connect was too strong. Hands swept—clutching, touching, taking.

'I missed you,' he growled raggedly. 'Missed you so much.'

She trembled as he pinned her, kissing her, caressing every inch as if he desperately needed to rediscover her every secret. Every want.

But then he slowed as he gently stroked her belly. 'This scares me.' He glanced up, hot, raw honesty tumbling from him. 'But it brought you back into my life and for that I will always adore it.' He kissed that soft curve and looked up at her again, vulnerability visible in the sheen of his eyes. 'I'm going to need your help. I don't know how to be a husband…as for a father…'

'We'll figure it out together,' she promised him, her throat so tight she could hardly speak.

'Make do with what we have?' A half-smile broke his strain.

She nodded and curled herself about him, holding him where she needed him—with her, sealed along every inch. 'Together, we have everything.'

They had such ecstasy. And it was so sublime she actually laughed as he claimed her—her joy was too intense to be contained. He smiled back—she loved his smile. Loved him. Loved *this* with him.

And then she couldn't laugh any more, she couldn't speak. She—like he—could only *show*. In every kiss, every caress, there was total love.

Later, cuddled close, she never wanted either of them to move again. But Theo wriggled; reaching down to the floor, he scooped up his jeans and got something out of the pocket before lying back beside her. He put the small box he'd retrieved on her stomach and then took her hand and slid the diamond ring from her finger.

'What are you doing?' she asked, but she couldn't move in case that other little box slipped off her skin.

He held the diamond in his hand for a moment before

placing it on the bedside table. 'I've regretted giving you this ring from the moment I did.' He shot her a smile at her barely stifled gasp of dismay. 'I thought if I kept everything impersonal, I could keep you at a distance. But you were already under my skin. I didn't choose that diamond. I didn't want to think about what you might like. I didn't want to think of you at all. But it was all I ended up doing. The more I wanted to hold you away, the more you flooded me—filling all those dark, empty corners, Leah.' He picked up the box on her stomach. 'I spent the last week thinking about everything I'd do differently and this is the smallest of the things that I can do differently. I chose this one—your favourite colour…not so secret any more.' His smile was a touch self-conscious.

The ruby was so richly coloured it was almost crimson. Flanked by square-cut diamonds, it was sensual and striking and her eyes burned with its beauty. She shook her head as the tears threatened again.

'You don't like it?' He actually looked anxious. 'We can change it. You can choose—'

'No.' She put her fingers on his lips, half laughing, half crying. 'It's beautiful, I love it.'

Not only because it was stunning, but because of what it signified. He wanted to please her. But that in itself made her panic again. 'But you know you don't have to give me things. I don't want you feeling like you have to please me…' She breathed shakily. 'You've spent so long trying to please, trying to be perfect just in case—'

'And you haven't?' He cupped her jaw. 'You *do* things for people, Leah. For everyone—your friends, family… You did things for me too—you wore those heels and drove me mad. But this is different. It's not only to please you, but me too. Because I love you like I've never loved anyone. I never knew it was possible. And it's scary and wonderful and I just want to give you everything.'

'The only everything I need is you. Just you.'

He leaned over her, mischief sparkling in his gaze. 'So you don't want the ring?'

She hesitated, loving his flash of humour. And she slowly smiled. 'Maybe we should just see how it looks.'

He pushed the ring down her finger until it nestled next to the wedding band and they both laughed. He looked into her eyes. 'Perfect.'

She nodded. 'Want to know what else would be perfect right now?'

'Oh, I already do.' His hands slid to where they were so sweetly welcome. 'Mine to have and hold.'

'For ever.' She'd never felt as content and secure and as loved.

'I never want to spend another night apart from you.' He trailed his fingers up and down her arm. 'We need to speak to Dimitri,' he said with a smile in his voice. 'He and I talked.'

'Really?'

'You were right. He'd guessed some, I told him more. He was sad but he was mostly concerned about me. And you.' He suddenly smiled. 'You're like this hot marshmallow, fitting perfectly between us to forge us into a real family. You've made us both melt. You're like the sweetest glue…'

'You think I'm a hot marshmallow?' She chuckled, but inside *she* was the one melting.

'So hot.' He nodded. 'And he'll be thrilled to see you come home with me.'

'We'll come back here often though, won't we?'

He sent her a look of total triumph and pleasure. 'You really like it?'

'You were right. Not prison. Paradise.' She looked at him, overwhelmed with emotion to see him looking so happy. That he felt as deeply for her? 'I love you so much it hurts.'

'I don't want it to hurt, Leah.' He swiftly kissed her, his arms tightening like bars around her. She was imprisoned in the paradise that was his love.

Perfect, profound peace settled deep into her heart. 'I think, as long you're holding me, it won't.'

CHAPTER SIXTEEN

Three years later

LEAH WATCHED THE helicopter descending over the island and put her sketchbook down. She'd not made much progress on her latest design today, too distracted waiting for this—Theo's return. There was a shriek from the other side of the pool where her daughter, Petra, had been dangling her feet in the water while her great-grandfather, Dimitri, read to her. Petra too knew what the helicopter meant.

While Theo never spent more than a night away from them unless he absolutely had to, he'd had to stay in Athens for a couple of days. Now, pulse skipping, Leah watched until he appeared around the corner from the helipad. His sleeves were rolled back and Leah's stomach flipped in that funny way it did when she saw him again. Three years of marriage, of making love every night, hadn't cured her helpless desire for him. Instead it had deepened and today the butterflies in her tummy were as skittish as that very first night they'd met. But as he moved across the terrace with that purposeful stride, it wasn't only Leah who was captivated by his appearance.

'Daddy!'

Laughing, he dropped his bag and crouched down as Petra ran towards him. Leah's heart swelled as he scooped their toddler up and swung her into his embrace. Petra's squeals of delight rang clear across the azure pool. Leah's eyes filled. Her lovely little girl had a father who adored her and was so demonstrative about it. He was everything Leah had ever wanted and he gave everything she could ever have wished for to their child—total, unconditional love. He gave that to her too. They'd learned together.

Summer on the island was sheer bliss. Her little family spent long, lazy days here, enjoying the sea and the sun and sheer fun of being together. In the last couple of years, Dimitri's health hadn't just stabilised, he'd been reinvigorated thanks to Petra. The little girl filled all their hearts till they overflowed, forcing them to beat stronger still.

Her brother had visited and they'd defrosted him from the lab. He'd then returned—coming at least a couple of times a year, which was wonderful. They'd seen her parents on one of their trips to England but didn't spend too much time with them. It hurt Leah less now she had too much else in her life to treasure.

With Theo's encouragement Leah had pressed forward with the plans she'd begun while they'd been apart for those terrible few days. She now owned an online knitwear company, but, as she had no real need to turn a profit, she'd established it as a charitable enterprise. For every item purchased, a second item was donated to those in need—they'd made and given children's jumpers, wool blankets, ballet crossovers for a dance school offering free classes in an underprivileged area in London… There were so many to help and she loved it. What was more, over a surprisingly short time she'd developed a really active online community who provided laughter and support for her venture. She'd begun selling her pattern designs and they'd become popular too so now she spent most of her work hours designing and knitting up samples…from beautiful baby shawls and cosy natural blankets to luxury silk sweaters and, of course, the original ultimate outrageous leg warmers. But right now, the thought of handling anything woollen seemed mad—she was hot inside and out from studying her too-stunning husband, waiting for the right moment to tell him her secret.

He called something to Dimitri and murmured something else to Petra, who smiled and ran back to her great-grandfather, who picked up the book again. Theo then casually grabbed his bag and turned towards Leah.

Finally.

Their gazes locked. Even from across the pool she sensed the heat flare within him, matching that which was building inside her. But she remained still as he slowly sauntered over to where she reclined in the shade. There was no denying it, right now she was living like some spoiled minor Greek goddess…and she loved it. He made her feel utterly adored. That familiar spark radiated from deep within her, igniting the need that always sat so close to her surface. He hadn't released her gaze and now he smiled a slow wicked smile. Her heart raced even faster.

'You're pleased to see me, *agape mou*,' he murmured.

She'd been counting down the hours more desperately than ever today. But she didn't bother to reply, instead she leaned forward and lifted her face towards him. He slid his hand to the nape of her neck and drew closer. His kiss was leisurely and thorough to the point that her toes curled. Luscious, loving and yet not enough.

'How was your day?' He sat on the edge of her lounger and she shifted her legs to make more room for him.

'Good,' she breathed. It was even better now he was back and still had his hand resting on her shoulder. 'Though I fell asleep this afternoon.' She giggled. 'Poor Petra was showing me her dancing skills but the music was dreamy and I just drifted away.'

'Hmm. You've been tired lately.' Something smouldered in his eyes.

A swirl of tension drew her closer. 'You've noticed that?' She licked her lips.

'I've noticed a few other things as well.' He traced a finger from her shoulder along the edge of her V-necked tee to rest at the top of her cleavage.

Her already oversensitive breasts tightened even more beneath his blatant inspection.

'Maybe with all this time on the island, I'm getting lazy.' She grabbed his hand to stop him teasing, but held it close to her chest. Her heart thudded harder.

'Maybe.' He cocked his head and sounded disbelieving, but his smile deepened.

'Too many late nights working on my new design?' she offered, but she sounded too breathless to pull it off properly and she had to look away from him and stifle her giggle.

'Maybe, but then, the last few nights you've been going to bed earlier than usual.' He bent closer. 'So maybe there's another reason.'

'Low iron?' She peeped a look at him from under her lashes.

He flicked his eyebrows, heightening that sinfully amused look. 'It's not that, Leah…'

She bit her lip, trying to hold back her giveaway laughter. 'What do you think it is?'

He chuckled delightedly. 'Perhaps I know you better than you know yourself.'

'You think…?'

He opened his bag and pulled out a box. 'You want to prove me right?' He presented the home pregnancy test to her.

Leah laughed and took the box from him with her thumb and index finger, only to swivel and drop it to the ground with a flourish.

'I don't need to, because I did one early this morning.' She couldn't hold back her joy and she leaned forward, threw her arms around his neck and all but sobbed, 'I'm pregnant!'

'I *knew* it,' he growled, swiftly seizing her by the waist and pulling her right onto his lap.

'At the *same time* as me, thank you very much,' she said with a squeak but tightened her hold back on him.

He kissed her again.

It was only when the gurgling laughter from their daughter across the pool impinged that he pulled back. Leah rested her forehead against his and looked into his brilliant eyes, unable to stop smiling. The love she felt for him? The connection they had?

'Leah,' he murmured.

She heard the depth in his voice, saw it in his eyes—he felt it the same.

'What you've done for Dimitri and me? The gift that is Petra, and now this baby?' He looked so happy. 'You've given me everything. Now I know how to love, how to be loved…and I *love* you.'

She leaned closer, resting against him—with him—so beautifully content.

* * * * *

RUMOURS BEHIND THE GREEK'S WEDDING

PIPPA ROSCOE

To Lady Penelope, a most excellent and definitely non-fictitious drinking partner.

This dedication is for friends and drunken promises.

Sláinte.

CHAPTER ONE

'*Bonsoir*, Chariton Endeavours.'

'I will speak with Célia d'Argent.'

'May I ask who's calling?'

'You can *warn* her that it's Loukis Liordis.'

'Consider her warned. What can I do for you *this time*, Mr Liordis?'

Only a brief pause hinted at any semblance of recognition from her client. And Célia d'Argent *meant* recognition. For Liordis would never lower himself to feel as human an emotion as contrition. If anything, the small moment had been one of reprimand, one that hinted it should have been for *her* to feel contrite. And normally Célia would be mortified to utter such a response. But this wasn't such an occasion. Loukis Liordis, Greek billionaire, renowned playboy and presently the biggest pain in her neck, had driven Célia beyond the brink of her usually impeccable civility.

'You answer your own phone?' he demanded as if such a thing should have been beneath her.

'I do when it is nine thirty at night, Mr Liordis.'

'What has that to do with anything?'

The absolute gall of the man!

Célia glared at her reflection in the windows of her office. Loukis might have been their first client, and might be the reason why she and her business partner Ella Riding had been able to achieve the success that they had enjoyed in the last few months, but that didn't mean she had to like him, or jump to his every command. Just the majority of them.

'You can explain to me how it is that you have spectacularly failed to deliver on your promise, Mademoiselle d'Argent.'

Célia frowned, mentally scanning through the lists of current events they had planned for him. 'I'm not quite sure what you mean, Mr Lio—'

'I will speak with Ella, then.'

Célia ground her teeth, not caring whether he heard the sound through the phone or not. She hated that his words had spread anxiety through her chest. Hated that her pulse was beginning to speed up and a wave of insecurity threatened to overwhelm her.

'I am afraid that is not possible.'

'Why not?'

'As I have explained—' *many, many times* '—Ella is presently on maternity leave.'

'Surely she is able to pick up a phone?'

'No, Mr Liordis. She is not. Now, if you could, I would like the opportunity to hear your concerns.' She wouldn't, of course. It was late, she hadn't even had dinner, and the hastily consumed half-lunch was now a distant memory.

'My concern is that you have not fulfilled your obligation.'

'Which obligation are we speaking of?'

'The one that would restore my reputation, Ms d'Argent.'

Célia dropped into the soft leather chair that was her favourite piece of office furniture and swirled round to her computer, absolutely speechless.

'You have nothing to say?'

'Forgive me, I was just checking the letterhead of our company stationery. At no point or place does it say that we are in the reputation business. Our role is—'

'I know what your role is, and don't be crass, Ms d'Argent. Ella—and by extension I presume you—knew exactly why it was that I signed on with your company. And the resulting publicity from my first event with your company was not positive.'

'I appreciate that. I do. While the charity event backed by you and your company has given the Erythra Foundation the ability to do some incredible things in the future, personally for you, it has perhaps not gone as well as we had envisaged. Quite possibly down to the fact that you did not deem it important enough to make an appearance.'

The line went completely quiet. Icy. Frigid even. And Célia suddenly realised that she had gone too far. It was not for her to question her client. No. The headlines following the event had done that well enough. That she and they appeared aligned in the belief that he had, once again, found himself in bed with his lady *du jour*—a lady probably of statuesque physique, impeccable proportions and in all likelihood platinum blonde—was neither here nor there.

'We will talk about this further.'

Before she could even offer the possibility of a meeting, the line went dead, and the phone went limp in her hand.

What had she just done?

She *never* spoke to people that way, let alone their most valuable client. But Loukis's constant hounding over the last few months, his absolute determination for everything to be perfect had driven her and her team out of their minds. In the months since Ella had signed him in Fiji, Chariton Endeavours had taken on even more clients and had been absolutely run off their feet working hard to fulfil their promise to both the business side and the charitable side of their organisation. They'd undertaken twelve events in the last month alone, and all without Ella, who was Célia's rock, sounding board and confidante.

In truth Célia was exhausted, which was the only reason that she had let her usually ironclad guard down and said exactly what had been on her mind. She ran a slightly trembling hand over her face and finally put the phone down.

Tomorrow she would have to do damage limitation. But for now, she needed to return to her apartment and sleep. Eat. Perhaps even indulge in a cool white glass of Australian Pino Gris.

That decision rose within her like defiance, as if she still had to justify something as silly as her taste in wine to her father, even if she did imagine a look of abject horror crossing the proud Frenchman's features. His distant disapproval a constant presence in their interaction. But as Célia looked out at the Parisian streets from her window, she mentally shielded herself from being drawn down that dark path.

She grabbed her bag, her keys, locked the front door of the ground-floor office and turned onto the street only to pull up short.

The absolute gall of the man!

In a dramatic turn of his recent luck, Loukis Liordis had found a parking space just outside Chariton Endeavours about thirty minutes earlier. He had terminated his call to Célia d'Argent only ten minutes ago and was now leaning against the sleek McLaren supercar he'd leased for his time in France, scrolling through the latest headlines pontificating on his absence from the charity gala last week. Each successive screenshot fuelled an ire ignited by the steely voiced Célia.

If it hadn't been for the barely audible gasp of indignation he might not have even noticed her departure from the building. He certainly would not have *noticed* her. But that was partly due to the fact that, dressed in what could only be described as a deeply unappealing beige top, she had been camouflaged by the stonework behind her. And had it not been for a pair of black jeans he might not even have known she was there. Especially since the moment she'd caught sight of him, she had pulled up short and not moved a muscle.

He resisted the urge to roll his eyes. Barely.

'Ms d'Ar—'

'What are you doing here?' she demanded.

He'd barely taken a breath before she continued, 'You *can't* be here.' Finishing the inhalation, slowly, he locked a well-honed, utterly devastating gaze on her and tried again. 'Ms d'Argent, as I said. We need to talk further.'

'Not *now*.'

'Yes *now*. I am needed back in Greece first thing tomorrow morning,' he said, checking his watch unnecessarily, as he perfectly well knew the time, but it was not bad for an on-the-spot dramatic effect.

Having done so, he levered himself from where he leaned against the car and held open the passenger door. 'Shall we?'

'No, we shall not,' she hissed as she skirted around him and away from the open door as if he posed some great threat. Fine. He closed the door.

'Célia,' he called out before she could get much further. 'We do need to talk.'

It must have been the change in his voice that stopped her retreat. It wasn't the charming playboy tone that had done him both great success and great damage only a few years before. Before everything he'd known had come crashing down about his ears. It wasn't the tone he'd used to seduce, or amuse, to charm, placate or cajole. Neither was it the autocratic arrogant, commanding, brook-no-argument voice he'd used on her earlier. Strangely enough it was none of the façades he'd adopted over the years, but the tone of his own true self that halted her departure.

He watched her take a deep breath and remembered just how beautiful he found her. Her face was almost startling in comparison to the bland taste in clothing. Broad features made the most of the sharp cheekbones that were contrasted with lips that were a small, delicate cupid's bow. Eyes, wide in shock, were of the purest amber. Her hair had been piled up as if thoughtlessly in a messy bun, but the little of what he could see hinted at rich auburn tones he wanted to investigate further. Her rich, creamy skin was covered in a light spattering of freckles that the horrid T-shirt did nothing for. But no matter how appealing and refreshing he found her, it was not why he was here.

'Mr Liordis. I am sorry, but I really do need to eat.'

'We have reservations at Comte Croix.'

'I… I'm hardly dressed for—'

'Anything other than paintballing? I had noticed. But as you'll be with me, I'm sure they'll make an exception.'

A blush rose to the creamiest of skin on her cheeks, blotting out the subtle shades of her freckles. He opened the door for her once again and as she passed before him he inhaled the sweet scent of orange and herbs, basil perhaps, and pressed down the urge for more. *More* was certainly *not* on the menu tonight. Or any other night, quite possibly, for the next ten years or so. In that moment he cursed his mother all over again and wished her safely and securely to hell.

Célia pressed herself deeply into the plush leather of the sleek supercar wishing she were anywhere but right there, next to Loukis Liordis. It was one thing to be sharp with him on the phone, but altogether something else to be within touching distance of such a…such a… Well, she wasn't blind. The renowned Greek billionaire playboy was utterly overwhelming in person.

From this angle she couldn't miss the thick waves of dark hair that had been pushed back from a proud forehead as if conspiring to show off his innate beauty. His brows were low above eyes that were busy scanning the lamplit Parisian streets. Eyes that she'd chastised herself already for comparing to rich espresso the one and only previous time she'd met him.

He'd come to the office before Ella's maternity leave and their brief introduction had sent seismic shock waves through Célia. Not because of any special attention he'd directed her way. No, in fact he'd barely raked a glance across her features. But that glance had fired something within her. Something she'd thought dormant. And it had been enough. Enough to warn her she would have to be on her guard around him.

Her eyes were drawn back to his tense jawline, strong enough to demand attention, despite the *keep away* aura that seemed to fill the car. The powerful angle of his cheekbones highlighted the bridge of his nose—the slight kink there hinting towards a years-old break, perhaps. But it was his lips that really got to her. They appeared ever so slightly pursed, as if intentionally drawing her gaze to the centre of his upper lip, where it swept downwards at the same point as his lower lip lent upwards just a little.

And then those lips moved. Quirking into a side-angled smile as he caught her openly staring at him.

Kill me now. Please.

She pressed even further back into the seat, trying to make herself invisible.

'If you want to move the seat back—'

'Non, merci.'

He simply nodded in response, never once having taken his eyes off the road, nor loosening the smile that quirked his lips.

She hated the painful blush that stole over her cheeks. Hated dealing with the rich clients Ella sourced, and wished for the hundredth time that day her best friend and business partner weren't on maternity leave. But no matter how much she did, Célia would never begrudge the happiness Ella had found with Roman. Despite a deeply rocky start, they had found their happy-ever-after. One that she couldn't ever imagine for herself. Not after…

Her thoughts were cut off as the car pulled off the road towards the large sprawling entrance of the famous Parisian restaurant. Taking a deep breath, she forced her mind into a semblance of order. 'So what did you—'

'We're here,' he announced, either purposely or unnecessarily interrupting her.

She clenched her jaw and took a deep breath in through her nose. He might be the most attractive man she'd ever seen, but he was also the most infuriating. As he exited the car, she grabbed her bag from the footwell, making sure she hadn't marked or scuffed any of the furnishings, wishing she could erase her presence from the car as much as the evening. She was about to reach for the handle when the car door swung open, to reveal Loukis standing there, offering her his hand.

Social etiquette did not compensate for rudeness, however it would be churlish to refuse, so she placed her hand in his, trying to disguise the momentary shock she felt as his fingers wrapped around hers. Tingles zipped up her hand to her wrist and forearm, raising the fine hairs as if she were in the midst of an electrical storm. A storm that held them both at the centre in a moment of complete calm. From where she sat looking up at him, he appeared to loom over her. His eyes intent, one brow slightly furrowed as if he was confused about something—a confusion she felt too as her heartbeat picked up speed to match his where she felt his pulse against her wrist.

She watched him carelessly toss the keys to a car worth more than she could dream of to the valet, and gesture for her to enter the restaurant. It was a move that even her obscenely rich father would never have made. No, there had never been anything careless about her exacting father's actions.

She felt Loukis's presence at her back as she made her way to the maître d', adopting a mask she hadn't used for years. One that implied that she was used to eating in restaurants like this for breakfast, lunch and dinner, no matter what she looked like. Even if, inside, she was experiencing an excruciating humiliation.

Over the hum in her ears she barely heard Loukis state his reservation, but she didn't miss the way the black-and-white-suited maître d' cast her a no-less-than-she-deserved disparaging look and a sudden wave of Loukis-focused resentment sliced through her. Of course she was not dressed appropriately for a restaurant of this calibre. Ten minutes ago she hadn't even known she would be here. She waited for Loukis to make some apology for her state of dress, but was surprised to find a steely glint in Loukis's eyes as if daring the man to object or find fault. Instantly his manner transformed to obsequiousness.

She followed behind the two men weaving between tables where hushed conversations, romantic assignations and even a few business deals appeared to be taking place and smiled thankfully at the now chastised man who pulled a chair out for her as if she were royal.

'May I offer you the *carte des vins*?'

'That will not be necessary. A bottle of the Pouilly-Fuissé and whatever fish main you have today.'

'Bien sûr.'

'Merci,' Célia added just before the man could beat a hasty retreat with the unseen menus. After all, she knew what it was like to be on the receiving end of Loukis's abruptness. Choosing to ignore the fact that he had not even thought to ask her wine preferences, let alone food wishes, or even possible allergies, she attempted to take at least some control back of her hijacked evening. Attempted to pull around her some of the confidence and self-assurance she felt when dealing with the charities that were her much preferred interaction.

'So, Mr Liordis, what is it that you wish to discuss?'

'I need another event.'

'Okay, did you have something in mind?'

He shook his head, his lips pulling into another moue of carelessness. 'Not particularly. Only that it must be within the next few weeks.'

Loukis watched Célia take in his directive, silently, but mind clearly racing. He had expected outrage, immediate dismissal, and certainly a great deal of objection, but no.

'It would not be realistic to expect to do so again with the Erythra Foundation.'

'Why not?' he asked, not to be petulant, but genuinely curious.

'In order to ensure that there was no oversaturation or fatigue with donations and press. Do you have another charity in mind?'

'No. But ideally it would be Greek.'

Célia nodded, pressing her hand to her rosebud lips and looking off to the side. At this angle, the length and curve of her neck were on exquisite display and he found himself almost thankful that she was wearing the horrid beige round-necked T-shirt.

The first time he'd met her, in the offices in Paris, he'd had to force himself to wrench his eyes away from her. Instantly he'd felt a pull of desire so strong and so sure that he'd been shaken by it. But even then he'd known that he couldn't entertain such a thing. Not only were they working together, but he just couldn't risk it. Not then, and certainly not now.

He was in the process of once again forcing his gaze away from that alluring curve when she turned her attention back to him.

'I would need more time than a few weeks. What is your absolute deadline?'

Loukis couldn't quite account for why her practical, no-nonsense, down-to-business approach to this conversation bothered him so much. After all, it was what he had wanted, and what he usually demanded from those he got into business with. But on Célia it seemed...unsatisfying.

'I need it done by the end of—' He cut himself off short, before revealing too much, and silently cursed the strange reaction she was provoking in him. 'By the end of June.' He had nearly said by the end of the school term. And that would have been unacceptable. It was utterly imperative that he did not reveal a single thing about why he needed this event to happen so quickly. Even the smallest detail would put everything at risk—and that he could simply not allow.

'So I have four weeks.'

'*Nai*—yes.'

'Do you have a preference over the type of event?'

'Only that it be as public and positive as possible.'

'How do you feel about art?'

'I have a few investment pieces.'

'Would you be willing to part with them?'

'If I have to.' He would be willing to part with anything if it helped his cause.

Célia's rapid round of questions was brought to a halt by the appearance of the sommelier. He proffered the bottle to him, but Loukis directed the tasting to Célia. He watched as she swirled the wine once and inhaled before tasting, then nodding her approval. Again, Loukis found himself bemused by a woman who looked as if her entire dress that evening was cheaper than the price of the bottle of wine they were about to drink. A feeling apparently shared by the sommelier, who filled their glasses modestly and left.

'What is more important to you in this event, the clientele and publicity or the funds raised for the charity?'

He knew that she would prefer the latter, but he couldn't jeopardise this. It was his last chance to bolster a ravaged reputation. Delaying the moment her displeasure would be revealed, he sidestepped the answer.

'Is this a test?'

'No, it helps determine what kind of charity to approach. If your goal is to make the greatest impact on the charity, then it would be best to approach one in great need, even if it were something that perhaps might not be on many people's radar. If, however, as I am inclined to believe, you are looking for a great *personal* impact, then a charity that could draw many celebrities, and therefore attention, would be where I start looking.'

If there was any hint of censure in her tone, Loukis could not detect it. 'No way to do both, I suppose?'

'Mr Liordis—I, *we*, match business leaders with charities. All money raised is a gift to them. And trust me, I will be charging you an obscene amount of money in order to achieve this. Money that will go towards the future investment of more money for more charities. Our endeavour may be hopeful and charitable but, make no mistake, it is also business minded.'

She was such a strange combination of steel encased in silk that he had to work hard to focus on the issue at hand and not on Célia herself.

'How obscene?'

'Very,' she said, with the smallest of smiles curving the rosebud lips upwards enticingly. She took a sip of her wine, her eyes narrowing a fraction, before putting the glass back down on the table.

'You don't like the wine?'

'I had started out the evening looking forward to an Australian Pinot Gris, a small bowl of soup and perhaps one episode of the period drama I'm currently watching. And yet…' She shrugged, her hands open before her as if to say, *Here we are.*

'Surely that is sacrilegious?'

'My preference in wine?'

He cocked his head to one side in answer to her question.

'Only for purists.'

It was on his tongue to probe the question of her purity further and realised instantly that he would not be talking about the wine. Three years ago nothing would have stopped the line falling from his lips. But three years ago he had been a very different man. At least the spell she seemed to have woven over him had not yet quite short-circuited his sense of decorum.

As if that self-imposed morality had returned, he suddenly felt guilty for disrupting an evening she seemed to have very much wanted. And for the first time that evening, he took in the signs of exhaustion about her eyes. Very well disguised, but still they were signs that he recognised, certainly in the first few months, if not more, when his life had been turned upside down by his mother three years ago. Not that he would take them back for a second. And that timely reminder put him back on track. Célia and her tiredness didn't matter. That she delivered what he needed did. Very much.

'So, you will arrange the event and the charity for the end of June?'

'Yes. On one condition.'

'Which is?'

'That you are present this time, Mr Liordis.'

Célia watched his eyes narrow. For a moment, it felt almost as if they had breached the business talk, as if Loukis's ruthless pursuit of a positive reputation had been forgotten. She'd felt as if he'd been about to ask something…but whatever softness, whatever sense of unmasking she had sensed had quickly withdrawn behind a look of fury.

'I do not make that request to be difficult,' she quickly added. 'If you are to achieve what you desire, then it is important that you are there.'

'I will be.'

The waiter arrived with their meals, but suddenly Célia was no longer hungry. The smell from the scallop and lobster tortellini with a bisque broth was incredible, but she couldn't shake Loukis's steady gaze. She forced herself to pick up her fork, cut into the silky pasta and the soft mousse of the filling, and as she raised it to her mouth she looked up to find his hawklike eyes still on her. As if daring her to consume it beneath his gaze.

Never had she been around a man who wielded his sensuality like an extension of himself. She couldn't deny the effect he had on her. But that didn't mean she needed to succumb to it.

The last time she had, it had proved devastating when she had realised it was not her but her father's money, her father's approval that had been her ex's end goal. She had vowed not to make the same mistake again and hadn't yet.

With that last determined cry ringing in her mind, she ate the first, second and third mouthfuls without acknowledging Loukis at all. She had focused her gaze on the plate before her and knew that the delicious meal was utterly wasted on her as her thoughts blocked the pleasure of taste.

Célia was so focused on getting to the end of the meal that, when she laid her fork down, she realised that Loukis had not only finished but was placing an alarmingly large number of euros onto the table.

'I will take you home,' he said, without sparing her a glance. Given where her thoughts had been it was hardly surprising that Célia momentarily thought he intended something else.

'That won't be necessary,' she claimed, having absolutely no intention of letting Loukis Liordis anywhere near her apartment.

He pierced her with a look that she was sure would have wilted many a woman throughout the years. 'That is not how I was raised.'

'And that has nothing to do with me. I can find my own way home, but thank you for the offer.'

He followed so close behind her as they wound their way out of the restaurant that Célia was sure that she could feel the heat of his body pressing against her, speeding her departure from Comte Croix.

He waited until she had arranged for the valet to call her a cab, spinning his keys around his forefinger not with impatience, but habit, she supposed. When the car arrived, he opened the door for her, and left it open as she settled into the sleek town car.

'I look forward to hearing from you as the plans develop

for the event. In the meantime, Ms d'Argent, do yourself and the world a favour and burn that T-shirt.'

He closed the door before she could even respond and disappeared into the night.

The absolute gall of the man!

CHAPTER TWO

Twenty-five days, four hundred and thirty-three emails, one hundred and twenty-eight hours of meetings, one hundred and nineteen invitations, and two flights later, Célia found herself in a stunning white-walled exhibition space overlooking the Acropolis in Athens.

If she had been tired the evening she had gone for dinner with Loukis, she was exhausted tonight. But in just a few hours, the event Liordis had demanded, negotiated, tweaked, argued and begrudgingly agreed to, would be over. And she could sleep. Finally. Perhaps even have *one* day where she didn't have to have a single tense conversation with the Greek billionaire.

Still, she could argue that what they had managed to achieve together in such an impossibly brief time was nothing short of miraculous. She might have managed to sound confident back in the Comte Croix in Paris, but the panic that had beset her once the anger from his comment about her clothing had receded along with the image of him standing there watching the car turn the corner had been swift and intense. And certainly enough to distract her from the devastating effect he'd had on her in person.

She passed between the two large stone columns that would greet their guests and onwards into the open white-walled space, contrasting against the dark granite flooring and rough concrete ceiling that lined the repurposed warehouse. It was a fairly new gallery, but absolutely perfect for the event.

The clean tones offset the collection of admittedly impressive pieces Loukis had managed to get his hands on, either from his own collection or donated from equally wealthy contributors. Bright colours screamed from the canvases of some of the world's most famous modern artists. Muted tones soothed from older masterpieces, and shadows were cast from inconceivable sculptures from throughout the last century.

For a moment, Célia was lost in the sheer beauty of what surrounded her until the click of high heels made their way towards her. She turned to find Sia Keating, the art valuer from the privately owned international auction house Bonnaire. As always, Célia found herself unable to look away from the glorious titian hair that haloed her face and neck.

'Célia, I'm so pleased I got to see you before I left,' Sia said as she took Célia into a warm embrace.

'Me too,' she replied. 'I can't thank you enough for doing this at such short notice.'

'It's my pleasure, and for a very good cause. Is everything in place?'

'Yes, each piece's documentation is present and correct and, if I may say so, *very* impressive.'

Célia smiled. That final check meant that the event could go ahead as planned. 'And having Bonnaire as backers for it is a real coup.'

Sia's smile dimmed a little. 'Well, they were happy to do so, provided I took the valuation on my own time.'

Célia frowned. 'On your own time?'

'I had lots of holiday to use anyway. And it's *almost* on the way to the Emirates.'

'I'm sure we could—'

'No,' Sia said with a genuine smile this time. 'Really, it's fine. It's nice to be part of something like this. And frankly I was lucky enough to get a job with them anyway.'

Célia placed a comforting hand on Sia's. They had become fast friends since first meeting at a charity gala event a few years ago and bonded over the difficulties with their parents.

'Dare I ask?' Sia questioned.

'I haven't seen either of them in five years,' Célia replied, knowing that Sia was asking after her parents.

An alarm beeped on Sia's phone and she looked apologetic as she reached into her handbag to retrieve it. Shaking her head again, 'I'm so sorry. The flight is due to leave in just a few hours.'

Wishing Célia the best of luck for the evening, Sia departed with promises to meet up soon in Paris.

Once again Célia was alone in the grand space. Only this time echoes of an old hurt were her companion. She flicked out her fingers from her hands as if she could expel the painful sensation gathering within her body as she walked amongst the pieces of art that would hopefully net the charity a large sum of money and, of course, garner a great deal of positive press for Loukis.

Three rooms over, towards the back of the gallery, there were forty-five staff hired for the evening preparing canapés and drinks for the attendees. The master of ceremonies for the evening had arrived and was getting himself ready. But just for a moment, Célia had the space to herself and she drew in a deep breath to calm the nerves roiling in her stomach.

Rarely had she been at the front and centre of events like this. Ella usually gloried in this role. Ella, who had been worried when Célia had called to update her on the event. She hadn't missed the brief pause that spoke of her concerns. She hadn't missed the carefully constructed sentences gently probing if she might be taking on too much, or whether she might actually not be able to pull it off.

All of which had only driven Célia further. She now had as much invested in the event as Loukis. A brief flare of irritation welled in her chest as her thoughts turned to him, especially as since she had last seen him, far too much of her time had suddenly seemed preoccupied with her own clothing.

She pulled a slight grimace as she looked down at her black trousers and white silky top. It was definitely better than the beige T-shirt but she was sure that Loukis would manage to find fault with it. A part of her had wanted to find something that would wipe the disdain from his face the next time they met, but she had neither the time nor the money to do so.

Every bit she earned went into either the company or her home. Living in Paris, alone now—without Ella to share the rent—she'd had to move into a new apartment and, although she loved it dearly, it was still a drain on her earnings. Ella and Roman had offered to buy somewhere in Paris but Célia couldn't, wouldn't, take that. It wasn't so much a case of cutting her nose off out of spite, more an awareness of how much she valued her own independence after all those years. Her father would be horrified to see the small loft apartment she had squeezed herself into. It was a far cry from the palatial estate she had grown up in as a child, before being sent to boarding school. And while it had been the height of luxury and status, she shivered at the memory of the way silence had echoed amongst the rooms. Seen and not heard, had been her father's idiom. And for the millionth time, she wondered if it would have been different had she been born the son that her father had so desperately wanted. The heir to the business that was her father's sole focus. Would that have prevented the endless well of disapproval she had felt from her father—even as she tried to emulate his path by going into computer sciences and engineering?

When she heard the determined clipped tones of shoes on the sleek flooring, she turned, wondering if Sia had forgotten something, and stopped short.

Loukis stalked towards her, his gait somehow both lazy and predatory, careless yet alluringly so. Dressed in a black tux, his white shirt undone at the collar, the tie balled in his fist, he looked as if he were just finishing his evening rather than starting it. As if he had just departed some mysterious woman's bed. The thought sent images crashing through her brain and short-circuited the carefully prepared welcome she had wanted to greet him with.

'Is everything ready?' he demanded across the space as if he already had somewhere else to be, someone else on his mind.

She took in a breath she hoped would calm the frustration that seemed to be a constant companion to his sudden appearances.

'Yes.'

'Kalós,' he said, scanning the space quickly with an assessing gaze before he reached her.

'Are *you* ready?' she queried, cursing her words the moment his eyes returned to hers and pinned her with an angry stare.

'Nai.'

'Really?' she asked again, despite his assurance. Somehow in all their conversations she'd become strangely touched by his use of half-Greek, half-English words, their meaning evident by the context. It was not the suave language of the playboy, but a signal of understanding, of trust in her and her abilities.

She held her hand out for the tie still clenched in a vice-like grip, wondering which Loukis she would get this evening. She had seen his determined side, she had seen the charming side as he had flirted over the phone with her usually sternly efficient assistant, the result of which was for her to descend into a useless heap of blushes and giggles. Only once had she seen what she thought might be the true Loukis. When he had said that they needed to talk in a tone that had stopped her hasty departure, before they had gone to Comte Croix.

Frowning, he held out the crumpled tie, which she smoothed before stepping closer to him and looping it up over his head. The move had begun as an automatic thing. The mirror image of a memory she had from her childhood. Of watching her mother doing this for her father before every dinner event they attended. Even as her hands crossed over the silky black material, looping it into a bow tie, Célia wondered what on earth she was doing, aching from the past and yearning for something she should not want from the present.

The scent from his aftershave, spicy and earthy, drifted towards her as if propelled by the heat from his body, crashing against her in waves. Refusing to look up at him, unable to face what must have been confusion at her actions, she concentrated on knotting the silks in the right way and just about resisted placing her hands on his chest once she had done. They fell uselessly beside her once she had pulled the silk tight and stepped back, looking out to what must have been a Hockney to disguise her own embarrassment.

'I don't think that anyone has ever done that for me before.'

Loukis watched her shrug a shoulder as if to say it was nothing, but the small gesture had exposed the sleek line of her neck and collarbone and obliterated any sense of casualness the moment might have conveyed. The moment she had looped the tie over his neck, she had brought them so close he could smell her shampoo, orange blossom and citrus. He'd had to look away, jaw clenched and body steeled against the sudden shocking wave of arousal she had ignited. If he'd been tense when he had arrived, he was now rigid.

But any thoughts of sensual delight provoked by Célia were doused with the reminder of why he had been so stressed upon his arrival. Sobbing ten-year-olds had that effect. Sobbing ten-year-old sisters tended to drive him beyond despair.

'Why do I have to go...? Why are you making me do this...? Please, Loukis, I don't want to go with her...'

The ache in his chest mixed with fury and an impotence, a helplessness, that Loukis simply refused to accept.

'The MC is here?'

Célia stepped away, as if sensing the swift change in mood from whatever had just passed between them.

'Yes.'

'And the—'

'Valuation has been done, the staff are preparing the food and drink for this evening. The red carpet is lined with a roaring crowd of paparazzi—in case you came in the back way—and all but three invitations have been accepted. We should have a full turnout.'

Loukis nodded, heedless of the way she had interrupted him.

'Good. We should go.'

'Go?' Célia asked. 'What? Why would we—'

'We need to make an appearance on the red carpet. My limousine is waiting at the back to circle around the block so we can make our grand entrance.'

The horror covering Célia's features would have been funny had it not been such a shocking waste of time.

'No. I'm not… I cannot—'

'You can and you will.'

She was shaking her head now and backing away from him as if he posed some great physical threat.

'I did not agree to that and…no. No, Loukis, I will not be walking the red carpet with you. I will not get drawn into whatever publicity you are courting. I can't be—'

'Associated with me?' Loukis demanded. As if he didn't have enough reasons to regret his wayward youth. A wave of exasperation rode over him, his usual defences having been brought down by Annabelle's recent misery. At one time in his life, he'd had nothing more to think of than his own sensual pleasures. With hindsight he could see the desperate need to escape, to lose himself in whatever delighted him after years of a bitter, emotionally neglected childhood. To protect himself, even, from all the hurt that it had brought.

He had immersed himself in whatever and whoever he could find, courting scandalous headlines even as he sought, almost childishly, to illustrate just how little he cared. How he had laughed as each of the world's news stations and papers had reported his latest exploit in competition with his even more scandalous mother.

But he did care. Cared that Célia seemed so horrified by being seen with the legendary playboy. It hurt, more, because in the last month they had worked so closely together on tonight's event, he'd inch by inch shown a little of his true self. He'd relaxed into her strangely satisfying blunt honesty and thought that just maybe she'd seen him as more than a headline. But he should have known better.

'No, Loukis, it's not what you—'

'It's fine,' he said, cutting off any further words with a hand slashed through the air. Without casting another glance her way, he spun on his heel and exited the room, pulling slightly at the bow tie's hold around his neck.

It was time to refocus on why this night was so important. Three years ago, his mother had unceremoniously dumped a seven-year-old girl on his doorstep, without any other explanation than 'sister', and departed. No return date, no apology, no financial assistance and no belongings—clothes even. Nothing. Until six months ago, legal documents bearing the word 'custody' plunged a knife into his heart.

By the time he'd walked through the kitchens and passed staff too preoccupied with their tasks to give him a second look, he'd managed to calm his breathing. By the time he slid into the back of the sleek limousine he'd decided it was better she was not by his side and was already cursing whatever accidental instinct had prompted such a demand. And by the time the town car had circled the building to draw up at the top of the red carpet, to a hail of flashbulbs, he had a particularly charming smile in place.

He opened the door to the limo himself, not waiting for the driver, and stepped out onto the carpet. Initially he'd been against the idea, but had been won over by the calibre of celebrities Célia had somehow managed to draw to the event. He was not so vain as to think for a second that it was because of him. Yes, his name held not inconsiderable weight in the business world, and his private fortune had amassed into the billions, courtesy of his father's years of hard work. But savvy, intellect and, as he'd once heard an Englishman say, gift of the gab had nearly trebled the shipping company's income.

All of which had made his board members very happy and his mother even more avaricious. Especially in the years since his father's death. But it was the years before his father's death that had created the most damage. Watching his father slowly lose a piece of himself each time his mother disappeared with yet another lover before he finally broke had taken its toll on Loukis, and ensured that the one surefire way of getting what he wanted—sole custody over his sister—was completely untenable. Nothing would persuade him to enter into the devil's bargain of unholy matrimony, not even to appease the court's outdated impression of what 'family' should look like. After all, that mirage of a family unit had done him no favours.

So no. The only conceivable way forward, the only way to change the tide of public opinion on a reputation he hadn't actually lived up to in the last three years, was this. This event. It had to be absolutely perfect. So as the flashbulbs strobed through the night, he smiled his most charming smile, waved and stopped to speak with reporters even though his skin crawled and his face hurt. Perhaps Célia had been right not to accompany him along the carpet after all.

'It's been such a wonderful event, Célia. You've done really incredible things here, not to mention the life-changing amount of money raised.'

'You're very welcome. Estía is a wonderful charity and it's one very close to Loukis's heart.'

The wryly raised eyebrow from Estía's CEO was hardly subtle, but he accepted her statement without comment.

'Loukis Liordis has been deeply involved with every decision on this evening's event. It was incredibly important to him that it was perfect.' Nothing Célia had said was a lie—it was, however, open to interpretation. And looking at the now thoughtful expression on Mr Sideris' features, she felt at least satisfied that she had worked hard to achieve both aims of the night. To help the charity *and* Loukis's reputation.

Throughout the evening she had caught glimpses of him

as he met and spoke with everyone present, celebrity and charity member alike. She'd tried to ignore the way that every adoring female gaze followed him—not that she could blame them. He was simply stunning—magnetic even as each woman present seemed to be drawn towards him consciously or otherwise. Célia had tried to block out how tactile he was, always touching someone on the arm, leaning forward into space Célia considered far more personal than not. But what she really marvelled at was how unconscious it seemed to be for him. He just…*did* that. For a person who shrank back into the shadows at every opportunity, Célia found herself oddly jealous at the ease with which he interacted with others.

'That's very kind of you to say, Mr Sideris.'

Célia jumped at the sudden and shocking proximity of the man she had just been thinking of. An action painfully visible to both men. She felt the blush rising on her cheeks and cursed her pale skin tones. Loukis speared her with an odd expression—one of either confusion, disdain, or even quite possibly both—before turning back to Estía's CEO.

'I very much look forward to doing business with you again,' he said, grasping Sideris' hand in his own.

'Likewise, Mr Liordis. Likewise,' returned the CEO, before departing with the wife that had been waiting patiently in the background.

Célia retrieved her phone from her trouser pocket, most definitely a benefit of her attire that evening, and clicked through the security pin code to retrieve the web browser she had found earlier.

'One roaring success, Mr Liordis.'

He took the phone from her hand, using the tips of his fingers as if not wanting to make physical contact with her. It made her plunge her hand into her pocket. It made her feel…hurt having seen him be so open with all the other guests present that evening.

'What am I looking at?'

'The online results for this evening's events,' she said, the excitement at their achievement that evening cutting through any preceding thoughts. 'With over two hundred and fifty thousand unique visitors to Estía's website in the last four hours—'

'Two hundred and fifty thousand? That doesn't seem that much.'

'Loukis, you're incredible. Truly. But you're not a Kardashian. It's great, trust me.'

'For who, Estía or me?'

'For *both*,' she replied, feeling like growling. 'If it helps at all, then the majority of those visitors' page impressions were to your bio on the site. But perhaps you'll be happier with the fact that you're currently across nearly every social media site, four international news agency websites and you'll be on the front cover of the early morning edition of *The Times*. In five different countries.'

'What about the American press?'

She was going to kill him. She was *really* going to kill him. His inquisition seemed solely focused on his own ego and it was destroying any sense of pride and accomplishment she felt at having not only pulled the whole event off—*in little less than a month*—but also ensuring it was actually a success, despite what Liordis apparently thought. She snatched her phone from his hands, unable to avoid that irritating zing that served only to fuel her ire, and walked away.

'Is it going to be in the American press?' he called after her.

'Why does it matter?' she tossed over her shoulder.

'It just does, Célia.'

He was using that tone again. The one that she instinctively knew was more *him* than anything else he'd said. It caused her to pull up short. Again. She didn't need to check her phone for the answer. 'Yes,' she said, finally turning back to him. 'Happy now?'

'Nai.'

He didn't look happy. He looked more determined and more than a little…triumphant? It was an odd expression. It was…utterly devastating. Her heart began to pound in her chest and she wanted to run. To get away from him as fast as possible.

'Where are you going?' he demanded.

'Back to my hotel. I have an early morning flight back to Paris.'

'I'll take you.'

'I can find my own—'

'I'll take you, Célia.'

She shivered, hating the effect of his words on her already overly sensitised thoughts. For a moment, the promise hung on the air between them—as if he, too, realised the double entendre. Purposefully sidestepping that thought, she wondered how she *would* get back to her hotel. Exhausted and not speaking Greek, she decided Loukis's offer was the easiest and quickest solution.

'Fine.'

'Then you are going the wrong way. My car is waiting in a side street. Best to avoid any further press.'

He held out an arm to guide her and although he didn't touch her, didn't place it against the white silk of her top, as she passed him she felt the heat of his palm as if he had rested his hand against the lower part of her back.

They made their way through nearly deserted kitchens and out into the alley where, as promised, Loukis's limousine was waiting for them. The driver leaning against the car hastily jumped to attention, but not quickly enough for Loukis, who opened the door and ushered her inside.

The warm, dark interior was a complete contrast to the shocking white walls and brightly coloured paintings that had decorated Célia's last six hours and she closed her eyes, taking the first nearly calm breath that evening, desperately seeking that sense of excitement and pleasure at a job well done. Anything other than the awareness of the man sliding in beside her.

'Champagne?'

'Non, merci,' she replied.

She hadn't touched a drop of the bubbly alcohol in years, because the nutty dry taste on her tongue embodied far too much the hurts of the past. To Célia it reminded her of disapproval, of superiority, of desperately waiting for the moment that her father would finally see her. Would finally recognise her. Love her.

She rubbed at the headache forming at her temples. Too much of that evening, too much of Loukis, seemed to remind her of that. Of powerful men who only wanted one thing…one thing that had never been *her.*

And she hated that sense of desperation yawning within her. Because of what it had driven her to; the times she had tried, and tried, to be what her father wanted, to choose a profession, a career that would somehow bring her closer to him. Choices that had led her to develop designs that had unwittingly caused such devastation.

And for the first time, she wondered how many charities she would need to help in order to pay off the taint on her soul. To compensate the damage done by her naïve technical designs. Ones she had hoped would help, but instead had been used for destruction. By her father. The man whose name she no longer bore. The man she had not seen in five years.

'Are you—'

Whatever Loukis had been about to say, as the limousine pulled out into the busy night-time traffic, was cut off by the ringing of his mobile phone.

'Nai?'

Before he could press on, Célia felt the temperature in the back of the town car drop to below freezing. A stream of urgent Greek poured into the space, causing her to shift and shiver in concern. Something was wrong. Terribly wrong.

Loukis leant forward, pounding on the screen to the driver, and seemed to be directing words both to him and down the phone.

Célia wrapped her arms around her waist, sensing that it would be impossible for her to interrupt and ask what was going on. As Loukis continued to bark words into the phone, his free hand went to his hair, shoving it back from his face in desperation. He looked as if he wanted to tear it from his head.

The limo pulled around in a shocking U-turn, sending her sprawling against him, her hand landing against his thigh and her chest pressing against the stiff outline of his shoulder. He reached to settle her, his hand against her forearm, holding her until the car had righted itself, and finally hung up the phone, staring ahead of him as if he had just seen a ghost.

Célia bit down on her lip, stopping the questions running through her mind.

'We have to… I…'

She had never seen Loukis stuck for words and could not even begin to imagine what had happened to cause him such…panic.

'We don't have time—'

'It's okay,' she assured him.

'I—'

'Loukis, it's okay,' she repeated, pulling herself from his grasp, knowing that they were no longer going to her hotel room, and very much hoping that what she had said to him was the truth.

CHAPTER THREE

LOUKIS LAUNCHED HIMSELF from the car before it could even draw to a halt. His blood was pounding so loudly in his ears that he barely heard Célia follow him from the car and up the steps of his Athens estate. The door swung open before he could grab the handle and the terrified face of the usually competent American nanny loomed in the doorway.

'Have you found her?' he demanded.

Her tear-stained cheeks trembled as she shook her head in denial. Tara had been with them for the three years since Meredith had deposited his sister on his doorstep, a seven-year-old who had spoken not even a word of Greek and had since found the language deeply difficult to master.

He bit out a curse and ran his fingers through already tousled hair. He stalked to the bottom of the staircase in the hallway and shouted, 'Annabelle,' as loudly as he could. Hoping that if she were somewhere in the house, the sheer ferocity of his tone would draw her out. That she would sense his fear and come running. But only silence met his call.

He spun round on the poor upset woman just as Célia reached the entrance to the estate, staring confusedly between him and Tara. He didn't have time for this, didn't have time—or words—to explain to Célia what he'd brought her into.

'What happened?' he demanded.

'I don't know…she had been upset all afternoon. She didn't want to go…' At this, Tara cast a look towards Célia, clearly unsure about what she could and couldn't say in front of this stranger. Loukis waved a hand—he'd deal with that later. Now, he just needed to find Annabelle. Tara took a deep breath. 'She doesn't want to go to her mother. I'd put her to bed at seven this evening, just like always, and when I went to check on her, she….' Tara's eyes welled and a half-wail threatened to undo him.

She could be anywhere. Panic, like he'd never known before, reached into his chest and pulled at his breath. His hands began to tremble as if he no longer had control over his own body.

'How old is she?' Célia asked, continuing in English, clearly grasping the situation from the brief conversation.

'Ten,' replied Tara.

'And did you go somewhere this afternoon, or are there any favourite hiding places she had?'

Loukis's mind flashed back to his own childhood. His own favourite hiding places and the many, many times that he'd run away himself. *Christos*, Meredith had been back in her daughter's life for only six months and the effect on Annabelle was already devastating. She had never run away before. She had never run from *him*.

He eyed a vase on the table stand in the hallway and wanted to throw it against the wall, anything to expel some of this fear, this anger, this rage.

'Did you check the pool house? I'm going to check the pool house.'

'Should we call the police?'

Tara's question stopped him in his tracks. Should he? He hated the fact that the first place his mind went was not the immediate safety of his sister, but the long term. If he called the police, it would be on record, and it would desperately affect the custody battle—no matter that Meredith would have been the main cause of it. But if something had happened to Annabelle…

'Do you think that she could have left the estate?' Célia questioned. 'Would she have been able to leave through the front door—or anywhere from the garden?'

Tara shook her head. 'I've been in the sitting room, so would have known if she'd passed me to get out through the front door. And the garden is walled and gated…' but she shrugged her shoulders helplessly.

Célia rubbed Tara's arm a little—a gesture of consolation and support for a complete stranger that struck him deeply for just a second, before all the fears and thoughts crashed through his painfully chaotic brain.

'Then we give it an hour, I think, before calling the police. But perhaps you could ask the driver to check the surrounding streets, or any parks she liked to visit?'

Tara cast a hopeful look towards Loukis, who nodded his assent. The nanny disappeared out into the night while thoughts of Annabelle being alone out there in the dark shook him to the core.

'Why don't you go and check the pool house, as you said, and perhaps any other places in the garden. In the meantime, I'll head to the top of the house and work my way down. Perhaps fresh eyes might help.'

He was as thankful for her calm efficiency as he was irritated by it. He was usually the calm head in the crisis, *he* usually knew what to do. But this?

'If I find her…'

'She speaks English fluently,' he said, before heading out into the night himself, his only thought to find Annabelle.

As Célia made her way up the large sweeping marble staircase, she struggled for some of the calm she had somehow been able to project on two people who seemed absolutely terrified beyond their wits. Had she made the right suggestion not to call the police? Was it actually the height of stupidity not to do so?

But that was only one path her mind took. The other was that Loukis had a ten-year-old child. He must have been quite young when she was born, not that that mattered. But the fact that he had apparently been living a playboy lifestyle while his child had been in nappies? Was it possible he had not known about her then? Indignation about his playboy lifestyle all the while he had a child reared in her mind. Could he have done that knowing he had a daughter? Her mind was spinning with all the unanswered questions.

As a child Célia had never run away. It had simply never occurred to her to disappoint her father even more than he already had been. She had grown up with impossible wealth, but the cost of it had been loneliness and emotional distance. Célia's birth was traumatic for her mother, who had then been unable to carry another child, thus failing to provide her father with the heir he had so desperately wanted. And so he had simply removed himself from her life, long before she could do and had done the same. She would spend hours trying vainly to catch even a glimpse of him when he finally returned from his office, or the few days he might be home at the same time as her boarding school holidays. All that hope, all that yearning still ran through the pain and anger she'd drawn around her in the last five years.

But she forced those aside as she came to the top of the large estate, sighing at the sheer number of rooms and spaces that a ten-year-old could hide in and not even knowing where to begin.

She walked along the hallway all the way to the end and opened the door to a master bedroom. Instantly she was hit by a familiar scent—Loukis's aftershave. Lit only by the moon, the room was cast in shadow, but she could make out an impossibly large bed with dark sheets, perfectly made. Everything about the room was neat and tidy, and Célia struggled with the feeling of imposing, of trespassing where she should not. But she did have a missing girl to find, so she quickly and efficiently looked wherever she thought this Annabelle might be able to hide. Beneath the bed, the deeply impressive walk-in wardrobes, the en suite bathroom. All the while unable to shake the sense of *him* around her. Having thoroughly investigated the space, she left, quietly closing the door as if somehow that could excuse the intrusion she felt she had made.

The next room down on the left was…completely different. The lights had been left on, so the beautiful soft pink walls seemed to glow. White, fluffy fairy lights hung against the wall beside another impossibly large bed with a princess canopy. Célia couldn't help but smile, thinking it close to every little girl's dream. Unlike the near ruthless tidiness of Loukis's room, Annabelle's was strewn with open books, stickers, pens and cut pieces of paper. Clothes were scattered on the floor, stuffed toys in various heaps marked the edges of the room, shoes and a dressing gown discarded lazily by the wardrobe.

Célia frowned. Surely if Annabelle had run away from the house, she would have taken her shoes and even the coat that still hung on the back of the door. Not knowing what could have set the girl off, aside from Tara saying that she hadn't wanted to go and see her mother, it was hard to say just how far she might have wanted to run. But Célia didn't think that she really would have gone far.

As she made her way out into the hall, she thought she heard something. A sniffle, perhaps? But not from the room she had just left. She glanced up and down the hallway, seeing several doorways that could lead off into more rooms. She was about to leave when she heard the sound again.

Torn between not wanting to scare the girl and letting Loukis know that she might have found the child, she realised that even Loukis would want Annabelle to be the priority. Célia popped back into the girl's room and retrieved the stuffed toy that took pride of place on Annabelle's bed and returned to the hallway, folding herself into a cross-legged position on the floor.

'Well, Mr Bear. It's very nice to meet you. But I wondered if you could help me, because I'm looking for a little girl called Annabelle. You see, Loukis is very worried about her…'

She held the toy to her ear, hoping that this would work. Otherwise, she really was going to look quite foolish.

'I know,' she said replying to nothing. 'It's very hard for an adult to be so scared.'

A crack appeared in a doorway a few metres from where Célia was sitting. It was just a sliver of darkness, but it was enough to give Célia hope.

'I'm sure it's hard for a bear to be scared too,' she pressed on, asking whoever it was out there to forgive her for laying such a guilt trip on a ten-year-old child.

The door widened a bit more and Célia was sure that she could make out a little foot at the bottom. Perhaps even a flash of pink pyjamas.

'But I am sure that Annabelle is okay, Mr Bear.'

'His name is Alfred,' came a voice from behind the door.

'Alfred,' Célia exclaimed. 'What a truly marvellous name. It is very nice to meet you Alfred. My name is Célia.' She shook the little bear's paw all the while studiously ignoring Annabelle and instead focusing on the bear as if he were the most important thing in the world. Célia's heartbeat had risen dramatically the moment she sensed Annabelle, but now she knew she was safe in the house, her pulse slowed even as she was desperate to call out to Loukis.

'Is Loukis very scared?'

'A little,' she said, finally turning to take in the girl. 'But nothing he won't get over,' she said with a smile at the little dark, curly-haired girl with tears shimmering in her eyes.

'I didn't want him to be scared.'

'I know, *ma chérie*.'

Annabelle came to sit beside her on the floor of the hallway. 'Why am I a cherry?'

Célia smiled, a true, wide glorious smile. 'Well, you are deliciously pink, and sweet and I think...yes, I can most definitely see a stalk growing from the top of your head.'

'No, you *can't*.' Annabelle giggled.

'Yes, I *can*,' Célia insisted, grasping nothing but air just a few inches above the girl's head. 'See?'

She couldn't help but laugh as Annabelle craned her neck to try and look above her head and was delighted when Annabelle joined in.

Through the bannisters, just over Annabelle's shoulder, she caught sight of Loukis, who immediately pressed a finger to his lips, clearly not wanting to interrupt. She saw him lean back against the wall, and inhale a silent, but shaky breath of relief.

And as the adrenaline crashed down through her body, Célia was torn between an irascible fury that he was foisting this sweet adorable little girl on a mother who she clearly did not want to see, presumably so he could go about his playboy ways, and the swipe of her conscience reminding her that it was none of her business either way.

'I think that Alfred is a little tired after all this evening's excitement. What about you?' she said to Annabelle.

Loukis closed the door to Annabelle's bedroom, putting the phone he'd just checked back into his pocket and heaving the deepest sigh of relief that he had ever breathed. The moment he had heard Annabelle's giggle from the floor above, he'd wanted to sweep her up in his arms and never let go. And it was precisely that which made him surer than ever that he could not let Meredith gain custody. Not even for a second. Annabelle had been so devastated by the return of her absent mother she had run away. She could have been…

He stopped his mind from reaching all the dark places that had nearly consumed him in the last two hours. She was safe. And he would do *whatever* it took to keep her that way. Especially in light of the press's recent and most devastating blow. He stalked down the stairs and into the living area where Célia was sitting having a drink with Tara, who was still looking deeply upset.

'Mr Liordis, I'm so very—'

He cut off her words with a slash of his hand through the air. 'It's fine. She's safe. You may go,' he instructed. He certainly didn't need a witness to his next conversation with Célia.

Tara put down her drink, casting a watery-eyed glance at each of them, before retreating upstairs to her room.

As Célia moved to do the same with her glass, he took a seat opposite her, leaning forward and resting his elbows on his knees. She seemed to realise that the gesture spoke of a future conversation and pulled the glass back to her as if unsure of what was going to happen next.

'I…' He stalled, trying to order his thoughts. Knowing what needed to be done and yet somehow wanting to put it off, if only for a moment. 'Thank you. For this evening.'

Célia nodded, but said nothing. He could sense a storm brewing behind that burnt amber gaze. It vibrated from her, lashing against his skin from across the space between them. Her cupid's bow lips had thinned, emotion had painted rose-coloured slashes on her cheekbones, and he welcomed it. Welcomed the fight he desired as much as she seemed to. Anything to release all this pent-up, unspent adrenaline.

'Out with it,' he commanded.

'It has absolutely nothing to do with me, Mr Liordis.'

He gave her a look that communicated the exact thought of, *Oh, come on.*

'Fine. Really? You leave a deeply distraught ten-year-old girl with a nanny who, by all accounts, was on the phone to her boyfriend for half the bloody night, while you were out there schmoozing with celebrities for what? Restoring your all-important reputation?'

'If you'll remember, one of your conditions about holding the event in the first place *dictated* my presence.'

'Not to the detriment of the peace of mind of a *child*.'

'Yet when I *did* do precisely as you ask on the night of the Kinley charity event, I was lambasted by both the press *and* you,' he ground out, barely able to keep the frustration from his tone.

Brows furrowed, Célia seemed to take in this new piece of information.

'Why not just say it was because of your daughter?'

'She's not my daughter.' He'd known that would have been her conclusion. It would have been anyone's conclusion. Especially for someone with his reputation. 'She is my sister.' He took a deep breath, knowing that he had no other choice but to come clean with the entire story—something he hadn't done with his closest friends, let alone a stranger. Though he couldn't really say that Célia felt like a stranger as such. But if he was to get her to agree to his plan, he would have to explain.

'My half-sister,' he clarified. 'Meredith, our mother,' he said, barely able to say the words without scorching disdain dripping from every syllable, 'had her five years after my parents had divorced.'

'Who is…?' Célia trailed off, appearing to regret her interruption.

'The father?' He shrugged. 'If Meredith knows, she's never said. I would imagine that he's not an option, otherwise Annabelle would never have ended up with me. Three years ago she was dropped off on my doorstep, with no belongings, clothing, books, toys or otherwise and I was told by Meredith, as she practically leapt into the waiting car, to "take care of her".'

'Annabelle has not seen Meredith or heard from her since that day. Until six months ago. Her lawyers got in touch with mine to demand her return. As if she was a package to be sent back to its sender.'

Loukis leaned forward into the space between them, placing his elbows on his knees. 'For three years, Annabelle has lived with me. I have seen to her every need from schooling, to holidays, to play dates, and music lessons. She barely remembers Meredith, aside from the ache of abandonment, and I have no intention of letting my sister be taken away to another country by a mother who all but eschews any semblance of maternal instinct.'

Célia seemed to consume the information readily enough, even though he knew that she could barely conceive of the part that she would, now, have to play in his obscene family drama.

'That is why you've been working to redeem your reputation.' It was a statement rather than a question, but he nodded anyway.

'But why keep everything such a secret?' she queried.

'Because I know what Meredith is like. I know how she twists and turns things, how her scheming little mind works,' he concluded, thrust back into the sealed records of his parents' divorce. How she had turned everything around to make every act, every word a mirror of what it had been in truth. 'And because I know, with everything in me, that this is just about money. She doesn't care about Annabelle one bit,' he said, concluding silently that the reason he knew this was because she had never cared about *him*. Meredith had eventually shown her true colours, and he half hoped that she would do so again, if it wouldn't inflict further pain on his sister.

'Then why are you telling me?' Célia asked, her amber gaze once again warily watchful.

'I need you to take a look at something for me.' He offered her his phone, open to the search engine tab that displayed the shocking headline *Liordis At It Again With Mystery Woman!*

The three grainy photos showed Loukis ushering Célia into the limousine, the car doing its sudden, urgent U-turn, and the two of them rushing into the house. The speculation about the urgency of their desire for each other was bald and blatant.

The shock that crossed Célia's features as she read, the way her hand went to her lips as if to stifle some inaudible gasp soothed a little of the anger coursing through his veins. Little, but not enough. Everything he had done in the past three years, all of the attempts to redeem his impossibly tarnished reputation, had burned to dust.

Célia took in the headlines and the black and white photos of herself and Loukis. She hated that some unseen person had followed them, had taken pictures of such a vulnerable moment for Loukis. When she was a child, her father had gone to great lengths to keep her and her mother away from the prying eyes of the press. But attending boarding school, she had seen so many students cowed and buckled under the weight of the paparazzo gaze. Every painful, awkward, embarrassing moment pulled out for inspection. And in her darkest nightmares, the moment that her crimes were published for the world to see brought an unimaginable terror to her. Even the thought that they might discover her father's identity, as shielded as it possibly could be, scared her, deepening her dependence on denial. They wouldn't, couldn't find out. She'd worked so hard to separate her life from before from her life now.

But it was precisely these thoughts that prevented her usually quick mind from putting two and two together to understand what any of what Loukis was saying had to do with her.

She looked up at him then, his fierce gaze studying her intently. The steely line of his jaw, tense, his hands braced as if forewarning her of some life-changing moment.

'What is it?'

'I cannot risk any further damage to my reputation. Not with Annabelle's happiness and future at stake. I *will* not let Meredith get her hands on her, even for a minute.'

She nodded, still not quite understanding where he was going with this.

'Which is why I need you to sign a non-disclosure agreement.'

The statement came as a bit of a surprise to Célia, but she would have been more than happy to agree to such a thing for the happiness of the little girl who had already begun to creep into her heart.

'Is that all?' she asked, half relieved that it seemed to be the case. She took a sip of wine to steady her trembling nerves.

'No. Sadly it is not. What I need of you now, in light of the press article, is your hand in marriage.'

CHAPTER FOUR

FORTY-FIVE SECONDS LATER, Loukis was wiping at the front of his wine-covered shirt and Célia was mortified.

She didn't think that actually happened, she'd honestly only seen it in films. But the moment Loukis had uttered his declaration, the gorgeous mouthful of wine Célia had just taken erupted in a half cough, half gasp that covered Loukis's chest from across the table.

'I'm so… Loukis, I…'

He cut through the air with a free hand, while the other maintained its hasty dabbing and then seemed to give up altogether. A painful blush rose on her cheeks, stinging in its intensity. Her hands were twisting around each other, as if hand-wringing was some age-old inherited act to express… Célia honestly didn't know what to think or to feel about Loukis's strange demand.

With a less than happy sigh, Loukis returned to his seat opposite her as if his five-hundred-dollar shirt had not been ruined and he was clearly determined to resume…negotiations?

'You want to marry me?' Célia asked, unable to prevent the slight trembling from affecting her voice.

'No! *Christos*, no.'

The punctuation of the second denial felt borderline cruel and unnecessary.

'We just have to be engaged, until the court awards me custody.'

Célia felt as if she were playing catch up. 'Why would

the court appoint you legal guardian over Annabelle's mother?'

'Because I will prove that she is deeply unsuitable to raise the child she abandoned over three years ago. You've already witnessed the lengths my sister has gone to in order to avoid seeing Meredith, let alone live with the woman.'

Célia couldn't argue with that. Even though it had taken little on her part to distract the young girl, she'd clearly been upset enough to cause a great deal of fear and worry on her behalf.

'But why do you need *me*?'

Loukis looked at her, clearly frustrated that she hadn't just jumped to his demand.

'That photo and the press furore around it will cut through every single inch of positive publicity I have spent the last few years clawing back. I have only two months until the court hearing and there is no time for damage limitation. This, as loath as I am to admit, is the only way to counter the negative impact and present to the court the exact kind of family unit they would need from me in order to grant custody.'

The headache Célia had managed to ward off earlier came back full force and struck her right between the temples. She pressed her thumbs there, ignoring the way that this seemed only to increase Loukis's frustration.

'I'm really not sure this is a good idea. I'm certainly not going to lie to a court judge, Loukis.'

'What would you be lying about? We'd be engaged. That's the truth,' he said with a shrug as if it were that easy.

'I would be lying by telling the judge that we plan to spend the rest of our lives together.'

'No more than any other couple entering into marriage. The road to hell is, after all, paved with good intentions.'

His cynicism regarding the institution was, while not

wholly unexpected, painstakingly obvious and for just a moment Célia felt a little sorry for him. And while she understood his attempts to indicate marriage was some form of hell, she didn't think he was so obtuse as to not realise that the same could be said precisely of the endeavour he was suggesting himself.

'And what about Annabelle? What would you tell her? You can't expect a ten-year-old to lie about something like that, and nor can you expect me to lie to a ten-year-old. Loukis, please,' she begged, 'there must be another way.'

'Oh, yes, absolutely. The other way is for the press to assume that you spent the night with a client. A client with a particularly sordid reputation of seducing and then abandoning all manner of women. I'm sure that would have a beneficial impact on *both* our reputations. I wonder how many charities would want to work with you then?'

Célia felt the colour drain from her face. 'But it could be explained.'

'It could,' he assured her in a tone so insincere her teeth ached. But the tenor of his next statement cast chills across her skin. 'But I have absolutely no intention of doing so. If I'm going down…'

Célia had seen Loukis as many things, but crude and cruel were new to her.

'That's blackmail.'

'Yes.'

His word was swift and assured, contrasting harshly with the threat he had conjured in her mind and the sea of emotions threatening to overwhelm her. For a moment, she was transported back to the last life-defining moment that had pushed her to a precipice she hadn't seen coming. The sickening realisation that she had been used against her will by the very last man she had ever expected it from.

For five years, she had kept her head down, had changed her name to cut all connections with her father, had swapped her university degree, had done everything she possibly could to avoid any kind of spotlight or attention. Instead, she had funnelled her every waking moment into creating a business that would give back…that she hoped would somehow compensate for her naïve actions five years before. The energy and determination that had taken had nearly consumed her. But this time, she couldn't run. This time, she couldn't hide.

Because she believed in her business, had carefully cultivated a rise from the ashes of her previous life. And she would not do that again. So clearly could she see the morning newspaper headlines, she was half convinced they had already happened. Her reputation would be in ruins. Everything she'd worked so hard to achieve, destroyed. By this man. Determination fired in her breast as she fought for control in a situation Loukis currently dominated.

'What do I get out of it?'

'I can pay you,' he said with a shoulder shrug that indicated it was nothing to him. The money, the coercion…

'I don't want your money,' Célia exclaimed with nausea and distaste vying for pole position.

'Then what do you want?'

She shook her head, utterly horrified by their conversation. Was she actually considering this? Could she even do this? Pretend to be his fiancée? She forced her chaotic thoughts into some semblance of order. Her business was her sole focus. It was the only way she could compensate for her past mistakes. The thought of being paid to be draped across his arm was utterly unpleasant. But if it could bring about more help for more charities…

'I want six new clients,' she decided out loud.

Loukis raised his eyebrows. 'Six?'

'If you want to make it ten, then—'

'Six is fine,' he interrupted hastily.

Loukis felt the pressure in his chest build. He was so close. Célia was, at least, considering his proposal. He had no idea where he might find six potential clients, but he would. He couldn't risk letting Célia realise how much power she wielded in that moment. She could ask for the moon and he'd have to make it happen.

'What does it actually entail? I mean, how do you see this playing out?' she asked, her quick mind leapfrogging ahead of his own. He'd been so focused on actually getting her to agree that he didn't have all his plans in place. But Loukis was used to thinking on his feet. He wasn't in charge of one of the world's top ten companies for nothing.

'A very public engagement for at least the next four months. After that, I'm sure we can manage a press announcement that outlines how we have decided to amicably separate.'

'Yes, but what does it actually mean? I have a business in Paris, a life there. I have upcoming events.'

Loukis bit back the scoff of derision. She had only one event, he very much knew that to be the case, but if it gave her the semblance of security to exaggerate her schedule, he would allow her that.

'You would need to relocate to Greece for the duration. We would need to be seen in public as much as possible. There would be an engagement party at least, but I would also be willing to accompany you to the...*events* you have in your diary.'

'How very generous of you,' she said with as much disdain as womanly possible. 'Just like that, you expect me to move to Greece?'

'We will, of course, have been keeping our relationship

a secret for the past few months. Not only to protect our privacy, but also your business interests. You were deeply concerned about the effect that this would have on the many fabulous charities you already work with.'

'Was I, now?'

'Are you not?'

'Yes, of course—'

'Then we are simply backdating a few things.'

Her pretty amber eyes flashed ominously.

'It is for your benefit as much as mine, I assure you.' His statement did nothing to dampen the narrowing of her gaze, or the warning it contained. He sighed, resisting the urge to place his head in his hands. 'I will obviously support financially any expenditure generated by this.'

'Oh, that's okay, then. Because of course my first concern was being out of pocket. Not the fact that you want me to lie to the press, a court of law and your little sister.'

'She is the reason I'm doing this. The *only* reason. Her happiness and security are my primary concern. I will find you six new clients. I will ensure that your time in this will not be detrimental to you or your business. I will do everything in my power to make this as seamless and painless as possible. Do you agree?'

'Do I have a choice?'

'Of course you do. If you make the right one, you'll be fine.'

The unspoken threat hung in the air between them. Loukis could honestly say that this was an all-time low, even for him, but he'd not been left with much of the same choice that Célia seemed to desperately want for herself. He held his breath until he saw her head bow and caught her gently muttered agreement.

'Great. I'll have the paperwork drawn up first thing tomorrow morning.'

No ring, no words of love, no undying declaration. Paperwork. A signature. What on earth had she got herself into?

Time seemed to move differently for Célia the moment she had aligned herself with Loukis. As if under his expressive hands it sped up and slowed down, bent to his will.

She hated that he had been right. Right about the reaction from the world's press, the accusatory headlines at first placing a notch beside her name on his bedpost. Then after a very carefully worded release from both his company and Chariton Endeavours, she was scrubbed out, removed from that particular wooden totem, and placed beside his name as some kind of wonder; the woman who had tamed the playboy.

He had also been right about the need for her to leave Paris, where her apartment simply wasn't prepared for the onslaught of nearly one hundred reporters armed with cameras and notepads. Her neighbours had all but requested her removal from the premises, not wholly unreasonably considering hers weren't the only rubbish bags that had been picked through with a fine-tooth comb.

But it was Ella that had surprised her the most. She had expected caution, concern, questions…not the high-pitched squeal of joy Célia put down to post-pregnancy hormones. Somehow she'd wanted Ella just to *know*. To realise that this was beyond Célia's usual behaviour. To understand that there were other forces, namely Loukis Liordis, at play. But Ella had only been full of questions Célia didn't feel equipped to answer. What was their first date like, their first kiss? When did she know he was 'the one'? The fact that none of these things had actually happened suddenly and painfully stuck in Célia's mind.

And then, after the litany of questions, came the deep

sigh and, *'I'm so pleased that you've moved on. It's been such a long time since Marc...'*

And that had been too much. Célia had ended the call, disconnecting the painful conversation so much easier than preventing the memories from surfacing.

Because they had surfaced and hung within her all the way through the flight to Greece. The hurt, the confusion… the way, just as everything she'd thought she'd known about herself and her life was shifting, Marc—her last mooring—had removed himself, all the while blaming her.

Which was why, when she arrived back at Loukis's estate just outside Athens, she wasn't prepared for the presence of a small, bespectacled woman, dressed head to toe in black, with a ponytail so severe Célia almost winced in empathy for her hair follicles.

'You see what I'm dealing with?' demanded Loukis, without even looking up at her from where he was furiously typing away on his laptop.

The woman's close scrutiny both up *and* down Célia's entire being was intrusive to say the least.

'I see,' the woman replied, drawing out the second word as if it could convey the gravity of the situation. What situation they were referring to, though, Célia had no idea.

She jumped when the woman approached with a feline grace and began to walk a three-hundred-and-sixty-degree circuit around her. Célia was speechless until the moment the bespectacled woman leaned in to within inches of her face and uttered a low hum.

'What is going on?' Célia demanded. She had always hated such close inspection. In fact, it was precisely why she continued to choose the most unassuming, blandly coloured clothing. She just didn't want to invite that kind of observation.

'Have her to me by three this afternoon.'

Loukis gave a wave of acknowledgement and the woman disappeared.

'Hello, Loukis. It's nice to see you. Yes, my flight was good, thank you for asking. No, I've already eaten and yes, I think I would like something to drink now.'

Finally he looked up, slightly confused.

Only the moment he did, she wished he hadn't. With his hair slightly tousled as if he'd run his hand through it more than once, his shirt loose at the neck…the moment that confusion cleared from his gaze, his eyes hit her like arrows. It was a little too much. She had forgotten the impact that he could make.

She fiddled with her handbag, aware that her few suitcases were being dropped off in the hallway behind her.

'What am I doing at three?' she asked, suddenly uncomfortable with the realisation that she had moved all her portable possessions into the home of Loukis Liordis.

He continued to stare at her as if something was wrong. She frowned, placing a hand against her cheek. Maybe she had something on her face? Finally he turned back to his laptop.

'You're going to a stylist.'

'A what?'

'We're going to be seen in a lot of very exclusive places and I can't have you wandering around in that.' He'd broken off his typing only to gesture to her roughly with one hand in a sweeping circular motion.

'But I—'

'I told you to burn that T-shirt.'

It had been perverse of her to insist on wearing it today, she'd known that. But she hadn't been able to help herself. It was an act of defiance. An act of revenge that for some reason had given her just a little of the strength she'd needed to get onto the plane in the first place.

Until the moment she saw herself through his eyes. Standing in his exquisite Athenian estate where sophistication practically dripped from the modern glass chandelier, beautiful swathes of cream and grey adding a surprising warmth to the impersonal wealth she found herself surrounded by, she felt…uncouth.

But more than that she felt hurt. That familiar sting that she had been found wanting. That once again, she wasn't living up to the perfection people wanted from her. People like her father, Marc, and now Loukis. She knew that Loukis wasn't being personal, but practical. And it shouldn't hurt, but it did. Now the T-shirt just felt petty. All her pride and defiance melted away and she gripped her jaw against the swelling tide of emotion she desperately wanted to put down to jet lag.

She cast about for a distraction. Anything that would remove the microscope from her and onto something new.

'Is Annabelle here?'

'She is in Texas.' His clipped tones as harsh as the sounds of his fingers bashing against the keypad of his laptop.

'Really?' she replied, half fearful and half disappointed that there wouldn't be a natural buffer between her and her new fiancé.

'The visit with Meredith was court appointed. And trust me, I tried to fight it.'

'Is she okay? You've spoken to her?'

Loukis didn't miss the concern in her voice and it touched him. He might not have set out on this path wanting a fiancée, but the fact that Célia, who by unhappy circumstances had unwittingly entered into that role, clearly valued his sister's happiness was a gift.

He just wished that he had more time. More time to get to know Célia, to have vetted her, to have…thought it through a little more? He hadn't invited a woman back to his estate ever. His affairs had been conducted far away from here. And that was *before* Annabelle.

Whatever the press might think, it had been three years since he'd lived up to his playboy reputation. A reputation he'd indulged and enjoyed greatly—as had the women who had graced his bed—until the moment he realised the damage it had done to his future.

But it was the damage from his past that had designed his present. All he had known of marriage had been harshly shouted arguments heard from his hiding place on the staircase. His nights were consumed with them. They would start almost immediately after his bedtime. He would be in that lovely hazy moment of near sleep when they would begin. His father complaining about his mother's drinking, which would escalate to her blaming him for the demise of her modelling career—and by extension Loukis. Then his father would retaliate by raging about her less than private affairs, her extended absence from the family home. On and on, through the nights and years they would go. Throwing verbal barbs and opening wounds, apparently careless of whether their son might be listening.

Marriage, to Loukis, had seemed a battleground. Relationships had become something that he'd never wanted to willingly entertain. Oh, he knew there were instances of couples that seemed to have found their joy in each other. But they were few and far between and dissipated beneath the pain and ferocity of his parents' own relationship.

But, as Célia peered at him from her stance taken up in the doorway as if ready to bolt at any moment, he reminded himself that he wasn't getting married. That this was a fake engagement to ensure that his sister never bore witness to such a thing. Was never tainted by that same feeling that he had been.

Meredith's abandonment of her three years before had already done enough damage. His sole focus, now, was to ensure that no more harm could be done to his sister.

'I'm due to speak to her later tonight. But she has arrived and is…well. With them.'

'Them?'

'Meredith has apparently found herself a rich Texan oil baron as her latest victim. I can only imagine that the man has strong family values, otherwise Meredith would never have returned for Annabelle. Children—according to my mother—have an aging affect that is deplorable to her.'

He recited the line by rote. One of the many accusations she had hurled at his father.

'I'm sorry, Loukis.'

He must have given himself away. Perhaps his mask had slipped to reveal emotions that were far too close to the surface for his liking.

'My housekeeper will show you to our room. Your bags should already—'

'Our?'

He frowned, wondering what had been unclear about his statement. 'Yes, "our" room.'

He could have laughed at the shocked look on her face, widening her beautiful amber eyes with something akin to horror. That was new. He'd never had that reaction to the suggestion he share a bed with a woman before.

'I'm not sharing a…room with you,' she replied, clearly stumbling over the moment she might have said bed.

Instantly the misstep threw up a riotous display of imagery, Loukis peeling away the straps of her bra, placing kisses across the delicate line of her collarbone, leading down over the gentle slope of her breast to—

Loukis cut off the errant chain of thought, desperately fighting the shocking streak of arousal that had shot through him and instead casting his gaze to the hallway to make sure that no staff were within hearing distance.

'Would you care to sit for this conversation?' he asked, gesturing to the seat opposite him.

'I'll stand, thank you,' she replied, as if waiting, bracing herself for some kind of penance.

'Célia, let me explain something to you. You have agreed to become my fiancée.'

'I don't remember being given much choice.'

'And as such,' he pressed on as if she had not interrupted, 'we need to be seen as a couple very much in love and ready to spend the rest of our lives together. And when I say "be seen", I do not mean just when we're out in public. Everything I have, everything I love, is riding on this engagement being believed. By everyone. By Meredith, by the courts, by my sister and I will not have that at risk because a member of my staff sees that we are using separate rooms.'

Although he had not raised his voice to a level that could be overheard, Célia felt the vehemence of his words right down to her toes. His insistence that they share a room became a primal demand within her, one she seemed powerless to deny.

Célia knew what he was saying made sense. That it was in her interest as much as his not to be found out. Because if they were, the damage to her reputation and business would be apocalyptic. But the thought of sharing a room, let alone a bed, with Loukis Liordis was terrifying. Not because she was in any way scared of the man. No, she was more scared of herself. Because somehow the thought of sharing such an intimacy with him thrilled her. It sent a cascade of electrical bursts through her body, ensuring that every inch of her was hyperaware, over-sensitised even. She hadn't even felt this way about Marc. And that was warning enough.

CHAPTER FIVE

Célia stepped out of the car that had picked her up from the stylist's and brought her to what she could only presume was one of Greece's most renowned restaurants—if the deluge of supercars on display lining the road was anything to go by. Ferrari, Maserati, Lamborghini, McLaren. The brands rolled off her tongue like a shopping list for the rich and famous.

Reluctantly she had to admit that four hours ago she would have been terrified to even get out of the car. But Layna, despite her severe and frosty demeanour, had been a revelation. Instead of being superior and dismissive, she had peppered Célia with a hailstorm of questions. What she wanted from her clothing, what colours she had in her apartment, did she have a favourite painting, what did she see clothing as being to her. All the different questions had initially seemed unconnected, but as Layna took her through the selection she had cultivated while Célia was getting her hair and make-up done, she realised how the woman had woven a select wardrobe built from *her*. How each piece reflected something of the answers she had given about her life, her tastes, her fantasies even. She couldn't deny how they flattered and had miraculously unfurled some hitherto unknown sense of pride and satisfaction in her looks.

Which had made her sad. Sad because, once, she had loved dressing in bright clothes, had relished a sense of her own beauty. Before she had cast aside her family name, been discarded by Marc, and hidden within bland, invisible clothing so as not to be seen. Not to be noticed. Because if she was honest with herself, Célia was a little fearful of what such close inspection would reveal.

She brushed aside a layered lock that she was just about getting used to. Before the hair stylist had got his hands on her, she had been unconcerned about the universally shoulder-length, light brown strands. And perhaps that had been part of the problem. The moment she had caught sight of herself in the mirror she hadn't been able to prevent the shocked gasp that had fallen from her lips.

'*Nai.* Good? Good.'

She hadn't even been able to muster any kind of resentment at the knowing gaze and asked and answered question from the hair stylist. Because he was right. Taking her hair a few shades darker, a rich, warm auburn shade of mahogany, had made her somehow more *her*. Her pale skin now seemed creamier, richer. And her eyes—they glowed. She glowed. But more than that, she felt it deep within her. A feminine pride she hadn't realised that she'd sorely missed.

As she got out of the car, she picked up the gorgeous forest-green silk of the dress's skirt so it wouldn't get damaged on the pavement. The moment she had seen the dress, her heart had thudded in her chest. She'd never usually wear such a thing, certainly couldn't usually afford such a thing, but Loukis appeared to be more than willing to fund the extravagance. The dress seemed timeless, having borrowed aspects from different periods, and rather than confusing was somehow eternally elegant. The halter-neck detail that swept from behind her neck, between her breasts and round to the low dip of her spine offered a more risqué design, while the style of the details, the small green jewels sewn into the overlaid cream fabric, suggested grandeur and delicacy.

Her make-up had been kept simple apart from a swipe of bright red matt lipstick and her only accessory was a golden clutch that—as yet—was completely empty. 'But appearances must be kept,' Layna's command echoing in her mind.

Her golden sparkly heels glinted in the street lights and as she straightened up, she caught the approving glance of the driver, before he quickly masked his features. It fired a little spark within her. Not because of the driver, but because it gave her a little hope as to what Loukis's reaction might be.

And momentarily she faltered, wobbling a little on her too-high heel. She shouldn't be wondering that. She shouldn't be blurring the lines at all. This wasn't some fairy-tale romance, with her own private Cinderella moment. This was a carefully constructed lie in order to get Loukis what he wanted. Hadn't he already proved the lengths he would go to in order to do so? Hadn't he already threatened her reputation and her business? No. She had to remember that he was proving himself to be just like her father, just like Marc. Only interested in her for what she could get for him.

It was precisely this chain of thought that caused the slight flattening of her lips, the barely perceptible tense line to her shoulders. None of the other diners in the restaurant would have noticed such a thing, all too readily consuming the beautiful vision she presented. But Loukis did. He noticed every single thing about her as she walked towards the glass-fronted balcony to where he sat at a table beneath the night sky, waiting but most definitely not ready.

The fierce red slash of colour on her lips was almost carnal and his hands clenched into fists as she swayed towards him provocatively on high-heel-clad feet. Her hair was a different shade, which seemed so much more natural than her previous colouring. The colour reminded him of autumn, but a glorious fireball of autumn that promised warmth…heat even.

Fire. He was playing with fire. Because he couldn't help but acknowledge that he'd found Célia strangely alluring even dressed in that horrible beige top. But that inner sense of beauty he'd known she masked was now on full display for all to see. And it was incredible.

Wordlessly, he stood as the waiter guided her towards him, as if presenting him with some great gift. He watched as she walked towards him. The streak of lightning that cut through him when their eyes met was something he tried hard to ignore. This evening had one purpose. Everything had been arranged, right down to the second. That should be what he was focusing on, not the way that her hips swayed beneath the deep green silk of her dress, the way that it veed down her sternum, revealing rather than hiding the dramatic slope of her breasts. Not the way it cut in at her waist, giving her a true hourglass figure and making his mouth water.

As she reached the table neither seemed capable of moving and, while the waiter discreetly retreated, they faced each other like combatants.

Breaking the spell, he rounded the table and pulled out her chair for her, his arms either side of her feeling the heat from her body through the thin linen shirt he wore, his sleeves rolled back so that the fine dark hairs on his arms pricked up. He lingered imperceptibly, pausing just long enough to try to identify the gentle swathe of perfume kissing his senses, one he vaguely remembered from before. It was a bitter-sweet citrus scent that was balanced by something fresh and delicious that reminded him of basil.

He felt her flinch beneath him and removed himself from temptation, skirting back around the table and resuming his own seat. He sighed. No one was going to believe they were engaged if she kept jumping every time he came within a hair's breadth of her.

'Did you—'

'You look—'

They had spoken together and each cut themselves off mid-sentence at the same time. Loukis frowned his discomfort. There was an awkwardness between them that hadn't been present before. But then, before, they'd been working together. Now they were…

He gestured for her to go first.

'Did you manage to get hold of Annabelle?'

Loukis clenched his teeth, not needing to vent his frustrations at this moment in time. He would wait until later for that. 'Meredith had decided to take her out for the afternoon, so I will have to try again later.'

She nodded and looked about. He wondered what she was seeing. The balcony of the restaurant jutted out from the building like an architectural feat, dramatically increasing the floorspace of the flat rooftop. He had reserved the whole area. For privacy and for other important reasons, not least because of the beautiful views of the Athenian skyline at night. Framed by the dark slash of the mountain range, the Parthenon was lit dramatically in the distance, its place high up on the hill drawing every gaze, tourist and local alike. Dusk had fallen, barely an inch of pale purple remaining as the dark promise of night bled into it.

Loukis took this all in in one glance, his gaze reluctant to leave her for more than a few seconds.

'You look beautiful.'

Her amber eyes flew back to him from the horizon, as if she was attempting to silently interrogate his meaning, his motivation.

'Better than the beige T-shirt, then,' she said, the sting

of the bitterness in her tone dimmed slightly by the sadness he didn't miss in her eyes.

'The item in question was offensive only in that it was painfully obvious what you were trying to hide.'

'And that was?' she asked, seemingly genuinely intrigued.

'Everything in you that is innately beautiful.'

He hadn't meant to say those words. He hadn't mean to be so truthful. But there was a vulnerability about her that night that called forth the only honesty he could give her.

He knew women well. Had made it his mission to study and understand them when his own mother seemed so impossible to predict, to identify. So he knew women who would hide their pain beneath brittle masks, knew women who displayed their sensuality like a glorious fan of peacock feathers, knew women who aggressively sought dominance where they had once lost it in the past, and knew women who hid their inner sense of power and sensuality, hoarding it protectively from view. And he very much thought that Célia was of the latter variety. But as if sensing it was too much for both of them, he picked up and perused the menu blindly.

'What would you like to drink?'

As if the waiter had sensed it was safe to return, he appeared on the balcony to take their order.

Célia seemed to take a deep breath, turned smilingly at the man and ordered a martini. It surprised him; her choice bold, the drink dry, and the request for a twist of lemon rather than an olive seemed to suit her.

'Same,' he stated to the waiter without taking his eyes off Célia, who was clearly uncomfortable with his constant gaze.

'I'm surprised that you didn't order for me,' she said, placing her hands on her lap beneath the table. Probably, he assumed, turning them within each other as she had done before.

'That was for speed and efficiency. This is not.'

'What is this for, then?'

It was then that he decided not to tell her of his plans for that evening. He would need her to be as natural as possible—and even before they had ordered drinks she'd had a streak of tension through her as if she were ready to bolt.

'This is so that we can get to know each other a little more.'

'Is that necessary?' she asked, still unable to meet his gaze.

He reached across the table and placed his hand on her neck to cup her jaw. As expected she almost jumped right off the chair. But he kept his hand in place, feeling the flickering of her pulse, smoothing it slightly with a swipe of his thumb that caused a sensation within him that he had to fight to temper.

'It is if you're going to stop jumping every time I touch you. We're supposed to be…we *are* engaged. And we're going to have to start acting like it. So,' he said, finally removing his hand, 'I have a game of sorts for us to play.' He waited for her to take this in. 'You will ask a question, and for each one I answer, I will touch you.'

The look of fear that crossed her face bit him hard. 'Not like that, not…' He shook his head, trying to find the words. Where was his usual charm? Where was the man reported to have seduced women in their hundreds? 'We're in public, Célia, it's not as if I'm going to ravish you. Consider it the opposite of aversion therapy. For every question of mine that *you* answer, you will touch me.'

Célia's heart thudded in her chest, her cheek still warm from where he had caressed her. She knew that he was right, that she had to stop being so…overly sensitive to his touch. They would have to put on a performance in public eventually. And out here, beneath the night sky, where the air was warm and there was no one to see them, was surely a safe place to…to…

'You agree?' he cut through her thoughts and she nodded her assent even as she feared what his first question might be.

'What is your favourite colour?'

She laughed then. At the ridiculousness of his question, of her fear. Couldn't help but catch the way his lips had quirked up in a smile as if he'd expected her reaction.

'Orange.'

'Really?'

'Yes,' she laughed.

He nodded, as if impressed somehow. 'I thought it would have been—'

'Don't you dare say it,' warning him away from saying beige.

'*Entáxei*—okay.' His eyes were lit with mischief and the laughter on the air between them had broken some of the tension that had built since she'd first felt the heat from his body as he held out a chair for her.

Loukis laid his arm on the table, his palm outstretched for her, challenging her.

She stared at it as if it were something strange and new. An inexplicable urge took over her then. The desire to touch, to feel, to know… She pressed her thumb into the palm of his hand and drew it upwards along the length of his middle finger, his palm curling in gently as if wanting to prolong their connection, her touch. His skin felt smooth and warm beneath hers and it sent little starbursts across her hand and forearm. She resisted the urge to shiver.

'Your turn,' he said, breaking the spell that had held her in silence.

Her mind strangely blank, she searched for something as bland and unchallenging as the question he had posed, not quite ready to delve deeper.

'What is your favourite food?'

'Baklava.' He answered too quickly for it to be a lie.

'Really?'

'I'm Greek. It would be criminal for me to say otherwise.'

Célia couldn't help but smile at the prideful, playful tone and the trace of starlight in his eyes.

Hesitantly she placed her arm out the way that he had done and laid her hand open on the table before him. It was then that she realised what he had done. That in allowing her to be the one to touch him first, he had ensured that she would not be subjected to anything he wouldn't receive himself. It made her feel…strangely safe. Until he touched her.

Receiving exactly the same touch that she had given sent sparks down her arm to her core, unable this time to prevent the shiver that wracked her body. Her palm flared then curled beneath his finger, just as his had done. Her nipples drew to stiff peaks as arousal, swift and sharp, pierced her and she flinched, withdrawing her hand suddenly.

He masked it quickly, but she saw something pass his features. Frustration, she thought, disappointment perhaps.

'I'm sorry.'

'Don't be. That's why we're doing this. We need to become accustomed to each other,' he stated simply as if he had not been devastated in the same way as she had by something so basic as one touch.

'My turn. Where did you go to school?'

Célia's body spun within some strange vortex as she

forced herself to answer the question. 'Switzerland. With Ella. Boarding school.'

'Not France?' he queried, probing for more details.

'No, my fa— My parents wanted me to go to "the best of schools",' she said, adopting her father's imperious tone. She cast a glance to Loukis, and if he noticed the slip, he was kind enough not to press.

He placed his arm on the table again, but this time face down. She hesitated again, then steeled herself for the impact, knowing what to expect this time. She placed her hand over his, smoothing her way up over his wrist and forearm, her fingers dipping beneath the rolled-up shirtsleeves, all the while braced against the sensations that drenched her.

Questions came and answers went, each time eliciting a touch here, there, an elbow, a little finger hooked around another, a thumb, a hand held, and a palm kissed gently. Loukis had moved his chair next to hers, so that the table no longer lay between them. Small plates of delicious food went ignored as the awareness and knowledge of each other deepened.

'What three things would you save in a fire?' Célia finally asked.

'Annabelle.'

Célia smiled. 'That's just one thing,' she chided.

'I don't need anything else.'

His answer struck her more deeply, more viscerally than any other from that night. And suddenly she feared him asking her the same question. Feared that she wouldn't be able to answer it because she didn't have anyone to take with her like that. Anyone who was enough. Belongings seemed insipid in comparison to his answer, the items in her apartment only five years old, nothing from before. Nothing from her childhood. Because in the last five years, she realised, she'd made herself an island. New, shiny, determined, but unanchored, untethered.

Loukis seemed not to realise that she hadn't taken her due, hadn't touched him in turn, because he pressed on with his next question.

'Why do you dress the way you do? What are you hiding from?'

His head was bent towards her as if listening to her unspoken response. *Everything*, she mentally replied, shocking herself. Inexplicably as thoughts of her father's betrayal, of Marc's desertion, of the absence of her mother from her present life rose up around her and she felt the hot press of tears gathering at the corners of her eyes.

Loukis reached up a thumb and gently swept away a tear that had escaped. The warmth and comfort of his palm against her cheek, this time so much more familiar, so much more wanted than earlier in the evening. His face was so close, the lips that had pressed into her hand, her wrist to answered questions, tempting her, teasing her, making her want them, making her want him.

Her heart pounded, crying and demanding for what he was so clearly willing to offer.

Breath left her lungs in defeat as she closed the distance between them, giving up the fight, which she had known would only end one way. Her supplication and his dominance.

The moment his lips met hers, her mind stopped. Thoughts were lost beneath the heady indulgent sensations of his mouth across hers, his tongue gently sweeping, asking and gaining entrance.

A need, shocking in its intensity, reared in her breast. *More.* She wanted more. Her hands rose to either side of his face, needing to touch, to explore. Her fingers threaded through the fine strands of his hair, relishing the softness, at the same time as riding a wave of something inexplainable, something almost euphoric.

A bright white flash cut through her closed eyes, startling her. Again and again it popped, causing her to rear back in shock.

Eyes wide, mouth thoroughly kissed, Loukis had never seen anything so beautiful, before something like fear covered Célia's features. Even though he'd known it was coming, he'd still felt the intrusion of the paparazzi's flashbulb. The photographs he'd assured would be taken, now unwanted and frustrating.

It was then that he realised that his bright idea, the one that would cement their engagement publicly and assuredly, was a mistake. He saw it as Célia would see it. A betrayal. But as his conscience lashed at him, his need to win, his need to secure custody of Annabelle over Meredith rose hard and fast.

He swiped his lower lip with the pad of his thumb, sure that some of her lipstick had transferred from her mouth to his. As he looked down at the red mark on his skin, he wondered just how badly he had wounded her this evening.

He pushed up out of his chair, ignoring the way that Célia stared out into the distance trying to find the invisible photographer who had caught them in such an intimate, private moment.

'What do we do?' she asked, her voice trembling in the same way that her body had beneath his.

'We leave.'

He placed a guiding arm around her and ushered her from the rooftop, back into the dimly lit interior of the busy restaurant. It seemed impossible to him that there had been upwards of one hundred people on the other side of the glass. He guided her through the tables, noticing the way her skin had become cold, goosebumps pebbled her arms, where previously soft warmth had been all he could feel.

As he stopped by the small desk to the right of the entrance, passing over his credit card, the manager looked up. 'Did you get what you need?'

'Nai,' Loukis said, swiftly cutting off anything further the man might give away. He felt, from where his arm was still placed around Célia, her body stiffen.

As he stalked from the restaurant towards the bank of elevators in the hallway, her footsteps slowed, her face transforming from confusion to disgust.

'What did he mean?'

'I'm sure that he meant to ask if we enjoyed our meal.'

'I don't think so. If that were the case, he would have used those words.'

Something horrifyingly like guilt lashed at him.

'What was it that you needed from this evening, Loukis?' she demanded.

The elevator doors swung open and he stepped inside, studiously ignoring her question.

'What, you no longer want to play your game?' she said, her voice hoarse with emotion as the doors closed behind her.

He inhaled, his mind a swarm of thoughts all the while he could still taste her on his tongue, her scent wrapping around him in the small enclosed space.

She pushed him then, double handed, shocking and no less than he deserved.

'Answer me!'

'I needed the press to have a photograph of us together. I needed us to be seen as a couple,' he growled through clenched teeth, the answers insipid and unsatisfying even to his own ears. 'It needed to seem natural. It had to be perfect.'

'But you didn't have to lie to me. You didn't need to set up some silly game just to get me to…' She seemed unable to bring the words to lips that he'd so thoroughly kissed. He watched her bring herself under control, tried to avoid the way her chest pressed against the silk lining of the dress as she levelled her breathing.

'No more lies, Loukis. I won't be lied to again.'

And something in her tone spoke of more than just his actions that evening. Something deeper and darker. But he refused to delve into it, no matter how much he might want to ask who had hurt her. He had done enough for now.

CHAPTER SIX

LOUKIS RAN A weary hand through his hair as his eyes focused on the bright laptop screen glowing like some unworldly portal in the dark room. He checked the time on the watch on his wrist. Two forty-five in the morning. Anger was keeping him awake. Anger, frustration and an unhealthy dose of discomfort swirled in his empty stomach. He now regretted not touching any of the delicious morsels that had been presented to him and Célia earlier in the restaurant.

In the car on the way home, he had messaged his housekeeper and given her a few days off, realising that there was no earthly way he could make good on his demand that Célia share his bed.

He might be many things, but crass was not one of them.

A few days would give them time to…adjust to one another. But by the time Annabelle was safely back from Texas and away from the clutches of his mother, there would most definitely have to be a united front.

He checked his watch again. Time had slowed to almost imperceptible increments as he waited for the moment when he could video call his sister. And after that, he would collapse into one of the spare rooms upstairs and hope that sleep would somehow dull the way that the evening loomed in his mind. It had taken on a technicolour quality, the vivid slash of Célia's red lipstick, the forest-green silks of her dress, the impact of their kiss still vibrating through him like earthquake tremors long after the fact.

He didn't regret his decisions that evening. The paparazzo was as necessary as getting to know and getting used to Célia. But just when their game had turned from one of necessity to one of expectation, want even, he couldn't tell. And even now he wondered at the answer to the question he had not had time to ask her. What Célia would have saved in the fire.

The screen of his laptop changed as Annabelle's video call appeared, the sudden pings echoing loudly, intrusively in the quiet estate. He grabbed a quick mouthful of cold coffee and accepted the call.

'Hey, Nanny,' he said, using the nickname they'd had for the last three years. Where or how it had come about forgotten beneath the impact of those first few months. 'Have a Texan accent yet?'

Her face filled the screen, bright, shining and happy. She was clutching a bright, torrid-pink fluffy bear, and Loukis's first thought was, *And so it begins.* The buying of Annabelle's affection would have been Meredith's first and obvious move.

'Don't be silly,' she laughed.

'And who have you got there?'

'His name's Jameson.'

'Jameson? That's an interesting name. I like his fur.'

Célia woke up, startled and unable to tell where she was or what had woken her. Her heart was pounding and a thin sheen of salty dampness was rapidly drying in the cool room. Loukis. The photographer. The kiss… All these things seemed to crash down in her mind.

It needed to seem natural. It needed to be perfect.

The word had sliced through her like a knife. *Perfect.* It had been too close. Too reminiscent of Marc, of her father. It was supposed to be different with Loukis. They had an agreement. She knew the terms. And now he did too. *No more lies.* She just had to hope that she could live up to her end of the bargain. To be the one thing that she had failed at before. To be…perfect.

Her mouth was bone-dry and she knew she'd not be able to go back to sleep now. She shrugged on her new silk robe and, on bare feet, made her way towards the staircase that led downstairs.

A sound pulled her up short. Startling and rich, Loukis's laughter cut through her. It was conspiratorial in a way that made her jealous. Perhaps he was on the phone to his lover. And she suddenly felt horrified. They'd never talked about that, and why wouldn't he have one? He was clearly a deeply sensual man—but he'd kissed her? She rubbed her forehead, her thoughts chaotic after an unsettled brief bite of sleep.

In a fit of unfamiliar pique, she continued down the stairs, not disguising her footfalls on the cool marble. She rounded the bottom of the staircase and saw Loukis through the doorway to the living room, illuminated in the darkness by a shaft of light from his laptop screen.

The moment she heard Annabelle's voice echo through the speakers, she felt guilty. Guilty and intrusive. She made to retreat, but the move must have caught his eye, because Loukis looked up, a smile lighting his features momentarily. And then, as if he too remembered how they had left things, how she had stormed off to the room and slammed the door shut on him as if she were a child, the brightness of his smile dimmed.

'Who's that?' she heard Annabelle demand. Almost reluctantly he beckoned her over and Célia, unable to refuse the command, went to stand behind where Loukis sat so that she could see the screen.

'Bonsoir, ma chérie,' Célia greeted the ten-year-old,

expecting and receiving the peal of giggles that the girl emitted.

'She calls me Cherry,' she cried to Loukis in delight.

'You're getting quite the collection of names, Nanny. I hope you can keep track of them,' Loukis said, jokingly chiding.

'Mummy calls me Annabelle, though.'

She felt Loukis jerk back in the chair as if struck.

'But mynewdaddy—' she seemed to roll the words into one '—calls me Anna. He's silly.'

Her statement hit the room with the force of a tornado Annabelle couldn't even have imagined.

'Your new daddy?' Loukis demanded, his voice shaking with anger.

Annabelle looked uncertain for a moment. 'That's what Mummy calls him. My new daddy,' she replied, as if confused and unsure as to why Loukis's reaction was what it had been.

'Are you having fun?' Célia rushed on, trying to cover his discomfort. 'What have you been up to?'

As Annabelle chatted away about visits to shopping malls, where she was given Jameson, and a trip to the zoo, where she saw tigers, bears and snakes—her favourite was Diego the skunk—Célia was painfully aware of the tension and frustration that filled the air on this side of the world, Annabelle thankfully oblivious to it. Or at least she had been until her voice trailed off a little and her small fingers started to twist in the bright pink fake fur of her toy.

'But I… I… They don't have dolphins. Not like the zoo in Greece.'

Célia's heart ached. For Annabelle and Loukis, both desperately trying to navigate this new dynamic.

'I don't think I've ever seen a dolphin,' she remarked into the awkward silence.

'You haven't?' Eyes wide and childishly outraged, Annabelle demanded that Loukis take her to see the dolphins *right now*.

'*Ma chérie*, it is nearly three-thirty in the morning. I don't think the zoo is open here yet.'

'But it's still light outside?'

'Not here, my love. You're so far away that the sun is in a different place and it's a different time. What are you doing tomorrow?' Célia asked, trying to get some of the happy enthusiasm that had filled the little girl's voice. But sadly it didn't quite work. Her joy was as dimmed as Loukis.

'How is Meredith treating you?' he demanded, his voice rough and begrudging.

'She wants me to call her Mummy.'

All the man beside her could do was nod.

'Is that okay with you?' asked Célia, keeping her tone as light as possible.

Annabelle narrowed her eyes, the weight of the question being given serious consideration.

'I think so?' She darted a look towards Loukis as if to check that she had the right answer and, once again, Célia's heart ached just a little more.

'You call her what feels right for you, *oui*?'

'Wee? Why did you say *wee*?' Annabelle cried, pealing off into another beautiful giggle.

'It is how I say yes,' Célia explained with a smile.

'You talk funny,' Annabelle accused.

'You have funny friends,' Célia replied, pointing to Jameson.

'He *is* funny. And silly. And pink!' she exclaimed.

After a few more minutes, Loukis too quiet to be able to continue pointless conversation, they agreed to video call again tomorrow and signed off.

When Loukis closed the laptop's screen, the living room

was shrouded in a sudden darkness that left spots dancing in the backs of Célia's eyes and a weight against her chest that burned.

She understood why Loukis was so angry, but also was frustrated that he'd revealed some of that anger to Annabelle. She was a ten-year-old child and shouldn't bear the weight of adult emotions. Not when she'd soon have enough of her own to deal with.

'What?' Loukis demanded in the darkness. 'I can practically feel the waves of your disapproval.'

'I… It's not my place,' she said, turning to leave the room.

Loukis leaned forward and switched on the lamp beside the laptop, the shaft of light cutting off her escape.

'Well, as my fake fiancée for now, you might as well spit it out.'

She turned back to him, as if reluctant. Her eyes large, glowing and wary as if she knew what she had to say would hurt him. Loukis almost laughed at himself then. *Christos.* What was it with the women in his life?

'It's just a shame, Loukis, that's all. I know you have a complicated relationship with your mother, but Annabelle looked like she was having fun.'

The silent accusation that he might have somehow taken away that fun cut him deep. Meredith was the danger, not him. He was doing everything in his power to protect his sister. And if that protection came at the cost of being spoiled rotten by a flaky woman whose only claim to motherhood was birth, then so be it.

'Oh, fun. Yes, I remember "fun" Meredith,' he bit out. Because he did. He remembered the mother who would arrive at the school, middle of the day sometimes, and whisk him away to the beach, on a yacht, or a trip to the zoo, or to shops full of the best toys. He remembered the way his room had filled with useless presents designed to prove her occasional affections, to make up for the rest of the time. He remembered a woman he thought had hung the moon and more, who made him feel as if he were the only other person in the world. Until something brighter and shinier came along to distract her. Usually a man other than her husband, with more money than sense, who might or might not have owned an island, or a villa in a different part of Greece, or even Europe. Then, he wouldn't see her for weeks. Her absence marked only by a new toy.

'But I also remember the Meredith who would leave me waiting in a playground for three hours before my father could come and get me. Not just once, Célia. Nearly once a week. I remember the Meredith who was too busy enjoying the delights of the Riviera to return for Christmas. Not just the day, the whole damn holiday. I remember the woman who walked out on her daughter one day and never looked back, until now. I remember the nights, weeks, months of Annabelle crying herself to sleep, asking where her mother was and why she wasn't coming back. It was nearly a year before she stopped asking after Meredith. And what do you think will happen to Annabelle, how do you think she'll feel, when Meredith tires of her returned plaything, and wants to drop her off again and disappear? What will Annabelle remember then?'

His voice had grown louder and harsher throughout and he realised he was shaking with anger. Anger for Annabelle, anger for himself, and anger towards Célia, who had only pointed out something he had already been castigating himself for.

He couldn't bear to look at her, fearing and resenting that she had called forth such blatant vulnerability from him. He never spoke about his mother, never spoke about his memories of her. She had left and not once looked back.

Not even for his father's funeral. So he had wiped her from his mind, cut her from his life as ruthlessly as a surgeon removing dangerous cells from the body.

He felt Célia's hand on his, and this time it was his turn to flinch. And just as he had done in the restaurant, Célia maintained the delicate contact between them, adding to it even, as she reached for his chin to guide his gaze to hers.

'I am sorry that happened to you.' The sincerity in her gaze scoured. It scoured because in some ways having her understand, having her apology, opened up the hurt in a way it had not been before. Desperate to stifle it, to shove the lid back down hard, Loukis turned back to where the laptop was open on his desk.

'But what if Meredith does actually want a relationship with Annabelle? What if she *does* want to be part of her life? Is that not worth exploring, even if just a little?'

Loukis couldn't help the bitter laugh that escaped at her naivety. 'That woman isn't capable of thinking of anyone else but herself.'

'That's possible. Even likely, given what you've shared. But…'

He was getting tired of trying to sift through her words to find the heart of what she meant. He both wanted and feared her spelling it out, because if he was honest, he thought he might know what she was about to say.

'Just say it, Célia.'

'She will need to make her own mind up, Loukis. She will need to figure out her own feelings about Meredith. And you need to be a safe space for that. You *need* to be non-judgmental as she works through it, because if you don't then you'll be the one creating the wall between you and her, not her and Meredith. If Annabelle's mother is as bad as you say, she'll reveal herself and it will devastate your sister. And she will need you for that.'

He met her statement with the clenched jaw of someone who knew he was in the wrong and she was in the right.

'But your reaction is totally normal. You're acting just like any other parent going through a custody battle.'

'I'm not a parent,' he ground out.

'Really?' she asked, her head to one side as if inspecting him for a deeper truth. 'You are looking to be granted full custody of a child you have spent three years feeding, housing, clothing and caring for and you deny that you're a parent? If not for that, then why are you doing this? Because, Loukis, if you're doing this just to get back at your mother then…'

Then you are just as bad as her.

The unspoken accusation hung in the air between them, a bell that had tolled its tale and rippled out into his consciousness. He shook his head against her words, trying to dislodge the barb that had hooked into his mind.

'I'm going to bed,' she said gently before leaving the room. He barely acknowledged her departure.

Was Célia right? Really? Was it vengeance driving him to seek custody of Annabelle, because of his own hurt feelings, teaching Meredith a lesson perhaps? Or had he told the truth, that his sole motivation was to protect his sister?

In the dimly lit living room, in a chair that after four hours was uncomfortable, he tried out each different chain of thought, listening to his mind and heart as he felt his way through the morass of his motivations. Reluctantly, Loukis was forced to admit that perhaps it was an unsettling mixture of both. But Célia was right. He had to make sure that he kept his own feelings for his mother out of it. Because Meredith would reveal herself soon enough and the blow to Annabelle would be devastating. Not that it stopped his plans for even a second, Loukis decided. He could at least hope to limit that damage by gaining sole custody and ensure that any interaction with Meredith was kept to a minimum.

The next morning, Loukis surprised her. Not only had he, himself, laid out a breakfast of delicious treats, hot and very strong coffee, but he also appeared to be in a good mood.

After the awkwardness from the night before, it was taking Célia a little longer to adjust to this new, charming fiancé. A dull thud hit her heart as she thought of the word. It hadn't been the first time that she'd had a near-fiancé. The word conjured images not of Loukis, but of Marc. Of how charming he'd appeared at first, how joyful and exuberant. All things that had disappeared the moment she'd rejected her father's name, money, and her own burgeoning technical career.

Torn between memories of the past and an unsettling present, it took her a while to realise that Loukis had said something. Or asked something? Because he was looking at her for an answer to some unheard question.

'I'm sorry, what was that?'

Loukis pushed aside the newspaper and leaned forward. Not before she'd got a look at the large black and white photo of them kissing on the rooftop of the balcony the night before. A headline, she was sure, screamed the news of their engagement and apparent happiness. An article, she was equally sure, dredged up the many references to Loukis's past conquests and more questions about who this strange woman who had claimed him was.

'Would you?'

'Would I what?' she asked, irrationally irritated.

'Would you like to go into Athens this morning?' he repeated pleasantly and frustratingly without…well, frustration.

'Oh. Yes, I suppose?'

'You don't seem sure.'

'Loukis, right now, to be honest, I'm not quite sure of anything. Why would we go into Athens?'

His answer surprised her. Silencing her. Making her suddenly a little fearful. Because his answer, his apparent purpose, was their engagement ring. A ring that would make all this so much more tangible. It would draw a line beneath the way she had been trying to pass this whole endeavour off as something not quite real.

Loukis's cheerful mood seemed to carry on through the morning. The journey into Athens in a chauffeur-driven town car had been full of twists and turns that only served to exacerbate the nausea building in her stomach. The Acropolis loomed high in the distance as they drew closer and closer to the city centre. Sleek buildings bordered the road as they wound through the streets, until they came to the sprawling sandstone building housing the Greek Parliament. It rose on one side of the car, large, proud but strangely removed of some of the pomp and finery of other countries' central government. It struck her as both beautiful and uncompromising. A little like the man beside her.

It was soon left in the rear-view mirror as the car took them further into the centre, smaller streets full of motorbike riders risking their lives swerving in and out of traffic, tourists doing much the same as they navigated the busy pavements and side streets. The limousine, drawing curious glances from pedestrians, drew to a halt at the corner of a street, and with lithe grace Loukis exited the car and came round to open her door for her.

It seemed to Célia that these small gestures, manners, were automatic for him and in some ways she preferred that. They weren't intended to ingratiate, there was no purpose to them other than it was simply what he did. It seemed doubtful that this was something his mother had imparted, but more likely that it had been his father. It was on the tip of her tongue to ask, but as she stepped out into the sunlight her mind halted beneath the incredible sight of a riotous waterfall of fuchsia bougainvillea. It was pouring from one side of street, clinging impossibly to a yellow-painted wall, as if challenging the white wisteria blooming forth from the opposite building. It was such a beautiful sight, she couldn't help but smile.

Even at ten in the morning, the street was bustling with people and tourists, and they soon had to step out of the way of the oncoming wave of pedestrians. The trees created a canopy above tables set out on stone-paved streets full of people with coffee and cigarettes and the hum of conversations drifted towards them.

Loukis seemed content to allow her to take her fill of the surroundings.

'You've not been to Athens before now?'

She looked up, smiling, and shook her head. 'I only flew in before for the gala and…well, was gone first thing in the morning, as you know.'

Momentarily his espresso rich coloured eyes darkened, before he schooled his features back to that practised smile and slipped on a pair of sunglasses.

'Come,' he commanded, his hand outstretched to hers. 'We have an appointment.'

She hesitated, momentarily cast back to the feel of his touch, of his kiss from the night before. The aching realisation that their intimacy was for public display returned and she sadly took his hand, chiding herself for the errant thought that she'd wished, for a moment, for him to take her hand because…because he just wanted to.

He led her up the gently sloping street, past restaurants and shops selling everything from ceramic masks of Greek mythology with impressive swirling beards, to leather sandals, and Grecian-style dresses of turquoise, white and fuchsia. The bright vibrancy was infectious and soon smoothed away most of the exhaustion from the night before.

She was thankful, as the heat of the sun began to warm the streets, that she had determinedly chosen her clothing from her new wardrobe. The wide-cut tan linen palazzo trousers and white T-shirt, more fitted that she would usually have worn, were a godsend. Loukis, too, was in linen, dark trousers and a white shirt, rolled back at the sleeves, with his jacket hooked on his finger and trailing over his shoulder. He looked every inch the charming playboy and for the first time she felt as if she might just fit in beside him.

They drew to a halt at a small building squashed between two others, one a restaurant and another selling antique books. The darkened windows looked closed to further inspection, but Loukis confidently ushered her through the door before him.

A small man who could not be any younger than eighty greeted Loukis like a long-lost friend, taking him by the arms in a deceptively strong grip and kissing both cheeks of her soon-to-be official fiancé.

A smattering of Greek filled the small room, which, as her eyes adjusted, she could see was absolutely full of the most incredible jewellery. Shafts of sunlight from the street picked out princess-cut diamonds, baguette cuts of what looked like blue tourmaline, pear-shaped rubies far outshining the cluster of tiny pearls in which they were set… it was as if she'd wandered into Aladdin's cave.

As the two men continued to chat away, Célia's eyes snagged on a marquise-cut diamond solitaire. A whisper of hurt wound out from her heart. It was exactly like the ring Marc had once pointed out to her.

'When I ask your father for your hand in marriage, that is the ring I will buy you.'

At the time, she'd been so overwhelmed, thought she'd been so happy, she hadn't realised that his 'proposal' had been more of a statement, and that he'd put her father first. The signs had all been there, she just hadn't wanted to see them.

'Really?'

Loukis's question interrupted her thoughts.

'*That* is what's caught your eye?'

'I was just looking. You don't like it?'

'It's not whether I like it, but it doesn't quite seem like you.'

How was it that this man, who she barely knew, who she had yet to even share a bed with, seemed to know her better than Marc, with whom she had spent nearly four years?

'What do you think would suit me best, then?' she asked, pushing past her bruised and battered heart.

He levelled her with a gaze so considered she wanted to turn away, fearful that he might somehow divine her thoughts. Finally, as if deciding something, he took her by the shoulders and guided her to a velvet ring display on top of the counter. The old man stood behind it with an exhilarated look across his features. She was distracted by that for a moment, before looking down at the single ring held by the dark velvet folds.

'Oh.' She couldn't have prevented the small sound of shock falling from her lips. It was beautiful; a thin gold band, set with bright green sapphires in a half eternity pattern. It was everything that she would have ever wanted for her engagement ring. And it was altogether too much.

The man behind the counter gently prised the ring from

where it lay and gave it to Loukis, gesturing for him to present it to his fiancée.

'I'm sure it won't…'

She trailed off as Loukis took her hand in his, his thumb unfurling her ring finger, smoothing away the slight tremors she felt across her skin, and slid the exquisite piece down to where it fitted, perfectly at the base of her finger.

She looked up at him then. She shouldn't have, but she couldn't resist. The look in his eyes, the dark promise, the undercurrent of something more than just an agreed upon fake relationship, shocking them both.

CHAPTER SEVEN

As Loukis exited the shop, he tried to ignore the residual feelings that had been brought on the moment he slipped the engagement ring onto Célia's finger. For a man who had been determined to avoid such a thing ever happening, he put it down to the fact he was going against his very nature. Rather than the fact that for a moment, in the shop, Célia had seemed utterly vulnerable. Without artifice or defence, her expressive amber eyes had contained too much. Had communicated too much.

He grasped her hand and placed his arm around her shoulders, persevering through the flinch he had expected, and settled her into his side, careless of the other pedestrians trying to rush around them in their haste.

He felt her head scan to one side, then the next, as much as he saw it from his peripheral vision, given that she barely reached his shoulder.

'What are you looking for?' he asked, curious.

'The press. Surely you wouldn't want them to miss this moment.' The bitterness on her tongue was harsh, but just.

'No press. Not today.'

'Giving me the day off?'

'I think you've deserved it,' he said, trying to keep his voice light. 'What would you like to do now?'

'I get a say in the matter, do I?'

He was beginning to get more than a little frustrated, so he drew her around to face him.

'Célia.'

'I know. I'm sorry, it's just all a bit too much.'

'Which is why I wanted today to be fun.'

She huffed out a laugh. 'Fun?'

'Yes, you do remember fun, don't you?' Although looking at her reaction, perhaps she didn't. 'How long have you been working on Chariton?'

She inhaled, the action tempting his gaze to her breasts, but he resisted. Barely.

'Three years, give or take. Ella and I were talking about it long before, when we were still at university.'

'When was the last time you had a holiday? Or just took a break?'

That she avoided both his gaze and his question told him enough. He sneaked an arm around her waist and guided her back up the street.

'Where are we going?'

'First we are going to Monastiraki, which has a flea market perfect for our purposes of simply enjoying the morning. Then we have lunch.'

Loukis had decided not to tell Célia about the lunch meeting he had arranged for her. He'd not missed the way that, if given too much time to think, Célia would over prepare, over question and over doubt. When she met the first prospective client he had arranged, as agreed upon as part of the fake fiancée deal, Loukis wanted her to be as natural as possible.

She dragged her heels for a while, but soon relaxed, guided by his arm around her shoulder, Loukis telling himself the touch was necessary for them both. Aversion therapy, he had said the night before. The problem was that Loukis was not in the least averse to touching her.

The smell of strong coffee and sweet treats filled the air, his mouth watering at expectation of the honey and pistachio of a baklava. As if Célia was having the same thoughts, her footsteps slowed, and he smiled.

'Coffee? Baklava?'

She nodded, smiling, and they took a seat at one of the free tables out in the street. Dappled light picked out shadows on the white tablecloth as it filtered through the leaves above. The warmth of early summer comforting. He loved Athens at this time of year. A little too early for the massive influx of tourists that would usually drive him and Annabelle from their estate out to the island. It had been the first property he'd ever bought. Somewhere that his mother hadn't tainted, his father's devastation hadn't touched, and where he initially and then, later, Annabelle had both found a peace…no. More than that. They had—for a while—found happiness. Suddenly, without warning, the looming custody battle set his heartbeat racing as he vainly tried to struggle with the fear, shocking and terrible, that he might lose Annabelle.

The waiter came with menus, but Loukis waved them away, simply ordering baklava, an espresso for himself and *frappe metrio* for Célia. He thought she would like the sweet iced coffee. As the waiter disappeared back into the restaurant, his attention was drawn by a father and son on the nearby table. The son was angrily wiping at his eye with one hand, as if trying to disguise his tears, and holding what looked like a small black electronic plane in the other.

He heard the father's reassurances, and almost felt the man's helpless anger as he tried to explain to the boy that there must be something wrong with it. That they just had to wait until they could go back to the shop. Though judging from the look on the father's face, he either didn't hold out much hope for a solution or feared the money it would cost. Loukis empathised with the man, clearly struggling with his child's hurt and pain. Since Annabelle had come into his life, he'd felt that constantly.

Célia turned to look behind her, her gaze seeming to snag on the same tableaux as his had done.

'What's wrong?'

Loukis shook his head, shrugging. 'Something wrong with the machine apparently.'

He watched as she cocked her head to one side as if trying to get a closer look at the machine, rather than the boy and his father, which struck him as a little odd. She shifted her chair a little, so she could better see, which drew the attention of the upset little boy and his father.

'Can you ask him what's wrong with it?' she said to Loukis.

Frowning, he relayed the question and the father's answer, all three of them looking rather bemused by Célia's interest.

She nodded, and held her hand out for the toy.

The boy looked to his father for permission and, once granted, passed the machine over to Célia.

It felt strange having a drone in her hands again. Strange, exciting, sad…a heady combination as she placed the lightweight black body on her lap and scrolled through the controller to switch the language from Greek to French. She was familiar with the cheap mass-produced brand—a family favourite that entertained children and adults alike. Checking that the drone was powered up, she scrolled to the status bar to find the compass setting. She had already checked the aircraft battery was above eighty per cent, so she was pretty sure that recalibrating the compass should be all that was needed. Looking for the solid clear light at the back of the drone, she put the controller aside, and picked up the body of the machine, turning it in her hands three hundred and sixty degrees until the light ran green. Pointing the nose downwards, she turned the machine again until the green light started flashing. Which was just as it should be.

She looked up at the boy, smiling, and passed him back the drone and controller after switching the language back to Greek.

The boy took it from her gingerly, placed it on the ground and experimentally started the drone up. It jerked upwards, startling some passers-by, and the boy let out a cry of joy, before guiding it up and into the air, running a short way after it.

For a moment, she indulged. Indulged in her own childhood memories. The hours she had spent playing with similar toys, and then later, the years she had spent studying, working towards more and more complex designs, GPS systems, loving the way that binary numbers combined with computer chips and the smell of a soldering iron. As her interest in the mechanical had turned into the way that signals could be sent and received to identify locations, the possibilities that could be achieved with such information had set her brain alight with wonder and excitement. The thrill of having an idea and of making it—

'What was wrong with it?'

Loukis's question cut through her thoughts, drawing her attention back to the present, back to him.

'The father wants to know, in case it happens again.'

'The compass needed to be recalibrated. It's a fairly common problem for that particular brand. He can look it up easily enough.'

It was only when she looked up at Loukis that she realised her mistake. Because how on earth would she explain how she had known that? His eyes didn't leave hers as he translated what she had said to the father. They didn't leave hers as the father proclaimed effusive thanks, tried to pay for their coffees—an offer that was dismissed by Loukis with a wave of his hand—and ran off after his happy son. No, it was Célia that broke the connection, unable to bear the scrutiny.

Over the past five years, only Ella had known about her drastic career change. She had been the only person to stick with her after her life had changed. Faces and so-called friends ran through her mind from that time 'before'. Hopes and dreams of trying to be seen by her father, be considered valuable, or even worthy in his eyes. But then he had taken her plans for agricultural drone technology for use in drought-affected areas of Africa and warped it, changed her good intentions in the most horrible way. Took them from her and used them for his true love: his own company.

She had spent the summer interning and impressing the research and development department in Paquet Industries as a way to try to be closer to her father. To impress him somehow. She'd inherited her father's genius, they'd all said. At the time she'd been pleased, so, so pleased. Only Ella had grumbled about being a genius in her own right. But Célia hadn't cared. Finally pleasing her father had been her only focus. Until someone had seen the technical specs she'd been working on as part of her degree over lunch one day. Closer and closer they had looked and once they'd realised what she'd done, they'd whisked her up to see her father. Her drawings, her ideas, had been pored over and over. At first by the manager, then by her father, then by other advisers and ultimately by lawyers.

God, she'd been so naïve. At first she'd been thrilled, excited, hopeful even. But then suddenly everything went quiet. People stopped talking about the project, behaving as if it had never happened. Her father became too busy to see her, to answer her calls even.

She'd wondered if perhaps they'd found something wrong with her designs and that had scoured her insides, devastating her in what she'd hoped to be 'the final' way, the 'only' way her father might find use or value, or even love. Three weeks after the internship had finished and she had returned to university, returned to Ella, who had comforted Célia in her bewilderment, she discovered what had happened. In the newspaper. The article had revealed a major deal between her father's company, Paquet Industries, and one of France's leading firearms manufacturers, proclaiming the revolutionising of drone technology as its key motivation.

What she was working on—designs to help agriculture in drought-affected areas, to allow better crop production, rapid identification of pest and fungal infestations, information on irrigation and so much more—had been used instead for murder. Justifications like *war on terror* and *border defence* and the little-known discipline of Measurement and Signature Intelligence had done nothing to assuage her guilt.

That her designs, her hopes and dreams had been so vilely abused had shocked her to her very core. Only Ella knew of the devastating guilt that had torn through Célia. That had seen her nearly drop out of college altogether. That had given her nightmares for months and months.

Her father had simply refused to speak of it, as if pretending it hadn't happened. Her mother had stood by him and, in Célia's mind, chosen his side. She hadn't spoken to her father in five years, her mother in three. And it still ached and twisted in her chest.

'Célia?'

Once again she had become so lost in her thoughts she had missed what Loukis had said. She brushed the hair that had fallen in front of her eyes aside, noticing how the green sapphires glinted in the sunlight, bringing her back to reality with a bump.

'Are you okay?' Loukis asked, a frown marring the near perfect features looking up at her.

'Yes. Sorry, what were you saying?'

'That we probably need to leave if we're going to make lunch.'

'Lunch?'

'Yes, you have an appointment.'

'An appointment?'

He nodded. 'One that would probably benefit from something more than you repeating my every word.'

Loukis stood from the table, but Célia remained on the chair.

'Is this a kind of sit-in?' he demanded, half amused.

'Yes. Until you tell me what's going on I'm not moving.'

'You sound like a child,' he said, now openly smiling, enjoying the slightly petulant bent to her tone. It had been much better than the series of emotions that he'd seen play upon her features after she had fixed the drone. Something that he had not forgotten and would most definitely be exploring at a later date. It was just that it didn't seem to fit. Not with Célia and who she was. And that made him uncomfortable. But he didn't have time right now for that.

'Lunch is where you are going to meet your next client,' he stated.

A look of horror passed over her features, new and different from before. 'But I'm not prepared. I don't know who they are or…anything. *Loukis.*' She used his name as both a question and punctuation. It was adorable.

'You are perfectly well prepared. You know your company inside out, you've got plenty of examples to draw from to illustrate any kind of point you need to make. And your soon-to-be new client has a low tolerance for unnecessary pomp, and a great deal of respect for straight talking. The two of you will get on wonderfully.'

Loukis gestured for Célia to go ahead before him, following behind a black-suited head waiter towards the table where Yalena Adeyemi and her husband sat, laughing quietly at something secret.

The moment Yalena caught sight of them, she stood from the table and greeted them both with a wide smile and excitement glinting in her espresso rich gaze.

'Loukis. It's been far too long,' she gently reprimanded. 'I'd be horrified that business has brought you finally back to socialising, if I wasn't so curious about the opportunity you've presented.' Without missing a beat, she turned to Célia. 'It's lovely to meet you, and *not* just because you're the "business opportunity",' Yalena said with genuine happiness.

Célia, who had been silent since he'd told her of their intended destination, came to life as if a switch had been flipped.

'Likewise. If I'm honest, I'm trying hard not to fan-girl at the moment. Your company has such a fantastic reputation and has achieved some really incredible things.'

Célia hadn't lied at all. She'd known of Yalena Adeyemi by reputation. As founder and CEO of one of the quickest growing peer-to-peer lending platforms, Yalena had been an inspiration for both Célia and Ella when starting up their own company.

'As does yours. Chariton Enterprises is steadily gaining quite a bit of notoriety, and,' she said, clearly noticing Célia's glance towards Loukis, 'not because of your recent exciting news. May I offer my congratulations on your engagement?'

Yalena gestured for them to sit, and Loukis made the introductions between Iannis, Yalena's husband, and Célia. Drinks were ordered, and small talk was made until they arrived.

'Iannis, why don't we leave the ladies to their business and go to the bar and gossip like the old miserable men that we are?' Loukis announced. Giving his wife a kiss on the cheek, Iannis followed Loukis away from the table and towards the bar as promised.

Célia was thankful for it. For some reason having Loukis there had put her on the back foot. As if embarrassed or worried about what he might think if he saw her in client mode. Which was doubly strange because he was a client himself. She looked across at Yalena. Her close-cropped hair highlighted incredible cheekbones, gorgeous wide eyes and a ready smile. But for all of that, Célia knew that her mind was razor-sharp and her focus fierce.

'I was not just paying lip service, Célia. I am impressed with what you've done with your company, especially such a young one.'

'Thank you. It means a great deal to Ella, my business partner, and myself.'

She nodded. 'May I ask why?'

'Of course.'

Over the next hour Célia and Yalena discussed everything from why they had started their own businesses, what they had wanted from them and where they would like to go in the future. Each had been struck by how closely their motivations and desires had aligned and celebrated the successes and understood the challenges faced by the other. They were both in the business of matching like-minded clients, for their mutual benefit, and had faced many similar obstacles. This might have been why Yalena had probed deeper and more thoughtfully than most of Chariton's existing clients and, instead of dismissing outright the charity areas that Célia believed were the best fit for her peer-to-peer company, allowed her to explain her reasoning and interacted happily with Célia's initial thoughts on what kind of events would benefit them.

Yalena leaned back in her chair, her hands sweeping circles on the smooth white cloth.

'I know that look,' Loukis said from behind Célia's shoulder.

Yalena's thoughtful gaze turned into an amused scowl. 'You're ruining the moment.'

'No, I brought more champagne to celebrate.' The confidence in his voice sparking the thrill of excitement and a burst of hope in Célia.

'Does that mean I should have the contracts drawn up?' asked Célia with a smile.

'Yes. Most definitely yes. But that is all the business talk done for the day. Now. I want to hear *all* about the proposal!'

The lunch had lasted long into the afternoon and dusk was beginning to fall as Loukis paid the bill, much to Yalena's mocking disgruntlement. With deft acuity, he'd been able to keep much of the focus on Iannis and Yalena rather than on Célia and himself, Yalena's husband more than happy to indulge in schoolboy memories shared by them both. And Loukis realised that he'd missed it. Missed the easy laughter of unweighted adult conversation. Much of the last three years of his life had been spent focused solely on Annabelle and shielding her from an outside gaze. Once Célia had realised that she'd secured not only another client, but one that had clearly inspired her, she had relaxed, joining in the gentle mockery between the two couples.

She had opened up under the gentle encouragement of

those around her and it had been glorious. But he hadn't missed how she skirted around her own past, her parents and life before Chariton Enterprises. There had been a few of her own childhood stories of a Swiss boarding school with Ella, and her friend's marriage and recent baby news, but of herself, very little. And he still couldn't quite work out how the drone fitted with the charitable endeavours.

Emerging onto the stone street from the restaurant, they were greeted by a swarm of paparazzi and a hail of flash-bulbs.

Yalena reached for him, kissing his cheeks in farewell. 'They're a little feisty this evening. Perhaps they caught wind of your news?' she said, sotto voce, to Célia and Loukis.

Célia looked towards him as if expecting an explanation, but he simply shrugged. 'It wasn't me.'

Iannis gave him a half-hug, ordered him not to let it go so long next time, turned to his wife and asked, 'Ready to run the gauntlet?'

The two disappeared and Loukis was a little disconcerted that they didn't manage to take any of the vultures with them.

He placed an arm around Célia's shoulder. 'The car should be waiting in the back street. Ready?'

She tucked herself a little more deeply into his side. He knew it was for protection, but he couldn't help the streak of sensation that fired up and down the length of his body.

The moment they stepped forward, the questions began. The shouts and flashes were enough to bring on PTSD. He felt Célia tremble beside him and realised how intimidating and scary this would be for someone not accustomed to it.

'Congratulations! How did he do it, Célia?'

'Did he get down on one knee?'

'Ms d'Argent—any comment on the news about your father?'

Célia stumbled, her foot twisting, and she would have fallen had it not been for his arm around her shoulders. Loukis bit back a curse.

'What does François Paquet think of his future son-in-law?'

The name of the renowned French defence contractor cut through his anger with shocking intensity. Paquet was her father?

'Any response to the claims you've bagged another billionaire, Célia?'

'When was the last time you spoke to your ex, Marc Moreau?'

At this, he'd had enough. He turned to the seething mass around him. 'Ladies and gentlemen—' though the friendly appellation stuck in his throat '—is it not a bit uncouth to ask about the father, ex-partner and current fiancé all in the same breath?'

His tone had been light and mocking, received with laughter by most. But those that knew him, were familiar with him, held a trace of unease. For that was when he was at his most deadly.

'I would love to expound on this further, but as we have already agreed to a private interview with a *reputable* journalist, you will have to read it alongside everyone else.'

'We have an interview?' she whispered, from where she remained tucked into his shoulder as they rounded the corner towards the safe haven of the limousine.

'We will once you tell me what the hell all this is about,' he bit out. 'Get in the car.'

Célia slid into the limousine, her body protected from the strobe lights of the paparazzi, but her thoughts flayed by the repeated bursts of shocking white.

Her heart pounded in her chest. The rush of adrenaline soured by self-recrimination. She should have known that they would find out. Should have prepared for it. Denial had not been enough to protect her from their piercing gaze.

The moment the door closed behind Loukis the sleek town car sped off, sending the sprawling mass scattering. The atmosphere in the dark interior was full of tension, as Loukis's barely leashed control seemed to strain against his hold over it. Her own pulse seemed to thump within the thick air.

'I...'

A gesture of his hand cut through the space between them, silencing her. She stifled back the words, unsure really where she would have begun anyway.

As the car wound its way towards Loukis's estate, the silence and tension filled the space between them to the point where Célia feared she might not be able to draw breath.

'Loukis—'

'François Paquet is your father?' he demanded.

All Célia could do was nod.

'And you—who demanded truth from me—didn't think to tell me?'

'He is no longer part of my life,' she insisted, as if she could make it true.

'Do you know what this fresh wave of interest from the press will do? They'll be frothing at the bit now. It will be impossible to keep the custody battle a secret, it will be impossible to...'

He trailed off. She knew he was thinking of how hard it would be to shield his sister from their penetrating gaze.

'*Christos*, Célia, if I'd known we could have come out in front of it, but now we're behind and...' His fury seemed to be working against his usual smooth calm, stopping words before he could form them. 'Why the hell didn't you tell me?'

'I haven't spoken to my father in five years. Not since I changed my degree, my name and left behind almost everything that connected me to that life.'

And with that she had lost any sense of family or belonging. As if she hadn't even realised until this moment just how isolated and lonely she felt, a sob rose in her chest that she desperately tried to stifle.

'Why? What happened?' He demanded explanations as if he could draw blood from a stone.

'I don't want to talk about it.'

'Tough,' he said mutinously. 'Because now I'm going to need to know everything. Including whoever the hell Marc Moreau is.'

The thought of what he wanted turned in Célia's stomach as they negotiated the bends in the road before pulling up to the estate. She watched him leave the car and stalk towards the front door of his home, realising that it was the first time that Loukis had not opened the car door for her. She was being punished, she realised. Or, he was so consumed by the shocking revelation that he had simply forgotten it. Either way it hurt, strangely.

Her feet felt heavy as she followed through the open doorway, closing it behind her and wishing she could just as effectively close down the events of that evening. She had been so happy! She had been so excited when she'd known she was having lunch with Yalena Adeyemi, and when she'd realised that they'd get a chance to work together? She'd been ecstatic. She should have known better. Because the last time she'd felt that excited, that thrilled, as if on the brink of something marvellous, everything had turned to ash. And once again, it was because of her father.

CHAPTER EIGHT

SHE FOUND LOUKIS pacing the living-room area with a drink already in his hand, his hair ruffled as if he'd run his hand through it several times before she'd entered the room.

'Sit,' he commanded.

'I'll stand, thank you,' she said, unconsciously echoing the last time they'd had an uncomfortable conversation in this room. It was, she realised, an act of self-preservation. As if her subconscious knew that flight would be easier from standing rather than from sitting on the plush soft sofa.

He looked at her as if to indicate that he had not *asked*, but she remained where she stood. Because now she was angry. How dared he find fault with a reputation not of her own making, when his was so debauched? She needed to cling to that anger, because beneath it was a layer of hurt and betrayal so deeply entrenched, she was terrified of hauling it out for inspection. But even that, she realised, covered a guilt that had motivated every single decision she'd made in the last five years. And no matter what, she knew she'd never reveal that to Loukis.

'Start with your father.'

'My father took something of mine and used it for his own purposes.'

He looked at her as if to say, 'Is that all?' and she wanted to scream.

'What, he withheld your pocket money?'

'Don't be crass,' she replied, this time very consciously echoing his own words once fired at her down the phone.

'What, then?' he demanded, his patience clearly wearing thin.

'He took my technical specs for a more efficient drone tracking system.'

The look on his face might have been comical had it not been so painful.

'What?'

She'd known he'd have trouble either understanding her or believing her, either way he clearly needed more of an explanation.

'Five years ago I was studying a graduate degree at the ENS in Sciences, specialising in mathematics and computer sciences. Please don't look at me as if I've just sprouted a second head. It's...patronising and infuriating.'

'I'm not being patronising,' he said defensively. 'I have clearly only known you as a successful humanities entrepreneur. The computer science thing doesn't seem to fit.'

'I happened to be very good at *"the computer science thing"*, thank you.'

'Which begs the question,' he replied, as if she had only proved his point.

'As a child, it became quite clear that I had an affinity with computers and technology. To me, they always made sense. There was clarity in ones and zeros, an unwavering logic. I liked the challenge they presented and revelled in working around and within them to get what I wanted. As part of my degree at ENS, I knew that I would have to find an internship to support my education and thought that Paquet Industries would be perfect.' She had told herself that then, and told Loukis the same lie now. But, really, it had been more than that—she just didn't want to open that painful truth to herself, or Loukis.

'I had been using their workshops to work on my dissertation project. One of the senior managers had seen what I was working on and the next thing I knew it was taken from me. Used in a…used in a very different way from what I had intended.' She felt the familiar rush of anger, the ache of her father refusing to speak to her.

'Because you had signed an intellectual property waiver for work done while interning.'

Surprised, she looked up at Loukis, immediately appreciating the quick mind that had made his own company such a shocking international success.

'Yes.'

'I get how that must have been frustrating, but, what? This is about money? Recognition for your designs?'

'No, it's not that!' She knew that was how it would have been seen had the news got out with no acknowledgement of the wracking guilt she still faced to this day. She couldn't, wouldn't share with Loukis what her plans had been used for, horrified by the sheer thought of his reaction, but she could try to make him realise why, could try to make him understand.

'I…growing up with my father wasn't…' She took a deep breath. This was so much harder than she'd thought it would be. 'He was a difficult man. Exacting, focused…'

'Demanding?' Loukis prompted.

'No, actually. He wasn't. Because he never really expected anything of me other than to be seen and not heard. He'd always wanted a son to pass on Paquet Industries to, but after me, my mother was unable to fall pregnant again. So, in a way, I became a representation of his failure, I think. I can only guess, because he hardly credited me with such an honest explanation or outpouring.

'And in my childlike logic, I thought that if I could prove myself of use, if I could harness my skills for my father's company he might… He might finally see me as worthy.'

She shrugged as if her innocent conclusion didn't hold such a world of pain within it.

'And Marc Moreau? Who is he?'

'He works for the Ministère de la Jeunesse et des Sports,' Célia said, trying not to flinch at Loukis's tone.

'The Ministry of Sport?'

'And youth affairs, yes.'

Loukis frowned, as displeased. 'Okay. Let's try this again. Who is he to you?'

'My ex-fiancé.'

'I gathered that much, Célia.'

She inhaled the tense air between them, trying to fortify herself. 'I met Marc at boarding school. He joined when we were sixteen and was…charming and playful. Fun. He could have had his pick of any of the female students, but he was only interested in me,' she concluded with a shrug. 'I was surprised, but flattered. I enjoyed his attention.' It had been a gift even then, before she'd realised just how distant her father was and how desperate it had made her for affection. 'He ended up at the same university as me and Ella. He'd wanted me to move into an apartment with him, but Ella and I had always talked about living together so I said no. But we went out, restaurants, clubs, parties. I didn't really enjoy it—' she could see that now '—my course required a lot of work, but he always seemed so disappointed when I would say no. Only after did I realise that the restaurants were always booked in my name, the VIP sections in clubs, the party invitations.' And she felt like such a fool.

'Over the four years we'd been together, he'd spent quite a bit of time with my family. He seemed to get on with my father, more than I did at least. He made a monumental effort with him. And I thought it was for me. Until I broke ties with my father. Until I changed my name. And somehow in his eyes, that made me a changed person. He refused to understand why what my father had done was wrong. Insisted that I try to make it up with him.

'When I refused, he began to retreat. Telling me I'd changed, telling me that I wasn't fun any more. He made me doubt myself, and it hurt to force myself to be with him, to keep a smile on my face I didn't feel surrounded by people I didn't know. Because I didn't want to lose him too.' She felt the ache building in her chest. Hating to admit such a thing, feeling so very vulnerable to tell Loukis this. But she knew that he deserved what little she could tell him. 'Slowly, bit by bit he removed himself from my life. I didn't notice at first, but then it would be days, or a week that I wouldn't see or hear from him. Ella convinced me to have it out with him, if anything just to let him know how I felt.

'It was awful. He said it was all my fault. The time and energy he'd put into me wasted. How he didn't want a *girlfriend*—you see, I'd been relegated by that point—who couldn't...*give* him anything. What use was I if I was not perfect?'

In that instant, she realised the truth of the past. As if saying it out loud had somehow conjured the shocking revelation that she had never been wanted. Not for herself. Only for what she could do and be for someone. She had been used by her father, by Marc...and each time she had failed to live up to their expectations, had failed to be what they wanted and in that moment she felt that she had never felt truly loved.

Loukis pressed a drink into her hands and she realised she was shaking.

'And I demanded the same,' Loukis said softly into the silence.

'Non,' she replied, shaking her head. 'I knew what you expected from the beginning. You didn't…'

'Lie?' he said, letting loose a curse that surprised her.

Loukis let out the burst of air locked in his lungs, trying to marry the two vastly different aspects of her personality—the technical expert and the head of a humanities charity—and make them somehow fit with the guilt stirring in his veins. Guilt because, no matter how much she might try to absolve him, he had taunted her with perfection. With the need to be everything that her father and ex-fiancé had unfathomably found wanting in her. Guilt because, even as he knew how much it cost her, he still needed that perfection. For Annabelle. And that scoured his veins and struck his heart. Because it was a hurt that called to him. A hurt that he recognised so painfully as a mirror reflection, in some ways, of his own.

His father had never disapproved of him, nor his mother—they had both been so preoccupied with each other, he had barely even been a consideration. Oh, his father had tried after the divorce, but he'd never been the same, just a shell of the man he once had been.

But he did know how that affected him. It had seen him spiral into a level of selfishness that had him desperate to indulge in every whim, every pleasure, everything he felt had been denied him in his childhood. Looking back now, he could see the mask that had hidden that childhood hurt. The rakish playboy, the careless façade had created a barrier between him and the world…him and hurt.

But all the while he had been indulging, had been consumed by satisfying his wants and needs with a selfishness that shamed him now, Célia had chosen a different path to direct her energies. He wanted her to see that. Wanted to help her realise that she was so much more. So worthy of more than whatever pittance her father had meted out.

'You know that what you've achieved since then is incredible.' It was a statement. A reassurance. 'You did it without the backing of a name and an existing company, which is far more than I've ever done.'

She turned aside, as if not even wanting to accept the compliment.

'Célia, look at me,' he commanded, bringing her face round to his with the crook of his finger at her chin. He took in her large, molten amber eyes, the same fiery colour shining from her hair. The pale, creamy skin blushed by a tint of peach, sweet enough to want to…

He stifled the wicked sensual pull he felt, the desperate urge to taste more than the simple starter he had experienced the night before, to delve into everything she had to offer. None of which he could do, or even entertain the thought of. Bringing anything more into the precarious agreement they had could bring the whole thing crashing down about them. As if torn between reluctance and the desire to touch, he reached his arm out around her shoulders and drew her to him, the action soothing something within them both.

'I mean it. You should be incredibly proud of what you've achieved. Yalena—'

'Was only interested in me because of you,' she interrupted.

'Yalena,' he pressed on, 'wouldn't have agreed to partner with you had it not been because you are worthy of it. She's a great friend, but she wouldn't even do that for me. You are the head of a company that has seen great success in the first three years because of the drive and determination you have brought to it and that should not be dismissed. You have a power that it pains me to see you don't realise. And no one, not your father, nor some stupid ex who didn't realise what he had before throwing it away, nor *I* can take that away. Only you can do that to yourself. And until you cast that aside, you won't realise just how much more you can achieve.'

As Célia felt the words settle about her, she began to feel it. The power that he had talked of, the pride that he had shown her through his eyes. It soothed, and it helped. But she couldn't deny that she still felt…still felt that she wanted more. More from Loukis.

'What happens now?' she asked, her voice still a little shaky from emotion.

'Now? Now I need to know how quickly you can plan an engagement party.'

Célia had laughed at the idea that an engagement party would distract the press enough from her notorious father's identity. But the moment it was announced, they had behaved exactly how Loukis had promised they would.

Célia felt a fresh wave of goosebumps crest across her skin. Not from the fresh sea-salt-laden air, but the nervousness for what was to come. Standing on the deck of the most luxurious yacht she'd ever seen, she couldn't quite believe that all of this was for her. *For them.*

The first guests were due to arrive any moment now and she felt poised on the brink of something she couldn't put a name to. In the last week, since the night of the press furore, things had been…easier between her and Loukis. She had feared that sharing a bit of her past would disappoint him, or disgust him. But it had been freeing. A weight had lifted. Not all, but some of it. She had taken his words that night to heart. Allowed them to settle around her and drawn strength from them.

She refused to turn for the sound of Loukis's footsteps

making their way towards where she stood at the balcony of the yacht, looking out over the port of Piraeus. The sun was hovering halfway between the zenith and the horizon, bright and still powerful even at this time in the afternoon.

She was amazed that she didn't flinch when she felt Loukis draw the silk scarf that had fallen into the crook of her arm upwards over her shoulder. All these little touches, the sheer proximity of him, sent a thrill through her, as if the power of them had built over the last few days. Something she had come to long for, as if the dizzying rush of adrenaline and desire had become addictive to her, and she just about managed to stop herself from leaning into him.

She did flinch, however, when he drew her to his side, just as she'd wanted him to. Not because of him, no. She flinched as the electric starburst cascaded through her the moment the bare skin at her side met his forearm.

Never before would she have dared to wear such a thing. But she had been unable to resist. The night of their conversation about her father, Loukis had made her realise how much she had buried in the last five years. It wasn't just her relationship with her parents, but with herself. Her sense of self. And she wanted that back. Wanted to be the powerful, glorious woman Loukis told her he saw. So she had chosen the most daring of designs and colours. The rich Prussian blue of the material suited her and the high-waisted long maxi skirt was a dream, unfurling from her in smooth, silky waves every time she moved. But the cropped top that clung to her curves and an area of her stomach she wasn't sure had seen the light of day for years had given her pause. Until she'd caught the way that Loukis had looked at her. Was, in fact, looking at her now.

That alone sent a shocking thrill to her very core.

'Annabelle is set up for an evening of junk food and

films,' he said, turning to look out on the horizon, breaking whatever sensual hold he had on her.

'Did you tell her I said hi?' she asked after she had navigated the sudden shift between them.

'She's rather attached to her new nickname.'

Célia smiled.

'Leya's parents will bring her over to the island on the boat tomorrow and Tara will arrive just before the custody hearing.'

Célia was curious about this island estate Loukis had told her they'd be going to after the party. Thankful that they'd finally be escaping the narrow-focused lens of the paparazzi after what felt like weeks of fighting headlines and photo opportunities, she heaved a sigh of relief tinged with excitement. And was also surprised to be looking forward to seeing Annabelle again. All of this had been with her shadow in the background. And once Loukis had seemed to take on board what she'd said about Meredith and his true motivations, he hadn't relaxed, exactly, but had been refocused in a way. More determined to ensure Annabelle's happiness. To a woman who had been so badly betrayed by her own father, it had touched her. Warmed her to Loukis, even when he was being his most autocratic.

But her thoughts went back to the island that was somewhere out there in the sea before her. He had told her about it, about the private beach, about a bit of the architecture… but he hadn't said anything about the bedrooms. About *his* room. And suddenly she couldn't shake the thought of it. Of sharing a bed with him. Of exploring where those touches might lead. This evening, tonight, she'd be sharing a room with her fiancé.

She wasn't sure if Loukis was aware of the way his fingers traced the bare skin at her side. He certainly couldn't know the chaotic thoughts it sent through her mind, the wants it sent through her body.

The sounds of a car door closing cut through the background noise of the port, and they turned in unison to see Ella and Roman making their way down the red-carpeted gangplank with something a little like awe on Ella's face, and easy acceptance on Roman's dark features.

Célia couldn't tell if it was Ella or herself that had let out the little squeal of delight when they finally saw each other, both rushing forwards for a hug.

From the corner of her eye, Célia saw the two men greet each other in the half-hug and back slap that had become internationally recognisable as the greeting of men.

For a moment, her breath caught in her lungs. Both men looked as if they'd just stepped out of a fashion shoot. Impossibly tall, painfully handsome, Roman dressed in a dark linen suit and Loukis in one of a blue that echoed her own clothing's colour, they were a sight to behold.

'Loukis,' Ella called across the deck. 'You may have her for the rest of your life, but for this evening, she is *mine*,' she mock taunted, with absolutely no idea of the effect her words had on Célia.

Her gaze flew immediately to Loukis, who seemed in an instant to understand exactly what had caused a streak of lightning to burst through her in shock. All these weeks, everything they'd done had been to promote their fake engagement. But the people gathering this evening, friends and family and others…they expected a wedding. They believed in a future that Célia would never have. A love.

Ella had whisked Célia off and then more guests had arrived, slowly filling the beautiful wooden deck, so much so that he only seemed to catch glimpses of his beautiful fiancée through tailored suits and exquisite dresses. The jewellery on display could have made the stars jealous, as if every person there had known that they might appear in the next day's newspapers.

The interview with *Hello!* Greece had been a six-page spread with posed portraits in a rented apartment overlooking the Acropolis. He ensured that the focus was not on Célia's father, but about what she had achieved, how she had wanted to do it herself without her father's influence. The piece was positive and glowing and not because of him, but the genuine interest and excitement from the journalist. Since the article had come out more than twelve international business figures had contacted Chariton, causing Célia to remark that he had given her a bonus. The way she made it sound, as if his part of the 'deal' was done, had unaccountably caused a sense of dismay within him, resentment—he reluctantly admitted—at the reminder of their agreement.

He caught another glimpse of her, with Yalena and Ella, the three women laughing together and it was a sight to behold. The moment he'd seen Célia he'd almost asked her to change. She was stunning in a way that made him want to keep her to himself. To hide her beauty, hoard it all for him. But saying that would reveal too much. Reveal just how much he was affected by the sensual torment he had ignited the first time he had touched her in the restaurant.

By the bar he saw Iannis and Roman and was just about to join them when another car drew up to the yacht's gangplank. They had been due to set sail at any moment, so he turned to greet the latecomers, ready—along with the staff—to hurry them onto the deck before the departure when he stopped midstride, shock and fury turning him rigid.

He purposefully released the clench in his jaw, aware that any slight reaction would draw the gazes of the guests.

He could almost feel the shutters on cameras clicking through a hundred photos as if the press had expected this moment, wanted it even.

Meredith walked onto the deck of the yacht like a queen ready to receive her due. In her wake followed a large, round, red-cheeked man improbably wearing a Stetson, grinning as if he was genuinely in ignorance of the horror show this was about to descend into.

Loukis couldn't let that happen. He didn't know what game Meredith was playing, he certainly knew that she hadn't been on the invite list, but he could hardly kick her off the boat, much as he wanted to, as the gangplank was rolled away and the ship's captain sounded the horn to announce their departure from the dock.

His mother's gaze found his and for a moment, just the barest of seconds, he couldn't quite decipher the look that crossed her features, before it was schooled in that same plastic fakery he was used to seeing splashed across the headlines that had decried her infidelity all those years ago.

She made straight for him. Unsurprising, since she had never seemed to shy from a fight with his father.

'Darling,' she called to him, drawing a few curious glances from those about him who knew about their precarious relationship. She placed a red-taloned finger on his forearm and leaned in for air kisses two inches from either cheek.

'What are you doing here?' he growled, keeping his voice low so that only she could hear.

'I came to wish my son all the happiness in the world for his engagement,' she said loudly enough for others to hear and in a tone that completely ignored the hostility rising from him in waves. 'Let me introduce Byron Fairchild.'

'Nice to meetcha,' he said, his Texan drawl so strong the

last two words rolled into one and sounded vaguely like a south American cocktail.

He felt the man's beefy hand encase his, and Loukis searched the man's features for something other than genuine delight. Had Meredith not told him anything? 'What a gal you've got here,' he said, casting his gaze around the deck, clearly speaking of the yacht, rather than Célia, who Loukis suddenly wanted to protect, to hide from his mother's piercing gaze as she, too, searched the boat with an equally assessing gaze.

'As is our Annabelle. She's such a sweetheart,' Byron said without awareness of how his use of our cut through Loukis like a knife.

Loukis felt a lurch in his stomach, from the propulsion of the yacht's engine or the reaction to his mother's presence, he couldn't tell. It had been three years since Meredith had deposited his sister on his doorstep. And before that? Fifteen years since the night she'd promised to come back for him, promised to take him with her. But then he'd heard the argument between his parents. Heard his father offer to pay her an obscene amount to leave Loukis with him. He'd been so sure she would refuse. So sure that she would be outraged and furious. But she'd agreed. And Loukis had never seen her again.

'It's been too long, darling.'

Not long enough had been on the tip of his tongue, when he felt an arm at his back, lending him strength and levelling him in the moment. Had she somehow sensed that he would need this?

'Hello,' Célia said, reaching out her free hand to greet Meredith, whose practised smile turned positively feline.

'So you are the one who has tamed the notorious playboy.'

It was a phrase he knew that Célia had both heard and

read many times, but to hear it from his mother, it cut him deep. Célia was so much more than that.

'Célia d'Argent, Meredith…forgive me, I don't know which name you're going under these days. It wouldn't still be Liordis,' he said, the bitter humour lacing his tone enough to make both women momentarily pause. 'And you never much seemed to care for your maiden name. Are you back to being Meredith Leda, or—'

'Timone,' she interrupted, clearly not caring for his words. 'I'm going by Timone.'

'But soon to be Fairchild, yeah?' the brash Texan said, shouldering Meredith in a way that she must have been braced for otherwise she would have been sent flying. Loukis happily caught the flare of frustration before Meredith schooled her features and hooked her arm around her fiancé's.

'Just think, the two of us, engaged and on the brink of such happiness,' Meredith said, not looking so much at Byron, but between Célia and Loukis.

He genuinely couldn't tell whether her engagement with Fairchild was as fake as his own, but whether Byron himself knew that or not was another matter. As the large man engaged Célia in a conversation, he finally turned to take in his mother.

Her hair was still the same brilliant blonde he remembered from his childhood—whether by artifice or nature, he couldn't tell. Faint lines around her eyes had escaped the pull of Botox he was sure had been used liberally across features that felt so devastatingly familiar. Seeing her in person was so much more…affecting than on the front page.

'Meredith—'

'Where is Annabelle?' she asked, looking around as if she might be there.

'Not here,' he replied, viciously enjoying the look of

frustration on her features. 'Why are you?' he demanded again.

'I wanted to talk to you about dropping the custody case.'

He scoffed. Loud and low and he could have sworn he saw her flinch, but instead he believed the avarice he saw glinting in her eyes.

'How much?'

'How much what?' she asked, her artificial confusion grating against the frayed edge of his nerves.

'How much would it take to walk away? Five million. Ten?' His tone spoke of boredom, all the while his pulse raged in his chest as she finally revealed her true intentions. He knew that this would be the way he could finally get rid of her. Because he would pay. He would pay whatever price she—

'I don't want your money, Loukis.'

'You don't need to play this game with me, Meredith. I know how this works, remember? I've been here before. What was it again? Twenty million for the divorce, and an extra ten if you left me behind?'

'Is that what this is about? You want to punish me?'

'No.' Although his inner voice cried liar. Loukis kept his voice low and his words lethal. 'I will not allow you to hurt Annabelle. I will do whatever it takes to ensure that she stays with me, safely and happily, because I love her and want the best for her.'

'Then you will understand that I will do the same. Because I do love her, Loukis.'

You just don't love me, he raged silently, cursing his own weakness.

She nodded to herself and turned, searching her fiancé out amongst the crowd from where Célia had guided him, summoning him to her as if by some previously agreed signal.

'We'll be leaving now.'

'We're in the middle of the damn sea, Meredith. But I should not be surprised to find that you already had your escape route planned. Leaving is something you are clearly very good at.'

She resisted the barbed comment, and as she waited for Byron, she took in Célia as well. Loukis felt even more alert, poised, ready to defend what was his against his own mother.

'I'm pleased at least that you have her. The way you look at her…' Meredith trailed off. 'Was more than I ever looked at your father. But I do mean it. I want Annabelle with me and I'll do whatever it takes to get her back.'

And on that cryptic note, she drew Byron away towards the back of the yacht, where he could see a smaller speed-boat had slunk through the barrage of press boats following in their wake, up behind the yacht, and was being frantically moored out of the way of the jet stream of the engine.

Célia looked up at him, the concern clear in her face, and he couldn't help himself. He needed it, he needed her. His lips crashed down on hers, shocking them both, each feeding off the adrenaline, drawing strength and more from the heady impact of the kiss.

CHAPTER NINE

DUSK HAD FALLEN, casting the sea about them in an inky darkness that was pierced by the bright lights strung overhead. The deck was still full of guests, though the staff weaving through them with silver trays of champagne and canapés had lessened in the last hour as Célia and Loukis's departure grew closer.

A boat was to meet them and ferry them to Loukis's island home while the yacht returned the guests back to the port at Piraeus. Célia drew the silk wrap around her shoulders to ward off the sea breeze, undeterred by the large heaters placed strategically across the deck. She wasn't sure what had passed between Loukis and his mother, but ever since they had left, her fiancé-for-now had been distant. Oh, he'd played his part well, smiled and laughed with the guests, pronouncing him the happiest man, the luckiest. But that kiss had been full of so much more than expediency or efficiency to communicate their 'engagement'. It had shocked her, the ferocity of need that whipped through her, that she felt from *him*. Had it not been for the wolf whistles that had cut the kiss short, she would have been lost. Lost to him and to whatever it was that he had called forth.

And since then, he'd remained just out of reach. Never staying long in the same circle she was, hovering some distance away, ready with some excuse to withdraw. Having become so accustomed to his touch, his presence, the feel of him at her side, Célia felt strangely adrift. As if she'd done something wrong. As if she was being punished, or denied something, without explanation or understanding. It had nestled into the space she kept reserved for her father and her ex. And she hated it.

Had he too realised what she had? That they had spent the entire evening lying to their friends, their loved ones? That the happiness of the guests had started to grate because they were celebrating something that was not to be? Célia's heart ached a little at the thought and she chastised herself for it.

One of the reasons she had been happy to agree to Loukis's demand was because she would know where she stood. That he would not demand anything more than appearance. That there were clear lines that neither would broach.

But she wouldn't lie to herself. Not now. She knew her body's reaction to Loukis. She knew that she had somehow come to want him more than anything she had ever experienced before. In the last few weeks she had understood, appreciated and even liked him more for his need to protect his sister. The kind of protection that had never been afforded to her. She wanted to know what that was like. To be able to rely upon a man so strong in his conviction, so powerful, so…enthralling.

She had come to want to be the woman he saw. The proud, accomplished, driven woman who was just as powerful as he. And as she tried that woman on for size she was surprised to find how intoxicating that sense of power was, how…hedonistic.

It was with painful irony that she realised this just as Loukis seemed intent on withdrawing from her and she now looked upon their retreat to his island estate with trepidation. She knew what she wanted…but would he give that to her? She was not naïve. She knew that she had seen the flame of arousal and need in him. Knew that he was affected as she had been, not just by the kiss earlier, but each touch and caress that drew them inexplicably towards a point of no return. But she could also sense the barrier between them. The one that held him on one side and her on the other—an immoveable wall that she wanted to tear down. But could she risk it? Could she give into her desires, but still protect her heart?

Her heart wasn't involved, she told herself sternly. It wasn't what Loukis wanted and it certainly wasn't part of the deal. The irony was that although he needed the perfect fiancée, it wasn't real…so perhaps she didn't need to be so perfect. And it was precisely that which gave her desires, her wants, free rein.

A smartly dressed man in a Captain's uniform appeared at her side, informing her that it was time. Célia knew he meant that the boat had arrived to whisk her and Loukis away from their guests, but she couldn't help but feel that it was also some internal battle cry. That it was time. For her finally to ask for what she wanted, to demand it from him.

The guests laughed as Ella gave Célia one last hug, shouting demands to Loukis to bring her friend back safely, as if they were going on a holiday or, worse, that he might actually keep her. For ever.

The words hung in Loukis's mind, taunting him. He shouldn't have done it. The kiss had been over three hours ago now and he could still taste her. Feel her lips beneath his, the spike in his adrenaline washing away the bitterness of his encounter with Meredith, consuming all his thoughts and focus on the sensual delight Célia offered. She had returned his kiss with a fervour that had both shocked and aroused. Until the wolf whistles of the guests on the yacht had cut through the moment of madness.

He hadn't touched her since. Not even in the little ways he had become accustomed to doing, in the name of…he had been a fool. Lying to himself. Those touches had nothing to do with her getting used to him and had been only about him laying a hand on her. Teasing himself, testing himself, trying to prove to himself that he wasn't the playboy any more. That he could resist temptation.

In the last three years he *had* resisted the temptation of many beautiful women. He was most definitely not the reckless playboy of his youth. The problem was *Célia*. Not him. She had called to him like a siren from the very beginning. Even now, as he waved goodbye to the guests from the speedboat moored beside the yacht, he remembered their first encounter. She had presented an unusual challenge and, despite the hideous *beigeness* of her T-shirt at the time, he had still seen the beauty she worked so hard to hide.

But the challenge had morphed in the last few weeks, until the bright point of its edge had cut through the sensual miasma between them and he'd realised that the real threat would be to act on his desire for her.

The way you look at her...

His mother's voice taunted him even as he did take his fill. The yacht's Captain had taken her arm and was helping her down into the speedboat beside him. He observed a brief glimpse of smooth pale skin between the high skirt and the cropped top she wore, the way her hips swayed as she took her first steps towards him and the smile across her features and a thrill in her eyes he wanted to turn away from. For it was not excitement at the boat ride towards his island home, but something else. A deeper, darker pull, tempting him. Taunting him.

But the risk was too great. Hadn't Meredith shown that tonight? Nothing could come between himself and his custody of Annabelle. Not even the woman coerced into helping him get that very thing.

As he pulled down on the throttle of the boat he was piloting himself, he relished the roar of the engines, hoping that in some way they would burn away the ferocious need that held him tight in its grip.

They had moored at a jetty after about forty minutes on the speedboat. The noise from the twin engines making any form of communication impossible. Not that Célia had tried. She might know her own body's desires, but she could also tell his. Loukis had built a wall between them ever since that kiss. One that she wanted to tear down.

It was as if a line had been drawn in the sand—one she would readily cross, yet he remained on the other side. But it was his fault. He had started this, he had drawn this impossible need from within her and now she was angry. Angry that he was seemingly walking away.

Once again, his automatic sense of chivalry had been lost as he forged ahead up the dark path, leaving her to follow in his wake. Célia had been shut out before, so many times that the feeling was painfully familiar. But she wouldn't have it. Not this time.

As Loukis opened the front door to a sprawling estate, she saw none of the beauty and opulence she had come to expect from Loukis. She saw nothing but his back as he walked further into the property she really couldn't care less for.

'Don't do this. Don't ignore me,' she called after him as he stalked through the dark rooms offering only shapes in the gloom to identify their use.

'The bedroom is upstairs. There's no one here, so you can—'

'Don't. Ignore. Me.' The words held a barely leashed anger that had been brewing long before she had met Loukis.

'What do you want from me?' he demanded, spinning

to turn on her. The moonlight glinting through impossibly large windows picking out the harsh lines of anger on his features.

'I want you to stop playing. I want you to stop hiding.'

'Hiding?' he breathed out on a harsh laugh. 'You accuse *me* of hiding?'

'Yes. Right now, I am. Because you *are* hiding.'

He shook his head. 'Go to bed.'

'I'm not some child you can easily dismiss. I will not be sent to bed.' Her breath caught before she issued a demand of her own. 'Unless you are in it with me.'

'No.'

'Really? You were the one who said—'

'I know what I said,' he interrupted as if not wanting the reminder of his own demands. 'But I was wrong.'

'That must have hurt.'

'What?'

'Admitting that you were wrong.'

'Don't be—'

'Crass?' It was Célia that interrupted this time.

'Naïve!' he countered with anger. 'Do you think I can risk this? Meredith showing up tonight—'

'Has nothing to do with what is going on between us. So. Next?'

'Next what?'

'Next excuse to avoid what is going on between us.'

Loukis shook his head again, wondering how on earth Célia managed to oscillate between proud and determined and fearful and shy. He couldn't be here. He couldn't stand here and see her like this, because she was simply magnificent. Demanding what she wanted, powerful and righteous. And it was the most devastatingly attractive thing he'd ever seen.

She was a siren. Calling to him, calling *for* him. But he just couldn't. The risk was too great.

'There is nothing going on between us, other than a fake engagement.'

'Liar.'

She stalked towards him, capturing his gaze as the silky material unfurled around her legs, as the sensual pull in her eyes demanded, cajoled, taunted. She reached him, her head lifted towards his, the scent of her perfume soothing as much as enticing, the feel of her body's heat crashing against him more forcefully than the waves he'd battled to reach the island.

'Kiss me.'

He said nothing.

'Kiss me. Without the paparazzi watching. Without being on display. Show me, prove to me that there's nothing between us,' she demanded.

'I'm not playing this game.'

'This,' she said, reaching for his fiercely clenched jaw, 'is not a game any more.'

He didn't move. He couldn't. Because everything in him wanted to act, touch, taste. And there would be no turning back from that. So he stayed stock-still, as if made from marble. He had to.

She reached up on tiptoes and pressed a soft kiss against his lips. He resisted the gentle pressure at his neck from where she had reached, guiding him to her, deeper into her, hating that it must have felt like rejection to her, but unable to give in to her demand.

But a hint of the sweep of her tongue against his lips pierced his defences. Kiss after kiss, her mouth opening further in fractions that made him mad with need. The warm press of her breasts against his chest, her thighs against his within millimetres of where his hands had fisted by his sides.

And then, as if sensing his reluctance, she pulled away. And the look in her eyes crushed the air in his lungs. The raw yearning, need, and sadness in the large amber orbs was too much. His hands flew to her face, holding her, stopping her retreat and at the precise moment he should have walked away, he stepped forward, his mouth crashing down on hers and greedily taking everything she had to offer.

He breathed her in, his tongue demanding entrance, glorying in the feel of her beneath his lips and hands. He drew her to him as if he could consume her, as if he could steal something from her and keep it with him.

Need became a primal roar, echoing throughout his body, crying more, crying now. Only the soft moans Célia made cut through the raging pulse in his ears causing him to stop, to try and pull back the control he had lost so shockingly easily.

Their harsh breathing echoed between them. He saw the flash of her white teeth digging into a bottom lip he had just thoroughly ravished. It was too much. He wanted it for himself. And that was the problem. This wasn't about the custody battle, the press, or even his mother. He needed Célia for himself. And that was untenable.

'Is that what you wanted, Célia?' he demanded. 'To bring me to my knees? To make me beg?'

He made to turn away, the words bringing forth shocking images of exactly what he wanted to do to her, *for* her, but her hand reached for him before he could.

He had expected words, pleading, impassioned perhaps. But instead the silence remained as she lifted his hand and placed it high on her breast, covering her heart where he felt her pulse rage against his palm. A beat that echoed within him just as incessant, just as demanding, just as out of control.

'I am the one on my knees. I am the one begging,' she said resolutely.

'You should never have to beg, Célia. You are worth more than that.'

'I know my worth. I know yours. And I know what I want.'

The heat from her body beneath his hand wrapped around him, drawing him towards her, even as he fought every inch of it.

'I know what is at stake, Loukis. And I promise you, I would not jeopardise that. Ever.'

'This isn't about Annabelle, Célia. It's about you,' he said roughly. 'I am not capable of giving you what you deserve. Not now. Not ever.'

He had to say the words. Force them to his lips. It was the truth, the deepest truth he'd ever spoken to a woman. Célia deserved so much more than this. She deserved a future and he couldn't give her that.

'I understand.'

He had thought that would do it. That she would finally walk away, but instead, she placed her hand over his, where it still rested against her heart.

'And it doesn't change a thing.'

Célia's pulse sped under the heat of his palm secured by her own. She knew what she was saying, what she was asking him for. Neither of them were ready or willing for anything more than perhaps just this night. But she would not walk away from this easily. If, for even a second, she thought this heady, half-mad desire was one-sided, she never would have raised it. But she knew. She knew he felt what she did, wanted what she did. It was as if acknowledging, owning, the truth of their desire was the only thing that could save her from the precipice she was hurtling towards. As if he were the only thing that could save her from it.

He searched her gaze as if hunting for a flaw, a contradiction, a doubt in her mind. But there was none.

She became so aware of his hand on her chest, resting beneath her own, as if that one point of connection bound them together on the brink of action or inaction. Her body overly sensitised, wanting more, desperate for more. But he had to choose this. She couldn't force this on him no matter how much she felt he wanted it.

This time she turned away, feeling as if she had lost the battle. Until his fingers wrapped around her arm, drawing her back to him in a kiss that obliterated the memories of all other kisses.

She opened her mouth to the pressure of his lips, his tongue, let him angle her head to where he wanted it, because it was so impossibly good. Everything in her rose to cry *yes*. This was what she had wanted. Loukis, unfettered, let loose amongst the pleasure they were seeking.

As his hands released their hold and travelled across her body, Célia revelled in the heat of them through the material, and then, when they reached the expanse of uncovered skin at her waist, his fingers hooking at her hip and pulling her against him roughly.

Gone was civility, gone was propriety, gone were the rules that had both bound them together and kept them apart. Every touch, every kiss made her feel worshipped. As if he were gaining as much from her own pleasure as she was.

It was a feeling she had never experienced before. The riotous cascade of sensation, desire, was hedonistic. Beneath her palms his chest was firm, as she fisted his shirt in her hands and drew him closer. It wasn't enough. She feared, silently, that it might never be enough.

He stepped back, pulling her with him, until he came up against the wall, imprisoning himself within her embrace. He reached for her knee beneath the silky folds of the skirt, hooking it over his hip and bringing her core against the hard ridge of his arousal.

Instinctively she arched against his chest, her hands moving upwards to frame his face, exulting in the feeling of his palms against the skin on her shoulders and arms, the warmth and security she experienced as he wrapped an arm around her and held her to him. It was an anchor in the storm of emotions that threatened to wash her out to sea. Because she trusted him.

The thought took her by surprise, momentarily stopping her. Loukis pulled back, releasing her from his hold, his breathing ragged, his eyes whispering concern.

'You want to stop—'

'No,' she said hastily, interrupting him. *Never,* she thought silently.

'Because—'

'I know what I want, Loukis. Do you?' she demanded as she stepped back from him, worried that his questions, his second guesses might be the undoing of her.

His dark gaze morphed from concern to absolute conviction. 'Yes. Célia. I know exactly what I want.'

He pinned her with a gaze full of predatory power.

'I want to see you.'

It wasn't a demand, or a statement. It was a wish, one she felt in her very bones. One that lent her a power over Loukis she could never have imagined.

She reached for the fastening at the side of her top and released the tight material binding a chest she wanted to bare to him, to his touch. She drew it over her shoulders and head and cast it aside, relishing the flare in his dark eyes as he took her in, his gaze sweeping over her midnight-blue lace bra, to the skirt at her narrow waist.

All of you.

He didn't have to say it. She felt it as if he had whispered it against her skin. She reached for the zip behind her and drew it down, releasing the band and allowing the silk to drop and pool at her feet. He stood there, as if holding himself back, as if fighting some invisible leash, straining against his desire for her and some last shred of resistance.

She stepped out of the circle of her skirts and walked towards him in her underwear and heels. Never before had she felt so powerful, so attractive, so much herself. She was owning it all, just as much as she was owning her desire for him.

His hands fisted by his sides, still holding himself from her. From what they could have together. Hers went to the buttons on his shirt, slowly releasing them from his neck, down to his waist, pulling at the shirt to release it from his trousers.

He let her push the cotton from his shoulders, until he stood there, shirtless. His body was a marvel of muscle, and she gloried in it, her fingers tracing over dips and swells, causing him to inhale swiftly as he flinched.

When her hands went to the buckle on his belt, it was as if the spell that had held him back had been lifted, and he reached for her, pulling her upward, causing her to wrap her legs around his waist. They sought each other's lips at the same time, the feeling of his tongue crashing against the sensations of skin against skin as he walked them through some darkened maze of furniture she couldn't have navigated.

He brought her to an open part of the living room, the plush soft cream carpet visible in the light of the moon, shafting through large windows that formed the side of the estate.

He laid her down gently, gazing at her from above, and she was unable to take her eyes from him as he made swift work of his trousers. He stood before her naked and glorious, and everything she'd ever wanted.

He came to her then, a kiss full of desire and want, drenching her in a need that she could barely contain. His body against hers, skin against skin, was almost, but not, enough. His fingers snapped the clasp of her bra and he drew the straps down her shoulders and cast it aside. His mouth tracing the path his fingers had made, pressing open-mouthed kisses against her skin, drawing cries of pleasure from her.

She arched into his mouth, his touch, gasped when his fingers found the taut nipple of one breast, then another. His hand swept down her body, between her legs, the firm pressure confident, shocking and devastating to her arousal.

She wished the thin material separating them gone, but his hand swept over her again and again, as if relishing the barrier between them, the last there was to be had, teasing them both on the brink of what they both desperately wanted.

He pressed kisses beneath her breast, trailing down over her stomach, her hip, and lower, to where he pulled at the band of her thong, following the path of its removal with his mouth. At her feet, he removed the scrap of lace, and took up her ankle, delighting in the slow play of undoing the clasp of her shoe, removing one heel and then another.

She looked up at him, knowing she was now completely bare to him.

He reached for his wallet, discarded with his trousers, and sheathed himself with a condom, his eyes not once leaving hers, the promise in them not once faltering.

She expected him to lean forward, to rush towards the end of their pleasure, but he didn't. He trailed his hands up her calves, over her knees and gently pressed at her thighs until her legs lay either side of his where he kneeled before her. His hand returned to between her legs, instinctively causing her to want to draw them together, to hold him to her or hide from him, even she couldn't tell.

She felt his thumb press gently against her clitoris, just held there as if waiting for her to get used to his touch, as if waiting for her to unfurl beneath him. Because that was what it felt like. An unfurling. Her hips shifted, trying to create the pleasurable friction he was withholding, and he smiled, as if knowing exactly what she wanted. His free hand went to her hip, holding her in place there too, and she felt utterly under his command.

He waited until she had stopped, until she had succumbed and then, only then did his fingers start to move. His dark erotic gaze not once leaving hers, as if he wanted to see what he was doing to her, as if it fed his own desire.

His thumb moved over and over and over her clitoris, and her head fell back under the onslaught of pleasure he was wringing from her. When his fingers entered her she gasped, desperately trying to hold on, desperately clinging to the edge of the precipice she felt herself hurtling towards.

Incomprehensible words, cries, pleas escaped her lips and she was unable to prevent her hips rising, giving him more, wanting more from him. He controlled her, he orchestrated every pleasurable sound and feeling, drawing a shiver of damp heat across her body. Trembling now, she was entirely his, owned, possessed, inside and out.

'Come for me,' he demanded of her. And she did. The waves of ecstasy crashing over her, body and soul wiped clean and mindless to anything other than pleasure.

* * *

In all his life, Loukis had never seen anything more beautiful, more humbling. The pink slashes across Célia's cheeks, the erratic rise and fall of her breasts, the way her legs had pulled tight against his thighs as she had reached her orgasm just made him want her more.

A need, painful in its intensity, stung the back of his throat, as he leaned forward to claim her mouth with his. He wanted it all, every gasp, sigh, cry, breath, captured by him. Positioning himself between her legs, he waited until her eyes found his once more. He wanted her with him in this, he wanted to see her as he possessed her, as surely as she had possessed him. When her tiger's eyes met his, desire blackening her gaze, he felt it in his soul.

Slowly, inch by inch, he pressed into her, relishing the incredible feeling of her, his heart stuttering in his chest as she tightened around him, until he could go no further. Just as slowly he withdrew, teasing himself and her. After the frantic pace of their kisses and her orgasm, this slow descent into sensual madness was indescribable and utterly unique to Célia.

Before he could question why, sensations and need welled within him, his body demanding action, demanding more, demanding *now.* But he held himself back, slowly weaving an intoxicating spell as he entered her and withdrew again and again and again.

Her body began to move, showing only a fraction of the restlessness he felt roaring through his body. He captured her mouth with his, before her pleas and moans of pleasure could undo him, drawing out the inevitable moment when their climax would end this. Because he realised he didn't want it to end. He delighted in her pleasure, his no less for it. In fact, his need was heightened by hers.

He felt her hands around his thighs, holding him deep

within her, she arching against him as if wringing more and more pleasure from it and no longer could he hold back. He thrust into her deep and fast, her cries of need urging him on, faster, deeper, until he could no longer tell whose cry demanded more, whose pleasure was greater, whose need was more. Until he realised that it didn't matter because, at that moment, they were one.

As if the very thought released the last vestige of his control, an orgasm more powerful, more incredible than any he had ever known roared through them both, calling for hers, demanding hers and together they fell beneath moonbeams and starlight.

CHAPTER TEN

CÉLIA WAS WOKEN by the sounds of conversation, slowly rousing her from the deepest sleep she'd had in years. When her eyes opened, the curtains, the bed beneath her, the partial view from the window jarred painfully.

She rose immediately, her mind taking a moment to catch up. She remembered Loukis picking her up at some point in the night, and bringing her to his bed, where they had once again lost themselves in each other. Her body ached, but it felt strong. She stretched, leaning into the echoes of the sensual pleasure he had drawn from her. A blush rose to her cheeks at the memories from the night before, warming her skin just as a peal of childish giggles filtered from down the hall.

Annabelle.

She cast a glance around the room, suddenly very conscious that she was naked. Wrapping the sheet around her, she left the bed and padded over to the wardrobe carefully concealed behind mirrors that had teased and taunted them last night as they had…

Célia cut the train of thought in its tracks. She pulled open a door, hoping to find something of Loukis's that she could wear, but once she caught sight of the contents she stopped, hovering in shock. The clothes she had chosen from the stylist lined the length of the hanging rail, shoes tucked neatly at the bottom, drawers—she saw as she pulled them open—full of underwear.

'You will share my bed.'

Last night had been her decision. And she had known that this was part of the bargain they had struck. But what did that mean for the forthcoming evening? And the evenings after?

As Célia showered, she was torn between concerns for the future and the heady memories of last night, her body certainly desirous of another night spent in his arms. Arms that had held her as she'd had the most powerful sexual experience of her life. Marc had been dutiful in bed with her, as if it were something 'to be done'. And she could see now that even that was part of Marc's plan. It wasn't and never had been about her, but what she could give him.

And no matter how differently Loukis saw her, treated her, she was still exactly the same to him. She could give him the reputation and the situation he needed for Annabelle. She couldn't, wouldn't let her heart make another mistake and think for a second it was about anything else. Hadn't Loukis himself said as much?

'I am not capable of giving you what you deserve. Not now. Not ever.'

She hated that the deepest irony was that it was Loukis that deserved more. Because she *wasn't* the perfect fiancée he needed. She could never risk him finding out the truth of what had happened with her father. Not only because of the damage it could do to his custody claim…but the damage she feared it could do to her.

After showering and dressing Célia made her way down the hall, towards the sounds coming from what she could only assume was a kitchen or dining room. It turned out to be both. A beautiful sprawling open kitchen and eating area backed by the most gorgeous view of the Greek island where Loukis had made his summer home.

The moment Annabelle caught sight of her, she jumped up from the table, rushed around and came to a startling halt about two feet from where Célia stood. A shy, but utterly thrilled expression on her face.

'Hi!'

'Bonjour, ma chérie.'

'I told you she'd call me Cherry,' she cried victoriously to Loukis, before rushing up the stairs in the far corner with indistinguishable words about wanting 'to show Célia'.

Célia finally looked to her fiancé. Her *fake* fiancé. He was studying her over the rim of the small espresso cup he held to his lips, stopped just before he could take a sip.

She met his eyes and her heart thudded wildly in her chest. His gaze was proprietorial as if, unspoken, he had claimed her. As if he knew that she knew it too. It was full of promise, of heat, reminding her of what he had whispered to her in the night. Of the things he wanted to do to her, for her, instantly igniting an arousal, a need, that only he could meet.

'Good morning,' Loukis said, his tone as rough and deep as her thoughts.

She nodded and took a seat opposite him at the table, forcing her eyes to the view from the window, rather than the one in front of her.

'Sleep well?' he asked, a smile playing at the lips that had ravished her for hours the night before.

As if the gentle taunt called forth some of the power she had felt that night, she replied, 'Very. And you?'

'Not so much. I was distracted a little by a—'

'Here! Look,' Annabelle said, rushing back into the room and dumping something small and fluffy on Célia's lap, cutting through the undercurrents of their exchange like a knife through butter.

'It's Mr Cat,' Annabelle said proudly of the distinctly dog-like toy.

'Mr Cat,' Célia repeated. 'Nice to meet you,' she said,

taking the strange fluffy figure's paw between her thumb and finger, shaking it in greeting, and trying hard to stifle the shocked, choking sound coming from Loukis.

'What happened to Jameson?' Loukis asked.

'He lives with Mummy. But Mr Cat can live with you,' Annabelle stated, seemingly ignorant of the slight flinch that shook Loukis's body. 'We're going to the beach today,' Annabelle announced, clearly of a mind that Célia would be in attendance. She was torn. Part of her wanted to spend the day whiling away the hours with Loukis and Annabelle, and the other wanted to hide, to retreat into work for the day, putting as much emotional distance between them as possible. Because this happy family unit…it was both tempting and terrifying.

Loukis had sensed Célia's hesitation at the breakfast table, but refused to feel guilty at joining Annabelle in her not so gentle persuasion. Protests about not having a costume were refuted by the simple fact he had made sure that there was swimwear included in her new wardrobe. Objections based on work had been cast aside as it was a Sunday. Unable to prevent himself, any further refusals were silenced by a quick, firm kiss on her lips, which had apparently delighted Annabelle, whose enthusiastic squeals were punctuated by fist pumps and cries of 'yes', and shocked Célia into agreement.

Perhaps he had underestimated his little sister's happy expectations and he refused to think of the time when that would come to a natural conclusion after the custody hearing. Because he was beginning to see Célia as more than a means to an end. Though what that actually meant eluded him.

For so many years he had remained firmly unattached. Determinedly so. Convinced that any kind of relationship was based on nothing more than delusional romantic notions that simply aligned with financial avarice, sexual desire and, on occasion, pregnancy—unexpected or otherwise.

But as he watched Annabelle and Célia play in the surf, the rolling waves crashing against the private beach, the sun-kissed skin across Célia's shoulders and the happy smile on his sister's face, he was beginning to understand the appeal. Walls were shifting within him as he felt a sense of something greater than himself and his goal of custody. But that only served to make him disconcerted, his natural inclination to turn away from a lifelong-held belief that would not be shaken by one night.

Not that it would be one night, he realised. Not now that he'd had an exquisite taste of Célia.

Annabelle had finally grown tired of handstands and underwater somersaults and made her way to where he sat ready and waiting with towels, drinks and, more importantly to his sister, crisps. Behind her, Célia seemed to drag her feet, as if reluctant to return to the tactile interaction of yesterday. Of before.

He made space for them to sit on the large beach blanket they'd brought with them, noticing that Annabelle seemed distracted as she wasn't head down in the packet of crisps.

'Nanny? You okay?'

She sighed in a way that made her sound much older than her ten years. 'If I…if the custurdy thing says I have to go and live with Mummy, what happens to you?'

Despite Annabelle's mispronunciation, it was on his lips to deny that she would ever go and live with Meredith, but he caught Célia's focused look. As if she knew what he was about to say and desperate for him to change it. He'd done and was doing everything in his power to ensure that the custody case went his way, but he wouldn't make a promise to her that he might not be able to keep. He remembered what Célia had said that evening after the video call. He remembered her warning to be there as a support for Annabelle and had taken it to heart.

'Annabelle, no matter what happens, who the courts decide you will live with, there will always be a safe place for you here with me.'

His answer didn't seem to solve whatever his sister was wrestling with.

'If you're worried, I'll do my best to make sure that what you want is heard.'

To his horror, tears glowed within Annabelle's eyes.

'But…what if…what if I don't know what I want?'

'What do you mean, *chérie*?' Célia asked, putting her arm around Annabelle's shoulders.

'What if I don't know who I want to be with?' Annabelle whispered, looking at Célia as if she was too fearful to look at him.

Pain cut through Loukis. Pain and anger at his mother. Anger that Meredith had caused so much confusion and hurt in his sister. Because all he could see was having to pick up the pieces. Again. Of the eventual moment that his mother abandoned her. Again. And deeper than that, the ache with which he viewed his future without the little girl who had come to mean so much to him.

Célia looked up at him then, as if willing him to say the right thing. There was compassion in her gaze, too, but that seemed to hurt just as much. He forced the words to his lips. 'Annabelle, if you would like to live with your mother—'

'No! Well, maybe? I don't know.'

'And that's okay, sweetheart,' insisted Célia. 'Even adults don't always know what they want. You had fun with Meredith in Texas?'

'Yes, but I have fun here with Loukis too.'

'I can see,' she said, smiling. 'And your friends…'

'Are here. At school and Leya—she's my bestest friend.'

'Byron seems nice,' Célia pressed on while Loukis didn't feel capable of forming words at all.

'He is. He laughs a lot and has a funny accent.'

'And your mummy?'

Loukis marvelled that Célia was managing to bring out exactly the information that he wanted from his sister, who shrugged and seemed to burrow into herself.

'I don't know.'

Célia laughed gently, breaking some of the tension gripping both Loukis and his sister in a fierce hold.

'I haven't known how to feel about my dad for nearly five years,' she confided.

'Really?' Annabelle returned, wide-eyed.

'*Really.* There are times when I remember good things. Happy things. And times when, I know that he made me sad. Sometimes they get mixed up together and sometimes they feel very far apart.'

It was, Célia realised, the first time that she'd admitted to feeling something other than betrayal from her father. Ever. But that didn't stop it from being true. She had loved, *did* love him. But that love had been damaged by his betrayal and she could only imagine that being half of what Annabelle might be feeling, and at ten she quite possibly had no idea how to explain that. Especially to Loukis who, until recently, had simply pushed through with determination to ensure that Meredith came nowhere near her.

'Do you still speak to him?' Annabelle asked.

'Not for quite a while.'

'And your mummy?'

Célia sighed, and smiled, not realising quite how sad she looked in that moment. 'We've spoken more recently.'

'I spoke to my mum yesterday. She looked pretty and said she was going to your party.'

'Nanny.' Loukis waited until he had his sister's attention and Célia's. He seemed to be struggling with what he had to say. 'No matter what happens, I will always be here for you. No matter where you are in the world, or who you are with. You are my family. Nothing will ever change that.'

Célia felt as if a giant bell had been struck within her and as it swung back and forth, shivering tremors in its wake, her heart lurched in time and in tune. They were the words she had never heard, nor felt from her own father, let alone her ex-fiancé. But to hear them from Loukis's lips made her want, made her ache to hear them spoken for her. By him. She looked away at the horizon where the sea met the sky to avoid Loukis's penetrating gaze. He would see, he would know.

As she'd watched him with Annabelle, seeing him with his friends Yalena and Iannis, and with her own, Ella and Roman, Loukis had morphed from an irascible client, a renowned playboy, into something more, *someone* more.

'I am not capable of giving you what you deserve. Not now. Not ever.'

'But you don't like her,' she heard Annabelle announce, even as Célia focused on a small fishing boat further out in the sea.

'How I feel about her doesn't affect how *you* feel about her, and it won't affect how…*she* feels about you.'

The conclusion of Loukis's sentence felt forced, but her heart soared that he was trying. Trying to present a blank canvas for his sister, so that she might be able to forge a relationship with her mother that was positive, even as she knew he would hate that.

But, as with all things that flew too high, they had to come down, and Célia's heart swooped when she realised that his words reminded her of her last conversation with her mother.

Célia had demanded to know why her mother had sided with her father. Why she couldn't seem to understand how betrayed and lost Célia felt and why she wasn't there for her.

'He is my husband, Célia. If I held him accountable for every little—'

'Little? You're saying this is little?'

'Non, ma fille. Pas du tout. *But over the years we have both made mistakes...parental ones. He has forgiven me mine as I forgive him his. Because my feelings for him, whether you like it or not, are separate from my feelings for you. One day, I hope, you will understand these mistakes and that they were not intended—'*

'This wasn't just a mistake, Maman. It was an act. An intentional, business-focused act that took my idea and used it for the most atrocious means.'

'And those "atrocious means" have funded our entire lives until now, Célia. You can't deny—'

'Célia?'

She looked up to find Loukis standing above her, his body blocking out the powerful sun, the items they had brought with them to the beach packed up and even Annabelle standing ready to leave.

Had she been the one in the wrong? Had she reacted to her mother's response and drawn a line in the sand between herself and her parents from her words? Célia had been so hurt and so betrayed, had spent so long feeling unloved and unwanted that it had felt as if her mother had chosen her father. But looking back on it now, she realised that her mother had been trying to tell her that she loved her and Célia was the one to reject that love. Suddenly it seemed absolutely vital that she speak to her mother. Now, before she could talk herself out of it.

'Why don't you go on? I'll join you in a bit.'

Loukis's gaze showed confusion and something almost like concern, but he nodded and took Annabelle's hand. She watched them make their way back up to the house before reaching for her phone with trembling fingers.

Something had happened on the beach. What exactly it was, Loukis couldn't be sure, but Célia was…different. Lighter? Her laughter mingled with Annabelle's and it sounded, felt, freer somehow. The looks she cast his way were unguarded, and what he saw in her eyes was beginning to burn through the barriers around his heart.

For the first time ever, he wanted more. More than the façade of a fake fiancée. More than just one night with her. More than just the time limit he'd placed on their relationship. He wanted long dinners with friends, wanted to show her the places he loved to visit, wanted to see her eyes widen with wonder and feel the rich sound of her beautiful laugh roll over his naked skin.

It had been a constant whisper throughout the day, seductive and enticing. But he wouldn't, couldn't, give into it. The custody hearing was only a few days away and he had to keep his focus on that.

But after? his internal voice teased. *What then?*

Over dinner he'd been distracted by images of a future with Célia, of years not months, of days as well as nights. Of her growing round with his child, of a family he'd never thought he'd want.

That was why he'd spent at least an hour in his study, after Célia had gone to bed. Because if he'd gone with her, he couldn't honestly say what he would have done. What he would have begged for, pleaded for. It was a weakness. It could be exploited. He'd done so only once in his life and he'd learned his lesson then and there. Everything had a price. Even love could be bought. His mother's certainly had. And the only price he could afford to pay at the moment was Annabelle's. Nothing more.

He glanced at the clock. Surely by now Célia would be asleep and he could persevere through the fresh torture of having her in his bed and not touching her. Even the thought of it sent need directly to his groin. Even the memory of the sounds she had made the night before drove an arousal so fierce he nearly shook with the need to restrain it. Just the thought of the delicious taste of her was enough to have him swallow the last inch of whiskey in an attempt to blot out the yearning to taste her again.

Enough. He had more control over himself than this. He could and would leave her untouched this night. And as if to prove it to himself, he stalked determinedly down the hallway towards his bedroom.

Two strides into the room, stealthily as humanly possible, the bedside lamp flicked light across the room and revealed that Célia was very much awake and very much expecting him.

'Thought I'd be asleep?' she asked, no censure or accusation in her tone, just curiosity and that openness that had taunted him all afternoon.

'Hoped,' he said with something like a grimace pulling at his features.

'Because?'

'Because I'd wanted to avoid this,' he replied honestly.

'My conversation is so terrifying to you that it kept you from your bed?'

He sat on the side of the bed, his back to her momentarily as he pulled off his shoes and reached for his belt. As his fingers gripped it, he remembered last night, he remembered everything.

'I spoke to my mother this afternoon.'

Her words struck him still. Frowning, he turned to look at her, searching for traces of hurt or sadness. The swift desire to protect her from any source of pain shocking him with its intensity.

'How did it go?' he couldn't help himself from asking.

She looked sad and happy at the same time. Both caused a shifting sensation in his chest. Her beautiful amber eyes were glistening with tears, but the smile across her lips was sure.

'Good. It was…' she sighed '…good. And I wanted to thank you.'

'Why?' Loukis replied, genuinely confused.

'I wouldn't have made that phone call had it not been for what you said, what you did, for Annabelle today.'

He felt the invisible tendrils wound tight around his heart begin to unfurl, even as he would call them back.

'I did only as you suggested,' he dismissed.

'But you gave her, you gave *me*, the space within which we could find…peace. Safety. I want you to know that.'

'I don't—'

'Please don't dismiss this,' she asked.

His jaw clenched, anger and something like fear rearing their heads at her words. He stood and started to stalk towards the bathroom.

'Wait. Please?'

He stopped, but refused to turn, bracing himself for what he knew was to come.

'I think… I think that it might be what you are doing too.'

He rounded on her then. 'One conversation with *your* mother convinces you that you know *me*? That you know my—' He cut himself off before he could release the word he refused to admit to.

'Pain? The pain of being ignored by a parent? Of being rejected?'

'I wasn't ignored by my mother, Célia. She chose to leave. She chose to accept the money my father offered her in exchange for sole custody.'

'What?' she asked, horror dawning in her eyes as her hand flew to her mouth as if to stifle a gasp.

'Ten million euros. That was the price my mother accepted to be free of me. I had no culpability in that whatsoever. It was not my doing, my offer, or my suggestion.' Because there was no financial amount that would have made him reject his mother. No matter what highs or lows she had inflicted on him. *That* was the weakness he feared. *That* was the bitter truth he'd realised about himself that day. That he would have done anything to keep her with him. Anything. And Meredith had done nothing.

'No. You're right. It wasn't your doing, Loukis.'

'I know that. I just said—'

'Do you?'

It infuriated him that she was so calm. She could have been talking about the weather. Her gentle words were tearing gaping holes in his heart and she sat there poised and perfect.

'Do you really?' she asked again. 'Or, deep down, do you blame yourself?'

'What do you want me to say, Célia? You want me to say that I didn't learn, at the age of fifteen, my value was ten million euros? That it didn't hurt to be sold to my father in exchange for her freedom? To admit that I wasn't enough to keep her?'

The words were ripped from his throat, burning and tearing at the soft flesh, making his tone guttural and harsh, even to his own ears.

'No. I want you to admit that you *do* deserve more. That you *are* worthy of her love.'

That you are worthy of mine, his greedy, desperate inner voice filled in the silence between her words.

'You might not be ready to and that's okay. But I want you to know that I think you are. Worthy. Of that, of more than what you have limited yourself to.'

He turned back towards the bathroom, his jaw clenched so hard, he feared he might crack a tooth. His fists balled where they hung at his sides, the pulse raging through his blood so loud it blocked out the sound of her leaving the bed and coming up behind him, so that when he felt her hand on his shoulder he flinched.

He let himself be pulled around to face her. Let her seek out his gaze, unable to shutter the effect her words had had on him.

'I see so much when I look at you, Loukis. I see—'

He cut off her words with a kiss fuelled with need, pain and want. Need for her, pain for himself and want for what he couldn't have. Because he couldn't, wouldn't hear the words that would follow. The promise of feelings, of love, he believed she wouldn't be able to fulfil, for the sheer simple fact that no one else in his life had done so. Not his mother, nor his father, changed for ever after his wife's betrayal. And if they couldn't…

His chaotic thoughts veered away from the darkness as a starburst of light burned through him at her touch, at the way her hands—placed either side of his face—anchored him to her, focusing him on her.

How did she do this? How did she take his hurt and wash over it with acceptance and more? How did she see to the heart of him, yet join him rather than abandon him? The answer, he feared, would be more devastating than any lie he could tell himself. Because if she could love him, then why hadn't his parents? Somehow that thought only compounded the pain. All of it.

Within the kiss, her tongue teased, and fingers taunted, the little moans of pleasure falling from her lips found safe haven within him as he greedily consumed everything she had to give, despite his thoughts and fears.

He was done roasting himself over hot coals, the sensual web Célia was weaving drawing him in deeper to her, demanding more. Demanding everything. And as he laid her back on the bed, he feared that he would do it. Pay any damn price for everything she had to offer.

CHAPTER ELEVEN

DURING THE COURSE of the week on the island, Célia had worked a magic over Loukis that he couldn't account for. Under her steady gaze, full of a confidence in something he didn't want to put name to, a sense of rightness that he'd never felt before settled in his chest.

It was for this, and this reason only, that he got out of the limousine, stalked round the back of the car, and opened Célia's car door with a smile full and secure despite the fact that they were about to walk into a court hearing where he would confront his mother. He knew, he *felt*, that it would all be okay. That the courts would see Meredith for who she truly was—the person who had abandoned not one, but two children, the person who was clearly only interested in playing at being a mother to secure a rich American fiancé with strong family values—and that he could put the whole thing behind him and move forward. Move forward with Annabelle *and* Célia.

She looked glorious today. In a russet-coloured dress that veed between her breasts and tied at her hip, the silk pouring over her gorgeous shapely legs. It wasn't overtly sexy, more…confident and assured. He loved seeing her like this. He loved the way her eyes flared as she placed her hand in his, the promise in them echoing from the night before and leading towards the night to come.

They met his lawyers at the entranceway to the building and made their introductions, before being led into a small office within the building that they had been assigned for preparation and briefings.

Never ones for wasting their obscenely expensive time, his lawyers got right down to business, outlining the way that the day would run, the rules and regulations of the court for Célia's benefit. Although they were in Greece, with so many English-speaking individuals involved the proceedings would be undertaken with a translator present if needed.

They outlined the strategies to counter the areas of contention, his reputation, the natural leaning for the court to side with the mother, both being met by his new engagement, and Meredith's previous patterns of behaviour. As Loukis's fiancée and therefore someone who would be a very important part of Annabelle's life and upbringing, she would be providing a character statement not only for Loukis, but of herself. They were scheduled for just before lunch and until then Célia would be able to sit in the gallery. Even though it was a closed hearing, in order to protect Annabelle from the intense public interest, the associated individuals were allowed to stay.

'And your investigators haven't been able to find anything on Byron?' he asked, hopeful of perhaps this last reprieve.

'Clean as a whistle. He's exactly who he appears to be. A rich oil baron, longing for a family and desperately in love with your—with Meredith. Loukis, I know that you had expected to receive a financial request from her. I'm assuming you haven't?'

'No,' he said grimly.

'Shame. It would have made things easier. But I'm confident that the judge will find for us.'

He felt Célia's hand reach for his, entwining her fingers with his, and the pad of his thumb brushed over her engagement ring. Suddenly he thought it *was* a shame. A shame that he had given her such a beautiful ring for show and not for her.

He shook his head. He needed to focus. There would be time. Time for Célia and for them later. Now, he needed to head his mother off at the pass.

'Ready?' demanded the lawyer.

With one last glance at Célia, who was glorious with belief and assurance ringing her eyes, he stood. 'I'm ready.'

Despite outward appearances, Célia was worried. It was only when she took her seat behind the table where Loukis and his lawyers faced the judge that she allowed her mask to slip a little. She knew that Loukis needed her assurance, her faith so she had given it freely. But she hadn't missed the way that Loukis had almost unfurled in the time spent on the island, relaxed into the strange unspoken forward step their relationship had taken.

The night after her conversation with her mother had been like the last burst of a dam, the water punching through its final barrier. They had spoken for a long time, and Célia had tried to explain what she'd been feeling then, why she'd reacted the way she had. And her mother had told her how she might have disagreed with her husband but was trying to love them both in her own way. And Célia had finally accepted that love. And with that had come the realisation that she loved Loukis. She had felt it, she had wanted to tell him then that she had fallen for him. For the wonderful, incredible man she saw when she looked at him. But he had prevented her words and at the time she had understood. But in the days that followed, his excitement, the eager anticipation for the forthcoming custody hearing, the little verbal slips he made in suggesting plans that reached beyond this point, beyond their allotted few months of engagement, had made her hope.

And it was that hope that scared her. Because she knew that she would have to tell him. Tell him the truth of what her designs had been used for. Only then would she be truly free to love and be loved. She had to trust that he would accept her. All of her, including her imperfections. She wanted it so much, she ached.

'All rise.'

After all the carefully orchestrated publicity stunts, the engagement party, the perfectly cultivated relationship between them, the court hearing seemed oddly mundane. The introductions by the judge and each of the lawyers held a patterned rhythm of formal decorum that swept away the early morning hours and all the while, Célia couldn't help but think of what Annabelle would be doing with her friend Leya. They had planned to visit the park and then the zoo, Annabelle now fixated on a future as a vet.

As Loukis took the stand Célia cast a look towards Meredith and Byron, the latter catching her gaze and producing a smile full of warmth, completely at odds with the antagonism palpable between Meredith and her son. Haltingly she smiled back, Meredith catching the shared glance and frowning before something passed across her features. Something almost victorious.

Nervously she focused her attention back to the answers Loukis was giving to his own lawyers. He outlined the existing housing and care he was providing for Annabelle, letting them guide his answers to how difficult and traumatic it had been for her to be abandoned by her mother. The raw pain he expressed at his initial feelings of helplessness at his sister's misery was felt by all. To her credit, a pale Meredith seemed contrite and distraught to hear of it. His lawyers didn't miss a single thing that would give them an edge over the opposing counsel.

It was Meredith's lawyers' turn next, probing gently at his own feelings towards Meredith, suggesting that perhaps it was his own abandonment that had coloured his feelings over the situation. Célia's heart pounded in her chest to see him so exposed, but to her surprise they seemed sympathetic towards him. Not even touching on his own reputation. Something that even Loukis seemed surprised by.

By the time they indicated that they had no further questions, Loukis, his lawyers and Célia were confused. All of their attention had been so focused on defending assumed attack from that quarter, the sheer fact that they hadn't gone down that path made it seem as if they didn't even want to win the case.

'Ms d'Argent? If you would?'

Célia took a deep breath, gratefully received a supportive smile from Loukis and made her way towards the chair to the right of the judge. Focusing on answering Loukis's lawyers' questions helped some of the nerves Célia felt rising within her, ebbing and flowing, sometimes jerking at the spike of adrenaline when she had to pause and consider her words and how they might be interpreted by the opposition. But she answered them truthfully. Yes, she had met Loukis through work, but that relationship had developed. Yes, she had met Annabelle and taken the lovely little girl into her heart. No, she didn't have personal experience in parenting, but understood what it would mean for her future with Loukis if he were to become guardian of Annabelle and was one hundred per cent in support of it and was looking forward to being in her life. Yes, she had relocated to Greece to be with him, and most definitely yes thought that Loukis would be a wonderful parent.

With their thanks for her time, Loukis's lawyers sat down and Meredith's stood.

'Ms d'Argent, you have not always been CEO of Chariton Endeavours, have you?'

'No, the company was formed three years ago with Ella Black, a school friend.'

'And before that?'

'Before Chariton?'

'Yes.'

Célia shrugged. 'I was at university in Paris.'

'And what did you study there?'

'A degree in Humanities and—'

'But you started out with a different degree, no?'

Célia frowned, her heart beginning to pound in her chest. She cast a glance towards Meredith, to see a vindictive edge to her gaze. She *knew.* She turned to Loukis, wanting him to make it stop, needing him to. Because if he didn't, Loukis would lose everything and it would be her fault. A cold sweat broke out across her shoulder blades, sending shivers along her skin.

'Ms d'Argent? Please answer the question.'

'I… My university education began with a degree in mathematics and computer sciences.'

'And it was that which led you to an internship with Paquet Industries.'

Although Célia was looking at the lawyer, she saw Loukis lean to the man next to him, a frown marking his features, and confusion emanating from their table.

I'm so sorry, Loukis.

Fear and rage welled within her, for him, for herself. She knew she should have told him. Told him the true extent of what her father had done with her plans. But she'd thought those records were sealed. That no one would ever find out.

'Yes,' she said meekly.

'And while you were there, you had worked on technical specifications for a missile guidance system.'

'No.'

The lawyer's eyes blazed with the same intensity as Meredith's had, as if sensing victory.

'Need I remind you that even though this is a custody hearing, anything you say must be the truth, or it will be seen as perjury?'

'You do not. The specifications I was working on were for drone guidance systems for agricultural use in developing countries,' she said shakily.

'There is no record of that.'

'Those records are sealed.'

'Which might have been the case five years ago, but six months ago, François Paquet licensed the patent for his missile technology under IEPRA guidelines and as such they became a matter of public record.'

All Célia could hear was the roar of her own pulse. She felt as if her chest were about to explode.

'So. Do you deny that you developed technical specifications for a drone missile system that has been sold by Paquet Industries—an international defence contractor—and used to take the lives of nearly four thousand people across the globe?'

Noise filled the room. Objections and cries of shock from Loukis's legal team, the judge's gavel pounding on the wood behind her in time with the raging of her own heart, and above all Meredith's shrill voice, proclaiming she would not allow a *murderer* to care for her daughter.

Célia's field of vision narrowed to her hands, shaking and suddenly frigidly cold. Her breaths were coming in short sharp pants and nausea gripped her stomach in a fierce hold.

She vaguely found herself pulled from the chair, Loukis's concerned face hazy, snatching glances at people who were staring at her, imagining their faces twisted in horror, as she was led from the room and back to the small office where they had started this day.

Murderer.

What the hell was going on? Loukis fisted his hands, wanting to lash out at something. Anything. Célia was hunched over in the chair he had poured her into. His legal team filled the room looking as concerned as he was. But in all likelihood their concern was focused on the custody case now completely hijacked from the last source he had ever expected it to come from.

But his mind fractured. He had seen Célia begin to tremble, still sitting by the judge. The way her skin had paled and he'd known. Known something awful was about to happen and he'd not been able to do a damn thing to stop it.

Snippets of conversations filtered through his mind.

'It was taken from me...'

'Very good at "the computer science thing"...'

'Used in a very different way from what I had intended...'

'I will not allow a murderer to care for my daughter...'

Someone was telling Célia to breathe and a distant part of him recognised that it should have been him. Him making sure she was okay. But he was held in a vortex of shock and fear. They should have known something was wrong when Meredith's legal team didn't go after him for all the things they had suspected they would. They didn't need to. Because they had Célia. His mother had used Célia to bring him to his knees.

At that precise moment, Célia finally looked up at him. Her eyes glistening with unshed tears, her breath finally coming back to some semblance of normality.

'Leave us,' he demanded of the lawyers. As if sensing the storm brewing, they filed out of the room leaving Célia and Loukis alone.

'Loukis—'

'Explain what just happened to me.'

'I…'

'I can't do this for you, Célia. I have no idea what just happened. So just…tell me.'

'My father took the technical specifications from me and used them to bolster the designs for Paquet's combat drone. One that has since been sold around the world as one of the top ten UAVs available—'

'UAV?' he interrupted.

'Unmanned Aerial Vehicle.'

'So they were right?'

'Loukis, I didn't do it,' she pleaded. 'My designs were never intended for combat or the defence industry. I had no idea—'

'But they are right.'

'Yes.'

'Why the hell didn't you tell me?' he roared, unable to hold himself back. Everything he'd done, all of it, to protect his sister, it was slipping through his fingers like sand.

'Because I thought the records were sealed. Because I thought my father left my name off the designs.'

'Just how naïve are you? It's a legal patent. Of course he would have had to put your name down on the paperwork.'

He was half convinced that he was now shaking as much as Célia. Only he was furious. And she was scared, he realised, desperately attempting to pull back on the leash that had been lifted from his anger. He was going to lose. He was going to lose Annabelle. And Célia…

'I didn't tell you because I was ashamed. Because I know what those drones have done and will continue to do. Why do you think I was so determined to counter that with the charity work I do?'

'Well, it's not like I would have been able to guess that with you keeping so many damn secrets.' The line was petty and he hated himself for it, but couldn't stop it.

'I didn't tell you,' she said finally, in the softest of voices, 'because you wanted the perfect fiancée. You didn't, in fact, want someone whose reputation is worse than your own.'

He couldn't deny her words. He knew she was telling the truth. That she had believed no one would find out. And he could see that she was destroyed by the revelation in court, by the knowledge of what her designs had been put to use for. But did it matter? Right now, to the granting of guardianship over Annabelle?

He turned away from her then, unable to bear the weight of her watery eyes. Each glint cut against him, burying into his heart, exposing a raw pain, a deeper truth. One that could not be denied. All this time he'd roared and railed against the pain of being abandoned, rejected in favour of money. His father left a broken shell by the divorce and never quite fully recovering. And Loukis, himself, left horrified and damaged by the knowledge of his worth in his mother's eyes.

But now this time, it was he who was being forced to make the choice. It felt as if he were being torn in two, a painful wrenching that he feared he might never soothe. Neither option would provide enough to compensate for what he would lose.

His mind worked furiously, trying to forecast the outcome of whatever his next move was, until he was dizzy with an infinite number of futures, all of which left him sacrificing something vital to him.

Fury raged within him as he realised that the price he would have to pay for Annabelle was Célia. This beautiful, impassioned, kind, supportive woman who had snuck beneath every single defence he had. And he couldn't have her. Not if he wanted to protect Annabelle from their mother.

Célia could see it. The moment that he realised what she, herself, had come to realise as soon as Meredith had cried out the word *murderer*. There was no way that she could stay. She was now the greatest threat to his guardianship over Annabelle. A far worse threat than any that Loukis could have represented, or even foreseen.

Loukis's chance at being granted custody had hung by a gossamer thread already. And she had effectively severed that thread. If she stayed.

'Don't,' he commanded as if hearing her thoughts.

'It's the only way.'

He didn't speak, but he was shaking his head as if refusing to listen. Refusing to do the only thing left to do.

She took a deep breath that trembled within her lungs. Oh, it hurt. So, so much. In her mind rose Loukis's words from the first night they had made love. Speaking them now, with her tongue, the words on her lips, she felt them down to her very soul.

'I am not capable of giving you what you deserve. Not now. Not ever.'

'That is not fair.'

'None of it is fair Loukis.'

She looked at him, his hair a chaotic mess, his eyes blazing, torn, but she could tell he knew, could tell that he would not stop her. And even in that, he looked glorious to her. The man who had given her strength, the man who had returned her sense of self to her. The man she had come to love. The man she was now destroying.

The horror she felt rising within her at the sheer fact

that she had accidentally brought this down on him was acute. That she was the one who had unconsciously betrayed him… She knew that precise poison betrayal could be, the self-recrimination, anger and helplessness when wishes, plans and hopes for the future were taken away and smashed against the floor. She knew the devastating anguish that would reap for Loukis and she wouldn't, couldn't, do that to him.

'You will return to the court, be as outraged as you like. You didn't know. You would never have allowed me any contact with Annabelle had you known. And you have severed our…connection. I will not be an impediment to your guardianship over Annabelle.'

He said nothing, staring at her so intently she had to break their gaze. Had to because she simply couldn't bear it.

'I'll go straight to the airport. You can send my things on and I'll give you the money—'

'Stop,' he commanded.

'No. Because I'm right and you know it. It's the only way.'

'Célia,' he begged, and she couldn't stand it. 'I can't—'

'I know,' she said, shaking her head, hoping to prevent more excruciating words. 'I understand, Loukis. Truly.'

She got up from the chair, her legs still a little shaky, but forcing the strength that he had given her into her body, heart and soul. She reached for her bag. 'I think you might have been right,' she said with a sad smile. 'Everything *does* have a price. And, Loukis, this is the one that *I* am willing to pay. For you. For Annabelle.

She turned to walk away, but a hand caught her wrist, pulling her back round to him, causing her to crash against his chest. His lips were on hers in an instant, demanding, punishing, as if trying to bend her to his will. His hands came around her face as if trying to anchor her to him, to keep her with him. And it hurt. The agony of what she was doing nearly buckled her. This one last time, this one last kiss, it was too much.

Weak as she was, she reached for him too. Her hands fisting in his shirt, clinging to him, to this moment as if wanting it all and knowing that it would never be enough. At first, she had flinched from his touch, then she had borne it and now she craved it with every fibre of her being. The only way she could find the strength to walk away from him was knowing that to stay would damage him irrevocably.

His thumb swept away a tear she hadn't even realised she'd shed. The bittersweet taste of his kiss haunted her and would continue to haunt her, she knew, for many, many days to come. She broke the kiss and gazed up into his rich dark eyes, but the sea of emotions storming within them was too much.

She left his embrace, turned and left the room, left the court building and blindly hailed a cab. All the while absolutely sure that she had left behind her heart.

CHAPTER TWELVE

BY THE TIME his lawyers came to find him in the court's small office, where Célia had left him, some unfathomable amount of time later, he could barely speak. They explained that a recess had been granted, but that it would be at least another five days before the case could be resumed. According to them, Meredith had not been pleased by the news and had nearly been admonished by the judge for her outburst. Even some minor victory over Meredith hadn't been able to shake him. They had put him in his car, and he'd even been blind to the concerned looks they shared between themselves as they sent him off to his estate in Athens.

Having to explain to Annabelle what had happened nearly eviscerated him as his little sister's eyes had welled, just like Célia's, and she'd run away too. He'd known how she'd felt at that moment, wanting himself to hide and lick wounds yet again inflicted by his mother. Though these particular wounds had a sense of self-infliction he just couldn't shake.

So many times in the last three days, he'd wanted to reach out to Célia. Wanted to call her, to see her, but with his lawyers on damage limitation, Annabelle nearly heartbroken at Célia's absence and the insecurity of the looming custody hearing, he barely found the time to eat, let alone sleep.

He was exhausted. He'd not been back to his room since Célia had left. The scent she'd left on his pillows, in the air of the room, he wanted to both avoid it and hoard it at the same time.

But it was more than that. He'd made his choice, that had been unquestionable. But living with it? Again and again he questioned how Célia had come to impact his life so much. Almost daily he wondered what she was wearing—if she had gone back to her beige T-shirt that he'd honestly give anything to see at that moment, or whether she'd continued to wear the beautiful bright clothing that brought out the colours of her eyes and hair. He wondered if she had spoken more with her mother, a reconciliation that he knew would be so healing for her. He missed the simple touches that passed between them as much as the deep passion that drove them to impossible sensual heights, a thirst that he had not come close to quenching.

More than all those things, though, he missed the way she would question him, challenge him to be better, to do more, to think his actions through. He couldn't shake the feeling that he was failing. Epically. Especially when it came to Annabelle.

He wanted her to tell him how to fix it. She had always seemed to know.

He heard the patter of Annabelle's bare feet on the marble staircase and waited until her pyjama-clad little self came into view.

Frowning at the clock, which read eleven-thirty, he turned. 'Everything okay, Nanny?'

Her little hands twisted in front of her, her eyes bruised by lack of sleep.

'Is Célia a bad person?'

Shock sliced through him and he had to bite out the demand for her to explain, forcing himself to think through the words Célia might have said in that moment.

'Why would you think that?' he asked, trying to keep his voice level.

'Mummy said she did a bad thing and that's why she had to go away.'

Every primal instinct to deny, to vent the sudden and shocking fury he felt, roared through him.

'No, sweetheart. She didn't do a bad thing. She…invented something that people used for bad things, but no. Absolutely not. Célia isn't bad at all.'

'Then, can you tell Mummy that so Célia can come back?'

Loukis forced a smile to his features. 'I…' He was about to explain that he had told Meredith, that he had defended Célia, when he realised that he hadn't. There had been no defence of Célia, not in the court and not since. Something twisted in his belly then. Something acidic and harsh and painful.

'You're right, Annabelle. I should do that. But I'm not sure that it would bring Célia back.'

'Why not?'

'Because Meredith doesn't want Célia to live with me while you're here. And sadly the judge might agree.'

'Then I… I think I should go and live with Mummy.'

'Is that something you want to do?' he asked, his voice level and compassionate even as everything in him trembled and shook.

Annabelle frowned. 'No,' she said, shaking her head. 'But then Célia could come back.'

'Why would you want that?'

'Because you are sad without her. And I don't want you to be sad.'

'But wouldn't you be sad, living with Meredith?'

She shrugged. 'I'd be okay.'

Loukis cursed silently. How could a ten-year-old contain

such stoicism? More than he ever had even five years older when Meredith had walked out on him and his father. And that thought brought a startling revelation. He was teaching his little sister, at ten years old, exactly the same lesson that their mother had taught him.

That love had a price. Annabelle was making her own bargain with him. His happiness for hers. And that devastated him. He couldn't do it. He couldn't allow this cycle to continue. No matter the cost to himself. But in order to break that cycle, he would have to risk everything.

He opened his arms to her and Annabelle threw herself into his embrace.

'So, how was it?' Ella's voice fed into her ear from where the phone was cradled between her shoulder and head as Célia pushed the plunger down on the cafetière.

She had rejected a video call, knowing that her friend would be horrified at the way Célia looked in that moment. She sighed.

'Weird, awkward, painful, but kind of okay.'

'Well, the *kind of okay* bit is good?' she asked, rather than stated, probing for more than Célia was capable of providing.

Célia had just got back from lunch with her parents. Both of them. Her father had aged so much in the last five years, she had been shocked. Shocked that the salt and pepper hair had transformed to a pure brilliant white. Shocked at how the lines on his face had increased in the time she had missed. Shocked that he had been so contrite, when—at the time—he had resolutely ignored any and all attempts to discuss the repurposing of her designs.

From words she'd been forced to read between, she realised that in his own way he had been hiding from the effects of his actions. A man wholeheartedly used to making quick, determined decisions about his company, he'd not quite been ready to interrogate the motives behind them.

It still hurt. That her father couldn't admit that he'd been wrong. Still awkward and distant in his feelings, he couldn't offer her the words of love and reassurance that she so desperately needed to hear. But if she wanted to be loved for who she was, she could hardly demand perfection from him. She too had to find love in imperfection, whether with her father, or herself. And that realisation had been the first step. In confronting the past she was so ashamed of. And in that bittersweet painful moment, she realised that she could no longer be bound by it. That she needed to live her life and stop hiding—as she had once accused Loukis of doing.

She poured the coffee into a mug and crossed the room of her Parisian apartment and curled up on her sofa, the phone still cradled between her shoulder and ear the way her hands now cradled the steaming cup of goodness.

'It is,' she said, finally answering Ella's half-question.

'Have you heard from him?'

Célia didn't have the energy to muster ignorance as to whom Ella was referring. 'No. But I didn't expect to,' she replied around the lump in her throat. 'Anyway, tell me about your gorgeous little one. How is Tatiana?'

'Teething.'

Célia groaned in sympathy. 'And Roman?'

'Loving everything about parenting. I'm lucky if I can get a look-in.'

'I'm sure he's just making up for the time he's away with work.'

'It's *him* I can't get a look-in with,' Ella replied quickly with a beautiful laugh. 'Tatiana only has eyes for him. For me, she has dirty nappies!'

Célia smiled, even as her heart broke. She'd have been

lying to herself if she denied that she had hoped that perhaps her future could follow a similar path to her best friend's and to one day find that same happiness with Loukis.

'Are you sure you won't come down to Puycalvel? Roman would send the jet in a heartbeat.'

'That's okay. Honestly. Yalena has returned the signed contracts and there is plenty of work to do now. It's certainly enough to keep me busy.'

'Life doesn't have to be all work, you know,' Ella chided, unconsciously cutting at Célia's heart. Because work was all she felt she had left now.

'Mmm-hmm,' she mused, noncommittally.

Célia heard a mewl in the background. One that was beginning to become insistent. 'You should go, Ella. I'll be fine. Promise.'

As she disconnected the call and placed her phone down on the table, the sapphire ring glinted in the dim light of what was quickly becoming a very late evening. She twisted the ring with her thumb, not in the least ready to remove it. It meant too much to her. The moment when she had felt finally *seen* by someone. Accepted. She threw her head back against the plush pillow resting against the arm of her sofa, growling at herself.

She had to let him go. She knew that. But she wouldn't deny the things he had brought to her. Never would she have known the feeling of empowerment resulting from being desired for who she was. Never would she have approached such an incredible client as Yalena, found a sense of pride in her work through that relationship. Never would she have reached out to her mother to ask her to arrange a lunch with her father if she had not met Loukis. If she had not realised that people made mistakes, sometimes not entirely their own fault. That love could be felt and wanted, despite events that shaped wishes into other things. Just as she loved and wanted Loukis, despite knowing her actions had brought about their separation. And though he was no longer going to be a part of her life, he had left behind those fundamental changes within her. Even as her heart ached, she felt transformed by him.

Glorious scent-laden steam wafted up from the cup of coffee. For the last three days, Célia had desperately tried to stave off sleep for as long as possible. Because at night, the dreams came. Memories mixed with fantasies, as Loukis kissed and caressed his way through the sleeping hours, leaving her to wake with tears on her eyelashes as she realised he was no longer a part of her life.

Her phone pinged with a message she would have ignored had it not been from an unknown number.

Leaning forward over the cup, she read the text.

can you call .me cherry

A spike of adrenaline sliced through her so quickly, it took her a moment to decipher the unpunctuated message.

She grabbed for the phone, immediately worried that Annabelle was in some kind of trouble, uncaring of the way she had slammed her cup on the table or the spill of dark caffeinated stain soaking into the plush white rug on the floor.

The moment the call rang through, Célia demanded to know if Annabelle was okay.

'Yes. No. Well, yes,' came the somewhat confusing reply. 'I am,' she concluded, perhaps realising how scared Célia had been in that moment.

Célia expelled a giant lungful of air and leaned back against the pillow again.

'Well, *ma chérie*, what can I do for you?' she said, somehow wrangling her voice under control, even as her pulse began a slow descent to normality.

Please don't talk about Loukis. Please.

Célia honestly didn't think she could bear it. But she was desperate to find out what happened with the court case after she had left. Had they awarded Loukis guardianship? Or had the damage been irretrievable? She drew her thumb to her mouth and bit at the nail to prevent all the questions from falling onto the shoulders of a ten-year-old girl.

'Can you come to Greece?'

'Now?'

'Yes?'

'I'm sorry, *ma chérie*, it's nearly midnight here. There are no flights. And even then, I'm not sure—'

'It's just that the judge is deciding the custurdy thing on Wednesday. I really need you there.'

'It hasn't been—?' She cut herself off. Clearly the court case hadn't been finalised yet, but it would the day after to-morrow. 'I don't really think I should be there, Annabelle.'

'But you have to be. You *have to*.'

Célia's heart ached more than ever.

'Because Loukis will be on one bench and Mummy on the other and no one will be with me.'

Célia felt tears forming in the corners of her eyes at the mournful voice through the phone.

'Does Loukis know you're asking me?'

'No. It's a surprise!'

Not one she could imagine Loukis being happy with.

'Please don't tell him that you're coming. It will ruin it. Please, Cici. Please? Pinkie promise? I need you there. With *me*.'

As Célia made her way up the stairs of the court building she looked around furtively, hoping that she wouldn't run into anyone. The feeling was ridiculous, considering she was about to return to the courtroom itself where everyone would see her.

She hadn't had the strength to refuse Annabelle. If it had been for anyone else, she would have found it somewhere.

'I need you there. With me.'

It had been too much. She defied anyone to turn down the pleas of a ten-year-old girl. She pushed through the heavy swinging circular door and followed the familiar hallway towards the chamber where Annabelle's future was to be decided. Where Loukis's future would be decided too. A future that she had, albeit accidentally, put at risk.

She had already decided that if he asked her to leave, she'd go. She'd go and never come back. But Annabelle's call had lifted a lid on Célia's hopes and all the hurt and fear that came with them. She needed to know what was going to happen today.

She looked up to find Annabelle standing outside the chamber, half hanging on the large wooden door, her other arm frantically beckoning her forward as if Célia was about to miss something.

Her reluctant steps picking up speed at Annabelle's urgency, she barely had time to say hello before the little girl had grabbed her hand and led her into the courtroom. She looked up fearfully at the table where Loukis and his lawyers sat. Only the suited men she recognised from the previous court attendance turned round. Far from the way they had looked at her before—as if she were a bomb that had detonated their case—they nodded, faces grim with protocol and severity, but without censure. The judge, mid-sentence, barely acknowledged the interruption, while Meredith and her lawyers seemed gleefully outraged. Byron, on the other hand, looked strangely miserable and deeply unhappy. Reluctantly her gaze was drawn to the broad outline of Loukis's shoulders, stiff and immoveable as if he were refusing even to register her attendance. He must have known, she realised, otherwise he would have turned. He would have wanted to know who had entered the court.

'I've already told them,' Annabelle said in a not-so-quiet whisper the way only a child could get away with. 'I've done my bit.'

'Your bit?' Célia asked, in a much more quiet tone. 'I thought you wanted me here for that? Am I late? You said ten-thirty?' Célia's voice gained a trace of panic as she realised that she had somehow let Annabelle down again.

'No. You're just in time.'

'Your Honour?'

Loukis's voice, rough and deep, as if he too had had many a sleepless night.

'I understand that it is time for my final statement, and, although it is an unusual one, I have a request.'

When the judge gestured for him to continue he said, 'I would like to call Célia d'Argent back to the stand to clarify some aspects of her statement.'

The whispers started between the lawyers, Meredith clearly unhappy with the new development, and Célia absolutely terrified. What on earth was Loukis doing? Was he planning to engineer a way to place *all* the blame at her feet? Was that the only way he could hope to win guardianship? If so, she could not blame him and would willingly do whatever it took to help.

Annabelle was smiling at her, pushing her forward and letting go of her hand. It was that loss that Célia felt most keenly. Unable to meet anyone's gaze, she kept her eyes on the floor as she approached the chair beside the judge. She feared that the moment she locked eyes with Loukis she might cry and that wouldn't help anyone. But when she looked up, rather than seeing hatred or vengeance in his eyes, she saw…something she couldn't hope to put a name to.

'Célia, thank you for coming today.'

She tried to keep the frown from her face, as it sounded as if he had known that she would be here. A quick glance at Annabelle's beaming face seemed to suggest that her plan was going winningly. A plan that was—contrary to her assurance—not some great surprise to Loukis.

'Five years ago, when you were working on the technical specifications for a drone tracking system, what were your hopes?'

'I'm not sure what you—'

'What was the intended use?'

Célia could give him this. She could see that he was trying to resolve the implications made the last time she was here. Felt somehow soothed by the fact that he was giving her the chance to explain. Even if it was too late.

'To help improve the tracking and data management of agricultural drones in drought-affected areas.'

'Areas such as…'

'Parts of Africa, Australia, areas in Pakistan…there are many places in the world that are drought-affected and that number is only increasing with global warming.'

'And you had no intention of that technology being used by the defence industry.'

'No. It was coursework for my degree but I had been using some of the equipment and time at my internship at Paquet.'

'And as such it was considered to come under their intellectual property disclosure.'

'Yes.'

'In fact, the use of the designs caused you great emotional stress?'

Célia bit the inside of her cheek before responding.

'Yes.'

'In what way?'

'I… It just did,' Célia replied, not quite sure what he wanted from her.

'In fact, it severely damaged your relationship with your father whom you were estranged from for nearly five years, it led you to leave a promising future in computer sciences and…it made you doubt yourself.'

His eyes bored into hers as if to say that he hated this. Hated hurting her. But she would bear it. For him.

'Yes.'

'Why did you leave me?'

The abrupt turn in questioning made Célia's stomach lurch.

'Excuse me?'

'Why did you break our engagement and leave?'

'I… Do we have to do this here?' she asked somewhat desperately.

'Yes,' he pressed resolutely. 'Why did you break our engagement?'

'Because it would risk your guardianship over Annabelle.'

'And why was that so important?'

Célia stared at him. As if she could demand to know what he was doing. Why he was putting her through this.

'Because I love you. And I've come to love Annabelle. And I don't want to see you both hurt because of my actions.'

As if the spell had been lifted, Loukis smiled, broad, wide, beautiful. His eyes sparkled and she'd never seen him look so wondrous.

'Good. Because I love you too.'

Célia's heart leapt.

'But I'll get back to that in a minute. I promise.' He turned to face the judge. 'Your Honour, if the courts are here to decide about protection, about family, then this is me. Protecting my family and fighting for the woman I love. I have a written statement from François Paquet completely freeing Célia d'Argent from any knowledge of what her technical specifications were to be used for. And I am devastated that she was so mistreated by the questions posed by my mother's lawyers, devastated that someone so good, so full of love and self-sacrifice was hurt by *my* actions and *my* needs. A woman who challenges me to be and do more each and every day, a woman who makes me a better person. And if this custody case is the price of Célia's love for me and my love for her, it is not one I'm willing to pay. Nor am I willing to teach Annabelle that lesson either. Annabelle has told you in her own words that she would like to stay with me. Would like to maintain her life here, with her friends and family that love her. I urge you to take this into consideration in your decision. But for now, I'd very much like to kiss my fiancée if that's okay, Your Honour?'

A rueful smile played at the mouth of the wigged judge and Célia practically fled the chair, at the same time as Loukis crossed the room, and they met in the middle in a kiss that Célia would remember for the rest of her life.

She gave no heed to the chaos that erupted around them, as his lips found hers and she felt the greatest well of love spring within her. Tears once again escaped her eyes, but this time they were full of joy.

'I love you,' he whispered against her lips.

'I love you too,' she whispered back.

Finally the commotion around Meredith's lawyers' table became too intrusive, Byron's anger boiling over and Meredith's panicked voice hastily trying to call him back. The large oil baron's arm cut through the air punctuating the word 'done', and he turned, taking a few short steps towards them.

'I'm so very sorry about how painful that must have been for you,' the American said. 'It should never have happened. And while I do love her,' he said helplessly, 'I cannot condone Meredith's actions. Other than to say that desperation made her…but it is inexcusable.'

As he left the courtroom, Célia looked towards the older woman, recognising some of the devastation across her features. Because she, herself, had looked like that over the last few days and, no matter what had happened, Célia's heart ached for the woman.

Her lawyers demanded a short recess from the court, and Loukis took Célia's hand in one of his just as Annabelle launched herself towards them. They were ushered from the room and back into the small office that was suddenly bursting with frantic laughter and happy tears from Loukis, Célia and Annabelle. But all the while, concern that Loukis still might lose custody beat in her chest.

'Are you sure?' she whispered to him as Annabelle wrapped her small body around Célia's waist. 'The risk, it's too great…'

'Not as great as the risk of teaching Annabelle that love has a price. That love *is* the price. I *won't* do that.'

They gazed at each other with love blazing in their eyes. It seemed to go on for ever, Célia refusing to break the heady, half-fearful, all-joyous and all-consuming feeling bursting within her.

Until one of Loukis's lawyers knocked on the door, and entered, the smile on his face as broad as she'd ever seen.

'It's over. Meredith has dropped the case. The courts are happy to award you full guardianship. Her only request was that she be able to see Annabelle a few times a year, with your permission.'

Célia's heart soared, to see the sheer happiness and relief across Loukis's features.

She felt Annabelle tug at both of them. 'Can I, Loukis?'

'Is that something you'd like?' he asked his sister.

'Yes.'

'Then you shall.'

'Can I…go and see Mummy?'

'Of course you can,' he insisted, his eyes returning to Célia's.

The lawyer stretched his hand out to Annabelle and the two made their way out into the hallway.

Loukis looked at the woman he loved, knowing that they still had more to say. That he did.

'Can you forgive me?'

She looked so adorably confused in that moment. 'What for?' she demanded.

'For letting you go. For not realising sooner. For putting you through—'

'There's nothing to forgive, Loukis. For so long, I was afraid of it all coming out. Of people thinking exactly what Meredith did. And I think I needed that. I needed to actually see it and feel it, to realise that it's how I see myself that matters. That I know that wasn't what I had intended. And that sometimes people do make mistakes. Unintentional ones. Like me. Like my father. How did you…?'

'I called him, told him what happened. That I loved you and asked him if he could provide a statement for the court. He was more than happy to do so and within twenty minutes of the end of our conversation, he'd emailed it through.'

'You did that for me?' she asked as if still incredulous at the lengths he would go to for her.

'I would do *anything* for you,' he replied, the promise on his lips soul-deep and eternal.

'Do you think the judge is still in the chamber?'

'No idea.' Loukis was confused as to the direction of her thoughts. 'Why?'

'Because I can't wait a minute longer to become Mrs Célia Liordis. I think it will be my most favourite name yet.'

Loukis's heart soared. This incredible woman wanted to be his wife, his future and his love. And Annabelle would be with them for every step of it. Family. The thing he'd avoided for so many years was now the only thing he wanted from the rest of his very happy ever after.

EPILOGUE

AUGUST HAD BECOME Célia's favourite month. Since their wedding—sadly not the day of the court case owing to licences and other frustrating legalities, but a beautiful day full of family, friends, flowers and the most gorgeous dress Célia had ever seen—Ella and Roman's family would come to the island for four whole magical weeks.

It hadn't been long after the wedding that Célia had discovered she was pregnant with their first child, Georgia, and then not long after their second, Antonis, much to Annabelle's great delight. With Ella and Roman's children, Tatiana, Adeline and Tikhon, Loukis would joke about opening a crèche.

But that wasn't what was occupying a large portion of Célia's recent spare time. She had gone back to university, deciding to honour her childhood dreams of computer sciences. She had no plans yet to return to the industry, but as she now well knew…plans changed and people changed with them.

Even Meredith, she ruefully acknowledged. It had taken a long time, but Loukis and his mother seemed to have found a balance and a sense of accord from their mutual love of Annabelle. The older woman had eventually apologised when she realised how much damage her actions in court had caused to others. It appeared she had truly been in love with Byron and in her desperation to be the perfect wife and mother he envisioned, she had gone too far. But Meredith had worked hard to prove her love for her fiancé as well as Annabelle and was even making tentative steps towards repairing her relationship with Loukis too.

It was the only thing that had prompted the hesitant suggestion from Loukis that perhaps the following August, they might invite Meredith for a short period. Célia had known how difficult that had been for him, but she also knew how important it was to forge those relationships—as she had done herself with her own parents. August had become the most precious time for them all. All business was put on hold and each company's workforce was given a month-long holiday to spend with their own families, because each and every one of them knew the importance of it.

As Célia checked and rechecked the fridge and pantry, ensuring that there was enough food for their first evening meal together that year, she paused—delighting in hearing the joyous sounds of Annabelle playing with Georgia and Antonis, their excitement at being reunited with Tatiana, Adeline and Tikhon. A last-minute addition of Yalena, Iannis and their family wouldn't even put a dent in all the food and produce Loukis had ordered.

'Do you think we've got enough?' her husband asked from over her shoulder.

'What, for the apocalypse? Yup. We should survive,' she replied drily.

'No one will go hungry in my house,' he declared.

'Little chance of that,' she assured him, turning towards Loukis as he reached his arms around her waist and drew her towards him. They never tired of the little touches that had brought them so close together in the early stages of their relationship. And Célia had never stopped wondering at the fact that something so wonderful, so pure, so loving could have come from such fake beginnings.

'Mmm…' she mused. 'Why is it that I'm thinking you're hungry, but not for food?' she teased.

'Because you know me so, so well.'

'I also know, *so, so well*, that our guests will be arriving in little under two hours and I've still yet to put the bedding in the spare rooms, tidy the sitting room, and clear away the playthings from the outside table.'

'Ella and Roman won't mind. They're used to it.'

'But Yalena and Iannis—'

'Will absolutely, one hundred per cent understand. Anyone who has taken one look at my beautiful wife would understand,' he assured her.

And it made her think of all the ways he'd seen her since that day in the courtroom. Flush with the excitement of their reunion, the passion he could tease from her, terrified and exhausted as her first labour went from its thirty-sixth hour into an emergency C-section, awed and infinitely full of love as she held their first child, then their second just a few years later. Grief-stricken when she had lost her father, but resolute and comforted by the way that they had found a peace between them and forged a loving relationship in those final years. But the best of it was each and every morning when she opened her eyes to find him looking at her as if he'd never seen anything more beautiful or more beloved.

The soft bent of her thoughts was yanked back to the present with an outrageous cry as he slapped her behind.

'Bedroom. Now,' he commanded with light, laughter and passion ringing his gaze.

The absolute *gall* of the gorgeous man she was proud to call her husband, the father of her children and the love of her life.

Her outrage died the moment she saw the impassioned look in his eyes and she raced him all the way to the bedroom and beyond.

* * * * *

THE MAID'S BEST KEPT SECRET

ABBY GREEN

This is my 50th title for Mills & Boon, and it's beyond shocking to write that down – let alone contemplate how it happened over the last thirteen years.

I'd like to dedicate this book first and foremost to my mother, without whom I wouldn't have inherited a love of reading, writing, and a very dark sense of humour.

To my writer tribe: Heidi, Iona, Fiona, Susan and Sharon. Without you all the writing world would be far duller and scarier to navigate. And Carol Marinelli – sounding board and car enabler.

To the McDermot and Mernagh clan, who adopted me into their family a long time ago before any of us knew how much I would need them.

To Susie Q, Eoin, Lucy, Lynn, Lorna, Lindi and Ruth, who encouraged me to take the leap into a new world.

To Hazel, who provides daily sustenance, free therapy and MUK online updates.

To Gervaise Landy, who planted the seed – and had 'that tape' – that led to me writing a Mills & Boon in the very first instance.

To my Mills & Boon editors, who have guided me and continue to guide me along the way: Tessa Shapcott, Katinka Proudfoot, Meg Lewis, Suzy Clarke and Sheila Hodgson. Without editors, writers are nothing.

And, last but not least, to you, lovely romance readers. I too am a romance reader, so we're all in on the secret that the romance genre simply is the best.

As long as people want to hear or read stories they will want romance. Because love – in all its myriad shapes and forms – is the most important thing.

CHAPTER ONE

MAGGIE TAGGART FELT RESTLESS. She'd finished washing up the dishes in the sink and looked around the vast and gleaming kitchen which was situated in the basement of an even vaster house. A stunningly beautiful period country house, to be exact. Set in some ten acres of lush green land about an hour's drive outside Dublin.

There were manicured gardens to the rear and a sizeable walled kitchen garden to the side. There was even a small lake and a forest. And stables. But the stables were empty. The owner—a billionaire tycoon—had apparently bought the house sight unseen on a whim when he'd had a passing interest in investing in horse racing, for which this part of Ireland was renowned.

Except he'd never bought any horses and he'd never actually visited the house. So here it sat, empty and untouched. Luxuriously decorated to his specifications. He hadn't even hired the housekeeper himself—one of his assistants had done it remotely.

That housekeeper had been Maggie's mother, and when she'd fallen ill she had been terrified of losing her job. So Maggie had quit her own job as a commis chef in a Dublin restaurant and come to help her and take care of her. Leaving her restaurant job hadn't been too much of a sacrifice, thanks to the head chef, who had been a serial groper of his female staff.

Then Maggie's mother had died suddenly, and when she'd informed the owner's offices an impersonal assistant had asked if she wouldn't mind taking over in the interim, while they found a permanent replacement.

Maggie had been in shock…grieving…so she'd found

herself saying yes, relishing the thought of a quiet space where she could lick her wounds and deal with her grief, not yet ready to face back into the world.

That had been three months ago. Three months that had passed in a grief-stricken blur. And she was only just emerging from that very intial painful stage.

Hence this sense of restlessness. Up to now the house had served as a kind of cocoon, shielding her from the outside world. But she could feel herself itching to do more than just tend to it. In spite of its lack of occupants, it was surprisingly challenging to maintain at the high standard demanded by the boss—should he ever decide to drop by. On another whim.

Maggie's soft mouth firmed. The impression she had of the owner—a man she wasn't interested enough in to look up on the internet—was one of gross entitlement. Who bought a lavish country house and then never even came to see it?

'Rich, powerful men who have more money than sense.'

Those had been her mother's words. And she had known all about rich, powerful men—because Maggie's father had been one. A wealthy property tycoon from Scotland, he'd had an affair with Maggie's mother and when she'd told him she was pregnant he'd denied all knowledge, terrified that Maggie's mother and his illegitimate daughter might get their hands on his vast fortune.

He hadn't offered any support or commitment. He'd offered only threats and intimidation. Maggie's mother had been too proud and heartbroken to pursue him for maintenance and they'd left Scotland and moved to Ireland, where Maggie's mother's job as a housekeeper had kept them moving around the country, never really settling in any one place for long.

To say that Maggie had a jaded view of rich men and their ways was an understatement. She sighed. However, she was being paid very generously to take care of an empty house by a rich man, so she couldn't really complain.

At that moment the peace that she'd so relished was shattered by a sound from upstairs—the ground floor. A banging noise. The front door? It was such an unusual sound to hear in this silent house that she almost didn't recognise it.

Maggie rushed upstairs and walked into the hall just as the knocker was slammed down onto the door again. She muttered, 'Keep your hair on…' as she switched on the outside light and swung the door open.

And promptly ceased breathing at the sight in front of her. A tall, dark man dominated the doorway, hand lifted as if to slam the knocker down again. His other arm was raised, and rested on the door frame. The late-summer sky was a dusky lavender behind him, making him seem even darker.

Maggie couldn't find her breath. Dressed in a classic black tuxedo, he was the most stupendously gorgeous man she'd ever seen. Thick curly hair and dark brows framed a strong-boned face…cheekbones to die for. His deep-set eyes were dark, but not brown. Golden. His skin was dark too. There was stubble on his jaw. The sheer height, width and breadth of him was heat-inducingly powerful.

She registered all this in a split-second—a very basic biological reaction to a virile male.

His black bowtie hung rakishly undone under the open top button of his shirt. Those dark eyes flicked down from her face over her body. A bold appraisal. Arrogant, even.

Maggie became acutely aware of the fact that she was wearing cut-off shorts and a sleeveless T-shirt, her hair up in an untidy bun. Her habitual uniform for when she was cleaning.

'This *is* Kildare House?' the masculine vision asked, with a slight accent.

His voice was deep and rough and the pulse between her legs throbbed. Most disturbing.

'Yes, it is.'

The man stood up straight. He had an air of slightly louche inebriation but his eyes were too focused and direct for him to be intoxicated. Actually, it was an air of intense ennui.

He turned away from her, and it was only then that Maggie noticed a taxi at the bottom of the steps leading up to the front door, engine idling.

The man addressed the driver, who was waiting by the car. 'This is the right place. Thank you.'

Maggie watched with growing shock as the taxi driver waved jauntily, got into his car and drove off.

She gripped the door. 'Excuse me but who *are* you?'

The man turned back to face her. 'I'm the owner of this house. Nikos Marchetti. I think the more pertinent question here is who are *you*? Because I've seen a picture of the housekeeper and you are most definitely not her.'

Nikos Marchetti. The owner she'd envisaged as middle-aged, paunchy, entitled. But this man was more like a Spartan warrior, sheathed in the modern-day trappings of a suit.

His eyes were dropping down her body again, with that insolent appraisal that should have disgusted Maggie but which was having an altogether far less acceptable effect on her body.

She drew herself up to her full five foot ten inches and crossed her arms over her chest. So far Nikos Marchetti was doing little *not* to live up to what she'd expected. Behaviourally, if not physically.

'I am Maggie Taggart—Edith's daughter. She died three months ago and your staff asked if I'd stay on until another housekeeper was hired. Something you're evidently not aware of.'

He looked at her, expressionless. 'I most likely wasn't

informed. My staff are briefed not to bother me unless it's something urgent, and clearly they felt that you could handle the job. However, I am sorry for your loss. Do you think I could enter my own property now?'

His casual dismissal and tacked-on condolences for one of the most traumatic events in Maggie's life—losing her beloved mother—made her stand her ground. 'How do I know you are who you say you are? You could be anyone.'

Nikos Marchetti looked at the woman in front of him and felt not a little shock and surprise running through his system. Along with something much more potent—the biggest jolt of insta-lust he'd ever felt in his life.

He'd just come from a black-tie event at Dublin Castle—leaving behind a room heaving with some of the most beautiful women in the world. And not one of them had turned his head like this…this fiery sprite.

Except she was too tall to be a sprite. She was strong. Supple. The full breasts evident under her thin T-shirt left little to the imagination, and she had wide hips and long pale legs that went on for ever. She was like a Viking queen—all woman and perfectly, generously proportioned—and Nikos's brain was melting into a heat haze.

Which was probably why he was still standing there, long past the time he would normally have indulged such impertinence.

It wasn't just her body, though. Unruly-looking red-gold hair was pulled up into a bun on top of her head and her bone structure was exquisite—high cheekbones, firm jaw, straight nose. Her face was dominated by huge blue eyes and a wide, generous mouth. Currently tight. Like the arms across her chest, blocking him from entering his own property.

'You've never even been here before, have you?'

Nikos arched a brow. 'I wasn't aware I had to account

to you for my movements—but, no, I haven't been here before.'

'Why now? Tonight? No one warned me you were coming.'

'As I own the property, and it should be in a state of readiness for my arrival at any time, I didn't see the need to forewarn or inform anyone,' Nikos drawled.

'It's late… I could have been in bed.'

Nikos was rewarded with a very unhelpful image of this woman lying back on a bed naked, hair spread around her head, welcoming him to explore her sensual body. Blood rushed to his already heated groin, making him hard—something he was usually much more in control of.

Now irritation prickled. 'Seriously? You're denying me entry?'

'I am until you show me some identification. If you are who you say you are, then surely you can appreciate the fact that I'm not going to let a stranger into your property?'

Nikos wanted to growl. There were very few instances when he wasn't automatically obeyed. Except she had a point. The fact that she apparently didn't recognise him was also a novelty that had an unexpected appeal. He was used to people targeting him because of exactly who he was: heir to a vast inestimable fortune and legacy.

But he didn't want to think about that now—it would only remind him of the feeling of ennui and claustrophobia that had driven him here in the first place, even though he'd almost forgotten about the Irish estate he owned.

He dug into his inside pocket and muttered, 'I can't believe I'm doing this…' before pulling out his passport and handing it to his housekeeper.

Who looked more like a cheerleader, with that supple body and fresh-faced beauty.

Before he could censor himself he said, 'How old are you?'

She looked up from the passport. 'Twenty-three. This is a Greek passport. I thought you were Italian?'

Nikos took the passport back. 'I'm half-Greek, half-Italian and I decided to go with my Greek side. Any more questions? Or can I now enter the property I own?'

Maggie couldn't believe she was being so antagonistic to the owner of this house. Because he *was* the owner.

Nikos Marchetti.

She scrabbled to recall the vague information she'd absorbed from her mother about him, but her mother's illness had taken most of her attention. He was heir to a vast fortune—the Marchetti Group. But even she knew who *they* were. The biggest conglomerate of luxury brands in the world. They also owned vast swathes of real estate—hotels, nightclubs, and entire blocks in places like New York.

Maggie stood back and moved aside. 'Please, come in, Mr Marchetti. It's a pleasure to welcome you to Kildare House.'

He made a rude sound and walked in, placing a small holdall bag down on a nearby chair. He was even bigger and more gorgeous under the bright lighting of the hallway. He looked around the hall and then proceeded to walk into one of the nearby reception rooms.

Maggie was still reeling from his scent, which had washed over her as he'd entered. Nothing manufactured—or maybe it was just expensive enough not to smell synthetic. Musky, woodsy and pure male essence…

She closed the front door and followed him to the doorway of the reception room to see that he had taken off his jacket and flung it carelessly over the back of a chair. He was at the drinks cabinet and opening a whiskey bottle, pouring a measure into a small tumbler glass.

'Would you like me to show you around?' Maggie asked,

aiming to sound professional and breezy when she felt anything but.

Whatever it was about this man, he'd lodged himself under her skin and she prickled all over. With awareness and something much more volatile.

He turned around. 'Sure.'

He walked towards her, taking a sip of the whiskey and keeping the glass in his hand. He looked thoroughly dangerous and disreputable and a little shiver raced over Maggie's skin.

Acutely aware of him, prowling behind her like a large, sensual jungle cat, she showed him the rooms leading off the circular hallway—more reception rooms, formal and informal, and a formal living room. At the back, overlooking the gardens, was a study, filled with state-of-the-art computers which had never been touched.

On the other side of the hall was a less formal living room, complete with media centre and projection screen for watching movies. It was possibly Maggie's favourite room in the house. Floor-to-ceiling shelves full of books lined the walls. Books that she'd surmised had been chosen purely for show. The works of Shakespeare… Dickens…

Nikos Marchetti faced her. 'Lead on.'

Maggie all but tripped over her own feet as she led him back through the hallway and downstairs to the kitchen. He barely glanced at that, clearly more interested in the gym and indoor lap pool on the same level. There were also rooms for massage or spa treatments. A sauna and a steam room.

He couldn't have looked more insouciant, with his open shirt, dangling bowtie and the glass of whiskey in hand, inspecting a property he owned but had never even laid eyes on before. So far every judgement Maggie had ever made about rich, powerful men was being proved right.

He turned to face her and drained his glass, holding it

carelessly between two fingers. Was it her imagination or did something in those mesmerising gold eyes flare for a second? She realised now that they weren't entirely golden, there were green flecks too. And hazel.

To her shame and disgust, she felt a wave of heat rise up through her body from her core, and she turned quickly before it could reach her face. As pale as she was, every passing emotion registered on her skin—much to her embarrassment.

'The bedrooms are on the first floor.' Maggie led the way back up to the main area of the house, not even checking to see if Nikos Marchetti was following her.

But he was. She could sense him—as if from the moment she'd seen him, she'd been plugged into a new awareness.

Nikos was finding it hard to notice much about the house when the tantalising vision of his housekeeper's bottom and swaying hips filled his vision as she climbed the stairs in front of him. Not to mention those long bare legs.

Theos. He was usually far more sophisticated than this. He just hadn't expected…*her* to answer the door of his country house in the middle of nowhere outside Dublin.

She was walking briskly down the corridor ahead of him now, opening doors and saying, 'These are all spare bedroom suites. Yours is here at the end…'

She'd opened a door and was standing back. He noticed now that she was wearing flip-flops. And that she had pretty feet. Toenails painted a coral colour.

He gritted his jaw and went into the room—but not before he caught her scent again: crushed roses and something much earthier. Musky. It made him grit his jaw even harder.

He barely took in the luxurious room, with windows overlooking three sides of the house, its gardens barely visible now in the rapidly gathering night. He recognised it from the photos he'd been sent by the interior designer after it had been completed.

This was the first house he'd bought—his other properties were apartments in the hotels his company owned. And now he was here he felt a little exposed—as if his motives for buying the house on the basis of a picture that had caught at his gut were being laid bare for this stranger to see.

He could feel her watching him. This woman with a body built like a siren and those huge blue eyes.

He turned around. Maggie Taggart's arms were folded across her chest again, which only pushed the generous swells of her breasts together under the thin material of her T-shirt.

The feeling of exposure was not welcome. Nikos didn't *do* introspection.

He deflected the attention back to her. 'Why are you dressed as if you're attending a barbecue?'

Her cheeks flushed. 'If I had been informed of your arrival you can be sure I would have dressed appropriately. However, considering the fact that it's well past official hours, I don't see why I have to justify dressing as I please. In light of the fact that your presence here is somewhat… irregular, I've taken the liberty of working the hours that suit me. I don't think you can fault the state of the house. I work seven days a week and it has been kept in a permanent state of readiness for your arrival.'

Nikos felt his conscience prick. Which was rare for him.

An innate sense of fairness made him admit, 'You *have* kept the house pristine. Look, can we start over?'

He walked over to where she stood in the doorway. Suddenly she didn't look so confident. He could see a pulse throbbing in her neck. *Not as spiky as she looked. Or behaved.*

He held out his hand. 'I'm Nikos Marchetti—owner of

this house. Sorry for the lack of notice about my arrival and thank you for keeping it so beautifully. Clearly you are doing an amazing job.'

He congratulated himself on keeping any mocking tone out of his voice.

His housekeeper looked at him suspiciously, but eventually she slipped her hand into his. Immediately Nikos felt the slightly rough skin of her palm, and the desire he felt turned into full-on arousal. Hot and pulsing through every vein. Instinctively he closed his hand around hers.

Maggie couldn't breathe again. What had this man just said? Her brain felt fuzzy. All she was aware of was how big his hand felt around hers, dwarfing it completely. Dwarfing *her*, actually. She was tall, and she'd got used to being described by various people throughout her life as *a big, strong girl*, but Nikos Marchetti towered over her, and for the first time in her life she felt…delicate.

Even in heels she'd barely graze his jaw—a fact which, though she hated to admit it, was a little intoxicating. It was rare for her to have to look up at a man. Not that she'd ever had much opportunity. A lifetime of moving around with her mother hadn't been conducive to forming a core group of close friends, and the few dates she'd embarked upon in a bid to broaden her social circle had invariably ended with a limp handshake when the men had turned out to be several inches smaller than her. Every single time.

So for that and a myriad other reasons—including her general mistrust of men, bred into her by her mother—she'd shied away from intimacy. But here…now…it felt very intimate.

She pulled her hand free. 'Have you eaten this evening? There's some leftover chicken stew. I can't remember if it's on your list of preferred foods, but you're welcome to some if you'd like me to heat it up?'

She was babbling—a habit when she was nervous and one she hated. She took a few steps back, putting some much-needed space between her and this man who was making her think about all sorts of things and...*intimacy.* He was her boss.

He shrugged minutely. 'Sure. I need to take a shower and change. I'll be down shortly.'

Maggie said, 'Your walk-in dressing room is stocked with a full wardrobe, should you need anything.'

She went downstairs and cursed herself for being so affected by him. He was undeniably gorgeous and sexy, yes, but he probably had the same effect on everyone he encountered. It was just proof that she wasn't immune to his very potent brand of sexuality.

She stopped in the hallway when she spied his overnight bag. It looked expensive. As she'd told him, he had a fully stocked wardrobe in his suite, but she should probably take his bag up too. Wasn't that part of the job spec of a housekeeper?

She went back upstairs and halted at his door, suddenly uncertain. It was half closed. She couldn't hear anything, so she knocked lightly and cleared her throat. It felt weird, after having had the house to herself.

There was no response, so she pushed the door open. Then she saw the door leading to the en suite bathroom was half open. There was the sound of running water, and tendrils of steam drifted out. He was in the shower.

Maggie crept forward and put the bag on the bed, turning to make a hasty retreat. Before she did, though, she looked in the direction of the bathroom and saw a tall, dark shape. The water wasn't running any more. And she stood, transfixed, as Nikos Marchetti's body was revealed in the sliver of space at the open doorway as the steam evaporated.

She couldn't move. There was a roaring in her head. He was naked and he was...*magnificent*. Breathtaking. Long, lean limbs. Hard-muscled torso. Every inch of olive skin gleamed and rippled. The hair on his chest led in a line down to the curling hair between his legs where—Maggie's face flamed—she could see the evidence of just how potent his body was.

And then he stilled.

Maggie's gaze moved up and she was caught in the beam of those dark gold and green eyes. Totally unperturbed, Nikos Marchetti reached for a towel and slung it around his narrow hips, covering his body. He didn't say a word.

As if someone had come along and slapped her across the face, to break her out of her stasis, Maggie got out a garbled, 'Sorry… I thought you might need…something… your bag…'

Then she turned and fled from the room, body and face burning.

Nikos drained his glass of the white wine that had accompanied a surprisingly delicious chicken stew. He hadn't realised how hungry he was until Maggie had placed it in front of him in the less formal of the dining rooms and the smell had made his stomach rumble. Food was rarely more than a means to keep going in his world.

He sat back now, ruminating on the fact that everything about this evening had been surprising.

Such as arriving here to find his housekeeper at least twenty years younger than he'd expected. And beautiful. And sexy in a way that caught at Nikos deep inside, where most women didn't impact on him. He liked to keep things superficial. Light. He wasn't in the market for anything deeper after a lifetime's learning that his emotional needs wouldn't ever be met. He focused on transitory pleasures and amassing his fortune—staking his claim on the family business.

Maggie reappeared in the doorway. She'd changed her

clothes since that explosive moment when he'd looked up and caught her staring at him as if she'd never seen a naked man before. Like a rabbit caught in the headlights. Her huge blue eyes big and round and fixated on that part of him that had refused to cool down in spite of turning his shower to cold for several long seconds at the end.

It was a good thing she'd left when she had or she'd have seen just how potent her effect on him was. He'd had to get back into the shower and turn it to cold for long minutes, resisting the urge to take the edge off his acute desire. He *wasn't* at the mercy of his body and hormones—no matter how tempting his housekeeper was.

She now wore a white shirt tucked neatly into black trousers. Flat black brogues. Hair pulled back into a bun at the back of her head. And, bizzarely, even though she was conforming exactly to the way he would have expected his housekeeper to behave, it irritated him intensely.

Yet he couldn't fault her. The house was pristine. And he had been out of line arriving without any notice. She worked here—she couldn't be expected to be in a state of readiness twenty-four/seven. That was just…not feasible.

She came over, avoiding his eye, and picked up the plate.

He said, 'That was very good. Excellent, in fact. You said you made it?'

Maggie was doing her best to avoid eye contact with Nikos Marchetti. But she couldn't ignore him. She forced herself to look at him. His hair was still damp and curling thickly on his head. Which only reminded her of *that moment…*

She said quickly, 'I used to work as a commis chef in a restaurant. That's what I want to do eventually…be a chef.'

Nikos Marchetti frowned. 'Why did you leave?'

Maggie wished that the clothes she'd put on—her uniform—felt like a barrier against that dark gaze. But when he looked at her she felt as if he was seeing all the way through her to where her blood was rushing and still felt so hot.

'Because of my mother's illness. Also, the head chef was too handsy for my liking.'

Nikos Marchetti tensed visibly. 'You mean he touched you?'

Maggie was surprised at his reaction. 'Me and pretty much every other female member of staff who came within a few feet of him. But my mother fell ill, so it wasn't a hard decision to come here to help her. She thought she could manage with my help. But then her illness progressed quickly…'

Nikos Marchetti stood up and took the plate out of Maggie's hands. He pulled out a chair. 'Sit down.'

Maggie hesitated for a moment, but then sat down. Nikos Marchetti sat down too.

'I'm sorry about earlier. Someone should have rung ahead to tell you of my arrival. And I'm sorry about your mother. You were lucky to have had her as long as you did. You sound as if you were close.'

Maggie looked at her boss. Maybe if she kept reaffirming that in her head—*her boss*—she would be able to ignore the way there seemed to be a million signals between them going on under the surface. Her awareness of him… the way he looked at her. It was illictly thrilling.

'We *were* close. She was a single parent and I was an only child.'

'Your father wasn't on the scene?'

Maggie shook her head quickly. 'No, he wasn't.' In a bid to divert him away from a subject she avoided like the plague, she asked, 'Is *your* mother still alive?'

Instantly Nikos Marchetti's expression shuttered. 'No. She died a long time ago. I don't remember her at all.'

For some reason Maggie had a sense that wasn't entirely true. But she said, 'I'm sorry. Losing a parent at any age is tough.' She reached out to take his plate again and stood up. 'If you'd like to move into the lounge I can bring you coffee, or tea?'

Nikos Marchetti looked at her and for a moment it was as if he'd forgotten she was there. He'd disappeared for a second.

Maggie suspected that the persona he projected—rich, careless—was a little bit of a construct, hiding something far more formidable under the surface. He was watchful, even though he carried that careless air of nonchalance.

'I'll have a whiskey. But on one condition.'

Maggie had been turning away and now looked back. Nikos Marchetti was standing up. 'What condition?' she asked. For some reason her heart tripped into a faster rhythm.

'That you join me for a glass. It's the least I can do after arriving unannounced.'

Maggie's hands tightened on the plate. She felt breathless again, just imagining inhabiting the same space as this man. Especially after seeing him naked.

'That's really not necessary.'

'Please. I've had more scintillating conversation with you in the last couple of hours than I've had with anyone in the last month. Indulge me.'

CHAPTER TWO

NIKOS WAITED IN the living room for Maggie to return. He didn't know if she'd take him up on his offer and realised it had been a long time since a woman had held any element of surprise for him.

He was used to not having to fight very hard or work very hard to get what he wanted—women or deals. He knew this was largely thanks to his genes and his wealth. He was under no illusions that if those elements were stripped away his life would be very different.

Still, life had become…boring of late.

He stood at the open French doors. The air was warm and still. Nothing was moving. A lone cow mooed in the distance. He couldn't recall the last time he'd been somwhere so peaceful, and to his surprise it wasn't making him itch for distraction—it was soothing his ragged edges.

No one knew he was here. That had been one of the indefinable things that had appealed to him about this house. The fact that it was so rural—a complete contrast to the life he usually led—had made his spontaneous purchase even more surprising. But he didn't want to analyse that now. And he certainly didn't want to analyse the sensation that he was in a place that felt like home, when nowhere had *ever* felt like home to him.

He didn't have a home and he didn't want one. *Home* was a myth.

He went over and looked at the bookshelves that lined one wall. Something caught his attention. He reached out and pulled a book off the shelf. It had been a childhood favourite of his, and it immediately and disconcertingly took him back in time to when he'd used books as a form of escape in his younger years.

He heard a sound and looked round. Maggie was coming in with a tray. Immediately he noticed the two glasses beside the bottle of whiskey. The rush of anticipation that coursed through him might have surprised him in another setting, but this evening had thrown up so many surprises that he barely noticed.

She stopped when she saw the book in his hand. She looked sheepish. 'Sorry, I put some of my books on the shelves. I hope you don't mind…'

Nikos put the book back. 'It's no big deal. I'm surprised you still have your childhood books.'

Maggie wasn't meeting his eyes now, as she put the tray down. He was used to women being forward, taking advantage of his interest. She was different. And he wanted her.

She poured whiskey into both glasses. She handed him one, kept one.

He lifted his. 'Cheers.'

She came closer, tapped her glass on his quickly. 'Cheers.'

She took a sip and made a face as the tart drink burned the back of her throat.

He smiled at her reaction. 'Not a whiskey drinker?'

Maggie shook her head. 'I've always wanted to try it.'

'So that's why you agreed to have a drink with me? In the interest of research?'

'Something like that,' Maggie said, hoping to sound careless, as if this interaction with the most dynamic man she'd ever met wasn't as intimidating as it felt.

She sneaked a glance at him. He was looking right at her. Her gaze skittered away again, but not before she saw what looked like a glint of humour in his eyes. As if he knew exactly what kind of effect he was having on her.

'So tell me—how did your books survive for so long?'

Maggie felt ridiculously nervous. 'We moved around a lot, me and my mother, when I was young. Books were my escape in a world that kept changing. My one constant. I'm kind of superstitious about them now. It's silly…'

'Not silly at all. I get it.'

'You do?' She was surprised. Again.

He grimaced faintly. 'I had those books too. But they got left behind long ago and I never really read much again. Didn't have time.'

Maggie felt a little ache near her heart that she shouldn't be feeling for a near total stranger. 'I wouldn't have had you down as a bookworm,' she remarked.

Nikos arched a brow. 'I'm more than just a pretty face.'

Maggie couldn't stop the smile tugging at her mouth. He'd said that with a definite mocking edge that he didn't need—because it was the truth. He was gorgeous. Overwhelmingly so. And she suspected that he was a *lot* more than just a pretty face. His eyes were way too sharp and knowing. Cynical.

Nikos had opened the French doors and everything was still outside. As if the rest of the world was very far away. But in spite of the stillness and the peace there was an electricity running through her veins. Dangerous. Thrilling.

He asked, 'You aren't bored here? It seems like an odd job for a beautiful young woman.'

Maggie's heart hitched. *Beautiful?* She told herself he must say that to dozens of women. An easy platitude. She felt self-conscious. Defensive.

'Since my mother died I've appreciated a…a quiet space to mourn her.' She wrinkled her nose. 'But in any case I'm not really the clubbing type.'

Except right now the thought of clubbing was almost attractive. A way to defuse the intensity of the atmosphere in the room between her and Nikos Marchetti. Which she had to be imagining. A man like him moved in circles far removed from country houses in quiet rural Ireland.

That prompted her to ask, 'Why did you buy this house?'

He arched a brow. 'I need a reason?'

Embarrassed, she said, 'Of course not…it just doesn't seem like the kind of place for a man like…' She trailed off, mortified now.

'It's an investment. I thought I might buy some race horses in the future, and I'd need a house with stables.'

Maggie didn't fully believe this perfectly plausible explanation. And she didn't even know why. She hardly knew this man.

'What prompted you to come here this evening?' she asked.

'Has anyone ever told you you ask a lot of questions?' he said.

Maggie flushed and smiled sheepishly. 'My mother—all the time. Maggie the Inquisitor, she used to call me.'

Once again Nikos was surprised by how honest she was, and the way she seemed to have no fear of him. It was refreshing. And arousing.

The truth was that he'd come here because he'd wanted to escape the claustrophobic confines of that function. He'd intended flying straight back to London, but the next scheduled flight wasn't until the following morning, and Nikos refused to use private air transport unless absolutely necessary.

He'd been about to book a hotel. But then he'd remembered his house. The house he'd never even visited. And so he'd come here feeling restless. Unsettled.

And then she'd opened the door and his brain had seized in a paroxysm of lust.

As if sensing the direction of his thoughts, she drained her glass and put it down on the tray. 'Thank you for the drink, but if you'll just tell me what time you want breakfast I'll have it ready for you in the morning.'

She looked at him and all he could see were those huge blue eyes. The two pink spots of colour in her cheeks. A pulse beating hectically in her neck. Breasts rising and falling under her shirt with her breaths.

The chemistry between them was so tangible he could taste it. He knew she wanted him as much as he wanted her. If there was anything he was expert in, it was women and desire.

He said, 'I couldn't care less about breakfast. Are you really going to pretend you don't feel it too?'

Maggie's heart stopped. And then started again in an irregular rhythm. Maybe she'd misheard.

'I'm sorry—what did you say?'

He smiled a slow smile and it was pure sin. She could feel heat creeping up over her chest into her cheeks. So much for hoping to create a more professional atmosphere by cutting this late-night drink short.

'You heard me, Maggie.'

Her name from his mouth… It trailed over her skin like raw silk, leaving goosebumps behind.

She swallowed. 'I don't know what you're talking about. If you'll excuse me, I'm going to go to bed now.'

She turned to leave, skin prickling and heart thumping, even as part of her ached to see just where his words might go. No man had ever had this effect on her. She didn't know how to handle it. How to be blasé, nonchalant. A man like Nikos Marchetti would chew her up and spit her out. Of that she had no doubt.

Before she reached the door, though, he said from behind her, 'Aren't you even curious? Do you know how rare it is to feel chemistry this powerful with another person?'

No! Because she'd never experienced anything like it before and it intimidated the hell out of her even as it thrilled her. She was a virgin, and totally out of her depth with a man like this.

Reluctantly she turned around to face him again. 'I think there must have been plenty of women at your event this evening who would have been only too happy to explore your mutual chemistry.'

He made a face. 'I didn't want any of those women. But the moment I saw you I wanted *you*. That hasn't happened to me in a long time.'

A shiver of longing went through Maggie before she could stop it.

Words, she told herself frantically, *These are just words to entice.*

He was playing with her. She was just a passing fancy.

Angry at herself for her out-of-control reaction, she said, 'I suspect that has more to do with your being jaded than with me personally.'

His mouth hitched at one side. 'You're not wrong. I *am* jaded. And cynical.'

Surprise that he was agreeing with her knocked her off-centre. She hadn't expected it of a man like him.

He shook his head. 'It's a long time since anyone surprised me. But you have, Maggie. If anything, you've reminded me that not everyone or everything is cynical.'

He put down his glass and came towards her. Maggie was rooted to the spot.

He stopped a couple of feet away. 'I'm not a man who plays games. I see what I want and go after it. I want you like I haven't wanted anyone in a very long time. You intrigue me. You excite me. But obviously this is not an ideal situation. Whatever happens is outside the bounds of your job. If you want this, it's between two mutually consenting adults and it's your call. Your decision. I'm getting the first flight back to London tomorrow. I don't know when I'll be back again.'

Maggie couldn't remember if she'd ever known anyone to talk so directly. Not even her no-nonsense Scottish mother. But she struggled to do the right thing over the pounding beat of her pulse. 'I don't think it would be a good idea…'

Nikos Marchetti took a step closer. So close that Maggie could see the gold and green flecks in his eyes. His scent tantalised her nostrils, making her want to move closer. She fought the urge.

'You're probably right—and normally I would never sanction mixing business with pleasure—but I find in this instance that I'm willing to take the risk. If you are.'

She swallowed. 'No, I don't think I am.'

There was a long beat and then he said, 'Okay. Your call. Goodnight, Maggie.'

He walked out of the room and Maggie turned to watch him go. He moved with lithe athletic grace. Broad shoulders tapering down to lean hips. Long legs.

When he'd disappeared she let out a shuddery breath. She lifted a hand and touched her mouth, almost expecting it to be swollen, as if he'd kissed her. He hadn't.

But you'd like him to, whispered a wicked voice.

Maggie groaned softly. Never in her wildest dreams had she imagined that this kind of scenario would present itself. She couldn't be more isolated from the world, and yet one of the sexiest, most dynamic men on the planet had more or less literally dropped into her lap.

He wanted her. And she had never felt this kind of physical attraction before. She'd believed it was a myth—a tale spun in the romantic novels her mother had loved. Maggie prided herself on her more practical outlook. She'd accused Nikos Marchetti of being cynical, but she knew she was cynical too. She was a cynical twenty-three-year-old virgin.

Another shiver went through her, but this time it wasn't one of awareness. Or desire. It was one of foreboding. She'd never intended staying here for ever, but three months had slipped by almost without her noticing. If she wasn't careful she would end up like Miss Havisham from *Great Expectations*—except she wouldn't even be lamenting a ruined relationship—because she'd never had one.

Nikos Marchetti is not offering a relationship. He's offering a moment in time, to explore mutual chemistry.

Maggie guessed that for a man like him—suave, experienced—it was second nature to act on impulses like this: seducing women he desired. He didn't seem like a man who denied himself. And was that such a bad thing? It wasn't as if he'd pretended there was anything else going on here.

On autopilot, Maggie went and closed the French doors. She collected the tray with the whiskey and empty glasses and took them down to the kitchen. Everything was silent and quiet. She could almost imagine for a moment that she'd dreamed up the events of the evening since Nikos Marchetti had knocked on the door so imperiously.

But the seismic changes in her body told her it hadn't been a dream. He hadn't even touched her, but she felt as if she'd been plugged into some vital force. She felt alive. Her skin was sensitive...hot. Her heart was still pounding.

Maggie cursed herself. She'd made a decision a long time ago to forge a different path from her mother, who had been dazzled by a powerful man and then cast aside as if she was rubbish. She'd vowed never to let herself be treated like that. If and when *she* had a relationship, it would be with someone who was her equal. Someone who shared her values—who wanted a simple wholesome life. Someone who took responsibility for their actions.

And if and when she had children she would want them to grow up in one place, safe and secure. Not wondering what they'd done to make their father hate them so much that he'd reject them for fear they'd lay claim to his fortune.

She wanted her children to grow up with two parents. She knew how hard it was to do it alone. She'd spent the guts of the last year caring for her rapidly diminishing mother, and some of her mother's last words had been about her regret that she hadn't met someone else, to give Maggie a more stable environment. Maggie had only realised then how lonely her mother must have been.

So the fact that she was even thinking about Nikos Marchetti and his outrageous suggestion was ridiculous. It was something she should be dismissing out of hand. He was the antithesis of everything she'd ever wanted. An arrogant rich man who bought vast houses on a whim and never visited them.

He's not asking for a relationship, reminded that small voice.

Maggie didn't have to be experienced to know that a man like Nikos Marchetti would not be looking for anything that wasn't transitory.

She felt hopelessly conflicted.

Would it really be so bad to take something for herself? When she'd never behaved selfishly in her life?

Just for a moment in time?

Nikos Marchetti was under this roof for one night. Based on his track record, he wouldn't be back for ages. If ever.

A million butterflies erupted in Maggie's belly and she put a hand there, as if that would quell them.

Maybe if she hadn't actually seen him naked…

But, no… She couldn't possibly be considering—*could* she? *No!*

She shut down her feverish mind and went and briskly turned off the lights, made her way upstairs. Her room was the most modest—tucked in a return, away from the main bedrooms. But she hesitated on the landing.

She could go into her bedroom, shut her door, and Nikos Marchetti would most likely be gone before she even woke in the morning. Temptation gone. The moment passed. Her world would never collide with his again. She moved in circles far outside of his sphere. By the time he returned to the house again she probably would have moved on to another job.

And still be a virgin.

As that stark thought sank in, a kind of recklessness she'd never experienced before rose up inside her. Nikos Marchetti was offering something decadent and illicit. He was offering life, and vitality. And, after seeing her mother wither away, Maggie desperately needed to feel that life force.

Almost of their own volition her feet turned in the other direction. She walked down the corridor towards Nikos Marchetti's bedroom. She stopped at the door, feeling slightly light-headed with the enormity of what she was contemplating.

She raised her hand and saw it was shaking. She lowered it again. She couldn't do this. She wasn't experienced enough to take what Nikos Marchetti was offering and remain unscathed. As tempted as she was, he would scorch her alive.

She turned away—and came face to face with fire.

Nikos Marchetti was standing in the corridor, naked from the waist up. Sweat pants hung low from his hips and he had a towel slung around his shoulders. His hair was damp. Face flushed. His dark olive skin gleamed. Dimly, she realised he must have been in the gym.

If Maggie had had a moment to resist then it had passed. He took a step closer and she could smell him. Musky and thrillingly masculine.

'Maggie?'

She dragged her gaze up from where it had been fixated on the dark curling hair covering his pectorals. 'Yes?'

'I presume you're not here to check if I have everything I need?'

She knew that she could quite easily step around him and continue on back to her bedroom. If she wanted to. Which she didn't.

Slowly, she shook her head.

'Do you know what you're doing?'

No, said an inner voice. But she nodded jerkily. 'I… I think so.'

Nikos Marchetti stepped closer. So close that she could see how his eyes glittered.

'You need to be sure, Maggie. I won't accept anything less.'

A deep, intense longing settled in her core. She couldn't turn her back on this. 'I am sure.'

'Nikos,' he said.

She blinked. 'You want me to say your name?'

He nodded.

Somehow it would have been less daunting if he'd just taken her face in his hands and kissed her.

She opened her mouth, took a breath, her heart thumping unevenly. 'Nikos,' she said.

Another shiver went through her. It felt unbearably intimate. His name on her tongue. He was no longer the owner of this house, and she wasn't his housekeeper. They were equal.

As if reading her mind, he said, 'When we go through that door we go as two mutually consenting adults, Maggie. You do not have to do anything you don't want. You don't owe me anything because of who I am. You are doing this because you want to. Because we both want this.'

She found that she felt quite touched that he was being so careful to make sure she felt in control of the situation.

Again, not something she would have expected of a man like him.

'I know what I'm doing. I want this.' Maggie's voice was husky.

'Good.'

Nikos came forward and took Maggie's hand in his. He led her into the bedroom, where lamps shed pools of golden light around the room. The sky was still a very dark lavender outside. On these summer nights there was only a few hours of total darkness.

He let her hand go and faced her. He made a face. 'I should shower.'

The thought of him turning away from her, even for a small moment, made her feel panicky—as if she might lose her nerve. 'No, you don't need to,' she said.

And he didn't. He smelled divine.

He pulled the towel off his shoulders and threw it down on a nearby chair. Then he said, 'Come here.'

Maggie took the step towards him, her skin tight all over, prickling with anticipation and awareness.

'Take down your hair.'

She reached behind her, as if in a dream, and pulled her hair loose. It fell around her shoulders. Unruly hair. Thick and unmanageable. Too much. But it was the same as her mother's so she loved it.

So, apparently, did Nikos. He reached out, taking a long strand and twining it around his fingers. 'Your hair is amazing…'

He tugged her even closer. Maggie's legs were like jelly. He slid the hand holding her hair around her neck, his thumb over the pulse that was hammering against her skin.

He tipped her jaw up. 'Touch me.'

Maggie lifted her hands and put them on Nikos's chest, felt his hair scratching her palms, his skin warm and alive. Muscles tensed under her fingers. Suddenly there wasn't enough oxygen in the room, even though Maggie felt a faint breeze coming from an open window.

Nikos put his other hand on Maggie's arm and bent his head, his breath feathering over her mouth for a moment. She smelled whiskey, and it rushed to her head all over again.

Everything inside her went still as she waited for his mouth to touch hers. She felt superstitiously that nothing would be the same after this… And then his mouth settled over hers and she knew it wasn't a superstition. It was truth.

Like dry kindling to a match, she went up in flames.

Nothing could have prepared her for how Nikos's mouth felt on hers—how it moved and enticed, encouraging her to open up so he could explore the very depths of her.

And the deeper the kiss got, the hungrier she became. It was as if she'd been starved her whole life until this moment. His hand was in her hair again now, tugging her head back to allow him more access, and Maggie moved closer, seeking more contact. She was responding instinctively, from a primal place of need…

Nikos was drowning in heat and lust. Maggie's mouth under his…hesitant and soft at first, and then becoming bolder… ignited his senses like no other woman ever had, blasting apart any jadedness or ennui.

Her body was quivering against his like a taut bow. Full breasts were pressed against his chest, and he itched to explore her curves, explore every womanly inch of her. Her height was a novelty he relished.

He found the front of her shirt, his hands uncharacteristically inexpert, and undid the buttons, pushing the shirt apart. He pulled back from her mouth and opened his eyes, groaned softly. Her eyes were still closed, lashes long and dark on her cheeks, and her mouth was plump and pink.

She opened her eyes and it took a second for them to focus on him.

Desire wound tight as a drum inside Nikos. When was the last time he'd kissed such a responsive woman? Perhaps when he'd been a teenager, fumbling and awkward?

He looked down and stopped breathing. Her breasts were full and high. Encased in lace. Her waist was small and her hips flared—she embodied a feminine sensuality that he suspected she wasn't even aware of.

She ducked her head but he tipped her chin up. 'You are *stunning*.'

Her cheeks were hot. 'I'm not wearing anything… special.'

Nikos had to control his urge to strip her bare and bury himself to the hilt, seeking immediate relief.

'Believe me, you are the sexiest woman I've ever seen,' he said.

She looked serious. 'You don't have to say things like that.'

'I'm not just saying it…' He meant it. The women he took to bed were usually so confident they required little or no compliments. Maggie seemed…*shy*.

Something occurred to him then and he went still. But he dismissed it out of hand. She might seem inexperienced, but she was probably putting it on—because in this day and age no one her age could be that innocent. She just wasn't worldly or sophisticated…

Maggie looked up at Nikos. For a second she wondered if he suspected how inexperienced she was, and she knew if she was going to say anything then this was her moment. She should tell him.

But all she could see in her mind's eye was the way he would look at her—with shock and then disgust. She felt panicky at the thought of him rejecting her. Surely he wouldn't notice?

A sense of desperation made her say, 'Nikos… I do want this… I want you.'

His eyes grew darker. He pushed the shirt off her shoulders, down her arms, and it fell to the floor. Maggie kicked off her shoes, undid the button on her trousers and pushed them down, stepping out of them.

Now she wore only her underwear, and Nikos's gaze travelled down over her body in a slow and thorough appraisal. Her hands itched and she clenched them into fists. She'd never felt so needy in her life.

With a brisk economy of movement Nikos shed the rest of his clothes until he was naked.

Maggie looked down and gulped. He was hard. Thick and long.

'Touch me, Maggie.'

She wanted to. But suddenly she was shy.

She reached out and traced a finger down his length, over a throbbing vein. She heard a low moan. Was it her or him? She couldn't think straight. She wanted to wrap her hand around him.

But he took her wrist and said, in a choked-sounding voice, 'I'm feeling a little underdressed here…'

Maggie looked up at him. He put his hands on her shoulders and turned her around, undoing her bra and letting it fall forward and off. He tugged her panties over her hips and down. They fell to her feet.

Her breathing was so shallow now she felt dizzy. No one had ever seen her as naked as this. She'd even been shy in front of her mother.

'Turn around, Maggie.'

Slowly she turned around, eyes down. She heard Nikos's indrawn breath. She bit her lip…saw his hand come into her line of vision. He cupped a breast, feeling its weight.

His thumb traced the areola around her nipple and it stood to attention. Tight and hard.

Maggie bit her lip so hard she could taste blood. It was excruciatingly intense, the sensation rushing through her body. She'd never expected it could be like this—slow, exploratory… Torturous in the most pleasurable way.

She looked up at Nikos. His eyes were heavy-lidded. Cheeks flushed.

She tried to articulate what she was feeling, 'I can't… I need…'

He looked at her, his hand closing over her plump flesh, trapping her nipple between two fingers. Maggie reached out, her hands landing on his biceps. She had to hold on to something. She was drowning.

'I need…you. More…'

Nikos took his hand from her breast and Maggie almost cried out. He led her over to the wide bed. The bed that she remade every week with fresh linen.

No, don't think about that now.

He came down on the bed beside her, and the clamour of needy voices in her head stopped when he covered her mouth with his again. He explored her with his hands, finding curves she hadn't even been aware of. His mouth moved down, leaving a trail of fire in its wake as he came closer and closer to where she ached most for him to explore: the throbbing points of her breasts.

When his mouth closed over one, encasing it in hot, sucking heat, she arched her back helplessly. Her hands were buried in his hair as he moved from one to the other, his hands plumping her breasts even more, feeding her to himself like some decadent pasha lingering over a tasty meal.

When he moved downwards Maggie was panting. He settled his body between her legs, opening her up to him. She'd never been more exposed, or so much at someone else's mercy, and yet she felt no sense of vulnerability or insecurity. Only a sense of wonder and awe.

He looked up at her and she could only describe the expression on his face as *wicked*—just before he dipped his head and she felt his mouth on her—*right there*—at the most intimate part of her body.

Maggie's hands, no longer in Nikos's hair, found the sheets and gripped them as he mercilessly demonstrated his skill. At one point the feeling was so intense she tried to close her thighs, but he kept them open. He put a hand on her belly, as if to soothe her, while his tongue explored her with a thoroughness that left her dizzy.

Everything inside her was winding tighter and tighter, bringing her to an edge she'd only ever explored on her own before. And then, with a rush, she tipped over the edge, her whole body spasming as a huge wave of pleasure undulated out from the centre of her being. She hadn't expected it to be so violent—like a force rushing through her body that she couldn't hope to contain. A force outside her control.

She looked up, dazed, as Nikos loomed over her. She'd heard the sound of foil ripping and looked down now, to see that he'd sheathed himself with protection. Her muscles quivered with renewed desire. *Already.* What was happening to her? She was insatiable.

Nikos looked at her. 'You're unbelievably responsive... do you know what a turn-on that is?'

Maggie couldn't speak. She could only shake her head.

Nikos moved between her legs and his thighs pushed hers apart a little more. She instinctively shifted, welcoming him into the cradle of her body, still sensitive after the rush of pleasure but already aching for more.

Nikos looked down at her, and then he slid an arm around her back, arching her up to him while at the same time guiding himself into her body, pushing deep in one cataclysmic thrust.

Maggie gasped, clutching at his arms, eyes wide as she absorbed the sensation of his body joining with hers.

Nikos went still, eyes narrowing on her face.

'Maggie…are you—?'

Reacting on pure instinct, and a desperate need for him not to say it out loud, she wrapped her legs around his hips, which deepened his thrust inside her. 'Please, don't stop…'

The sting of pain was fading as Nikos's body pulsed inside hers. She could have cried with relief when he started to move out and then moved back in. She welcomed him, her body flowing and adapting around his as an instinctive rhythm caught their bodies up in its timeless dance.

Nikos held her thigh against him as his thrusts became harder, deeper, faster. And Maggie could only cling on as the storm leapt and danced within her, whirling her higher and higher into a vortex of gathering pleasure that she couldn't escape. Didn't want to escape.

Her body arched up into Nikos's as tension held her taut for a long moment, the pinnacle beckoning, making her desperate for release. And then it broke, hurling her high over and over again, not letting her catch her breath as her whole being pulsated and throbbed in the aftermath.

Nikos knew she wasn't even aware of him tensing over her body as he, too, found his release, his body spasming deep inside her in the strongest climax he'd ever experienced, turning him inside out.

It tore through his body so powerfully that for a moment he could ignore the truth that had seared itself onto his brain before she'd pushed him over the edge and to the point of no return.

She'd been a virgin.

CHAPTER THREE

MAGGIE LAY ON the bed, unable to move. The aftershocks of what had just happened still rippled through her, inside, where Nikos's body had filled her to the point of almost pain…and then such pleasure as she'd never known could exist.

He'd gone into the bathroom, and Maggie was glad of a moment's respite to try and absorb what had happened. How it had made her feel. She hadn't expected it to be so… so intensely exquisite. So bone-shakingly desperate.

She heard the bathroom door open and pulled the sheet over herself. Nikos emerged with a towel slung around his waist. The sheer magnificence of his body made her mouth go dry. To think that a man like him had wanted her…

And then he spoke.

'Why didn't you tell me you were a virgin?'

He'd noticed.

Maggie's insides dropped like a stone. Of course he'd noticed.

She looked at him and couldn't speak. Not yet. Still too shocked at what had happened. The speed at which she'd gone from dealing with the unexpected arrival of her absentee boss to this moment was truly mortifying. As was her total and absolute capitulation. He hadn't even had to touch her to seduce her!

Now he looked the opposite of seductive. He looked positively icy. Condemning. A cold shiver went down her spine. *What had she done?*

She made her mouth form the shape of a word. 'I…'

'You…?' he said, impatience and something else less definable making his tone sharp.

Maggie's brain wouldn't function. She dragged her gaze away from his naked torso. 'Can you put some clothes on, please?'

He emitted a curse in some language that sounded guttural. She took advantage of the fact that he'd moved towards where his trousers lay, in a crumpled heap on the floor to pull the sheet up over her breasts.

He came back, hitching his trousers over his hips, pulling up the zip. 'Well?'

Maggie wanted to point out that his top button was still open but she resisted the urge. She swallowed. Focused on his question.

Virgin.

'I didn't think…' She trailed off.

That had been the problem, from the moment he'd appeared on the doorstep earlier she hadn't had a rational thought in her head. First of all she'd sparked off him, and then…then she'd wanted him.

He opened his mouth, but she didn't want to hear that sharp tone again so she said, with a little sheepishness, 'I didn't want you to stop.'

I was afraid you'd stop. Those words trembled on her lips but she clamped her mouth shut.

'*Theos,* Maggie. You should have told me. I thought you were experienced. I don't sleep with virgins. I am the last man who should initiate a woman in her first sexual experience.'

Maggie's body disagreed. After what had just happened, the thought of another man being the one to initiate her in the ways of lovemaking almost made her feel nauseous.

And that was an earth-shattering revelation.

Wasn't Nikos Marchetti the antithesis of everything she wanted in a man?

At what point had she succumbed to his wicked temptation?

It was all fuzzy now, but Maggie knew that somewhere along the way she'd justified having sex with him. And now she felt exposed. She'd had sex with a man who was the same as her father: rich and powerful. And she'd done it without a second thought.

She said, 'Could you pass me a robe, please?'

Nikos looked at Maggie for a long moment, feeling conflicted between anger and desire. She looked thoroughly and utterly debauched. Her skin was still pink from his touch. Her hair was in a wild tumble around her shoulders. Her lips were swollen. Her eyes were huge with the same conflict he was feeling, but there was also something slumberous. And dazed. As if she couldn't believe what had just happened.

Neither could he. He hadn't had such an erotic encounter in a long time. If ever. He'd never felt such desperation to join his body to a woman's.

He emitted a frustrated sound and retrieved a robe from the bathroom door, handing it to Maggie, who scooted into it awkwardly, trying not to show her skin.

It didn't really work. Nikos still got a view of one plump breast and recalled how his hand hadn't been able to contain its bounty.

His body tightened again. He ran a hand through his hair.

Maggie belted the robe and stood up from the bed. It was no consolation to see her legs wobble slightly. His own didn't feel much steadier.

Nikos shook his head. 'How were you still innocent?'

She shrugged minutely, avoiding his eye. 'I just…never met anyone I wanted to…' A blush stained her cheeks red.

'Have sex with?' he supplied, with a tone that he knew was astringent.

She looked at him. 'Something like that.'

There was something defiant in her eyes now. Proud. It

impacted on Nikos down low in his gut, pulling everything tight again. Making him want *more.*

Then she said, 'That was a mistake.'

The strength of the rejection he felt at hearing her say that surprised him. He shook his head. 'Oh, no, *angeli mou*—it's a bit late for regrets. We knew what we were doing—or are you now going to claim that you didn't?'

His conscience struck him. She'd been innocent, so technically she hadn't really known.

Anger eclipsed his conscience. He said again, 'You should have told me you were a virgin.'

She looked at him. 'You're right. I should have, maybe then we would have come to our senses.'

The thought of the dilemma Nikos would have faced had he known of Maggie's innocence wasn't lost on him. Would he have had the strength to deny himself? In spite of his lofty assertion that he didn't sleep with virgins?

And his pride was piqued. 'Do you really mean that?'

She flushed pinker. 'I'm disappointed in myself for sleeping with someone like you.'

Shock and indignation rocked through Nikos. No woman—*ever*—voiced regret for sleeping with him. The opposite, in fact.

He folded his arms. 'Someone like me? Please elaborate.'

Maggie regretted saying anything, but she couldn't escape or prevaricate. Nikos's laser-like gaze wouldn't allow it.

'Someone rich and entitled. Privileged.'

Her conscience pricked. She knew her judgement of him wasn't entirely rational, but from the moment she'd seen him he'd got under her skin and impacted on her in a place where no one ever had before.

After the lessons learnt in her own life, and from her mother, she'd hoped she'd be immune to the lure of a man like him. Cynical. Street-smart. But apparently not.

'Being rich and privileged isn't always all it's cracked up to be—or haven't you read the books and watched the movies about poor little rich kids?'

Maggie's skin prickled uncomfortably. There was a mocking tone to his voice, but also something almost bleak.

She said, 'You're right—that's not fair. It's just…you turned up here, on your first visit to a house you bought sight unseen—'

'Which is really none of your business.'

Maggie clamped her mouth shut, afraid of what might come out next.

Nikos moved closer. The chilly atmosphere warmed slightly.

'The truth is that even if you'd told me you were innocent I'm not sure if I could have resisted the temptation. Are you really saying you're stronger than that? That if you'd had a moment to think about it you would have changed your mind?'

Maggie couldn't look away from those leonine eyes. Who was she kidding? She *had* had a moment to think about it and she'd chosen *him*.

She shook her head jerkily.

'Neither of us were prepared for this chemistry,' he said. 'What happened was mutual, and I for one do not regret one moment. Regrets are for losers. Own what you want, Maggie. You can't go back—only forward.'

'Forward…' she repeated.

He nodded, and as he did so he reached for her, putting his hands on her robe, tugging her towards him. Treacherously, she didn't resist. So much for her brave declaration.

'What I propose is that we live for the moment and enjoy this very potent mutual desire. Or do you want your initiation to end here?'

Maggie's insides tightened and her skin prickled. Heat licked at her core, making her feel needy and greedy again. Would it be so bad to indulge? One more time? *Did* she want her initiation to end here? Even if it was with the kind of man she'd always sworn she would steer well clear of?

She gave him the only answer she could. 'No…'

Nikos's hands went to Maggie's belt and he slowly undid it, looking at her as if to make sure she really wanted this. Now that she was being honest with herself she felt almost impatient. She wanted to seize every moment of this…whatever it was. One-night stand. Interlude.

Nikos pulled the robe apart and looked at her. The heat at her core spread outwards and enflamed every nerve-ending and cell. She reached for Nikos's trousers, pulling down the zip. She tugged them down, over his hips and they fell to the floor, revealing his naked potency.

He pushed the robe from her body. They were both naked, and in that moment Maggie felt something emotional wash through her. No matter how conflicted he made her feel, she wouldn't have wanted to share this deepest intimacy with anyone else. She was glad it was him. He was a man she barely knew, and yet she felt she knew him in a way she couldn't really understand.

He pulled her down onto the bed and they landed in a tangle of limbs, hard against soft. Her breasts were pressed against his hard chest.

He put a hand in her hair and tugged her head back. He smiled wickedly and said, 'Don't give yourself a hard time, Maggie. I'm quite irresistible.'

She might have huffed at that assertion—but then his mouth was on hers, and his other hand was on her breast, and she could only agree.

Hours later, when dawn was breaking outside, Maggie lay in a half-slumber, sated beyond anything she'd ever felt before. Her bones felt as if they had liquefied. Nikos's heart beat a steady strong rhythm under her cheek, where she rested on his chest.

That emotion she'd felt earlier was still there, and she knew how dangerous it was to be feeling anything for this man. But she couldn't help wondering about him. Where would he go from here? What was his life like?

A thought chilled her—he could have a mistress, a girlfriend? Although *girlfriend* sounded far too pedestrian for a man like Nikos Marchetti.

As if he could hear her thoughts, he lifted her hand and brought it to his mouth, pressing a kiss to the palm. Which did not help her rogue emotions.

'Okay?' he asked.

Maggie's heart thumped. He was just being solicitous. Again, not something she would have expected.

She lifted her head and looked at him, nodded.

He flipped them so that Maggie was under him. He twined her fingers with his and held her hand above her head.

She couldn't help blurting out, 'Are you seeing anyone at the moment? I mean, is there a girl—*woman*—somewhere? Because I wouldn't like to think that we...' She trailed off, feeling self-conscious.

Nikos went still. 'No. I'm not. I can be accused of many things, Maggie, but I don't sleep around on women.' Then he frowned as he looked down at her. 'But you need to know this doesn't go beyond this room...tonight. Now. I don't do relationships, Maggie. I'm not interested in settling down, or romance, or happy-ever-afters. They don't exist—or they certainly don't exist with me.'

His words sank into her like cold little stones. She longed to ask him why, but she caught herself. He was telling her what she needed to hear—Nikos Marchetti wasn't the type of man she should want anything more with. Not in a million years.

And yet she'd been drawn to him like a moth to a flame. What did that say about her and her standards? That she was as susceptible as the next woman to his particular potent brand of masculinity?

That she was like her mother, dazzled by the charisma of a powerful man.

A need to protect herself from that too incisive gaze made her say, as lightly as she could, 'Don't worry, I'm under no illusions as to what this is. Anyway, you're not the kind of guy I see myself with long term.'

Nikos was surprised as a little dart of something pierced him. It couldn't possibly be *hurt.*

He moved over her, using his body to push her thighs apart. He heard her indrawn breath, felt the way she arched against him.

'I'm not?' he asked.

She shook her head, her eyes turning a darker blue. 'No way.'

He nudged her thighs further apart and notched the head of his erection against where she was hot and wet. He knew he had to slow the tempo or he would lose it even before he entered her.

'So…who is this paragon who will serve you for the long term?'

She moved under him restlessly, but that dart of emotion he hadn't welcomed made him torture her a little.

She said breathlessly, 'I don't know…someone kind. Respectful. Considerate. Dependable.'

Nikos made a face. 'Sounds boring.'

Maggie reached up with her free hand and traced the muscles in Nikos's chest. 'Boring is good for long-term happiness.'

Nikos caught her thigh and hitched it up, bringing Maggie's body into closer contact with his. He looked down at her and forced himself to hold back, even though he could feel the sweat breaking out on his brow.

'Just so we know where we stand… Later you can have as boring as you like, but right now…in the short term… you have *me*.'

He surged deep inside her and Maggie's whole body arched up to his, heightening the mind-melting sensation of joining their bodies.

Nikos let the physical momentum clear his mind of the fact that his encounter with this woman was way out of his usual comfort zone. And every coherent thought dissolved as they raced once again to the shattering peak of pleasure.

Nikos stood looking down at the sleeping Maggie for a long moment. Not the kind of behaviour he usually indulged in. A prickle of unease lay under his skin. He was reluctant to leave. When he *never* stayed. He always moved on.

He didn't like this. *At all.* He felt out of control. At the mercy of a force outside of himself. Exposed.

He blamed the uncharacteristic sense of restlessness that had been plaguing him recently.

He reminded himself that, as erotic as this encounter had been, and as surprising as Maggie had been, she wasn't any different from other women. *She'd just been a virgin.* That was it. That had to be the element that had elevated this experience above all others, distracting him when he knew he should have left already.

She was just a woman, and she'd piqued his interest briefly. Within a few days he'd have moved on and she would have become a dim memory.

The sense he'd had here of coming home was an illusion, and she'd been part of that illusion. A moment of craziness. But just a moment. Which would not be repeated.

Nikos injected ice into his veins and turned and walked out, already thinking ahead to the things he *should* be thinking of, and not lingering on a virgin Viking Queen who had given up her innocence with such artless passion.

When Maggie woke up the sun was streaming into the bedroom. She was disorientated—and then it all came back. She was in the master suite. Because she'd slept with the master.

She looked around. No sign of Nikos Marchetti. Everything felt very silent and still. The sheet was over her breasts, as if someone had pulled it up.

She came up on one elbow, her hair falling over one shoulder. She felt hollowed out from an overload of sensation, her body aching in places she hadn't known she had muscles.

She saw the robe at the end of the bed and reached for it, pulling it on and getting out of the bed. She noticed that Nikos's clothes weren't scattered on the floor as they had been before.

The nape of her neck prickled.

The bathroom was empty.

She went out of the bedroom and down the corridor. She checked the kitchen. But even before she checked the study and the main living room she knew that she was alone.

He'd gone. Left.

Maggie went into the hall, and it was there that she saw the card propped up on the table, addressed to her with a slashing line in dark ink: *Maggie.*

She opened it.

Thank you for last night, I enjoyed it.

I apologise for the lack of notice. It won't happen again.

Remember, no regrets.

If you need anything, contact my team.

Nikos

It took a long moment for the full impact of the note to hit her. It was like a slow punch to her belly, spreading outwards and making her feel cold. He hadn't even left her his personal number.

Contact my team.

He couldn't have made it any clearer that what had happened had been a very transitory moment.

But isn't that what you signed up to? asked a small voice.

Maggie put the note down. Yes, it was exactly what she'd signed up to—so she shouldn't be feeling this…this wrench.

She just hadn't expected him to be so tender. Generous. Passionate. She hadn't expected sex to be such a transformative, transcendental experience. She hadn't expected to…to *like* him. She hadn't expected to want to know more about him. To sense that his very charming exterior hid a far more steely interior.

Maggie's history had taught her to be wary, but Nikos had turned her preconceptions and her fears on their head.

Before she knew what she was doing she found herself in the study, turning on the main computer.

She put Nikos's name into the computer search engine. Hundreds of hits came up straight away. Business deals… A new casino recently acquired in Monte Carlo… Lurid headlines alluding to his playboy reputation.

There were other headlines too: speculation about him and his two half-brothers, about who really held the reins of power in the family business.

She barely glanced over the few pictures of him with his half-brothers, who looked equally physically impressive. Her eye was drawn treacherously to the pictures of him with dozens of different women on his arm at various events. They were all beautiful—stunning—and well out of Maggie's league. Not one woman appeared twice.

She felt a little nauseous now when she thought of how easily he'd seduced her. Had he just been intrigued because she wasn't as polished as the women he usually hung out with?

Clearly he was a renowned playboy—as if she hadn't deduced that for herself when he'd left her the way he had. When he'd seduced her with such ease. The fact that he was *known* for this kind of behaviour only took the sting away slightly.

But she shouldn't be feeling any sting. No doubt she was already just a blip in his memory as he flew high over the Irish Sea back to his jet-set lifestyle. A lifestyle that didn't impress her or tempt her in any way.

If anything, she should be feeling lighter. She'd lost her virginity to a consummate master of the arts. The problem was she had a sick feeling that he'd ruined her for any other man.

Nikos's words came back. *'I don't do relationships... I'm not interested in happy-ever-afters.'*

She welcomed the reminder—because the last thing Maggie Taggart wanted was for history to repeat itself and for her to fall in love with a rich and powerful man. Or, worse, have his baby. Nikos Marchetti was a man in her father's mould—avowedly anti-relationship and anti-family. The kind of man Maggie had promised herself she wouldn't ever seek out.

So, if anything, she should be grateful that Nikos Marchetti had spelled it out so brutally—because he was the last man she would ever consider as a long-term partner or as a father for her children.

Literally the last man.

CHAPTER FOUR

A year later

THE CHAUFFEUR-DRIVEN CAR wound its way through the small country roads, tall hedges on either side. The sky was turning a dusky lavender as the sun set and the smell from the farming fields around them was pungent.

The sense of déjà-vu was strong. As was the sense of anticipation that Nikos could not push down.

But she wasn't there.

She'd given in her notice about two weeks after that night they'd spent together. Him and the Viking Queen…

In spite of his best efforts to forget her she'd haunted him all year. His memory of that night was so vivid and potent that she'd ruined him for any other woman. His shock and surprise that any lover could linger so effectively in his memory had turned to serious frustration—so much so that he'd even looked for her.

To no avail. She'd disappeared and she hadn't given his staff any contact details or a forwarding address.

This was unprecedented for Nikos. The fact that he could still want a woman after one night and that she wasn't pursuing him. He wasn't so arrogant to think he was irresistible, but his wealth and fame made him a seductive package to most women.

But she'd been different. A virgin. Sparky. Not intimidated. Passionate. Responsive. Theos. So responsive.

In the back of the car Nikos's body hardened at the memory. He cursed again, then said to the driver curtly, 'How much further?'

The driver's eyes met his in the mirror, 'Almost there, Mr Marchetti.'

Nikos sat back, feeling on edge. His fingertips drummed impatiently on his thigh—a habit he hated and strived to hide around anyone but himself, fearing it showed some kind of weakness.

He was only here because he'd accepted an invitation to his friend's end-of-summer party at a house nearby. It was the same friend who had encouraged him to buy Kildare House and invest in horse racing. An investment he'd never followed up.

As the car finally swept in through the gates of the house Nikos vowed to put the property up for sale as soon as he returned to Paris. It was ridiculous to keep it now. Ridiculous to have kept it for so long.

They pulled up at the bottom of the steps leading to the main door. Nikos took his compact weekend bag out of the boot before the driver could do it.

He knocked on the door, and in the few seconds before it opened he found himself holding his breath, wondering if just maybe…

The door opened. His sense of disappointment was a further mockery to his already jagged edges. This housekeeper couldn't have been more different from Maggie Taggart. For a start he was a man. And somewhere in his fifties.

'Mr Marchetti, how nice to welcome you to Kildare House.'

Nikos stepped inside, aware of how this welcome was so very different from last year's, when he'd had to prove his identity. 'Thank you—Mr Wilson, isn't it?'

'Yes. Here, let me take your bag. I've prepared some coffee and snacks—they're in the living room. I can show you the way—'

Nikos was already striding out of the reception hall, 'I know where it is.'

He went inside and moved straight to the bookshelves. Maggie's books were gone. For a moment something prickled at the back of Nikos's neck. Had he dreamed it all? Dreamed her? Was he so jaded and burnt out from years of carousing and living down to the scandalous reputation he'd so painstakingly built that he'd conjured up a virgin to—

'Will there be anything else, sir?'

Nikos turned around. Mr Wilson stood in the doorway. Not Maggie. The disappointment was as unwelcome as it was acute.

'Just my tuxedo for this evening, please—and let the driver know we'll be leaving in an hour.'

'Of course.'

Nikos looked at the coffee on the tray on the table and made a face. He needed something stronger than coffee to burn away those memories. And what he needed was the taste of another woman to wash the memory of Maggie from his mind and body once and for all. Tonight at the Barbier party there was bound to be at least one woman who would stir Nikos's libido back to life.

Maggie's arms were aching, but she kept a smile fixed to her face as she walked through the crowd, holding the tray full of canapés that she'd helped to make earlier in the Barbier kitchen. Part of the reason she was serving was to gauge the reaction to the canapés.

The scene was magical—an end-of-summer garden party to celebrate the latest successes of the Barbier racing stables and stud. The garden was thronged with men in tuxedoes and women in glittering evening gowns, artfully lit by thousands of candles and fairy lights attached to an elaborate system of webbing that stretched over the garden from tree to tree, creating an intricate canopy of light above their heads.

Maggie saw the hosts in the distance—Luc Barbier and

his wife Nessa, who had been a champion jockey until she'd had children. A rush of emotion caught Maggie unawares. They had been so good to her, offering her a job, and then, when she'd—

Her thoughts scattered as she saw a new guest arrive, walking down the steps to be greeted by Luc and Nessa. He was tall and dark. Almost as tall and dark as Luc. Familiar. Ice prickled over her skin.

It couldn't be.

She stopped walking so suddenly that another waiter almost crashed into her.

'Maggie, watch it, will you?'

She didn't even notice someone helping themselves to a canapé. She had to be imagining it—*him*. Her all too frequent dreams had turned into a hallucination. She blinked. Opened her eyes. He was still there, head thrown back now as he laughed at something Luc Barbier was saying.

Women were turning and looking. Whispering. Openly admiring. Lustful. And no wonder. The two men were tall, dark and easily the most gorgeous men in the vicinity—but all Maggie could see was one man. Nikos Marchetti. And all she could remember were those cataclysmic hours when he had transformed her from inexperienced naive virgin into a woman. More than a woman.

Her hands tightened on the tray so much that it shook.

There was a voice near her ear, soft and concerned. 'Maggie? Are you okay? Here, let me take that for you.'

The tray was taken from her hands and Maggie tore her gaze from the man who had moved closer and was now just a few feet away. Nessa Barbier was putting the tray down on a nearby table. Maggie hadn't even noticed her approach.

Nessa's hand was on her arm. 'You look like you've seen a ghost—are you okay?'

Maggie tried to speak, but nothing would come out. This was too huge. Too potentially devastating.

Nessa frowned. 'Maggie, what is it?'

'I… I have to go inside. I need to…' She was babbling, making no sense.

But before she could leave, eyeing up her escape route by skirting around the edge of the crowd, an incredulous voice called her name.

'Maggie?'

Dread pooled in her belly—along with a very belated spark of emotion. *Anger.* She turned around and came face to face with the man she'd tried her best to forget—because he sure as hell hadn't been interested in remembering *her.*

She should have known what to expect. She of all people. But she forced a smile. 'Mr Marchetti. Fancy seeing you here.'

She barely noticed that he looked as shocked as she felt.

'What are you doing here?'

'I work here.'

'You two know each other?' Nessa sounded intrigued. 'I thought you said he'd never been to Kildare House?'

Maggie winced inwardly. She hadn't actually said that, but she'd been deliberately vague about Nikos's visit last year.

Nikos said, 'I visited the house last year…briefly.'

Yet he'd left a lasting impression—very lasting.

Maggie went cold again as the full significance of Nikos's presence sank in.

Nessa was saying, 'I can't believe you didn't tell us, Nikos…'

Maggie backed away, needing to escape. 'If you'll excuse me…?'

She turned and almost ran towards the house, not even caring what Nessa must be thinking. Because that wasn't important. What was important—

Maggie's hand was caught by another, much bigger hand. 'Hey, wait a second.'

She stopped, felt her heart palpitating. For a big man he moved quickly and quietly.

She pulled her hand free and looked up. She'd forgotten how tall Nikos was. Tall enough to tower over her own not inconsiderable height.

They were near the kitchen entrance of the house and it was dark in this part of the garden. The staff were using another entrance to ferry drinks and canapés from house to garden. Maggie cursed herself for leading him here. It was too quiet…intimate.

Nikos was shaking his head. 'I can't believe you're here.'

Maggie's insides were somersaulting all over the place. Had he always been so broad? Why was she still so aware of him? She needed to remember—not let him distract her.

'Well, I *am* here. Was there something you wanted, Mr Marchetti?'

Electricity crackled between them. The air seemed to grow even heavier, as if there was no oxygen.

His mouth tightened. '*Mr Marchetti?* Really? After—'

'Look,' Maggie cut in, desperate not to have him say it out loud. 'I'm working. I really should get back and—'

'Do you really think they'll miss one waitress for a few minutes? Why did you hand in your notice? Was it because of what happened?'

Maggie swallowed. After two weeks of mooning around the house like a lovestruck calf, in spite of her best intentions, she'd realised that Nikos Marchetti had really meant what he'd said. *Contact my team.*

She'd had a sudden vision of him arriving back at the house at some point in the future with a woman and she'd felt sick. So she'd handed in her notice that day.

She tipped up her chin. 'I was never meant to be your housekeeper. I just took over after my mother died—it was never going to be a long-term thing. It's not as if I had ambitions to be a rich man's housekeeper.'

Nikos's eyes flashed at that. Maggie could see the glint of green and gold in the dim light and it sent fires racing all over her skin.

'So moving down the road to serve finger food at the Barbiers' summer party is a step up?'

Anger sizzled in Maggie's belly and she welcomed it as an antidote to the awful crazy urge she had to plaster herself against this man and beg him to kiss her.

'I'm doing a lot more than just serving canapés. I'm actually making them.'

Nikos took a step closer.

Maggie refused to move back.

'You could have stayed at Kildare House. You didn't have to leave.'

Maggie shook her head. 'No, staying was never an option.'

Why was she suddenly breathless? As if she'd been running.

He tipped his head slightly to one side. 'Actually maybe it *is* better that you left.'

Maggie's brain wouldn't function properly. She couldn't take her eyes off Nikos's firmly sculpted mouth. 'Why?

'Because now there are no issues around me being your boss.'

She dragged her gaze up. 'Why would there be issues?'

'For when we do this…'

He was so close now she could see those hazel glints in his eyes, slightly more gold than green. His hair was a little shorter than last year. There was a day's worth of stubble on his jaw. She had an urge to reach up and feel the prickle against her palm. She curled her hand into a fist.

He reached out and caught a lock of her hair which had escaped the rough bun she'd put it into earlier. She hadn't had her hair cut in…months. It was seriously untamed. Unstyled.

He said, almost to himself, 'I can't believe you're here, right in front of me. You've been a thorn in my side for a year, Maggie Taggart.'

She shook her head, feeling as if she was in a dream. This couldn't be real.

'How…? Why?'

He put his hands on her arms and tugged her towards him gently. 'You've haunted me, mind and body, and I can't exorcise you until I have you again.'

'Have…have me?' She was stuttering now, the meaning of what he was saying too huge to compute.

He nodded. 'Not one other woman has made me want her the way you did from the moment I saw you. The way you still do. We have unfinished business…'

Maggie was stunned into silence. This was the man who had left her sleeping in his bed a year ago with only a note telling her she should have '*no regrets*' and to contact him through his team if she needed anything.

A million things bombarded her—chiefly indignation. But as his scent wrapped around her she was hurtled back in time and there was a beat thrumming through her blood, drowning out those concerns.

Nikos's head came closer, and then his mouth was covering hers, and as the reality of him flooded her senses Maggie couldn't deny that he'd haunted her too—even though she'd die before admitting it.

His mouth moved over hers as expertly as she remembered, all-consuming. Heat and madness entered her head and body. *Need.* His tongue swept in and sought hers, demanding a response that came willingly, rushing up through her body before she could stop it.

Her hands clutched at his jacket, either to pull him closer or steady her legs—she wasn't sure which. All she knew was that she never wanted the kiss to end. The hunger she felt was greedy, desperate.

But a sense of anger added an edge to her desire. The anger that had been bubbling under the surface at the way he'd left her a year ago, because it had hurt her when it shouldn't have.

Their bodies cleaved together—when had they even moved that close?—chest to chest, hip to hip, thigh to thigh. She felt unbearably soft—liquid next to his steely strength. She was reminded of how small and delicate he made her feel.

He surrounded her, and when he shifted his hips subtly, so she could feel the press of his arousal against her, her lower body clenched in reaction and a spasm of pleasure caught her off guard. It was as if she'd been primed for the last year for exactly this moment, and now it was here and she was ravenous.

How had she survived without this?

What had she been doing?

Nikos's hand was moving from her hip, caressing her waist, then cupping the solid weight of her breast in his hand. Maggie moaned into his mouth as he squeezed gently. Her flesh was aching. *Sensitive.* And it was sensitive because—

Maggie pulled back abruptly. Reality and the present moment eclipsed the lure of the past.

'What are you doing?' Her voice was husky.

'You mean what are *we* doing?'

The full impact of the fact that he was here, and that within about a nanosecond she had been in his arms again, combusting all over, was not welcome. She saw the stamp of very male satisfaction on his face and it incensed her.

She pushed free of Nikos's arms. 'Oh, my God—you're so arrogant you really thought you could just pick up where we left off a year ago? Is this some kind of fetish you have for menial staff—?'

'Stop that.' His voice was like the lash of a whip.

Maggie's skin was hot and tight, her heart hammering. Between her legs she was slick and hot. Her breasts were aching.

But suddenly she remembered and she turned around. 'I have to go. I don't have time to stand here and be mauled by a rich playboy who gets his kicks from—'

'Now, wait just a sec—'

'Maggie, *there* you are. I've been looking all over for you.'

Maggie came to a standstill. There was a young woman standing in the doorway leading into the kitchen, holding a baby in her arms. He had dark hair and dark eyes and his legs and arms were windmilling frantically.

Immediately everything else was forgotten and Maggie instinctively reached for him, cradling him in her arms, checking him over. 'Is he okay?'

'He's fine—I think he's just hungry. We ran out of your expressed milk.'

Maggie looked at Sara. She was from Merkazad, the country in the Middle East where Nessa's sister lived with her family.

'Okay—thanks, Sara, I'll feed him and put him down. Can you do me a huge favour and let Nessa know I won't be back to the party this evening?'

'Sure. No problem.'

Maggie saw the girl's eyes go behind her and widen as she took in Nikos Marchetti. *Damn.*

Sara left and Maggie slowly turned around. Much as she would have preferred to keep going in the other direction she knew she couldn't.

Her breasts were tingling again, but for entirely different reasons now. If she hadn't been so distracted by this man she would have noticed the signs and gone to her son before he'd had to be brought to her.

Nikos was looking at the baby with a mixture of shock,

incomprehension and horror. His bowtie was askew. Hair mussed.

Had she done that?

Mortification sent a hot wave of shame through her body. She had so much to say to this man, and yet when the moment had come she'd said nothing. Just climbed all over him like a lust-crazed monkey.

She lifted her son and put him over her shoulder, patting his back with an unsteady hand. 'I need to go. I have to feed him.'

She turned, but of course she didn't get far.

'Wait just a minute.'

His accent was thicker, and somehow that made Maggie's heart race again. What was wrong with her? She was in a moment of real crisis and her feverish brain was stuck in a lust loop.

Nikos came and stood in front of her. 'What the hell, Maggie…? Who is this?'

'He's my son. Daniel.'

My son. Her conscience pricked.

Nikos was shaking his head. 'So you had sex with someone else…? Who?'

The fact that he was trying to deny knowledge that he'd been told about her pregnancy sent her hormones into orbit.

'Someone else? Would that have been bad thing? When *you've* undoubtedly had sex with a legion of women in the past year? I don't have time for this—please get out of my way.'

Nikos moved aside without even realising what he was doing. Maggie swept past with the baby on her shoulder. He automatically followed her, in shock.

She'd had a baby. With someone else. She'd slept with someone else right after him—it would have to have been. The baby only looked a few months old.

That realisation curdled in his gut. Along with her accusation that he must have slept with countless women. If only!

The baby's dark eyes regarded Nikos steadily over Maggie's shoulder as she strode back in through the kitchens and up the stairs into the main part of the house.

Nikos was barely aware of staff around them. He felt as if he'd been in an explosion and he couldn't hear properly. Everything was muffled. Distorted.

Suddenly Maggie stopped and turned from the step above him. 'Why are you following me?'

He heard her perfectly, and for the first time he heard the panic in her voice.

He went still inside. She'd attacked him when he'd asked her about the father.

His gaze moved from her to the back of the baby's head. Dark hair. Maggie was fair. His mother had been fair, but his father's darker, stronger genes had won out. He'd had dark hair as a baby. Not that there were many photos of him.

His gaze shifted back to Maggie. She was pale. Something else curdled in his gut now. Suspicion.

'Who is the father, Maggie?'

'I'm not having this conversation here.'

She turned and kept on hurrying up the stairs, entering a corridor on the first floor. Nikos followed her. She went through a door. He stopped on the threshold. It was a spacious bedroom with a cot in the corner. For the baby.

She was looking at him, eyes wide. No longer antagonistic. Hunted.

'Maggie, who is the father?'

'You know you are—why are you asking me as if you don't know?'

Nikos looked at her. It was as if he'd heard her words but they were still hanging in the air between them. Not impacting fully.

He frowned. 'I *know* I am? What are you talking about?'

The baby's back stiffened and he made a mewling sound. Maggie looked distracted. 'I have to feed him. Can you wait outside?' When Nikos didn't move she said, *'Please?'*

Feeling blindsided, Nikos just watched as she came towards him. He stepped back over the threshold and she closed the door in his face. He heard her making comforting sounds as she presumably tended to the baby, baring her breast—the same breast he'd just cupped in a heat haze of lust.

Theos.

He walked away from the door, dazed. He paced down the corridor and back again, one word circling through his mind: *father*.

His only association with the concept of fatherhood was a toxic and complicated thing. His own father had been many things, but a father in the true sense of the word hadn't been one of them. He didn't even know what having a father felt like.

He reeled as the significance of this sank in.

If it was true.

One minute he'd had his hands full of Maggie, feverish with lust, her curves even more delicious than he remembered, and the next he'd been looking at a baby in her arms.

He was back outside the bedroom door now. He could hear Maggie's voice, indistinct, making crooning noises.

Nikos looked around. Nothing but an empty corridor and the woman behind this door with a baby who might or might not be his. And what had she said? Something about '*you know you are*'? That made no sense to him at all.

Nikos looked at the end of the corridor, the stairs leading back downstairs. He heard the muted sounds of the party outside—soft jazz playing, laughter, clinking glasses. The soundtrack to so much of his life up till now. Strangely, though, he didn't feel an urge to escape back to it. He wanted to stay right here and quiz Maggie until what she'd said made sense to him.

Minutes passed and Nikos paced up and down. He felt pressure on his chest. As if someone was sitting on it. Constricting him. He went to loosen his tie but it was already loose.

How long did it take to feed a baby?

When his frustration was about to boil over, Nikos stood outside the door, hand raised, ready to knock. Suddenly it opened and Maggie stood there. Pale. No baby. He looked behind her and could see the shape of the baby in the cot. She'd dimmed the lighting.

She stood back. 'You'd better come in.'

Maggie wished she felt calmer after the shock of seeing Nikos again…kissing him, him seeing the baby…but she didn't. She still felt jittery. It had taken her ages to settle Daniel, because he'd obviously sensed her tension.

Nikos walked in. He looked grim. Maggie directed him to another door which led into a small sitting room. She closed the adjoining door to the bedroom and watched as Nikos prowled around the room like a magnificent caged animal. A panther.

He stopped at the bookshelves, his back to her, hair curling over the back of his jacket. He said, 'You took your books with you.'

She hadn't expected him to notice. Her gut clenched as she remembered that moment last year. 'Yes. They come everywhere with me.'

He turned around. 'Did you leave Kildare House because you were pregnant?'

Maggie shook her head. 'I told you—it was never a long-term plan.'

Nikos gritted his jaw, making it pop. 'How did you end up here, then?'

She swallowed. 'I got to know Nessa Barbier from living in the area. When she heard I was leaving Kildare House she offered me a job here to tide me over…and shortly after I arrived I found out about…about the baby. She insisted I stay. They have a créche here, for the children of their staff. Nessa herself has two children. I worked in the kitchen under the head chef until a few weeks before I gave birth. Then she offered me a deal so I could keep doing some part-time work after the baby was born—they have staff here to mind him. Like this evening…'

Amidst the tension Maggie felt emotional, thinking of how supportive both Nessa and her husband had been. Unlike the man in front of her, who had never contacted her even though—

'You're saying the baby is mine?'

'His name is Daniel, and, yes, he's yours.' The insulting assumption that he might be another man's—that she would have so quickly jumped into bed with another man—hit Maggie anew.

'I never planned on having children.' Nikos said.

Why? Maggie pushed the question aside for now. 'Well, you do have a child.'

'If you're so sure he's my son then why didn't you tell me before now? The moment you fell pregnant?'

The affront made Maggie's spine rigid. She had agonised over whether or not to tell him—especially in light of her experiences with her own father—but ultimately she'd decided that she didn't have the right *not* to tell him, even if that came with the risk of not knowing how he would respond.

'I went to your offices in London—I even checked to see if you'd be there. You didn't leave me a personal number to contact you.'

Nikos frowned. 'I didn't see you.'

'No,' Maggie said, feeling bitter and humiliated all over

again. 'Because I didn't get further than your secretary on the top floor.'

'When was this?'

'When I was about six months pregnant. Last February.'

Nikos looked as if he was trying to figure something out. 'What was the secretary's name?'

'Chantelle.'

Maggie would never forget her fake smile and patronising tone. She'd looked pointedly at Maggie's distended belly and told her, *'Oh, no, Mr Marchetti is far too busy to meet with you today, but I'll be sure to pass on your note to him.'*

Maggie said, 'I wrote you a note.' *Like you left me a note.* 'She said she'd pass it on.'

'Well, she didn't.'

Maggie frowned. 'But I saw you with her—I waited for a while outside your offices, hoping I might catch you leaving—'

She stopped there, recalling how it had felt to see Nikos emerge with the tall, blonde woman who had been everything Maggie hadn't in that moment: slim, elegant, beautiful. Coiffed. They'd disappeared into the back of a sleek car before Maggie had been able to move towards them.

Nikos was shaking his head. 'She didn't give it to me.'

'But...' Maggie absorbed this. She sat down on the small two-seater couch behind her. 'She told me she'd pass it on.'

Nikos unfolded his arms and paced back and forth. He stopped, funnelled a hand through his hair, clearly agitated. 'I fired her around that time.'

'Why?'

'Inappropriate behaviour. She was sending me naked pictures of herself. It doesn't surprise me that she might have suspected we'd had a relationship and gone out of her way to disrupt it.'

'If you can call one night a "relationship",' Maggie muttered.

Nikos either didn't hear her or chose to ignore her comment. 'What did your note say?'

'It said that I was pregnant with your baby and we needed to talk.'

Nikos paced back and forth again. He muttered something that sounded suspiciously rude. Then he stopped and faced her again. 'I used protection that night.'

Maggie's face grew hot. 'I know. It must have failed.'

Nikos was struggling to contain the sheer magnitude of this news and what it potentially meant. 'You could have tried again…once the baby was born.'

'It's all been a bit of a blur since the birth, to be honest.'

Nikos hated to admit it but he could see the faintly purple shadows under her eyes now. And when he thought of how she'd felt in his arms just now… In spite of those curves he could tell she'd lost weight.

But if anything she was more beautiful. It was as if she'd grown into herself in order to embody something earthy and impossibly sensual.

Everything in him resisted her pull on him in the midst of this bombshell. Rejected this news. He did not want a child. Not now—not ever.

Maggie continued, oblivious to Nikos's inner turmoil.

'I didn't try again because I believed that you'd got my note and weren't interested. But I don't regret what happened. I don't regret having Daniel for a second, even though I know it's not what you want.'

The fact that she was echoing his thoughts wasn't welcome. 'First I need to confirm that he is my son—then I will decide how to proceed.'

Maggie looked hunted. For the first time in his cynical life Nikos had to acknowledge that he suspected Maggie was telling the truth. Not that he should trust her word alone, of course.

And in spite of all of this he was still burningly aware of her. This bombshell hadn't diminished his desire for her one iota. He was afraid he might give in to the impulse to haul her into his arms and kiss her into relaxing the rigid line of her spine…kiss her into apologising for turning his life upside down in the space of a couple of hours.

He needed to leave now. His emotions were too volatile, mixed with an even more volatile desire. He needed to leave before he could do something he would regret.

He said, 'I'll arrange to have a DNA test done as soon as possible. You'll be hearing from me.'

CHAPTER FIVE

NIKOS WAS GONE before Maggie could say another word. She let out a shuddery breath. The sounds of the party were a faint hum in the distance. She wondered if he had gone back to the party. Why wouldn't he? He was a playboy after all. But he hadn't looked like a playboy just now—he'd looked shell-shocked.

Which was about as much as she'd expected. He hadn't said anything about taking responsibility—which was also what she'd expected. It wasn't as if he hadn't been brutally honest.

She just couldn't help feeling sorry for Daniel, who was destined to suffer the same fate she had. No father on the scene.

The fact that he'd never got the note she'd left him had taken some of the fuel out of the anger she'd nurtured over the past few months, and without the anger there was just a sense of disappointment. Which was as dangerous as it was unwelcome.

Once he had confirmation that Daniel was his, and inevitably left them to get on with their lives as he would his, she would pick up the pieces and tell herself that it was enough that he knew.

In many ways she could handle this—she knew how to deal with an absent and uninterested father. She wouldn't know how to handle Nikos if he actually wanted to be involved. The man came within ten feet of her and she couldn't think straight, so this really was for the best.

Nikos threw back another measure of whiskey, poured from his decanter into a tumbler in his living room at Kildare

House. The fact that he was even using a tumbler and not drinking straight from the decanter didn't say much about his level of control, which felt very frayed.

Twenty-four hours ago he'd been blissfully ignorant. Blissfully ignorant of the fact that the woman who had been haunting his X-rated dreams for a year had become a mother in the interim. The mother of his child. Potentially.

It was disconcerting to think of his father's very dominant dark Italian genes appearing in this baby. The only hint Nikos held of his mother was in his hazel-green eyes. Those strong Italian genes had wiped his Greek mother out in more ways than one.

His father had been dark physically and morally, thinking nothing of stripping Nikos's mother of her fortune to further his own ambitions.

When she'd realised that Domenico Marchetti—handsome, charming, ruthless—had only married her to get his hands on the vast Constantinos inheritance she'd killed herself. Nikos had been two, and from that day to this he'd depended solely on himself.

Hence the reason why he'd always vowed not to have children. No way did he want to be responsible for the welfare of an innocent child.

And yet already Nikos could feel a resistance in him to the idea that Daniel might *not* be his son. Which was as shocking as it was unnerving. This was not a scenario he'd ever expected to face. He was the least likely among the three half-brothers to settle down…have a family. And yet if Maggie was to be believed he was well on the way to that situation.

If Maggie was to be believed.

Nikos had seen too much and experienced too much of human nature to trust for a second in a woman he'd spent only one night with, no matter what kind of persona she'd projected. Sweet. Innocent.

He felt a prickling sense of exposure. Had he been played? Spectacularly? A year ago and now? By a woman looking to feather her nest?

Nikos drew out his phone from his pocket and made a couple of calls.

Within a few minutes his phone pinged and he looked at the link that had been sent to him by his security company. He saw grainy CCTV images of Maggie, taken in early February. She could be seen entering his office building, wearing jeans and a coat, her pregnant belly evident. Her hair fell down over her shoulders in wild waves.

Nikos's gut clenched on seeing this evidence of her visit, of her attempt to tell him about her pregnancy. And he felt a pang of regret that he hadn't witnessed her body growing and ripening with his child. Something he had never in a million years expected to experience.

He put away his phone and poured himself another whiskey. But this time it left an acrid taste in his mouth. The truth was, all the whiskey in the world couldn't prepare him for what was coming.

His son would be a Marchetti, with all the baggage that entailed. And, as much as Nikos didn't welcome the thought of a child—had never planned to have a child—he knew one thing: no child of his would ever suffer the abandonment he'd suffered. Or the persistent feeling of standing on the periphery of his own family.

He and his half-brothers had always been kept apart from each other. His older half-brother, Sharif, had grown up mainly in his Arabian mother's country—but as eldest son he'd been groomed by their father to take over from a young age. Nikos's younger brother, Maks, had grown up in Rome, with his Russian mother and younger sister, and as Rome was their paternal ancestral home Nikos had always felt envious of him for having that link to their shared past.

Maks's younger sister had since been proved not to be

their father's daughter—not that Nikos had ever had a chance to get to know her anyway…

But that was enough about his brothers and a sister who was not even his sister. If this baby *was* his it would have a claim on the Marchetti legacy through Nikos. And for the first time in his life he felt a sense of destiny and a tangible sense of family that he'd never really had before.

The next day Maggie drove up the drive to Kildare House. She hadn't expected to be back here again and her heart lurched when it was revealed at the top of the drive. She'd always liked this house over any of the other houses her mother had worked in, where they'd inevitably lived either in a gate lodge or in cramped staff quarters.

The first time Maggie had seen it she'd loved it. It was the kind of house she'd always dreamed of living in one day, and living there so long without its owner in residence she'd developed a false sense of ownership.

But then Nikos had arrived. Asserting his ownership of the house. *And her.*

A shiver of memory went through her when she thought of what had happened.

For a while, in the aftermath of that night a year ago, Maggie had blamed grief for the reason why she'd acted so uncharacteristically—jumping into bed with Nikos Marchetti after little more than a brief conversation and some whiskey.

But if she was honest with herself she knew it hadn't been grief at all. Or the alcohol. It had been the man and the seismic effect he'd had on her the moment she'd opened the front door to him for the first time.

Maggie parked the car. She was here to meet with the local doctor and Nikos. The doctor would be taking swabs for a DNA test.

She sucked in a deep breath and got out, extricated

Daniel's baby seat. Before she could knock on the front door, though, it opened, and Maggie was surprised to see a middle-aged smiling man, dressed in smart dark trousers and a white shirt.

He said, 'Hello, you must be Miss Taggart. I'm Andrew Wilson, the new housekeeper. It's lovely to meet you—and this must be Daniel?'

Daniel smiled gummily, oblivious to the circumstances.

Then Nikos appeared behind the new housekeeper, and Maggie wasn't prepared to see him.

He said, 'We'll have some tea and coffee in the living room please, Mr Wilson.' He held out a hand to her. 'Here, let me take help you.'

Maggie was tempted to insist that she could manage, but that felt petty. As she handed over the baby seat she noticed how Nikos was careful not to look too closely at Daniel.

He led the way to the living room, turning around. 'Where should I put him?'

Maggie came over and took the baby seat from him, placing it safely on top of a table so she could keep an eye on Daniel.

She looked around. For a moment the sense of déjà-vu was almost overwhelming. Even though it was bright outside and not dusky night, the scene was acutely familiar.

Nikos glanced at his watch. 'The doctor will be arriving any minute. She'll take swabs for the DNA tests.'

Maggie bit her lip. Anyone with eyes could see that Daniel was this man's son. But of course he'd need proof.

'What then?' she asked.

'Then we wait for the results. And then…depending on the outcome…we discuss what we do.'

'He's your son.'

'I can't afford to trust you on your word alone. Too much is at stake.'

Anger at herself for having succumbed to the charms of

such a man—the kind who didn't trust and who demanded DNA tests—made her say caustically, 'Well, the feeling is mutual. I don't trust you either.'

'You trusted me enough to let me be your first lover,' he supplied silkily.

Maggie flushed all over. 'That was a moment of flawed judgement.'

He arched a brow. 'That was chemistry, pure and simple. Don't tell me you're still holding out for your boring hero?'

Maggie squirmed. She'd told him so much. *Too* much.

At that moment the doorbell chimed. Within a minute Mr Wilson was showing the doctor into the living room.

Maggie welcomed the distraction, getting Daniel out of his seat.

The procedure was done with the minimum of fuss and within minutes the doctor stood up. 'It'll take a couple of days for the results to come back. I'll let you know as soon as I have them.'

Nikos saw the doctor out and Maggie patted Daniel's back absently. Everything was about to change irrevocably. Nikos came back and she turned around to face him. She noticed that he was looking at Daniel. For the first time she had to appreciate what a shock this must be for him.

Impulsively she said, 'I'm sorry that you found out like this. But I did try to tell you.'

He lifted his gaze to hers. 'I know.'

'You know? How?'

'I got my security team to check the cameras and someone has been in touch with Chantelle. She confirmed it.' Nikos shook his head. 'She did a lot of damage.'

Maggie shrugged minutely. 'It's okay. You know now… or you will know soon.'

Nikos looked at his watch, suddenly businesslike. 'I have to go to London for some meetings. I'll come back when I have confirmation that he's mine.'

The abruptness with which he was going to leave again made Maggie feel a little winded. She had no doubt that if Daniel should prove not to be his baby she wouldn't see him again. Whatever passion had blazed between them was well and truly snuffed out. But Daniel *was* his, and she would have to see him again and accept the consequences of her actions.

Nikos followed her out to the car and Maggie noticed him looking at Daniel again for a long moment through the window. She couldn't help asking, 'Did you really never want to have children?'

He stood back and looked away from Daniel to her. 'The short, brutal answer? No. But if he is mine I will accept him fully and things will be very different.'

He turned to walk back inside and Maggie said, 'Wait just a second. What does that mean?'

He came and stood close. Hands on his hips. She sensed volatile emotions under the surface and to her mortification shivers of awareness ran through her blood, recalling his volatility a year ago.

He said, 'It means exactly what I said: if he's mine, rest assured that I will not shirk my responsibility.'

Three days later

Maggie walked into the plush Dublin city centre hotel. One of the city's oldest, and situated on St Stephen's Green, it oozed timeless elegance and sophistication. She'd been delivered here in a chauffeur-driven SUV—summoned by Nikos Marchetti.

The spurt of rebellion she'd felt earlier, when preparing to come and meet Nikos, had galvanised her to dress down for the occasion. But now that felt like teenage theatrics. She'd be surprised if she wasn't thrown out on her ear before she even reached the reception desk.

But no one stopped her. In fact a suited manager approached her and said, 'Miss Taggart?'

How did they know?

Maggie nodded. He smiled. 'Please…let me show you to Mr Marchetti's suite.'

Maggie dutifully followed him into a rococo decorated lift and her stomach dropped as they ascended. She really wasn't prepared for whatever was going to come next. But she couldn't go back now.

The manager led her out of the lift, down a luxuriously carpeted corridor to a room at the end. A light rap on the door and it opened almost immediately.

Nikos looked serious. Shirtsleeves rolled up, hair mussed. Dark trousers. His dark gaze swept her up and down.

'Maggie.'

'Nikos.'

The air was charged. Thick with sudden tension and filled with an awareness that she did not welcome because it was one-sided.

The manager cleared his throat. 'Can I send some refreshments up?'

Nikos didn't take his eyes off Maggie. 'Just some tea and coffee.'

Maggie looked at the manager. 'Thank you.'

He left and Nikos stood back, holding the door open. Maggie tried not to breathe in his scent as she passed him, but it filtered through anyway, precipitating dangerous memories.

She went straight over to one of the windows overlooking the green park. The suite was vast. She caught a glimpse of a bedroom…rumpled sheets. She felt hot.

'Where's Daniel?'

Maggie's heart hitched. *Daniel.* He knew he was his son now.

She turned around. 'The Barbiers' nanny, Sara, is minding him. I expressed some milk.'

She didn't know why she felt defensive. But it was as if now that he had confirmation of Daniel's parentage Nikos thought he had a right to ask her questions about him. About her. About her mothering. Would Nikos even know what expressing milk was?

He gestured to a couch. 'Please, sit down.'

He stood with legs apart, every inch the bristling Alpha male. A million miles from the teasing seductive playboy who'd turned her world upside down in one night.

Maggie swallowed. 'It's okay. I'm comfortable standing.'

He folded his arms. 'So, when *would* you have told me about Daniel? Would you have waited until he was walking and talking before you got around to it?'

No beating around the bush. Now he knew for sure, and he was angry. A muscle pulsed in his jaw. She was surprised at the emotion—she hadn't expected it. She hadn't expected a lot about this man, though, and he consistently surprised her.

She had to be honest. 'I don't know. I believed you knew but weren't interested. I guess I might have tried again when Daniel was a bit older.'

He paced back and forth, energy crackling. He stopped and faced her. 'I know it's not entirely your fault, but while your low opinion of me is refreshing, when I'm usually surrounded by sycophants, I can't believe that if I hadn't turned up at the Barbier party I might easily have missed out on a year of my son's life? Two years? More? As it is I have missed the birth of my own son. His first few months.'

Anger spiked at his accusatory tone. 'All you left me a year ago was a note—not even a personal number. You couldn't have made it clearer to me that you weren't interested in anything beyond that one night. And now you expect me to believe that you would have been interested in the minutiae of the birth of a baby you didn't believe was yours? You really don't have to pretend to be interested now. It's just us here. I know how this goes. My father—'

Nikos's voice was like a whip. 'Your father? What's *he* got to do with this?'

Maggie cursed her runaway mouth again. But it was too late. 'My father was rich—very rich. He had an affair with my mother and when she fell pregnant he denied all knowledge. Threatened her into staying away. He had no desire to be a father or to share any of his fortune.'

Nikos arched a brow. He'd never looked more imperious. 'And that pertains to me how? Because I'm rich too?'

'That and the fact that you told me specifically that you're not into relationships or families.'

His brow lowered. 'Well, that was before I had a son.'

A shiver went through her—a sense that once again Nikos was going to do the opposite of what she expected.

On impulse, she asked, 'Why didn't you want a relationship or children? Was it because you lost your mother?'

Nikos was so full of conflicting emotions and so full of desire for the woman in front of him that it was hard to think straight. Even though she was dressed like a hippy. Wearing worn dungarees and a singlet vest. Sandals. Hair up in an untidy knot.

She looked as if she'd just come from serving up lunch at an ashram. And yet he'd never seen anything sexier. It incensed him. He needed his wits about him, and all he wanted to do was carry her into the bedroom and spread her on the bed for his delectation.

Desire was a heavy, hot knot inside him, but he forced himself to focus. He debated giving Maggie some platitude, but for some reason he felt the urge to be brutally honest.

'I never intended to have children because I didn't want any child of mine to go through what I did.'

'What *did* you go through?'

His skin prickled. He would never entertain such questions from anyone else—much less a woman he had slept with—but this situation demanded a different response. She deserved to know what she was getting into.

'My mother killed herself when I was two—driven to it by my father, who had married her only for her inheritance. She believed he loved her. Soon after she died he married again, and his new wife had no interest in taking on his dead wife's son, so I was sent to live with my grandparents in Greece. They never forgave me for my mother's sins—for running off with her Italian lover and giving him her fortune. When I was old enough to be of some use my father took me away from Greece and sent me to boarding school in England. I was moved around like a pawn. A poor little rich boy who rebelled as a means of getting his father's attention. To no avail.'

Maggie's eyes had widened and were now full of something that Nikos had never seen before. Genuine emotion. It impacted on him in a way that made him feel on edge.

She said, 'I'm sorry you went through that.'

'Don't be. It did me a favour. I learned early on that the only person you can count on is yourself.'

Nikos saw the shimmer of moisture in Maggie's eyes and reacted instinctively, needing to take that emotion out of her. 'Don't do that—don't look at me like that.'

'Like what?' asked Maggie.

What he'd just told her had torn down some vital defence, leaving her exposed, vulnerable. She'd also learnt not to trust anyone outside of herself and her mother from an early age. Her father, who should have been one of the most important people in her life, had also let her down badly.

Nikos said now, 'I'm not a very nice person, Maggie.

Don't look at me like you care. Do you know what's on my mind right now? How much I want you.'

Maggie's thoughts skittered to a halt. *He wanted her.* She felt breathless. Tight inside.

'You…? Even now, with the baby…?'

He nodded. 'I've wanted you for a year. Only you. I told you—you haunted me.'

You haunted me.

Maggie's mind was melting. She didn't believe him.

'You're just saying that.'

Nikos looked imperious again. 'Why would I lie?'

He moved closer. The air thickened. Suddenly Maggie couldn't recall what they'd been talking about. It didn't seem important…

Nikos reached out and cupped her jaw, moving a thumb across her lower lip. Little fires raced across her skin and an intense longing made her sway closer.

Now he was so close that she could smell him. Their bodies were almost touching. Every pulse point was going crazy, making her head light. She was sensitive all over. *He wanted her.* The sharp lance of relief should have shamed her, but it didn't.

'I need to know that you want this too,' he said.

Nikos's blunt demand struck right to her core. Did any woman *not* want him? Impossible. Could he not see how she hungered for him, even though she wished she didn't? She couldn't think straight…she could only say what she felt.

'Yes.'

She had a moment of déjà vu. Thought back to that first night when he'd asked her if she wanted him. Made sure of it.

The past and the present were meshing. So when he snaked an arm around her waist and pulled her all the way into his body, and she felt her softer curves moulding to his far steelier strength, she had no other thought in her head except, *Yes, please.*

His mouth touched hers and she fell into his kiss like a starving woman, tongue tangling with his, teeth nipping at the firm contour of his lower lip. He surrounded her with a heat and an intensity that thrilled her to her very core.

That she craved.

That she'd missed.

He pulled back. She was panting, but she didn't care. His eyes glittered and his cheeks were flushed. His hands were on the straps of her dungarees, undoing them so that the front fell down. Maggie didn't even have time to think about the fact that she was wearing a breastfeeding bra, because Nikos was pulling up her top and baring her to his hungry gaze.

'*Theos*, Maggie, I have dreamt of this…of you.'

He undid her bra at the front and it sprang open. He took her breasts in his hands, thumbs moving back and forth across nipples sensitive enough to make her gasp. All she could see was his broad chest in front of her—still covered up. She needed to see him…to feel the heat of his skin against hers.

She reached for his buttons, undoing them. Volatile emotions swirled inside her, making her feel reckless like he'd made her feel a year ago, helping her justify making love to him.

But this wasn't last year, this was now. A year later. Not past—*present.*

Realisation hit and her hands stopped.

Daniel.

She dislodged his hands, dragged her dungarees top back up to cover her breasts. 'Wait…we shouldn't be doing this.'

Nikos looked at her, hair ruffled, cheeks lined with colour, eyes glittering. 'It's inevitable whenever we're in close proximity, Maggie.'

His shirt was half open, and even now her hands itched to reach out and touch the part of his chest that was bared.

She shook her head, even though every cell in her body protested at the interruption. 'The last time we did this I got pregnant.'

Nikos felt dazed, drunk with lust, but her words cut through the fog of desire.

Maggie took another step back and he had to curb the reflex to reach out and tug her back. *Christos,* what did this woman do to him? He struggled to regain control, cool his blood. But it was hard when her breasts were all but falling out of her clothes and her face was flushed.

'You're right—this isn't the time or place.'

His voice came out harsh and he saw how she winced. His conscience pricked but he turned around and did up his own clothes. This was not him. He was usually in control. Almost detached from proceedings. He never lost it so much that he seduced housekeepers and got them pregnant—

He cursed again.

He turned around when he had done up his shirt and tucked it in. He battled to cool his libido, but it was next to impossible while Maggie stood only a few feet away, clothed again but no less sexy for it.

The urge to throw caution to the wind and haul her back into his arms and finish what they'd started was overwhelming.

He resisted it.

'I hadn't intended that. I did intend just to talk.'

Eventually she said, 'I… Okay.'

He was more sophisticated than this. What *was* it about this woman that short-circuited his brain and sent it straight to his pants?

He raised his gaze to her flushed face and her wild

hair—tumbling around her shoulders now. Her eyes were bright blue and full of things that still made his skin prickle uncomfortably. It was those eyes and the emotion that he'd seen in them that had made him want to turn it into something else.

Passion. Not emotion. He could handle passion.

She was looking at him warily now. He reacted against her silent accusation.

'What just happened was mutual, Maggie.'

Maggie was struggling to regain a sense of composure but it was hard. Those last few cataclysmic minutes in Nikos's arms had flayed a layer of skin off her body. The knowledge that he still wanted her thrummed through her body like a drug, giving her an illicit high.

But that wasn't why she was here.

'We need to talk about what happens next,' she said.

Nikos folded his arms across his chest. 'Yes, we do need to talk. Now I know that Daniel is mine we can move forward.'

'What does that mean?'

The dark gold and green lights in his eyes glinted. 'Marriage, Maggie. It means we need to marry.'

CHAPTER SIX

OF ALL THE things Maggie had been expecting, she'd never—

She stared at Nikos, wondering if she'd heard right. 'Did you really just say *marry?'*

Nikos nodded, watching her carefully.

Maggie's legs felt suspiciously rubbery, but she locked them in order to stay standing. 'That's the most ridiculous thing I've ever heard. We barely know each other.'

Nikos's mouth firmed. 'And yet we've shared an intimacy that has resulted in a child. Some would say that constitutes knowing one another just fine. People in other cultures marry for a lot less.'

Maggie felt shaky. Panicky.

Seizing desperately onto anything to try and make him see sense, she asked, 'Is this what you want? Really? When you've told me what happened to you?'

There was a long moment of silence, and then Nikos said tightly, 'It's because of what happened to me that I'm determined to be there for my son. My father failed my mother and me—I won't do that to you or my son.'

Shock reverberated through Maggie as she absorbed this. She wasn't sure what was worse: a father who didn't want anything to do with them or a father who would take responsibility out of a sense of duty and nothing more?

'Do we need to get married, though? Can't we just come to some agreement?'

'There's more at stake than just us.'

She frowned. 'What are you talking about?'

'The Marchetti Group. Even though some time has passed since my father's death, people are still watching to see how us three half-brothers will work as a cohesive unit. We're all single, which makes us inherently less trustworthy to our largely conservative shareholders who are growing more nervous as the years pass. Stability of the brand and its image is everything.'

His mouth twisted.

'When the press find out about you and Daniel they'll have a field-day. It won't come as a huge surprise to many that I've fathered a child, but it will make the shareholders even more nervous.'

Maggie shelved his comment about people not being surprised. 'So you want us to get married purely to shore up the image of the Marchetti brand?'

'It won't just be for that—although that is a big part of it, yes.'

Panic threatened to rise again. Nikos sounded so implacable. Her mind raced, trying to take this in.

'But I don't know anything about you...' The memory of looking him up on the internet made her blush. Quickly she said, 'I mean, what about your family? You have two brothers? Are you even close?'

Nikos's face turned to stone. 'I have two *half*-brothers—one older, one younger. We all have different mothers. And in a word? No, we're not especially close. But we're all committed to the Marchetti Group.'

That sounded so...*cold.*

In as reasonable a tone as Maggie could muster, she said, 'I understand why you want to do things differently—so do I—but you of all people know the damage a bad marriage can do. We don't love each other.'

Nikos's face became derisive. 'Love? If anything can destabilise a marriage it's love. Love is for naive fools.'

'It's not naive to believe in love.' Her hands balled into fists at her sides. 'I loved my mother and she loved me. She did everything to protect me. It almost killed me when she died. And when Daniel was born…the love I felt for him straight away is like nothing I can describe. All-encompassing. I would do anything for him.'

Nikos heard Maggie's words, but she might as well have been speaking another language. He had no idea what she was talking about. He didn't dispute her feelings, but he'd never felt anything like what she was describing.

When his grandparents had died he'd felt nothing. They'd bitterly disapproved of him and had always seen him as evidence of their daughter's foolishness. They'd let his father take him away when he'd turned twelve without even sparing him a backward glance.

He didn't have to be a psychologist to know that a lot of his rebellion had been as much to do with testing the boundaries—seeing what it would take to get him expelled from the family completely—as it had with getting his father's attention. And, if he was honest, his half-brothers' attention too.

But Nikos didn't welcome this introspection, and he had a sense that Maggie was seeing far too much.

'You say you'd do anything for our son? I can offer you and Daniel a secure and stable life. A luxurious life. That's more of a guarantee than love will ever give you.'

Maggie's teeth worried at her lower lip and Nikos had to curb his urge to reach out and tug it free. The waves of desire that had beat so furiously just a short while before were still there…just under the surface.

'We have something far more potent and tangible than love between us. Desire. And a child.'

'Desire won't last for ever, though…and then what?'

Nikos didn't have an answer for that, and it irritated him intensely. He usually had no problem getting people to agree to whatever he proposed.

Maggie spoke again. 'This is a lot to think about.'

Frustration at how off-centre she made him feel made Nikos's voice sharp. 'You've had a year to think about it.'

She paled and he felt a stab of conscience. *You should have tried harder to find her.*

He pushed the inner voice down and forced a more conciliatory tone into his own voice. 'I think we can do better for Daniel. He deserves better.'

'You've barely looked at him.'

Nikos's chest constricted when he thought of that tiny vulnerable body. That dark hair.

'I have no experience with babies. It'll take me some time to adjust.'

Maggie couldn't say anything to that. He was right. She'd had a year to adjust to being a mother. She'd had the experience of carrying Daniel inside her. Giving birth to him. Bonding with him instantly. Even though motherhood still terrified her, she'd found it an easier adjustment than she'd expected.

But what Nikos was suggesting was a quantum leap into a dimension she'd never considered.

'If I did agree to marry you how would it work, exactly?' she asked.

'I think five years would be enough time to give a lasting impression of stability and create a secure base for our son. Then we can come to an arrangement about custody.'

Five years.

Maggie felt breathless. 'And where would we go…where would we live? I don't even know where you're based.'

'I'm mainly based in Paris, but I have apartments in New York, London and Athens. My apartment in Paris overlooks the Eiffel Tower.'

The perfect location for an international playboy.

Maggie felt a bubble of hysteria threatening to rise. Worse, she could still feel the imprint of Nikos's mouth on hers. Hot and demanding. He might have implied that he hadn't slept with anyone else since he'd slept with her, but she'd be naive in the extreme to believe that.

'Can I think about this?' she asked.

Maggie could see the struggle on Nikos's face. Evidently he wasn't used to not being given answers in the affirmative straight away. Well, tough.

'You can—but we don't have much time before the press sniff around and find out what's going on. What I'd like is for you and Daniel to leave with me when I return to Paris tomorrow afternoon.'

Maggie felt winded. 'Daniel doesn't even have a passport.'

Nikos waved a hand. 'I can arrange all the travel documents. We'll be flying privately, which makes things easier. Things move fast in my world. The sooner we can contain and manage this situation, the better.'

So she and Daniel were a *situation*?

Any vaguely romantic notions Maggie had entertained about meeting a nice, kind, dependable man were truly incinerated by now.

Feeling a little shell-shocked, she said, 'I need to get back to Daniel. And I need to think about all of this...'

To her relief, Nikos went to the suite door and opened it. She felt so raw after that kiss and the ensuing conversation that she knew if he touched her again she would have had no defences in place at all.

He said to her, on the threshold, 'You know what's best for our son.'

She looked at Nikos. She did—that was the problem. And the other problem was that she didn't trust herself around Nikos, and agreeing to his plan would put them in close proximity, and close proximity spelled danger, because everything was turned on its head now and she was facing a scenario she had no idea how to navigate.

Marriage.

As if reading the turmoil in her head, Nikos said, 'I have yours and Daniel's best interests at heart. You'll be a very wealthy woman for the rest of your life, and life with me won't be boring—I can guarantee you that.'

Oh, she was sure it wouldn't be boring. Every second with this man was a rollercoaster of emotions and sensations.

'Maybe I *want* boring,' she said.

That cynical look came into Nikos's eyes. 'Then I'd have to say it's too late. You made a choice last year and you didn't choose *boring* then, did you?'

No, she hadn't chosen boring last year. She'd jumped into the fire and got burned in the process.

In the end Maggie knew she didn't really have a choice. She'd expected Nikos to want to have nothing to do with them—in fact that would almost have been easier, in some perverse way.

Because he affects you.

And not just that, Maggie thought, feeling guilty, but because it was what she knew.

But more importantly there was Daniel. And the fact that Daniel's grounding years could be spent with two parents—together. Giving him a start in life that neither Maggie nor Nikos had had.

How could she argue with that?

She'd called Nikos late last night and told him over the phone that she would agree to marry him.

There'd been a beat, and then he'd said in a deep voice, 'You're making the right decision, Maggie.'

His car had picked her and Daniel and their paltry belongings up earlier that morning.

It had proved surprisingly easy to extricate herself from the life she'd built at the Barbiers' stud. Which had been a reminder of how her mother had picked up and moved with each new job, and a reminder that Maggie wanted more for her son.

She knew she had to live with the consequences of her actions. Yesterday in that hotel suite had been an example of how little control she had around Nikos. She'd all but thrown herself at him. Seduced by his sheer charisma. By his power.

Like mother like daughter.

She resisted the snarky voice.

'Are you comfortable enough?'

Maggie's head jerked around. She'd been watching Dublin drop away beneath the private plane, still reeling from the sense of just how different her life was going to be.

It had hit her when they'd arrived at a private airfield and she'd seen the gleaming black jet inscribed with the Marchetti Group logo. And when she'd seen the plush cream leather interior. Solicitous staff had offered Maggie everything from tea and coffee to champagne.

Now they were in this luxurious bubble high above the world and Maggie wondered if she'd ever touch the ground again.

'What's going on in that head of yours, Maggie?' asked Nikos. 'I can't read you and it makes me nervous.'

'And you can read everyone else?' she asked, in an effort to deflect him.

His mouth tipped up on one side. 'I'm an excellent poker player.'

Maggie wondered if his ability to read people had been born out of growing up in a relatively hostile environment, surrounded by people who didn't care for him. She hated that it had an impact on her, because Nikos seemed immune to needing *anyone*.

'What if Daniel doesn't want to be heir to a fortune?' Maggie asked, feeling a little desperate as this new reality sank in and thinking of her tiny, vulnerable son.

'Would you deny him his heritage?'

She opened her mouth and shut it again. Of course she wouldn't deny him. 'It doesn't matter to me if he doesn't have a fortune. It only matters if he's happy and healthy.'

Nikos's mouth firmed. 'A noble thought, but not very realistic. Think of the opportunities I can provide our son.'

Our son.

Maggie looked at Nikos. Even like this, lounging in his seat, he oozed barely leashed energy. His face was stamped with generations of arrogance and pride. He was from a long line of men who were used to being obeyed.

She desperately wanted to see him show some kind of emotion for Daniel. To have some inkling that he wasn't viewing him like some abstract object.

She said, 'I'm not interested in marriage if you're not going to be a father to Daniel. All the stability and security in the world can't protect him from a father who doesn't love him. I don't know if I can trust you to do that.'

Nikos's gaze flicked briefly to Daniel, where he lay in Maggie's arms. An expression she couldn't decipher passed so quickly across his face that it was gone before she could wonder what it was, or why she'd felt it like a soft blow to her belly. She wondered if she should have been so blunt… But surely Nikos Marchetti was cynical down to the deepest part of his marrow…

Wasn't he?

Nikos didn't like the sensation that Maggie could see right inside him to where he had his own doubts about whether or not he was capable of being the kind of father he'd never had himself. All he knew was that the thought of not being in his son's life made his chest tight.

He said, 'I didn't know until a few days ago that I even had a son. I think you owe me the benefit of the doubt as

I try to have a relationship with him. The last thing I want to do is cause him harm.'

Maggie's cheeks pinkened. 'I guess that's fair enough.'

It struck Nikos then that he was renowned for brokering huge deals with the most recalcitrant people in the world—and yet here, with Maggie, even that grudging concession felt like a massive victory.

The thought that he'd met his match in more ways than one made him edgy.

The seat belt bell pinged, indicating that it was okay to get up and move around, and Maggie undid her belt, and the one clipped around the baby, and stood up.

'I'll go into the back and feed and change Daniel.'

Nikos watched her walk down the aisle of the plane, Daniel safely in the crook of her arm. He wasn't unaware of the irony that not so long ago it would have been a very different scenario for him on a jet like this—featuring him and a woman, sometimes even two, unencumbered by anything but the mutual desire to lose themselves for a brief moment.

Because that was all it had been—a brief moment of respite from his ever-present sense of rootlessness and dissatisfaction. And those moments had never filled him with anything but an aftertaste of ennui.

Sleeping with Maggie hadn't felt like that.

No. She'd lingered on his body and his brain for months. Making him ache.

She was the woman he wanted. And she was the mother of his child.

When he'd found her at the Barbiers' stud he'd had no idea about the secret she kept. *His son.* But he was nothing if not skilled at adapting.

He'd learnt young not to expect people to accept him or want him. But he knew Maggie's reluctance for this marriage would turn to acquiescence when she saw the life he could provide for her and his son.

* * *

'When you said "apartment", I assumed you meant an actual apartment—not an apartment in a hotel.'

Maggie was standing at the wall of a terrace at the top of an ornate baroque building looking out at the Eiffel Tower. It was so close she could almost touch it.

She'd only been to Paris once before, on a school trip. She couldn't quite believe she was here, in this sophisticated and beautiful city.

Ireland had been enjoying an unnaturally warm summer, but this heat was on another level. A trickle of sweat pooled between her breasts and at her lower back as she looked at people strolling on the plaza near the Eiffel Tower wearing little sundresses and eating ice-cream. She was envious.

'Everyone local leaves Paris in August,' Nikos had told her as they'd driven into the city. 'They'll return over the next few days and the city will come back to life after the *vacances*.' He'd gestured to the crowds thronging the wide boulevards. 'These are all tourists,' he'd said, in a tone that signified disdain.

Maggie had been too distracted by the exquisite architecture, the tall and majestic buildings…

Nikos came and stood beside her now. 'All my apartments are in hotels that we own. The MG Hotel Group. I've found it more…convenient.'

Maggie looked at him, glad of the sunglasses hiding her eyes. 'You own this hotel?'

He nodded.

She should have guessed. When they'd arrived Nikos had been fawned over like visiting royalty.

She thought of something. 'So the house in Ireland—that's the only house you own?'

If she hadn't been looking at him she might have missed the flicker of an expression she couldn't decipher across his face, the slight tension in his body.

But he sounded nonchalant when he said, 'Yes. Like I said, I bought it when I thought I might invest in horseracing.'

Maggie sensed he was being evasive and wondered why her question had pushed a button for him…

But now he stood back and said, 'Let me show you around.'

Maggie followed Nikos back into the apartment. Daniel was asleep in his baby seat, so she left him where he was. It was much cooler in here, with the air-conditioning.

She tried not to let her jaw drop as Nikos showed her the vast apartment. The gleaming state-of-the-art kitchen had her hands itching to try out the ovens.

She said, 'I suppose you don't use this room much?'

'No. I'm not ashamed to admit I just about know how to boil an egg and that's it. I'm certainly not at your level of proficiency. That's all Mathilde's domain.'

'Mathilde?'

'The housekeeper here. She looks after a couple of the apartments and lives in one herself. She comes and goes. You'll meet her tomorrow. There are some prepared meals in the fridge.'

Maggie made a note to explore later, following Nikos again as he led her through a media room and into a long corridor with rooms off each side. His office, a gym with a lap pool, and then the bedrooms.

He opened a door, letting her precede him. 'This is yours and Daniel's suite.'

She avoided his eye, stepping inside. She wasn't sure what she had expected, but she told herself she was relieved she had her own space. There was a small room for Daniel beside hers, an en suite bathroom and a walk-in wardrobe. Empty at the moment.

He was leaning against the doorframe. 'I've never shared

my bedroom with a woman, and even though we'll be married I think it best that we have our own space.'

Maggie kept her expression carefully neutral. 'That's fine—I'd prefer that.'

And she told herself she meant it, even though she felt a little hollow inside. Of *course* a man like Nikos would feel stifled by something as domestic as sharing a bedroom with his wife.

He straightened up from the door. 'After you meet the stylists tomorrow they'll stock up your wardrobe.'

Maggie felt self-conscious. 'I have clothes.'

He responded smoothly. 'I know, but you'll be expected to dress to a certain…*standard*—and naturally I don't expect you to pay for that. Plus you'll need evening dresses for functions like the one we're going to tomorrow night.'

That stung—but what had she expected? Nikos owned part of the world's largest luxury conglomerate. Of course she'd have to look a certain way.

And then she thought of what he'd just said. 'Wait… what function?'

'It's a gala charity event—we'll use it as an opportunity to appear in public as an engaged couple for the first time.'

Suddenly Maggie felt insecure. 'I don't think I'm going to fit into this world very well.'

Nikos took her in: the plaid shirt, the worn jeans. Her hair up in a haphazard knot, with tendrils falling down. No make-up. Scuffed sneakers. Yet still she managed to exert a pull on his libido that was unprecedented. Not even her scruffy attire could hide her very natural beauty.

'You'll fit in just fine with a little polish. I've already released a statement announcing our engagement and the fact that we have a son, so the news is out. We were already papped on the way in here. Impossible to escape them in Paris.'

Maggie had the sensation of a net closing around her. 'Why didn't you tell me you were doing that?'

Nikos looked perplexed for a moment—and then Maggie understood.

She answered for him. 'Because you're not used to deferring to anyone else. Well, for starters, you can inform *me* of anything that affects me or Daniel before you tell the rest of the world.'

Nikos looked unrepentant as he said, 'Then I should probably inform you that I've arranged for us to be married next week by special licence.'

Well, she'd asked for that.

Her legs felt suspiciously weak. 'When did you organise all this?'

'Yesterday after you left the hotel and while we were on the plane.'

She absorbed this.

'Maggie?' he said.

She looked at him, feeling as if things were spinning out of her control. 'I know I've agreed to marry you—I just hadn't expected things to move this fast. Why does it need to happen so quickly?'

Nikos's mouth firmed. 'Because image is everything in this world, and the sooner we put out a united front, with Daniel, the sooner any speculation or gossip will die down.'

'Image is everything in *your* world, you mean,' she pointed out tartly.

'It's your world now, too. Yours and Daniel's.'

She seized on something. 'I can't go to this function with you—what about Daniel?'

'I've arranged for some nannies to come tomorrow morning for you to interview. You'll have to get used to leaving him.'

The speed at which Nikos was turning their lives upside

down made Maggie feel panicky. 'I'll only leave Daniel if I feel I can trust someone.'

Nikos looked as if he was about to argue, but then he said, 'Fair enough.'

As if on cue there was a cry from the sitting room. Maggie welcomed the distraction from their disturbing conversation and hurried back to the main living room. It was more like a vast luxurious waiting room, with big modern canvases on the walls and low glass coffee tables covered with big books featuring photos of beautiful people, beautiful houses, beautiful scenery.

Nikos had followed her into the room and stood near the open French doors leading out to the terrace, watching as she tended to Daniel, settled him to feed.

She suddenly stopped and looked up. 'Is it okay to feed him in here?'

'Of course. This is your home now too, Maggie.'

She privately wondered if he'd still say that if he knew that Daniel might quite easily upchuck all over the expensive fabrics, but the baby was restless, fussing, and she needed to feed him. He latched on with unerring accuracy, making her wince slightly.

'Does it hurt?'

Maggie looked up again. She'd preserved her modesty by placing a muslin cloth over Daniel's head and her breast, but she still felt as if Nikos could see right through it.

She was surprised at his question. 'No, not really—I've been lucky. Some women can't breastfeed at all. But it's just…a little sensitive.'

He said, 'You should make a list of things you need for Daniel and I'll give it to an assistant.'

Maggie nodded, but she was distracted by her view of Nikos, with the backdrop of Paris behind him. She could just see the top of the Eiffel Tower. He had his hands on his hips and he couldn't have looked less domesticated.

He looked like what he was: a titan of industry with all the natural attributes of a sex god.

Fresh panic hit her at the thought of how easily he affected her and at the enormity of living this new life.

'We don't have to stay here, you know. I'm happy to stay somewhere else with Daniel. It's a bit grand for us.'

Nikos's gaze narrowed on Maggie. He'd caught a glimpse of voluptuous breast before she'd started to feed the baby, and even that very *un*-inflammatory view had sent his blood spiralling downwards.

He cursed her silently for the ability she had to reduce him to some sort of horny teenager.

She was looking at him, waiting for a response to what she'd said. Either she was the world's greatest actress or she really was something he couldn't understand—an unmercenary person. But then his cynical reflexes kicked back into gear… No matter what happened between them, she was made for life.

The insidious thought that she might prefer to avail herself of his wealth but not have to spend time with him was rejected outright. She wanted him. He knew that much. And she knew they would have to put on a united front.

A memory assailed him before he could push it away. His father, visiting him in Athens at his grandparents' house when he'd been about eight. Nikos had asked why he couldn't return to Paris with him, and his father had replied, 'I have a new family there. You're better here with Mama's family. You want for nothing—don't be greedy, boy.'

After he'd left Nikos had watched the empty driveway for a long time, with an ache in his chest and a tight throat, wondering what it was about him that made everyone want to push him away…

A chill wind skated over his skin and Nikos pushed the

memory down deep. It was a long time since he'd thought of those days. He'd become expert at insulating himself against them with a lot of noise and activity to drown them out.

He folded his arms across his chest, noting how Maggie's eyes darted to his biceps. A shard of lust went to his groin and he welcomed it as an antidote to that memory.

'You've agreed to be my wife,' he said. 'We live together, not apart.'

Maggie expertly switched Daniel to the other breast without revealing any flesh. She said, 'I'm just saying that we don't need all this…'

'It comes with the territory, I'm afraid. You'll get used to it.'

She couldn't *not* get used to it. It was human nature. He almost lamented the fact that he was going to corrupt her.

You started her corruption a year ago, pointed out a voice.

Maggie's head was bent towards the baby, her hand cradling his head. Something about the image made an ache form in Nikos's chest. He didn't even realise he was so fixated until she lifted the baby up and placed him on her shoulder, patting his back.

Daniel emitted a loud burp and Nikos frowned. 'Is he okay?'

Maggie smiled. 'Totally normal. He needs to be winded after he feeds so that air doesn't get trapped in his belly.'

He saw that Daniel had a little bald patch on the back of his head—presumably from where he lay on it. The baby simultaneously terrified him and intrigued him. He had no frame of reference as to how to feel about a baby, a child. His half-brothers were single, like him. Every time he looked at Daniel he felt a curious mix of terror, protectiveness, and some emotion he couldn't name.

Maggie had done herself up again and stood up, Daniel

cradled in her arms. She saw him looking at Daniel. 'You should hold him,' she said.

Nikos looked at her in horror. *Hold him?* This tiny vulnerable thing? He wanted to turn and run in the other direction but knew he was being ridiculous. It was a baby. Not a bomb.

The innate confidence that Nikos had taken for granted most of his life was suddenly in short supply. Maggie was looking at him with those big eyes, seeing his vacillation. He couldn't *not* hold his baby—how hard could it be?

'How do I…?'

Maggie came closer. Her scent tickled his nostrils, but not even that could distract him right now.

'Here, crook your arm…make sure his head is supported.'

She placed Daniel onto his arm and his other hand came up instinctively, to hold him from the bottom. The first thing that impacted on him was the solid weight of his son. He hadn't expected him to be so heavy.

Daniel looked up at him with steady, dark long-lashed eyes. Totally guileless. Totally trusting. And just like that, before he could stop it, Nikos felt a sharp pain near his heart, as if it was expanding and cracking apart. For the first time in his life he had the sense that he was utterly insignificant. That this baby was literally the most important thing in the world. And he would do anything to prevent any harm coming to a hair on his head.

Daniel moved then, and Nikos's heart stopped as he instinctively tightened his hold on him. He realised how fragile he was. How easily he could be hurt. And Nikos felt fear.

The tendrils of that disturbing memory snaked around him again. Surely his father had had a moment like this? Holding Nikos in his arms? Feeling the same things? And yet he'd still abandoned his son. As had his mother.

It was as if Daniel could see all the way into his soul, to where Nikos had always felt so hollow. To where he'd been abandoned by his own parents because he hadn't been good enough…lovable enough. How could he give this child something he'd never experienced himself?

Cold sweat pickled over his skin and Nikos handed Daniel back into Maggie's safe arms.

He barely heard her say, 'That was really good…you're a natural…'

He had to get out *now.*

He left the room and went straight to the bathroom and locked himself inside. It took extreme effort and willpower not to be sick. He looked at himself in the mirror, but didn't really notice how wild he looked, his skin pale and clammy.

Eventually the nausea subsided and his chest felt less tight. *Theos.* He couldn't even hold his own baby without almost having a panic attack. And he hadn't had one of those since he'd gone to boarding school, where they'd been beaten out of him by the older boys.

After a few minutes there was a light knock on the door.

'Nikos? Are you okay?'

CHAPTER SEVEN

NIKOS'S HANDS TIGHTENED on the sink. He took a deep breath. The door opened behind him.

'Nikos?'

He lifted his head, saw Maggie reflected behind him in the mirror. Her hair was a vivid splash of red and gold against the white marble of the bathroom. He turned around. He still felt shaky, as if a layer of skin had been peeled away.

Maggie came further in and Nikos wanted to tell her not to come any closer. Because he knew what he needed right now, to eclipse this pervading spread of vulnerability, and it was something only she could give him.

Even that unsettling revelation wasn't enough to jolt him out of this mood, so he said nothing. He let her keep coming. Closer. Like Red Riding Hood approaching the big bad wolf.

She was frowning. 'What *was* that, Nikos? You looked like you'd seen a ghost.'

'Is Daniel okay?' he asked.

She frowned again. 'He's fine. He's already asleep. Nikos, you didn't hurt him.'

He shook his head. 'It wasn't that… I just…'

'What *was* it?'

Nikos put up a hand. 'You shouldn't come any closer.'

Maggie could feel the unmistakable electric charge in the atmosphere. Her body was reacting to it, making her want to move closer to Nikos even though the warned her not to.

She knew she should turn and leave—clearly he didn't want her here—but there was something in his face, in his eyes, that told a different story.

He needed her.

She didn't even know how she knew that—she just did.

She could only guess that holding his baby for the first time had been about as cataclysmic as it had been for her when Daniel had been born.

She tried again. 'What just happened?'

He shook his head. 'I can't explain it… *Theos*, Maggie, just get out.'

Maggie's heart spasmed at the raw tone in Nikos's voice. 'Why?'

'Because if you don't I'll have to touch you.'

Her pulse tripped and started again at a faster rate. 'Why would that be a bad thing?'

Nikos's jaw clenched. 'Because I don't feel very gentle right now.'

His warning didn't scare her—it excited her.

She told him without words that he could touch her if he wanted to by stepping right in front of him.

Nikos said warningly, 'Maggie…' But there was something unguarded in his expression. In his voice.

She lifted a hand and touched his jaw, felt the stubble tickling her palm. He caught her hand and turned it, pressing a kiss to the centre, flicking out his tongue. Her insides seized on a spasm of lust.

When he bent his head she was already reaching up, meeting him halfway. Mouths collided as her arms slid around his neck. She was arching her body even closer. Nothing could hold her back from this.

She was vaguely aware of Nikos lifting her and settling her onto a hard surface. The bathroom counter. It put their mouths on the same level. He tugged at her shirt. She heard something ping. A button? She didn't care. She just wanted Nikos's hands on her bare flesh.

He pushed off her shirt, opened her bra, cupped her breasts. Laved one peak with his tongue and then the other.

They were so sensitive… Maggie gripped Nikos's head, her whole body tingling.

His shirt was open—had she done that? She reached for him, pushing it off his wide shoulders. It fell to the ground and she half slipped, half slithered off the counter to reach for his trousers, undoing the belt, then the button, the zip, pulling them down. She was infused with a kind of confidence that would have shocked her if she'd been able to appreciate it.

His erection was long and thick. 'Touch me, Maggie…'

She wrapped her hand around him and he pulsed against her fingers. She moved her hand up and down experimentally and heard Nikos hiss a breath through his teeth.

He reached for her now, opening her jeans, tugging them down, taking her underwear with them. Then he lifted her again, back onto the marble surface. Her hands were dislodged from his erection and they went to his chest, fingers tangling in the dark hair curling over his pectorals.

A very feminine part of her exulted in his virile masculinity. It roused something that felt very primal in her. He pushed her legs apart, coming between them, and at the same time captured her mouth again.

He put his hand on her, between her legs. She could feel how hot she was. How damp. She might have been embarrassed if she hadn't felt so needy. She pushed against him, silently begging him to—

She gasped when he answered her silent plea, exploring her with his fingers, sinking them deep into her slick body.

But it wasn't enough. She pulled back and reached for Nikos's body again, wrapping her hand around him, drawing him to where she wanted him to fill her, to eclipse all the questions and fears in her head.

'Please, Nikos…'

He took his hand away and put his arm around her back,

nudging her legs even further apart. And then, with one powerful thrust, he was there…deep in the heart of her body…where she'd dreamt of him for a whole year.

Pleasure exploded outwards to his every extremity. *This*, Nikos thought as he plunged deep inside Maggie's tight, slick body. *This* was what he needed. Over and over again.

And then she was quivering in his arms, both their bodies slick, their breath coming in short, sharp gasps, as with one final thrust Nikos's thoughts went blank and were replaced with pure ecstasy. The kind of pleasure and transcendence that went above and beyond anything that could be synthetically made by humans. Pleasure in its purest form.

Maggie's body convulsed powerfully around his, causing him to shudder against her as another tide of pleasure swept over him.

Maggie was barely aware of Nikos extricating himself, helping her off the marble counter, handing her her trousers. Her shirt was open, her bra undone. She felt…turned inside out. The whole thing had been fast and furious, and yet she was suffused with lingering pleasure and a sense of satisfaction that made her want to lie down and sleep for a hundred years.

She could sense the tension in Nikos. When she'd put on her underwear and jeans and pulled her shirt together she looked at him. He was grim-faced. The suspicion that he regretted what had just happened made her feel exposed. She'd all but thrown herself at him…lust overriding every other thought.

'What is it?' Her voice was croaky.

'We didn't use protection.'

Maggie struggled to make her brain work. She wasn't unduly concerned. 'I haven't started my periods again yet… I won't while I'm breastfeeding. It's highly unlikely that we're in danger.'

'I was careless. I won't be next time.'

Because he didn't want children.

Reality slid back like a traitor as she remembered what had precipitated this explosive interlude.

She moved past him to the door. 'I should check on Daniel.'

As she went back out into the apartment she realised the magnitude of what had just happened. They hadn't even been in the apartment for an hour and they'd made love. *Combusted.*

Daniel was still fast asleep. Maggie went onto the terrace, feeling raw. She wasn't in her right mind around Nikos. She couldn't see straight…think straight.

She wasn't sure what she'd hoped for when she'd put Daniel into Nikos's arms—maybe, naively, some kind of idyllic bonding moment, with him weeping tears of emotion as he lifted his baby and proclaimed, *My son!*

She heard a sound behind her and turned around. Nikos was watching her. She felt vulnerable.

'Maggie…that shouldn't have—'

She put up a hand. 'It's okay—you don't have to tell me it shouldn't have happened. I know.'

He frowned and walked towards her. 'I wasn't going to say that. I was going to say it shouldn't have happened *like that.*'

Maggie knew she should let this go. She really didn't want to hear Nikos articulating that he couldn't bond with his son, but she had to know what she was dealing with.

'Why did it happen? What was going on with you?'

For a long moment he said nothing. Then he moved to the wall, putting his hands on it. Maggie turned around to watch him. Nikos didn't look at her.

'I've never held a baby before. He's so small and defenceless. But *strong*. I felt it…'

He turned around, a stark expression on his face.

'I wasn't loved, Maggie. By my parents or my grandparents. Even if my mother *did* love me I was too small to remember what that felt like.'

He shook his head.

'I don't want Daniel to experience what I did, but already I know he won't. Because he has you and you love him. I just can't promise to…to give him something I never experienced myself.'

Maggie took this in and tried to ignore the ache near her heart at the thought of Nikos as a lonely child. 'But I know you felt something powerful just now when you held him. I saw it.'

'I realised how vulnerable he is. And how much I want to protect him.'

Nikos looked tortured. A million miles from the careless charming playboy she'd first met. She wanted to tell him that wanting to protect his son *was* a form of love, but knew it would sound like a platitude.

'Okay,' she said after a moment.

'Okay?'

She made a little shrugging motion. 'That's good enough.'

Was it good enough, though?

Nikos said, 'I'm committed to making this relationship work for the sake of our son.'

Committed. In a way, Maggie couldn't fault Nikos. He was already offering more than her father had ever offered *her*. And she had seen powerful emotion affect him just now, so it was surely only a matter of time before he realised that what he felt for his son *was* love. Even if he didn't think he wasn't capable of it.

To her shame, she felt a dart of something like envy. For

her own son. Because he'd sparked something in Nikos that would flower to life. It couldn't *not*. But as for her…? Why was she even thinking of herself in this equation? She didn't even—

Her thoughts stopped there.

The problem was that she *did* have feelings for him. She'd had them since that night a year ago, when his note the next day had been like a punch to the gut. And then each day of a whole year had followed and he hadn't made contact—a further punch to the gut. Even knowing now that it hadn't been his fault, because he'd never got the note, it didn't diminish the hurt. Because he wouldn't have contacted her anyway.

Maggie knew she needed to cut off all these nascent tender feelings she had for Nikos, because he'd told her more than once that he just wasn't capable of returning them. He never would have offered her a relationship if it hadn't been for Daniel. The fact that he might come to love his son would have to be enough for her.

She said, 'I'm committed too.' But the words tasted tart on her tongue.

Nikos moved closer and sneaked a hand around the back of her neck. Her traitorous heart leapt, along with her pulse.

'I think we have a lot going for us, Maggie. I like you, and I want to be a good father for Daniel. We have insane chemistry. We want each other. We're going into this with eyes wide open—no illusions. That's as good a foundation for marriage as any I know.'

I like you.

Maggie longed to be able to pull back and tell Nikos that liking wasn't good enough. But this wasn't about her. And she was afraid that he would touch her again and see how close to the surface her emotions were.

She reached for his hand and pulled it down. 'I think I'll go and get Daniel settled in our new rooms.'

Nikos looked at her as if he was trying to figure her out. Then he took a step back. He glanced at his watch. 'I should go to the office to catch up on some work and clear my schedule before the wedding. Help yourself to dinner and make a list of things you need for Daniel. I'll make sure you get everything you need.'

Maggie watched Nikos walk out and exhaled once she was alone again. Her body was still over-sensitised and her heart was still bruised. As if on cue, to remind her of what was at stake here, Daniel made a sound, and she went in to find him awake. He regarded her with those steady dark eyes. Dark eyes with hazel flecks…

She pushed everything else out of her mind and tended to her son, telling herself that she and Daniel had a lot to be thankful for. Nikos might have proved to be just like her father, uncaring and uninterested. The fact that he wasn't should be a relief. To want anything more—like love and a real family—was just being greedy.

The next day Maggie stood in front of a full-length mirror, but the woman reflected back at her was a stranger. It was her—but not her. She was tall and svelte, with sleek wavy hair twisted up into an elegant chignon. She'd never thought her hair could behave like that, but the hairdresser in the hotel salon had cultivated it into something far less wild.

And she'd had a pedicure and manicure.

But the dress…

Maggie had never worn a long dress before. Not even for her end-of-school dance. Because she hadn't gone as she'd had no date. None of the boys had wanted to ask 'Beanpole Maggie' as they'd have looked small next to her.

The dress was black and off the shoulder, with little dropped sleeves that rested on her arms. Maggie had tried pulling them up but the stylist had said, '*Non, non, cherie*—they're meant to be like that.'

A sweetheart neckline showed more skin than Maggie had ever shown before. The tops of her breasts swelled against the bodice in a way that felt indecent. The material clung to her breasts, her belly, waist and hips, before falling to the floor in a swathe of material. When she moved a slit up one side revealed her leg.

She felt very pale, and wished she had more colour.

There was a movement behind her and she saw Nikos, reflected in the doorway.

Her heart stopped. He was wearing a tuxedo and she felt a rushing sensation in her head, remembering the first time she'd seen him lounging against his own front door, looking like the devil himself.

He looked no less innocent now, even though his tuxedo was pristine. He oozed sophistication and masculine elegance, yet with that ever-present edginess that hinted at something much darker and more intense.

He came into the room and she couldn't take her eyes off him.

His dark gaze swept her up and down. 'I knew you were beautiful, Maggie…but like this you are even more than I imagined.'

Maggie couldn't even take in what he was saying. It was so far removed from her reality.

Her old reality.

'You look…lovely.' She winced inwardly. What did one say to one of the most ridiculously handsome men on the planet?

Nikos quirked a smile. 'Thank you.'

She wanted to scowl. 'You know what I mean… I'm not used to this.'

Nikos's smile faded. He reached out and touched Maggie's jaw. 'I know. You'll be fine. I promise. Everyone will be captivated by you.'

'I don't want to captivate anyone.'

Don't you? whispered a small voice.

She ignored it.

Nikos took his hand away and moved behind her to the boxes laid out on a table. Maggie hadn't even noticed them before.

He opened one of them up and stood back. 'What would you like to wear with the dress?'

Maggie walked over and was almost blinded by the bling. Diamonds… A necklace with square rough-cut diamonds and matching earrings. A bracelet.

She looked at Nikos. 'My ears aren't pierced.'

He responded smoothly. 'Okay, the bracelet and necklace, then.'

He plucked them out and moved behind her to put on the necklace. She felt its heavy cold weight against her collarbone and touched it.

Then he came in front of her and lifted her arm, fastening the bracelet around her wrist. It too was heavy. Substantial.

'What if I lose them?' she asked.

Nikos looked at her. 'Don't. They're worth the annual debt of a small country.'

There was a glimmer of humour in his eyes, though. And then he picked up another, much smaller box.

Maggie looked down at it. 'What's this?'

'This evening is primarily focused on introducing you as my fiancée. You'll need a ring.'

He opened the box and Maggie sucked in a breath. She'd never really been interested in jewellery, but the ring nestled against a white satin cushion was exquisite. It was a square-cut emerald, with small square diamonds on either side, in a platinum setting and band.

Maggie said, 'It's beautiful.'

'I could have let you choose, but I thought this one would suit.'

Nikos took it out of the box and reached for her left hand. She held it out and he slipped the ring onto her ring finger. It fitted.

She looked up. 'How did you know it would fit?'

He let her hand go. 'A lucky guess.'

A little shiver went down Maggie's spine. This was all falling into place so easily.

Nikos stepped back. 'Ready?'

Maggie nodded, but was suddenly reluctant.

Nikos noticed. 'What is it?' he asked.

She bit her lip. 'Daniel… I hope he'll be okay.' She'd left him before, for brief amounts of time, but this was a whole new milieu.

'You like Marianne, don't you?'

She nodded. In the end none of the nannies who'd come for interview had been suitable, and then Mathilde the housekeeper had suggested her twin sister—newly retired from being a schoolteacher and already bored. They'd met, and Maggie had liked her immediately, warming to her easy maternal warmth. And Daniel had liked her too.

'We'll only be gone for a few hours. Mathilde is staying here with Marianne to help her out. And you've expressed milk, haven't you?'

Maggie wasn't unaware of the irony that Nikos was speaking those words out loud: *you've expressed milk*. A far cry from the lexicon of his previous experience.

'Yes.'

'Then let's go. The sooner we go, the sooner we're back.'

Maggie put her head around the door of the kitchen area, where Marianne had Daniel in her arms, making faces at him. He was gurgling and kicking his legs. She caught Maggie's eye and made a shooing motion. Maggie forced a smile, even though she felt physical pain at the thought of leaving Daniel behind.

In the lift on the way down Nikos said, 'It'll get easier. He'll be fine.'

Maggie suddenly felt at odds…out of her depth. Tetchy. 'And you know this because suddenly you're an expert in babies?'

He cast her a look. 'I might have more experience if I'd had more notice.'

Maggie clamped her mouth shut. She felt immediately contrite. 'Sorry. That wasn't fair. It's just hard to leave him behind. What if he—?'

Nikos took her hand, surprising her.

'Then Mathilde or Marianne will call and we'll come back straight away.'

He kept hold of her hand until they were outside, where a sleek car was waiting.

The air was warm and the sky was turning dusky, imbuing the surrounding buildings with a magical light. Maggie got into the back of the car on one side, Nikos the other. The interior was cream leather, sumptuous. When the doors were closed and they moved into the traffic the noises outside were just a dim hum. It was like a luxurious cocoon.

Maggie looked out of the window, taking in the wide elegant streets. They were crossing the Seine. She noticed something in her peripheral vision and looked to see Nikos's fingers drumming a staccato beat on his thigh.

Without thinking, she reached across and put her hand over his.

Nikos couldn't move his fingers. He looked down to see a pale hand over his, stopping his fingers drumming in that beat that he always felt gave him away.

Maggie's hand was cool on his. She took it away. He looked at her. She was pink.

'Sorry, I don't know why I did that.'

Nikos was more disturbed by her noticing his nervous

tic and wanting to soothe it than he cared to admit. He covered it up by drawling, 'Feel free to touch me whenever you want.'

She grew pinker.

Nikos wanted to shake his head. How had he, of all people, ended up with a woman like Maggie? Innocent, gauche. But surprising.

She surprised him now.

'Do you not enjoy social occasions?' she asked.

For the first time in his life Nikos was aware of a sense of reluctance about walking into a room full of people and...*performing*. Because that was what he'd been doing all his life. Performing to try and make his grandparents love him. Rebelling to make his father notice him. Charming and smiling and seducing his way through endless parties, functions and events and women, to perpetuate the myth of being a playboy while taking advantage of anyone who underestimated him.

He was inclined to give Maggie some pithy response, but he surprised himself by saying, 'Would you believe me if I said not as much as people might think?'

Maggie regarded him and shook her head slowly. 'No, I believe you. Why do you do it, then?'

Nikos shrugged, feeling the need to escape Maggie's piercing blue gaze. Was it more piercing this evening? Because of the artful make-up that had elevated her from beautiful to breathtaking?

'It's expected of me. It's an integral part of the world I grew up in and the business we have only enhances that.'

'You'd really have me believe that all these countless premieres and parties where you're photographed with beautiful women are pure torture for you, then?'

Nikos suspected that Maggie had intended that to sound lighter than it had. She looked self-conscious. It reminded him that she was different.

He took her hand and laced her fingers with his, feeling the inevitable tug of desire. 'They're not torture, no. It would be disingenuous to claim that. But those women were passing fancies. Diversions.'

He saw her expression change as his meaning sank in. They might be announcing their engagement tonight, but he still wasn't in the market for anything deep and meaningful.

She pulled her hand from his and looked away—and then she tensed. 'Oh, my God—is that where we're going?'

Nikos looked out of the window to see a hotel entrance lit up like Mardi Gras by the popping flashbulbs of photographers, which were almost out-dazzling the shimmering dresses and jewels of the guests being disgorged onto the red carpet.

'Yes, that's it.'

He looked at Maggie again and saw she was deathly pale.

He took her hand. 'Maggie, look at me.'

She tore her gaze from the scene they were fast approaching. 'I don't think I can do this.'

'Just hold my hand and smile. We're going to stop for a couple of pictures. All you have to do is smile, okay?'

For the first time Nikos felt a prickle of unease. He hadn't really considered what jumping into the deep end would be like for Maggie. Now he felt protective, and it was disconcerting.

Maggie nodded. She looked terrified.

He said, 'Relax. It'll be fine. I promise.'

The car stopped and the door was opened by an usher.

Nikos said, 'Wait there. I'll help you out.'

Maggie's heart was palpitating so hard she felt light-headed. She hadn't really considered the enormity of what this would be like. She'd had some notion that they'd walk anonymously into a function room. Not be paraded in front of the world's media.

Nikos was waiting, holding out a hand. Reluctantly she reached for it and let him help her out. The dress fell around her legs and she walked carefully in the high heels, not used to them, clinging to Nikos's arm to stay upright as much as to disguise her trembling limbs.

They were approaching the entrance now, lined on either side by photographers. Then they stepped onto the red carpet and the world exploded into blinding light.

'Nikos! Nikos!'

Maggie was in shock, clinging on to Nikos as voices came at her from all sides. She couldn't understand French, which was probably a good thing. She felt like Alice in Wonderland—as if she'd landed in a new and scary universe.

Nikos's arm was around her waist, pulling her close. It was enough to distract her momentarily, and then he said in her ear, 'Good… Now just smile and pretend this is normal. Let them see the ring.'

Maggie placed her hand as strategically as she could over Nikos's arm and the flashbulbs increased in intensity. So much so that she felt blinded.

After what felt like an eternity Nikos was saying something back to the photographers and leading her into a thronged foyer which was mercifully absent of flashbulbs. Her ears were ringing.

'Okay?'

She nodded, even though she felt stunned. Dizzy.

Waiters dressed in black were handing out tall, slim glasses of champagne. Nikos handed her one. She took a sip, aware that she shouldn't really drink too much, but she relished the alcohol fizzing down into her belly and sending out a little warming, calming glow.

Nikos looked as if he was about to say something else, but then they were joined by a tall man—as tall and dark as Nikos. Intimidatingly good-looking with deep-set dark eyes. He also looked slightly familiar, which was odd when Maggie knew he was a stranger. He had a forbidding expression.

Maggie sensed Nikos's tension. Then, 'Maggie, I'd like to introduce you to Sharif, my brother.'

So that was why he was familiar-looking. Maggie could see the resemblance now. The same high cheekbones. Strong bone structure. Thick hair. Arrogant air.

He put out a hand. 'It is a pleasure to make your acquaintance, Maggie. And I believe congrautlations are in order? On your forthcoming marriage and also because you've made me an uncle?'

For the first time Maggie had a very real sense that she and Daniel had joined a family.

She shook Sharif's hand, more than a little intimidated. 'Yes, thank you. His name is Daniel. He's three months old.'

Sharif let her hand go and slid a look to his brother. 'I look forward to meeting him soon. Perhaps at your wedding?'

Maggie nodded. 'Of course. He'll be there.'

Sharif addressed Nikos. 'So, are you still okay to do the tour or do I need to talk to Maks?'

Nikos answered. 'It's fine. We'll have a brief honeymoon and then I'll resume my work commitments.'

Sharif gave Nikos a nod, then made his excuses and walked away.

Maggie turned to Nikos. 'What was he talking about… the tour? And a brief honeymoon? Why do we need any honeymoon?'

Nikos said, 'We need a honeymoon to make our marriage look authentic, so we're going to spend a couple of days in Athens. The tour he spoke of is a showcasing of various aspects of the Marchetti Group in Rome, Madrid, London, France and Monte Carlo—from the launch of a new perfume to welcoming a new head designer for one of our fashion houses and hosting various charity benefits. It'll be a quick, fast-paced tour, over two weeks. We're building up our exposure for the thirtieth anniversary of the group next year.'

Maggie arched a brow. 'And was any of this going to be discussed with *me*? I know this marriage is just for show, and for Daniel's sake, but I do deserve to know what's happening.'

To her surprise, Nikos said, 'Yes, you're right, and I'm sorry. I'm not used to having to explain my schedule to anyone else.'

She was a little mollified by his response.

And then he asked, 'Do you think it's feasible for us to do the tour with Daniel?'

Maggie shrugged lightly. 'If we have Marianne with us it should be okay. He's portable at the moment. Obviously as he gets older things will be much trickier. We'll have to have more of a base.'

Maggie felt a pang as she said that. Nikos's apartment wasn't exactly the kind of home she'd envisaged. But maybe she needed to be more accepting of this new life and give it a chance.

After that they were sucked into a round of greeting people. Maggie was aware of lots of stares and whispers and did her best to ignore them. At first she tried to remember names and faces, but it soon became impossible so she gave up.

She noticed that Nikos had an assistant on hand, to help jog his memory with a name in case he forgot. What hope did she have?

'Ready to go?' asked Nikos.

Maggie looked at him, feeling guilty. Had he noticed her moving from one foot to the other to relieve the ache in the balls of her feet? Had she looked as bored as she'd felt over the past couple of hours?

'Can we?' she asked.

He nodded, then took her hand to lead her through the crowd. When he stopped suddenly she collided with his back.

He turned around. 'You did really well this evening.'

Maggie looked up at him, feeling a ridiculous flush of pleasure warming her insides. 'Really?'

He nodded and, to her surprise, reached out and tucked a wayward lock of hair behind one ear. His hand lingered and then caught behind her head. Before she could prepare herself his mouth was covering hers in a searing brand of heat.

Maggie swayed towards him, the kiss making her feel more drunk than the half-glass of champagne she'd had at the start of the evening.

When he pulled back she looked up. 'What was that for?' He didn't strike her as the sort of guy to indulge in a PDA.

'There's a photographer over there. I thought it would be good to give him something.'

The flush of heat in Maggie's body drained away. He'd kissed her for a photographer. Not because he hadn't been able to help himself. Of *course* a man like him wouldn't indulge in PDAs.

Maggie tugged herself free. 'I need to get back to Daniel.'

She walked towards the entrance.

Nikos watched her go for a second. It had been harder than he'd expected or appreciated to pull back from that kiss just now. It might have started as something strategic, but it had become something else as soon as their mouths had touched.

She cut an effortlessly graceful figure now, walking

through the crowd with a sensuality Nikos felt she wasn't even aware of. Who could have known that such a swan had been hidden under that casual appearance?

For a man who would usually abhor kissing a woman in public—even a lover—it had been surprisingly easy to turn to Maggie and kiss her. Not just because of the opportunity presented but because he'd needed to after an evening of her surprisingly easy presence by his side.

The crowd was closing in behind Maggie and she'd disappeared from view. Nikos moved to catch up, not liking the way he couldn't see her bright hair. He was almost at the entrance before he saw her again, and the feeling of relief that went through him was uncomfortable.

What was wrong with him? She wasn't going anywhere. She was his. Daniel was his. And he *would* make this work.

They were almost back at the hotel when Nikos asked, 'What is it, Maggie? You've barely said a word since we left.'

She was still angry—*hurt* by the calculated kiss. 'I don't appreciate being used as a PR stunt. If you're going to do that again then please tell me in advance.'

When she glanced at him she saw he looked blank.

'The kiss?' she prompted.

Comprehension dawned. 'You thought I just kissed you for that?'

'That's what you said.'

'I took advantage of an opportunity that presented itself—but, believe me, I didn't kiss you just for that.'

'What does *that* mean?'

'It means that right now there's nothing strategic to be gained but still I want to kiss you.'

'Oh.'

'But this isn't the right place.'

Maggie's heart palpitated. 'No.'

He took her hand and lifted it up. His warm breath feathered across her palm. She shivered with awareness. He pressed his mouth there, his tongue flicking out to touch her skin, inducing another shiver.

As the car stopped outside the hotel he said in a low voice, 'That kiss might have started out as a strategic thing, but it didn't end up as one. I never do anything I don't want to, Maggie.'

He let her go then, and got out of the car.

She didn't even look at him the whole way up to the apartment in the lift. She went straight to her bedroom, firmly closing the door behind her. She rested against it for a moment before she went to check on Daniel, her pulse racing, skin prickling all over.

Damn Nikos. She would have to be so careful around him or he would incinerate her.

CHAPTER EIGHT

THE DAY OF the wedding a week later was warm and sultry. Maggie and Nikos were travelling together to the civil register office. Daniel was in the car behind them with Marianne.

Nothing so romantic as her groom waiting at the top of an aisle to greet her. She was surprised at the pang of regret she felt that she wouldn't get to have that experience of watching someone she loved turn to greet her as she walked towards them.

It irritated her that the only person she could envisage in that scenario had all too familiar dark and devilishly handsome features. Thick curling hair…

'Why are you scowling?'

Maggie looked at Nikos. She'd barely seen him since the other night. He'd been working until late each evening—which Maggie had appreciated but also felt conflicted by, not liking the way she'd noticed his absence so keenly.

But she'd been busy herself—settling in with Daniel. Making sure she had all she needed for him. Doing up his room. Going through the clothes that the stylist had stocked her walk-in wardrobe with, feeling totally intimidated by all the silk and chiffon and elegant trouser suits. Chatting with Mathilde and Marianne, who were becoming good friends.

Mathilde had confided in Maggie that she was glad to see Nikos settle down, because she'd always felt he cut such a lonely figure. Maggie had smiled and said nothing, knowing that Nikos would bristle at the idea that anyone thought he was lonely.

Nikos was looking at her. She rearranged her features into a smile.

'That's marginally better. Aren't you delighted to be marrying the man of your dreams today?'

She could handle this charming Nikos, who mocked her. It reminded her of the man who had seduced her so easily.

Maggie affected a look of surprise. 'Oh? The man of my dreams is here? Where is he?'

She pretended to look around and Nikos emitted a short laugh. 'Don't tell me you're still holding a torch for Mr Nice and Boring?'

'It's a bit late for regrets now—and someone once told me regrets were for losers,' Maggie said lightly even though she wondered if Nikos was a mind-reader.

'That someone must have been very intelligent.'

Maggie was sorry for goading him now. It only reminded her of his note, and the fact that she wouldn't be here if it wasn't for Daniel.

The car was pulling to a stop in a square now. Maggie suddenly felt nervous. Nikos took her hand. She looked at him.

'You look beautiful. And, for what it's worth, I hadn't ever expected to be in this situation, but I'm glad it's with you.'

Maggie couldn't tear her gaze away from Nikos's. She couldn't fault him for leading her on with false hope and promises. He'd been very clear they were doing this for Daniel.

'Ready?'

Maggie nodded and tried to swallow her nerves.

She waited till the driver had opened her door and Nikos was waiting to help her out. She was wearing a fitted white blazer over a very simple but elegant white silk dress, cut on the bias. It fell to just below her knees and she wore satin kitten-heel shoes.

Her hair was up and she wore a small hat with a piece

of net that came down over her eyes. Clip-on pearls in her ears and her engagement ring were her only jewellery.

Marianne got out of the car behind them and Maggie went over to make sure Daniel was okay. He looked adorable, in a romper suit in a royal blue that matched the same blue in Nikos's three-piece suit.

She knew she couldn't delay any longer, so she shot Marianne a smile—the nanny smiled back reassuringly—and went over to Nikos, who took her hand to lead her into the office.

Maggie was surprised to see more than a few people there. She recognised Sharif, and there was another tall man, very lean, with short dark blond hair. Spectacularly gorgeous. He had to be Maks. Beside him was a young woman.

Maggie was too nervous to dwell on who everyone else was and tried to focus on the ceremony, led by a registrar who conducted it in English for her benefit. She made a mental note to learn French as soon as possible. After all, Daniel was a quarter Greek and Italian and would be growing up in France. A true child of Europe.

'You may now kiss your bride.'

Maggie panicked. It was over already?

She turned to face Nikos. He tipped up her chin with a finger and pulled her close. She cursed him for putting on a show.

He smiled. 'No regrets, Mrs Marchetti.'

Before she could say anything he was kissing her, and her brain fused with heat. She hadn't built all the sophisticated defences she'd need around Nikos yet. She probably never would.

When they walked out of the office some minutes later Nikos warned her, 'There'll be a few photographers. Not a crowd like the other night, though.'

Sure enough there were a handful, and they stopped

and posed for pictures. One of them called out, *'Baisez!'* and Maggie soon figured out what that meant when Nikos pulled her close for another kiss.

By the time they got to one of the most exclusive Marchetti hotels in the centre of Paris for the wedding breakfast Maggie's whole body was one big mass of quivering nerve-endings and overload of adrenalin.

'So you're Maggie?'

Maggie turned around, a smile fixed on her face. It was the blond man she'd noticed standing near Sharif in the register office.

She held out her hand. 'Yes—you must be Maks?'

'Guilty.' He shook her hand. He was very different from both Nikos and Sharif, and yet similar. More guarded. Intense grey eyes.

'I'd say welcome to the family,' he drawled. 'But that would imply that we're some kind of functioning unit.'

He looked over Maggie's head and she followed his gaze.

'That's my younger sister, Sasha.'

Maggie took in the woman she'd thought might be his girlfriend. She was beautiful in a way that made Maggie suspect she tried to hide it. She was dressed almost frumpily, in a long skirt and a high-necked blouse, but she recognised the bone structure. Maggie felt an affinity with the girl, even though they hadn't yet met. She recognised something about the way she was trying to hide herself.

'You look alike,' she said.

'We take after our mother. Nikos and Sharif bear the brunt of the Marchetti genes. Sasha has a different father from me and my brothers. She made a lucky escape in that regard.'

Maggie was just absorbing this, and how complicated this family was, when she heard a voice.

'Filling my wife's head with nonsense, Maks?'

She felt a jolt at the words '*my wife*'. Nikos slid an arm around her waist.

Maks smiled, but it didn't reach his eyes. 'Not at all, I was merely welcoming Maggie to the firm.'

Nikos made a sound that might have been a laugh or a snarl. 'If you don't mind, I need to steal my wife away. We're leaving for our honeymoon.'

Maks inclined his head. '*Bon voyage* and best wishes to you both.'

Nikos made efficient work of saying goodbye to everyone, and soon he was leading Maggie out of the hotel and into a waiting car. He undid his tie. Marianne had gone ahead with Daniel to the private plane, taking Maggie's expressed milk with her to feed the baby. They were going to Athens for a couple of days—ostensibly for their honeymoon, but also so that Nikos could check in on his Athens office.

There was a brooding energy surrounding him that she tried to dissipate by saying, 'Maks told me about Sasha… that she's not your sister.'

Nikos glanced at her and then away. 'I never spent any time with her growing up in any case—she made a lucky escape.'

'That's what he said too—or something like it. Was your father really so bad?'

Nikos made a slightly strangled sound. 'Yes. The only thing he did for us was to create a legacy that we must nurture and grow.'

'So what's Maks's role in the business?'

'He's involved in the fashion and branding end of things.'

'It's a pity you and your half-brothers aren't closer. It was just me and my mum. I always wished I had siblings. I don't even have cousins.'

She was about to add that she'd always intended having more than one child, but clamped her mouth shut.

* * *

Nikos usually resented any intrusion into his personal life, but Maggie was now his wife. He also didn't like being reminded of when he'd been younger, when he'd wished that he and his brothers were closer.

But reluctantly he confided, 'It was as if our father deliberately did all he could to keep us apart. Probably to keep us from uniting against him. I think he was afraid that we might do a better job than him, and while he wanted us to succeed him, he only handed over full control through his death.'

He looked at Maggie. 'What's your impression of my brothers?'

'Maks is intense. Sharif is impenetrable.'

'And me?'

Maggie went a bit pink. 'Charming—but you're hiding something much more serious. That evening you arrived at Kildare House, on first appearance I thought you were drunk. But you weren't drunk at all.'

Nikos was surprised at her assessment.

She saw too much.

He needed to deflect her attention from him now.

'The one thing me and my brothers have in common is that our father let all of us down.'

'That's sad.'

Nikos shrugged. 'Is it? Maybe it's better to find out early who you can depend on in life.'

Hours later, Maggie still felt an ache near her heart to think of Nikos and his half-brothers growing up separated by an insecure and domineering father. They'd arrived a short time before at the penthouse apartment of the most exclusive hotel in Athens—one of the Marchetti Group's jewels.

A grand classic building, it stood on one of Athens' oldest squares, and from its penthouse they had unimpeded views of the hilly city of Athens and the Acropolis.

Marianne was walking around with Daniel, oohing and ahing at the view. Nikos was due to take Maggie out for dinner and she'd just expressed some more milk for Daniel.

She'd changed out of her wedding outfit and into a pair of long trousers and a matching long-sleeved silk top with a round neck. Simple, but elegant. Her stylist had called ahead to the boutique at the hotel and ensured that Maggie's wardrobe there would be stocked with suitable clothes.

Now she had taken her hair down and was massaging her skull, which was sore from all the pins holding her hair up.

'Sorry, I had to take a call.'

She turned around to see Nikos walk in, adjusting his jacket. He'd changed too, into a steel-grey suit, and he looked so vital and handsome that her breath caught. He looked up, and that gaze raked her up and down. A flash of heat sizzled straight to her core.

He said, 'You look beautiful.'

Maggie was embarrassed. She wasn't used to compliments. She wasn't sure she'd ever get used to them. 'Thank you.'

'Ready?'

'Will there be paparazzi?'

'Most likely.'

Maggie swallowed her trepidation. She'd jumped into the deep end with this man a year ago, had his baby three months ago, and married him today. She could handle some photographers. She'd get used to it.

She'd have to.

'Would you like to go dancing?'

Maggie looked at Nikos across the table. *'Dancing?'*

He sat forward. 'Yes—you know… Somewhere they play loud music and people move energetically in a communal space.'

Maggie made a face, but her pulse was racing. This evening…this restaurant…had been the kind of date she'd never dreamed of, because it would have been way beyond her fantasies.

The restaurant Nikos had taken her to was high in a glass building with views of the Acropolis lit up at night. The lighting was golden and everyone in the place looked impossibly charismatic, beautiful. Gilded.

People had stopped and stared as Nikos and she had entered. She'd stumbled a little on the way to their table. But Nikos had put a hand to her back to steady her.

The food had been exquisite morsels of the freshest ingredients Maggie had ever tasted. She'd longed to go to the kitchen and talk to the chefs.

During dinner, Nikos had said to her, 'It's refreshing to be with someone who actually likes food.'

Maggie had looked up, her mouth full. When she'd been able to speak she'd said dryly, 'I'll take that as a compliment, shall I?'

She was in danger of being seduced all over again on another level. She put down her napkin now and looked at him suspiciously. 'Why do you want to take me dancing?'

A look passed across his face so fast she couldn't decipher it. Then he leant back and said, 'Full disclosure? For two reasons. One, because I would like to dance with you, and two, we will be seen—and that's a good thing to keep the gossip websites happy.'

Something deflated inside Maggie. Of course. She kept forgetting that everything was really an opportunity to be seen. Most likely even coming to this restaurant.

She shrugged as if she didn't really care. 'Okay, sure.'

* * *

As they walked out Nikos was aware of the fact that that had probably been the least enthusiastic response he'd ever got from a woman, and that not only was he drawing looks on the way out, so was Maggie.

And who could blame them? She stood out, with her height, her pale colouring and russet golden hair. Like a magnificent Valkyrie.

Nikos couldn't even recall the type of woman he'd wanted before. They had literally paled into insignificance in his memory.

He only wanted *this* woman.

But he'd never wanted another woman exclusively beyond for a night or two. Uneasiness prickled over his skin and he dismissed it. Whatever this was with Maggie, surely it was a *good* thing that he wanted his wife? He wanted to make this relationship work. He wanted to be a good father to his son.

The thought of anything deeper…he didn't know if he was capable of that.

Maggie wasn't sure where the pounding of her blood stopped and the pounding of the bass began. The beat was moving through her and it was infectious.

They'd taken a short journey to this club, where Nikos had been waved in like royalty. It was a big, cavernous space, with VIP areas around the edge of the first floor, from where they could look down on the dance floor filled with people dancing sinuously.

Maggie was fascinated, sipping her mocktail.

Then Nikos stood up, holding out a hand. 'Come on.'

Maggie put down her drink. 'Down there?' Her voice squeaked, which thankfully he wouldn't notice over the music.

He nodded.

Reluctantly Maggie took Nikos's hand and let him lead her down. As they got to the dance floor the beat changed to something much sultrier and slower. Maggie wasn't sure whether to be relieved or not. She'd dreaded looking like a fool—but now, when Nikos pulled her close, she dreaded him seeing how much of an effect he had on her.

He placed his hands on her hips, bringing her in close to where she could feel every part of his whipcord body, and as they started to move she felt the evidence of his desire.

Naturally her arms went around his neck, bringing them into closer contact. Heat and need suffused every cell in Maggie's body. Surely this had to be the definition of dirty dancing? She tipped her head back to look at Nikos. His eyes were glittering…his jaw was tight.

She wasn't aware of the hundreds of other people around them. It was as if they were in a bubble. He bent his head and after an infinitesimal moment, covered her mouth with his.

The music seemed to be pounding in time with her heart.

Nikos's hands smoothed down her back, the slippery material of her shirt making her skin tingle all over. His arousal pressed against her and Maggie thought she might melt into a puddle right there.

Then she remembered where she was, and with whom. She pulled back, dizzy. 'Is this for show?'

He shook his head. 'No. It's because I want you. Let's get out of here.'

Maggie was about to say, *But we just got here!* but Nikos was leading her back upstairs, picking up their things and leading her outside.

The cool air was like a slap to her face. Waking her up. Nikos's hand was still tight on hers. It was truly shocking how easily he affected her, spinning her out of all control.

His car appeared and he opened the door for her, letting her go. By the time he got into the other side she felt marginally composed again. Composed enough to realise just how much had happened in one day. They were *married.* And this man was still such an enigma to her.

When they got back to the apartment Nikos turned to face her, stark intent on his face. 'Maggie, I want you.'

It was the hardest thing in the world to resist the effect of those words, coming from that man, with *that* look on his face, He was overwhelming. But she had to resist. She needed space to absorb everything or she'd lose herself entirely.

She shook her head. 'I'm quite tired. I'm going to bed.'

He came close. 'This is our wedding night, *agapi mou,* and I want my wife. Believe me, the irony of being married and wanting my wife is not something I ever expected to experience.'

If he could have said anything to firm her resolve it was that. This wasn't a real wedding night and she suddenly realised that she wanted it to be. And if he touched her now he would see just how much her emotions were affected.

She stepped back. 'It's been a long day.'

Nikos's mouth thinned. 'I don't play games, Maggie.'

'I'm not playing games. I wouldn't know how.'

Believe me.

Nikos reached out a finger and trailed it over her jaw. Maggie felt her nipples tighten into buds of need. She gritted her jaw.

Nikos said, 'Oh, I don't doubt for a second that you'd become as proficient as any other woman, given the right circumstances.'

Maggie jerked her head away. 'Don't you ever get tired of being so cynical and suspicious?' She was *glad* she was resisting him now.

Nikos let out a tortured-sounding laugh. 'Believe me, I used to be a lot worse. You're doing something to me. Addling my brain. You've enslaved me, Maggie—does that make you happy? I haven't been able to look at another woman since I met you.'

Nikos's words took a moment to impact on her, and when they did she said faintly, 'I didn't think you meant that.'

His face was stark with need. 'I told you, Maggie. You haunted me for a year. You ruined me for any other woman. I only want *you*.'

Maggie's heart stopped and then started again. She looked at him. He wasn't lying. Why would he? Surely if he wanted to boost his pride he'd claim she'd been only one of many?

'Wow…'

He arched a brow, his mouth turned up wryly. 'Wow?'

Then, to Maggie's surprise, he took a step back.

He said, 'I won't ever make you do something you don't want to do, Maggie. But we are married and we want each other—a bonus in this marriage. Like I said, I don't play games.'

He turned and walked away from her. She had to clamp her mouth shut in case she called out and told him she'd changed her mind. Then he really would think she was playing games. And she needed this respite.

Nikos's words reverberated in her head. He was a proud man—she knew that. And yet he'd just told her that she'd ruined him for all other women.

Before she did something stupid she went into her room. Checked on Daniel—the reason for this whole union even if Nikos *did* want her. And she wanted him…

It took her hours to fall asleep that night. And the revelation that he hadn't slept with anyone since her hit her anew when she woke in the morning. She knew it really shouldn't mean anything, but she couldn't help her silly heart beating a little too fast every time she thought about it.

She knew it was dangerous to contemplate, but the fact

that he wanted her and she wanted him… Surely it went beyond the purely physical? Or could?

But Maggie grimaced. He still hadn't really bonded with Daniel. If he couldn't bond with his baby then what chance did *she* have?

When Maggie emerged into the breakfast room with Daniel, Nikos wasn't there. But there was a note and a mobile phone.

Your new phone. I've sent you a text. N.

She picked up the phone and read the text.

We're going to a party tonight. Need to be ready to leave at six p.m. Is this okay?

Maggie figured that at least he was *asking* her. Not ordering her.

She typed back a quick text.

Yes, fine. X

Then she quickly deleted the X and sent it.

'You didn't say we were leaving Athens to go to the party,' Maggie commented drily as she preceded Nikos back into the apartment later that night.

Her insides were still swooping after their return journey in the small sleek helicopter that had taken them to the island and back.

To her surprise it had been an enjoyable evening, an informal event celebrating the eightieth birthday of an old friend of Nikos's grandparents. Alexiou Spinakis.

The small, rocky and idyllic island had been covered in wild flowers and was full of exotic scents. They'd arrived as the sun was setting, and it had been the most magical sight Maggie had ever seen. And then they'd returned to see Athens lit up underneath them like a glittering carpet of jewels.

She slipped off her heels, giving a small groan of relief. She turned to face Nikos, whose shirt was open, his jacket off and slung over his shoulder, held by one finger. He looked thoroughly disreputable, and Maggie's body tingled all over after an evening spent in such close proximity with him.

In a bid to defuse the ever-simmering physical awareness, Maggie said, 'I really liked Alexiou. He was sweet.'

Nikos smiled. 'He liked you—the old goat.'

Maggie made a face. 'It wasn't like that. He really loves you, you know. And I can see that you care for him.'

Nikos's face became impassive. 'He was kind to me.'

'It's more than that—he considers you family.'

Maggie felt vulnerable all of a sudden, when she realised that she'd seen a totally different side to Nikos that evening. He'd been at home in his environment, relaxed in a way she'd never seen before. And clearly, he cared for the older man who'd evidently been more of a grandparent to Nikos than his own blood family.

With each layer stripped away he was revealing more of the complex man underneath, and she felt she had to protect herself more.

Terrified that he might touch her, or see even a hint of the vulnerability she felt, she stepped back and said, 'I should go and let Marianne know we're back. I told her not to worry about the night feeds tonight.'

Maggie turned and walked away and Nikos had to battle with himself not to beg her to stop and stay. Her words *he considers you family* reverberated in his head. He didn't need family. But the truth was that Maggie was his family now. And Daniel. No matter how alien it felt. No matter how terrifying.

He watched the green silk of her dress billowing around her body. She'd taken her shoes off and carried them in one hand. Her hair was loose and wild. That dress had been driving him crazy all night, making his hands itch to slide underneath it and cup her breasts.

He wanted nothing more than to go after her and sink deep inside her, where he didn't have to think. Or feel. But their son needed her.

For the first time in Nikos's life he had to acknowledge the novel sensation of someone else taking precedence over him. He also had to acknowledge that, as much as he wanted Maggie, he didn't relish those far too incisive blue eyes searching his soul for why he always felt such a mix of emotions when he saw his old friend, Alexiou.

He'd always been there for Nikos in a way his family never had. Alexiou used to visit him at boarding school, whenever he'd been in England on business. Even though Nikos had been an angry, surly youth.

The older man would ruffle his hair and say, '*You can't push everyone away for ever, Nikky. Sooner or later you'll have to let someone in or you'll die alone, like I will.*'

Nikos had always felt a pain in his chest when Alexiou left each time, and had always hoped that he would come back—even though Nikos hadn't seemed to be able to help but do everything in his power to push the man away. But he always had come back. And because Alexiou had never married or had children, Nikos knew that he saw him as a sort of son.

Nikos cursed and turned around, going into his own room. He didn't need this introspection and he certainly didn't welcome it. He needed to take a cold shower and numb the desire and the knot of emotion making his gut tight.

Rome, two days later

Another penthouse apartment at the top of a luxury hotel in one of Rome's most iconic buildings, this time with views of the Colosseum.

Maggie patted Daniel's back where he lay against her shoulder. She shook her head and smiled wryly to herself. If she wasn't careful she would get too used to arriving in a new city with everything she needed laid out for her, a cook to prepare their food and spectacular views. Her walk-in wardrobe was even stocked with clothes again, as it had been in the Athens apartment.

They were here for only one night, before moving on to Madrid tomorrow.

Nikos came into the room behind her. 'I have to go to a meeting now, but I'll be back to take you to the function at six p.m.'

Maggie turned around. She noticed how Nikos's eyes went to Daniel and then away again. He hadn't held him since that first time in Paris. A cold weight settled in her belly. She really didn't want her son growing up with a father who couldn't bond with him…

Nikos frowned. 'Is it too much for you?'

She shook her head and pushed down her concerns. She wanted to make this work. How was Nikos going to bond with his son if he wasn't with him?

'What is the function this evening?' she asked.

'A gala ball to fundraise for a group of charities that help combat homelessness and poverty. The Marchetti Group is its biggest benefactor.'

'Black tie?

He nodded. 'I've arranged for a team from the salon here at the hotel to come up and help get you ready.'

Maggie was simultaneously piqued at his implication that she needed help and relieved. 'Okay, thanks.'

Nikos turned away, and then he turned back. 'What are you going to do today?'

'Marianne and I are going to check out the Colosseum—she's never been, and nor have I.'

'You don't want to go shopping?'

Maggie shook her head. 'Why would I? I have everything I need for me and Daniel here. I'd prefer to see the city.'

Nikos stood at the vast floor-to-ceiling windows at the Marchetti Group HQ in Rome and took in the view—he could see the Colosseum in the distance. He imagined Maggie walking around the ancient site with Marianne. And the baby most likely in a sling, across her chest.

That feeling of restlessness was back…itching under his skin.

'Nikos?'

The fact that Maggie hadn't wanted to leave Daniel with the nanny and spend the day shopping really shouldn't have surprised him, but it had. It also shouldn't surprise him that she wasn't taking advantage of the fact that she knew he wanted her by using it as a device to manipulate him.

In his world any kind of desire was a weakness to be exploited. And yet she didn't…

'*Nikos?*'

Nikos turned around. The long table was full of board members who were looking at him. He felt exposed. He *never* let a woman compromise his focus—not even his wife.

He sat down at the head of the table and stared down anyone who might doubt his ability to be a member of this group—largely through his own careless actions.

For the first time in his life he regretted the fact that he'd created this persona. His own voice mocked him: *Re-*

grets are for losers. He could imagine Maggie saying it, teasing him.

Ruthlessly he pushed her image out of his head and said, 'Clearly whatever you were discussing couldn't hold my interest. I suggest you frame it in a more interesting way and start again.'

CHAPTER NINE

'YOU LOOK...AMAZING.'

Maggie wanted to blurt out, *Really?* But she forced herself to be gracious and say, 'Thank you—so do you.'

It was true. Nikos was wearing a white tuxedo tonight, with a black bowtie, and he'd never looked more urbane or gorgeous.

'Ready?'

Maggie nodded and walked forward, the long velvet dress moving sinuously around her body. It was high at the front, but completely backless. Which Nikos hadn't noticed yet. Her hair was up in a high ponytail, and she wore clip-on earrings and a sapphire bracelet which matched the blue of the dress.

When she reached Nikos he put a hand on her back to guide her and stopped dead. '*Theos*, Maggie.'

His hand was warm on her back. 'What?'

'Your dress...it's...'

'Backless?'

Nikos gritted his jaw.

Maggie might have felt like giggling if his hand hadn't been having such an effect on her blood. 'The stylist assures me it's perfectly respectable,' she said. She was sure that she'd seen pictures of Nikos escorting women in far less clothing to events.

He said, 'It's fine, We should go.'

In the lift on their way down Maggie could still feel the imprint of his hand against her skin. Awareness of him formed a tight ache in her lower body, which only got worse when he put his hand on her back again to guide her out of the lift and through the hotel lobby.

Resisting him was becoming harder and harder, and right now she wondered how long she could last before she didn't care if he saw her vulnerability or emotion.

A car was waiting outside and they'd soon joined the chaotic Roman traffic to move across the city to the stunning medieval palace where the gala was being held.

Maggie's jaw was almost on the ground as they walked through an open courtyard and into a palatial frescoed room lit by hundreds of candles and chandeliers. Mirrors on the walls reflected the sheer glittering opulence of the room and the people in it.

'This is amazing…' she breathed.

'Is it?' Nikos said, sounding almost bored.

She stopped and looked up at him. 'Are you really so jaded that you can't even appreciate how impressive this is?'

He looked at her. 'More impressive than the Colosseum?'

'Oh, no…well, that was just…mind-boggling. I mean, you'd have to agree that there's nothing quite like it.'

An expression that looked almost wistful crossed his face, and then he plucked two glasses of champagne from a passing waiter's tray, handed her one and said, 'I've never been in it, actually.'

Maggie's jaw dropped again. 'How can you never have visited the Colosseum? What about school trips? There were loads of schoolkids there today.'

Nikos shrugged. 'I had a tutor in Greece and then I was sent to boarding school in England. By the time I got to Rome I was more interested in staking my claim in the business and being a thorn in the side of my father by behaving outrageously than in sightseeing.'

'And after he died?'

Nikos's jaw tightened. 'I had a reputation to live down to and I was working hard.'

Maggie felt an unexpected lump in her throat. She took a quick sip of champagne to push it down.

'Nikos Marchetti! The very man!'

They were interrupted by a tall man who clapped Nikos on the back and looked at Maggie with undisguised interest. Nikos put his hand on her back again and Maggie wanted to groan. How was she going to handle an evening of Nikos touching her bare skin? This dress had been a terrible idea.

'Count Alfredo Pizzoli—please meet my wife, Maggie.'

The man held out his hand. 'A pleasure, my dear. So it wasn't an urban myth, then, your marriage?'

The man guffawed and Nikos said a few more words to him before expertly guiding Maggie deeper into the room, where she was introduced to many more people. This was a very different milieu from Alexiou's friendly and lively Greek birthday party. There was a more cynical edge here.

After a sit-down dinner, and some speeches by various guests about the work that the charities were doing, everyone got up and started milling around.

Nikos stood up and held out a hand for Maggie. He led her towards a room where she could hear soft jazz. It was another ballroom, with a band in the corner on a raised dais. Couples were dancing, bathed in the soft golden light of lots of candles. It was incredibly romantic.

'Like to dance?'

Maggie looked up at Nikos. 'Do I have a choice?'

He led her onto the dance floor even as he said, 'You always have a choice, Maggie.'

Yes, and she'd made a profound one last year, when she'd chosen to succumb to this man's seduction.

Yet even now—finding her way in his world, uncertain about his relationship with Daniel, with *her*—could she regret it? Not for Daniel's sake, obviously. And not even for her own.

Even if he never loves you? asked a voice.

He wants me, she answered herself almost desperately.

He pulled her close against his body, his hand moving

over her back, one hand high against his chest. They fitted. Even in high heels her head came to just below his jaw.

And I want him.

Maybe that was enough? She knew she was fighting a losing battle, resisting him. She wanted to sink into him now and let him take her whole weight. So she did—and it was the easiest thing in the world. Too easy…

She looked up at him, admitting wryly, 'I was afraid I was attracted to you because of your charisma and power. My mother always said that was what dazzled her about my father—until she saw what he really was… But after meeting the people here this evening I know it's not that. They have charisma and power, but they're not nice people.'

Nikos's mouth tipped up at one corner. 'Are you saying you like me for *myself*?'

Maggie heard the mocking tone in his voice and ignored it. 'Would that be so bad?'

Tension came into his body. His hand stilled on her back. But his voice was light. 'I keep telling you I'm not that nice.'

'I don't think that's really for you to decide.'

Nikos stopped moving, 'Don't do this, Maggie. Don't think that I'm different from these people. I'm one of them. I come from this world. You're a romantic—you're trying to make me fit into the template you have for a happy future. You *know* I can't promise you that.'

His cynicism rubbed her raw—especially when her whole body ached for fulfilment. 'Don't patronise me, Nikos. Maybe let's just see what kind of future we can have before writing it off, hmm?'

She pushed free of his arms and went to walk away, but her hand was grabbed and she found herself being whirled back into Nikos's arms. It would look as if they were still dancing, but the tension between them was thick.

Before Maggie could do or say anything else Nikos was

cupping her jaw and holding her close. And then his mouth was covering hers.

At first Maggie resisted with everything she had. But it was futile. She wanted him too much, and she hated it that knowing he hadn't been with anyone else since here made her desire for him even more potent.

Anger at him for having such a cataclysmic effect on her made her accept his kiss, and she felt a surge of adrenalin rush through them both as she wound her arms around his neck and matched him. Pressing close. Tongues duelling.

They both pulled back at the same moment, breaths coming fast and hard. Hearts pounding.

Nikos just said, 'I want you. *Now*.'

Maggie didn't feel conflicted any more. She felt needy. Aching.

She said the only word she could. 'Yes.'

Nikos took her hand and led her off the dance floor and out through the main ballroom, still thronged with guests. Maggie's cheeks were burning—surely their desire for each other must be glaringly obvious?

They went straight out to where the car was waiting. As soon as Nikos joined her in the back he said something to the driver, who raised the privacy partition before they drove off.

Nikos reached for Maggie, putting his hands around her waist and pulling her towards him so that she was on his lap. Their mouths fused and then Maggie's hands were pushing at his jacket, reaching for his bowtie to undo it but only getting it tangled.

Nikos drew back and huffed out a tortured-sounding laugh. 'Would you believe I'm usually a lot more sophisticated than this?'

Maggie said, 'I don't care.'

Nikos drew her up. 'Pull your dress up and straddle me.'

She did it, knocking her head on the roof of the car.

She could feel Nikos's arousal pressing against her and she moved.

He groaned. 'I want to see you…this dress…'

He reached for it at the top and pulled it down from her shoulders, revealing bare breasts that had been supported magically by the boning of the dress. They fell free now… heavy, aching.

Nikos cupped them and licked her nipples, first one and then the other, sending shards of exquisite pleasure down to Maggie's groin. She reached beneath her to Nikos's belt and trousers, fingers clumsy as she tried to release him.

Eventually she rose up and he took her hand away, releasing himself. She could feel his heat and strength and she almost wept with need. The fact that they were in the back of a car, being driven in loops around the city of Rome, was a decadence she couldn't think about now.

Nikos pushed her underwear aside and ran a finger along the seam of her body. She bit her lip—and then she felt the thick head of his erection.

Nikos said something guttural in Greek, but she understood instinctively.

She came down on his length until every hard inch was embedded in her body. They were both breathing fast. Her hands were on the seat-back behind Nikos as she tried to control her movements, coming slowly up and down again. His hands were on her waist, helping her. It was the most erotic experience of her life and she couldn't last.

Sensing how close she was, Nikos took her, holding her hips as he thrust up. Deeper than before. Harder. And Maggie came, over and over again, barely aware of the warmth of Nikos's explosive release inside her.

She slumped over him, spent. Sated. At peace.

Nikos never wanted to move again.

What the hell was that?

His body was still semi-hard. Still embedded within Maggie's snug embrace. If she moved—*Theos*, he would want her again. Already. The control this woman had over him was not something he wanted to dwell on…

He carefully extricated himself, wincing as the connection between them was broken. Maggie made a little sound that almost had Nikos hauling her back into his arms, but he forced himself to pull her dress up, to hide those magnificent breasts from his gaze.

She moved off his lap and then snuggled into his side like a cat. Nikos had instinctively wrapped his arm around her before he realised that this was the kind of behaviour he'd never indulged in.

Before.

But Maggie was his wife. Things were different now. That was all.

When Maggie woke the next morning she could hear Daniel gurgling in the apartment—presumably with Marianne. She lay on her back for a long moment, reliving the urgency of that coupling in the back of the car.

Nikos had had to carry her in from the car. Her legs had been too weak to hold her up. He'd brought her to her room and she'd been reaching for him again when Daniel had emitted a cry in the room next to hers.

Nikos had been the one to pull back, stand up. 'You should go to him.'

Maggie could only give thanks now that she hadn't exposed herself spectacularly in her ravenous need for *more.*

She turned over and buried her face in the pillow, groaning softly.

A few hours later they were on their way to Madrid—but without Marianne. She'd had to go back to Paris for a minor family emergency and wouldn't be able to join them again until they were in London.

In a way, Maggie was glad of the reprieve. She wouldn't have to attend the event that evening with Nikos. She wouldn't have to try and hide the fact that each outing only seemed to expose her more and more in her growing need for him. Physically and emotionally…

Madrid

Nikos came back to the apartment after midnight. He'd missed Maggie by his side tonight. It unnerved him how quickly he'd become used to her presence. How natural it felt and how unnatural not to have her there.

He opened his tie and the top button of his shirt, shucked off his jacket. He felt restless—a different kind of restlessness from the kind of dissatisfaction that had plagued him for the last few years. He hated to admit it, but it usually dissipated in Maggie's presence.

The way it had dissipated the first time he'd set eyes on her.

He poured himself a shot of whisky and opened the sliding doors that led out to a terrace which looked over the majestic capital city of Spain. He recalled Maggie's awe and wonder at the Roman medieval palace. He could barely remember a time when he'd felt that same kind of awe. He'd been so angry for so long. And since his father had died, he'd focused solely on work and pleasure. Nothing in between.

He heard a sound and tensed. It sounded like a cry. He went back inside and put his glass down. He heard it again.

Daniel.

Nikos walked down the corridor to the bedrooms and stood outside Maggie's door for a moment. He could hear Daniel gurgling to himself now. Following an instinct he couldn't ignore, he pushed the door open. One low light was on. Maggie was in bed, asleep on her back, hair spread out around her.

Nikos went over and stood by the cot. Daniel was on his back, arms and legs kicking. Eyes wide open. Dark. Nikos put his hand over Daniel's belly and at the same moment the baby smiled up at him. A wide, gummy smile.

Nikos felt as if he was falling. Falling with nothing to cling on to. It was exhilarating and terrifying all at once.

Daniel gurgled again and Nikos looked over at Maggie. She frowned in her sleep. He could see the shadows of tiredness under her eyes even from where he was, and so he did the scariest thing he'd ever done in his life. He put his hands under his son and lifted him up, cradling him against his chest.

He took him out of the bedroom before Maggie could wake, and walked back into the main living area. And then he stood there and looked at his son in his arms. And he felt a kind of awe infuse him, washing aside any hint of restlessness or dissatisfaction.

When Maggie woke she sensed immediately that something was wrong. She looked over and saw that Daniel's cot was empty and jumped out of bed, instantly awake.

Marianne wasn't here and Nikos had gone out. Where could—?

She left the bedroom—and came to a stumbling halt in the doorway leading to the living room.

Nikos was standing on the terrace, just outside the French doors, and she could see Daniel's head in the crook of his arm. Her heart stopped and started again. She was afraid to breathe in case she disturbed the moment.

She could hear Nikos talking to his son in a low voice, in Greek? Italian? Saying…what? She didn't care. The fact that Nikos had actually taken his son in his arms… Her chest felt tight and she put a hand to it. This was huge.

After a moment she walked further into the room and stood in the doorway leading out to the terrace. He must have sensed her presence, as he tensed and turned around.

'He was a awake. I was afraid he'd wake you too.'

Maggie smiled. 'That's okay. Thank you.'

But now, sensing his mother was near, Daniel let out a cry, and Nikos looked suddenly uncertain. 'What did I do?'

Maggie reached for him. 'Nothing—it's just time for his feed. That's why he was awake. You bought me a few more minutes of sleep.'

Maggie sat down in a nearby chair and undid her night-dress buttons, helping Daniel to latch on without baring too much of her breast. She looked up and saw Nikos had an arrested expression on his face.

She said, 'Would you mind getting me a muslin cloth from the bedroom? There should be some on the nappy changing table near the cot.'

'Of course.'

Nikos left and came back quickly with a couple of cloths. Maggie took them. Nikos sat down on a sofa nearby.

'Do you want me to get you anything else?'

She shook her head. 'No, thanks. How was the event?'

'Not as much fun without you there.'

Maggie's heart hitched. 'I'm sure that's not true.'

They settled into a companionable silence, the sound of Daniel feeding the only thing breaking the silence. It felt intimate in a way that she hadn't felt with Nikos before.

When she'd finished feeding him she put Daniel on her shoulder and stood up. 'I'll put him down again.'

She went back into the bedroom and winded and changed Daniel before putting him down. He was already fast asleep. She felt wide awake now, and couldn't stop thinking about how Nikos had looked at her as she'd fed Daniel.

She'd fully expected that Nikos would have gone to bed, but she found herself going back to the living room. *He was still there.* He was lying on the couch, shoes off. Arm above his head. Was he asleep?

Maggie went over and closed the French doors. Nikos hadn't moved. She couldn't help standing and watching him for a moment, even though she felt like a voyeur. He looked so much younger in sleep…his brow smoothed. She felt an urge to place her fingers against his lips and stepped back before she could do something stupid.

But as she was turning away her hand was caught.

'Where do you think you're going?' His voice was a rough growl.

'I thought you were asleep.'

Nikos tugged her down onto the couch beside him. He came up on one elbow. She could feel his gaze on her as he brought his hand up and flicked open the couple of buttons on her nightdress that she'd just closed.

It had to be the most un-erotic piece of clothing—a white cotton nightdress with buttons strategically placed to make it easy to breastfeed—but suddenly it felt like the most provocative thing in the world.

Nikos looked at her as he put his hand underneath the cotton to cup her breast. She sucked in a breath. It was still sensitive after feeding. But deliciously so.

He brought his hand up then, catching her hair and looping it around his fingers, tugging her down towards him until she was flat against his chest and her mouth hovered above his. Their breaths intermingled. He was like steel underneath her.

'Do you want this, Maggie?'

It freaked her out how much she wanted him. All the time.

She nodded.

He reached up and their mouths touched. She groaned. He speared her hair with his hands, angling her to make the kiss deeper, more explicit. Maggie wanted to rub herself against him like a needy cat.

Urgency gripped them both. Nikos pulled back for a second, grabbed her hips and pulled her on top of him so that her thighs fell either side of his hips. She wasn't wearing any underwear. He reached down and found this out for himself. They both gasped.

Maggie unbuttoned his shirt, needing to feel his chest. Nikos undid his trousers, lifting himself up to pull them down. And then she felt him there, released and hot and hard against her hungry flesh.

He opened the rest of the buttons on her nightdress, releasing her breasts into his hands, and she rose over him and took him in her hand as she guided herself onto his rigid length.

Her hands were spread on his chest as she rode him, tentatively at first and then with more confidence, biting her lip against the spasm of pleasure as he touched a point deep inside her.

He massaged her breasts, coming up to take one nipple and then the other into his mouth. That sent her into a frenzy, and her movements became less slick, more frantic, as she chased the peak that teased her…

She must have sobbed, or pleaded or something, because Nikos clamped his hands on her hips and took control, holding her still while he thrust into her over and over again until she collapsed against him and pressed her mouth to his in a desperate kiss, pleading silently for him to stop and yet never to stop.

And then it came—the moment when everything went still and taut before a quickening rush of pleasure so intense that she could only submit to its power and wait for the storm to pass.

When Maggie woke the next morning she was back in her bed, with only the vaguest memory of Nikos carrying her there. Daniel was awake and kicking his legs happily in his cot. She lay there for a moment, wondering if actually that had been a particularly intense dream last night.

But, no. Her body was tender in secret places.

She turned on her side and looked at Daniel, recalled seeing him in Nikos's arms. Emotion gripped her again. And something almost fearful.

The force of need she felt around Nikos and the fact that it wasn't diminishing was overwhelming. She'd heard that desire burnt itself out eventually, but this didn't feel as if it would *ever* burn out. For her. But would it for Nikos?

Of course it would. It had to be a fluke that he still wanted her. Some weird aberration.

He hasn't slept with anyone else since you.

She hated that voice in her head, making her think of things like that. Things that gave her hope. That made her wish for other things, like a proper relationship with Nikos—not separate bedrooms and moments snatched while they were on this whistlestop tour around Europe.

Once the tour was over…when things calmed down… surely then things would settle into a routine? Although *Nikos* and *routine* didn't really go together. He seemed very much at home with this peripatetic existence, but Maggie knew she couldn't live like this on a regular basis.

But maybe now…maybe now that he seemed to want to bond with Daniel…things could change?

Maggie laughed and Daniel gurgled. 'Honestly—he won't break. Just take his legs together in your hand and lift him up…good…then wipe his bottom with the baby wipe. That's it. Make sure it's dry and clean. Put the nappy here…'

The concentration on Nikos's face as he mastered the art of changing a nappy was nothing short of comical. It told Maggie a lot more about him than she'd bet he would ever want anyone to know.

He placed Daniel down on the clean nappy and pulled

it up between his legs, then secured it over his belly with the sticky tapes on the sides.

'I did it!'

After about ten attempts.

Maggie didn't say it out loud. Daniel had been amazingly patient. As if he'd sensed his father was trying to make an effort.

'You did.'

Nikos pulled on Daniel's Babygro and secured the buttons, then scooped up his son, carefully supporting his head, and walked out into the apartment with him.

Marianne was standing in the doorway and she sent Maggie an expressive look. Maggie returned it, with a smile and a small shrug, and followed Nikos out. The other woman had just arrived back from Paris, so hadn't yet witnessed Nikos's new interest in his son.

Maggie knew she shouldn't really be surprised that someone as focused as Nikos was taking to his role as a father with an expert zeal and a speed that left her breathless. They'd arrived in London earlier that day, and on the plane over from Madrid he'd fed Daniel from a bottle. And winded him. And when Daniel had vomited down Nikos's back he hadn't even cared. He'd just changed his shirt.

And then, on their drive to the hotel from the airport, she'd overheard him rescheduling a meeting for later in the day so he could come with them to the apartment and spend some time with Daniel.

Nikos turned around with his big hand across Daniel's back. 'Hyde Park is nearby—we could go for a walk and get a coffee?'

Maggie tried to tamp down the surge of happiness. 'Sure… If you have time?'

'Of course I have time.'

They went out with Daniel in his compact pram. The temperatures were starting to turn cooler after the summer and there was a freshness in the air. There was also, although Maggie hated even to think it, a sense of hope.

When they'd walked through the park for a while, and found a place to sit down and have coffee—decaf for her—she said, 'So what's on the agenda this evening?'

He took a sip of espresso. 'It's the opening of a new designer store on Bond Street—one of our labels.'

He mentioned the iconic name and Maggie's eyes widened. It was a byword in extreme luxe fashion—one of the most timeless brands in the world.

'That's one of yours?'

Nikos nodded. 'It won't be that formal an event, though. It's just a party to welcome the new head designer.'

Immediately Maggie felt anxious. 'What does that mean? What should I wear?'

Nikos looked wicked. 'Something very short and very sparkly.'

CHAPTER TEN

THANKS TO THE stylist at the boutique in the London M Group hotel Maggie had been able to fulfil Nikos's brief, and when they arrived at the event on Bond Street she was wearing a very short and sparkly green dress paired with vertiginous heels. He'd instructed her to leave her hair down.

Maggie clung to Nikos's hand as they ran the gauntlet of photographers lining each side of the short red carpet. They were calling her name as well as Nikos's now.

'Maggie, love, over here!'

'Maggie! Pose for us!'

'Who are you wearing?'

Thankfully an award-winning actress appeared behind her and their focus shifted to her.

When they got inside the noise faded and was replaced by chatter and pulsing music. The store was cavernous—more like a gallery space than a shop.

Maggie was still clinging to Nikos's hand. She let go, embarrassed. 'I wasn't expecting them to call out my name. It feels weird that they know who I am.'

He looked at her. He was darkly sophisticated tonight, in a dark blue suit and white shirt, no tie. Shirt open at the neck. 'They just call out your name to get a reaction. You'll get used to it.'

She didn't really relish the thought of this kind of experience becoming a regular feature in her life. But she shelved her concerns. More than any other event they'd been to, this one was seriously star-studded. Actresses, supermodels, politicians… She'd even spotted a very popular ex-American President and his wife.

She sensed Nikos tense beside her, and then a familiar face appeared. 'Maks!' she said.

He bent towards her to give her a kiss on the cheek. 'Maggie, how are you? Still putting up with my brother?'

Maggie heard the mocking tone in his voice—not unlike his brother's. 'Well, it *has* only been a couple of weeks…'

He looked from her to his brother. 'Nikos.'

'Maks.'

Maggie lamented the tension between the brothers. It made her heart ache to see how similar they were, to know how much they'd missed out on not growing up together.

Maks said, 'You didn't show for the board meeting today.'

'I was busy.'

'Luckily for you the wholesome pictures circulating of you and your new family seem to have done wonders for our stock prices.'

Maggie was confused. 'Pictures?'

Maks took out his phone and showed her a tabloid news site. There were pictures of them in Hyde Park from only a few hours ago, underneath a headline: *Reformed playboy spends afternoon with new family. How long before he gets bored?*

Maggie felt sick.

Nikos said something to Maks that sounded like a snarl and took her hand, pulling her away. They moved into the crowd and Maggie desperately tried to push out of her mind the insidious suspicion that Nikos had engineered that trip to the park specifically for a photo opportunity.

She'd seen the way he looked at Daniel. The way he was bonding with him when no one was watching. She had to give him the benefit of the doubt and trust him. Give them a chance.

He stopped a waiter and asked her what she wanted to

drink. She pasted a bright smile on her face. 'Just sparkling water, please. I have to feed Daniel later.'

Nikos took champagne. 'Okay?' he asked.

She looked up. She longed to ask him if he'd gone out with her today knowing they'd be photographed, but at the last second she said, 'Fine.'

After that they were sucked into a round of introductions and conversations that Maggie did her best to keep up with. But she couldn't deny she was tired. Travelling with a small breastfeeding baby was catching up on her, and at one stage, when Nikos had been spirited away by an assistant to meet someone, she couldn't hide a huge yawn.

'I don't blame you—these events bore me to tears too.'

She turned to find Maks beside her. He looked at her assessingly.

'Nikos seems different…less distracted. Maybe you and the baby will be good for him and the business. I'm sorry I showed you those pictures, it was unecessary.'

Maggie made a face. 'That's ok, I probably would have seen them anyway. What about you? Do *you* want a family?'

Maks's expression turned grim, the bones in his face standing out starkly. 'No intention of it. In fact I'm glad Nikos has done us all a favour in that regard.'

Maggie said, as lightly as she could, 'You never know. I don't think it was Nikos's intention either, but…' She blushed. 'Things happen.' She coughed, mortified that the conversation had taken this turn.

The grim expression faded from Maks's face and he looked at her again. 'Did you know it's Nikos's birthday tomorrow?'

She shook her head, realising there was still so much she didn't know. 'No.'

Maks said, 'In a funny twist of fate—or not so funny—all of us three half-brothers have birthdays in the same month. Nikos is first, then Sharif, and me at the end.'

'And your sister Sasha? Is she here tonight?'

'God, no—you couldn't pay Sasha to come to an event like this. No, her birthday is in spring.'

Then Maks's expression changed again, his eyes narrowing on someone across the room. He muttered almost to himself, 'What the hell is *she* doing here?'

Then he was gone, cutting a swathe through the crowd before Maggie could see who he was talking about.

Nikos reappeared. 'I saw you talking to Maks again—he didn't upset you?'

'No, actually, he was sweet.'

Nikos made a rude sound. 'I wouldn't have ever described Maks as *sweet*.'

'He apologised for showing me the pictures.' Maggie looked at Nikos carefully, but he showed no sign of discomfort or guilt.

'Did you know there would be photographers in the park?'

Nikos shrugged. 'I guess I took it for granted that they might be. Does it bother you?'

'Of course it bothers me that we can't go for a walk without being photographed. That's not normal.'

He shook his head. 'It's normal for us now.'

Maggie felt angry at his laissez-faire attitude. She stood directly in front of him.

'Does it have to be, though? Just because you all grew up under the glare of the media, it doesn't mean your own child has to. I don't want Daniel living his life in a fishbowl. He deserves as normal an existence as we can give him. Plenty of rich and famous people have families and manage to keep them out of the public eye.'

Nikos was taken aback by Maggie's passion. She looked like a warrior mother, protecting her young. The kind of champion he'd never had.

An unexpected and unwelcome surge of emotion made him suddenly reject the thought of Daniel being subjected to what he'd experienced. 'You're right. There's no reason why we can't live differently—or at least do our best to.'

She arched a brow. 'Even if pictures of a happy family outing are good for your stock prices?'

Nikos's conscience pricked. He'd taken more than Maggie's innocence.

But he forced himself to say lightly, 'Now who's being cynical?'

The following evening Maggie was nervous. The next day they were due to travel to the South of France and nothing had been scheduled for tonight. Except *this*. The thing that was making her nervous.

When Maggie heard the sound of the door she and Marianne quickly lit the candles on the cake and waited for Nikos to appear. As soon as he did they both started singing *Happy Birthday*—but they trailed to a halt at the look of utter horror on his face.

He looked at Maggie and she'd never seen him so haunted. 'What the hell is *this*? How did you know it was my birthday?'

'Maks told me last night,' Maggie replied. 'I baked you a cake.'

'He shouldn't have told you.'

Nikos turned and left the room and Maggie looked at Marianne, beyond bewildered.

Nikos couldn't breathe. He pulled at his tie, opened a couple of buttons. But that tight fist was around his chest, squeezing tighter and tighter.

He rested his hands heavily on the desk, breathed as deeply as he could, exactly as his friend had told him—an ex-French Foreign Legionnaire who had looked at him one day and said, 'How long have you been having panic attacks?'

That friend had known because he'd recognised the signs.

To Nikos's surprise, the symptoms started to fade—far more quickly than they usually did. He straightened up and went over to the window that looked out over London.

The shock and horror of seeing that cake, lit with candles, and then Maggie and Marianne singing… It was quite literally his worst nightmare. But for a tiny, treacherous moment he'd been transported back in time to *before* the day had become tainted for ever.

He never mentioned his birthday. He never acknowledged it. Why the hell had Maks told her?

Because his brother didn't know.

There was a soft knock on his study door. He tensed.

The door opened. 'Nikos? Are you okay?'

Nikos felt conflicting things. He wanted to snarl at Maggie to leave him alone and yet he wanted her to come in, so that he could pull her close and lose himself in her scent and silky body.

He bit out, 'I'm fine,' and went over to his drinks cabinet to pour himself a measure of whisky.

He was aware of her coming in. Wearing jeans and a T-shirt. Hair down. She could wear a sack and he'd want her. The desire wasn't burning out. It was burning up.

'Nikos…?'

Even her voice was enough to distract him, make him clench down low to try and control his body's response.

He said curtly, 'I'm sorry. You weren't to know.'

'Know what?'

He turned around. 'That I despise my birthday and any mention of it.'

She sat back against his desk as if winded. 'Why?'

Why, indeed?

Nikos walked over to the window, his back towards Maggie. His own face was reflected to him. Distorted.

He said, 'I never even knew it was my birthday until I was about five and my father turned up in Athens to take me out to a restaurant. There was more cake and sweets than I'd ever seen in my life—my grandparents didn't allow sweet things. My father encouraged me to eat my fill. I thought he had come to take me home with him. I was so happy.

'But I'd eaten too much cake, and I started to be sick. My father was naturally disgusted and sent me home with my nanny. I was sick for a week and I thought that was why he hadn't taken me home with him… Then, every year on my birthday he would show up and take me to a restaurant and order cake—even though I'd developed an aversion to it after my first experience.

'I came to dread the annual event, even as I lived in hope that he would take me away with him. But he never did. He would just put me back in the car and send me back to my grandparents' villa, to be sick for a week. That cake came to symbolise his disregard…the perpetual disappointment.

'And then one year he took me out and told me that he was taking me away. I thought he was finally taking me home with him. I knew he had a new wife and a son and a daughter—Maks and Sasha—and I was ecstatic at the thought of siblings. I was so lonely at my grandparents' house… But he didn't take me to tmeet hem. He took me to boarding school. One of the most remote schools in England.

'I never saw my grandparents again. They couldn't have cared less. And my father didn't visit me on my birthday any more. I discovered that my birthday is also the date of my mother's death. She killed herself on my second birthday.'

He turned around then, to face Maggie. Her face was pale, blue eyes huge.

'So that's why I have an aversion to birthdays, and anything sweet.'

Maggie stood up. 'Nikos, your father was some kind of sadist—and as for your grandparents…they didn't deserve the title. They rejected their own daughter and then you.' She came closer. 'I'm sorry. If I'd known—'

'How could you?' His voice was harsh. He modulated it. 'You couldn't have known. No one knows. Not even my brothers.'

She bit her lip and pulled something out of her back pocket. An envelope.

Nikos looked at it suspiciously. 'What is it?'

She pushed it towards him. 'A present.'

Nikos shook his head. He wanted to push it back. 'You don't have to give me anything.'

No one had ever given him anything.

'Please.'

Nikos took it reluctantly and opened it. It was a card with a nice bucolic scene.

Maggie said, 'It reminded me of the garden at Kildare House.'

Nikos opened it. Inside there was some kind of a printout. He picked it out and read it and his chest felt tight again. It was a voucher for a personal tour of the Colosseum.

Maggie said quickly, 'We can do it the next time we're in Rome—or, you know, whenever…'

Nikos saw a message on the card.

Happy Birthday, Nikos
Maggie and Daniel
XX

He put the card and the voucher down. He felt lightheaded after revealing more than he'd ever revealed to anyone.

'You're sweet, Maggie. Too sweet for me.'

I can't have sweet things.

She shook her head. 'I'm not too sweet—I'm just not as hardened and cynical as everyone else you know. I'm normal, Nikos. Most people out there are like me.'

No, she was more than that. Most people weren't as sweet as her. She was unique, and Nikos knew that he had no right to any of Maggie's sweetness. And yet he'd gorged himself on her.

He felt toxic.

'Go back and enjoy the cake with Marianne. Thank you, but it's not for me.'

Maggie felt a chill go down her back. Nikos was more remote than she'd ever seen him. He'd retreated to some place she knew she couldn't reach.

She moved towards him and he stepped back. A sharp pain lanced her gut.

'We'll be having dinner soon, if you want to join us.'

Your family.

Nikos shook his head abruptly. 'I don't need dinner. I have calls to make before our trip to France.'

The villa that Nikos had hired in the south of France was jaw-droppingly impressive, hugging the edge of a steep hill with views over the Mediterranean. A thoroughly modern structure, it was white and steel and sleek and impossibly sexy.

Maggie hated it.

And she was tired after a sleepless night with Daniel.

She and Marianne had decided that at almost four months he was starting to teethe—which had to be the reason for his tetchy humour and the fact that he would only take milk from her breast. He wasn't interested in a bottle.

Marianne was looking after Daniel now, in between feeds.

Nikos appeared on the terrace and Maggie had to steel herself not to react. But it was even harder today, when he was in faded worn jeans and a white polo shirt which showed off the olive tones of his skin and his musculature.

He barely looked at her, though, and glanced at his watch. 'Staff are coming to set up soon and the guests will be arriving from five p.m. I've arranged for a team to come up from a salon in Cannes. Clothes have been ordered—they should be in your wardrobe.'

'Yes, they're there.'

She'd seen the glittering array of dresses. Each one as beautiful and intimidating as the next. Even though she was getting used to the process she still felt like a fish out of water—and even more so now, when she was feeling fatigued and concerned about Daniel.

'Are you okay?' Nikos asked.

Maggie looked at him. She felt like asking if he really cared. He'd barely said two words to her since that conversation in his study in London. But now probably wasn't the time to get into anything.

'I'm fine, just a bit tired. And Daniel—'

Nikos frowned. 'Is he okay?'

'He's fine—we think he's starting to teethe.'

'Is that serious? Does he need a doctor?'

Maggie smiled. 'No, it's not serious—it's perfectly normal. All babies teethe. It just makes them cranky.'

'Let me know if it's anything more. Maybe you shouldn't come this evening—maybe you should stay with Daniel?'

Maggie smarted at the suggestion that she should absent herself. Which was crazy. Obviously Daniel was more important, but—ridiculously—she felt jealous of her own baby, who seemed to be commanding Nikos's attention with more skill than she did.

Earlier, on the plane, she hadn't been able to soothe a fractious Daniel. Nikos had put down his papers and held out his arms. 'Here, let me try.'

Almost immediately the little traitor had stopped crying and promptly fallen asleep in his father's arms.

It was something that should have sparked joy within Maggie. Alleviating her worst fears. But instead it had made her feel redundant. If Daniel and Nikos bonded, where did that leave *her*? She hadn't ever anticipated that scenario.

The suspicion that he was punishing her for intruding—going too far with the birthday celebration—was like acid in her stomach. A man as proud as Nikos wouldn't thank her after telling her the sorry facts of his lonely childhood.

She forced those thoughts out of her mind. 'Daniel will be fine. Marianne is with him and I can feed him when I need to.'

'I'll leave it up to you—just don't feel obliged.'

Maggie watched as he walked off. So now it didn't even matter if his wife was by his side? When it was supposed to be part of the reason for this marriage…? She couldn't escape the feeling that the ground was shifting underneath her and she had nothing to cling on to.

A few hours later Maggie looked at herself critically in the mirror. Make-up had covered the circles under her eyes, but she knew she still looked a bit washed out.

Her hair was caught back in a low bun and she wore a strapless light blue sheath dress, down to the knee, with matching sandals with kitten heels that were mercifully easy to walk in.

She left a sleeping Daniel with Marianne and went downstairs, nervous of Nikos's reaction now that he was in this strange aloof mood. He turned as she came down and she saw the flare of something in his eyes before his face became impassive again. She felt a treacherous little flicker of hope.

He hadn't appreciated having to open up. That was all it was.

'Is this okay?'

'It's fine.' His voice was gruff.

He wore a steel-grey suit and no tie. Casual, but elegant. And unashamedly masculine.

Staff had been busy in the interim. They'd decorated the space with flowers and she could see a long table outside in the shade, set for dinner.

A new scent infused the air. She wrinkled her nose, 'Is that—?'

Nikos grimaced. 'Yes, that's the new perfume—a little overpowering, but it's one of our biggest sellers already.'

Maggie saw cars starting to appear in the driveway, and as everyone arrived she got split up from Nikos. She did her best to mingle and make small talk with people, but found that this crowd looked at her as if she were a curiosity, and seemed more interested in speaking behind her back when she walked away.

She caught more than a few snide glances from other women. And one woman looked at her and openly laughed. To Maggie's intense shame, she was transported back in time to when the girls and boys at her school would laugh at her and call her *Beanpole.* And even though she wasn't the tallest woman here, in this place, that old feeling of exposure was hot and crippling and immediate.

She had a sense of having been found out. She was a fraud. She wasn't from this world and they knew it. She didn't belong here—she would never belong here. And that was the realisation Nikos had come to too. The only thing keeping them together now was—

Suddenly Nikos was there, looking at her. Specifically at her breasts. He came forward and took her arm, leading her to one side.

'What is that? Did you spill something?'

'What's what?'

Maggie looked down and groaned. There were two wet patches over her breasts. She was leaking milk. She'd ignored the signs of her breasts growing tingly and heavy, too intent on making a good impression at the party. Now she'd made an impression, all right.

Mortified, she said, 'I need to feed Daniel.'

She pulled away from Nikos and hurried upstairs, conscious of whispers and muffled laughter. Face burning, she went into the bedroom.

Marianne took one look and handed her Daniel, saying, 'I'll find you another dress.'

Maggie undid her dress and settled Daniel on her breast, taking a look down at the terrace, where all those honeyed people were milling about.

She shook her head when Marianne came back in with an armful of clothes. 'No way. I'm not going back down there—they're piranhas.'

Marianne made a huffing sound. 'He needs you.'

Maggie could see Nikos, head and shoulders above everyone else. Surrounded by sycophants.

'Does he? I don't think he does, Marianne. And clearly I'm not really suited to this milieu.'

Marianne said enigmatically, 'All the more reason for you to go back down and remind him of that.'

The last thing Maggie wanted to do was expose herself to that snooty crowd's ridicule again, but she wasn't that shy, over-tall girl any more. She was a woman. A wife and a mother. And she'd made a pledge to honour her husband even if theirs wasn't a love match. *And never would be.*

So when Maggie had fed and changed Daniel and put him down, she changed into a black silk maxi-dress and flat sandals. She shook her hair loose, put on some red lipstick and went back to the party.

All the guests were sitting at the long dining table. Waiters were serving. Nikos was at the head. As one, everyone seemed to stop and look at her when she appeared on the terrace. For an awful moment Maggie thought she couldn't do it—and then Nikos stood up and held out a hand.

'Everyone, if you haven't yet met her, this is my wife, Maggie.'

She walked towards him, his gold and green eyes holding her. Whatever was going on with him, and this new distance he was putting between them, she would be grateful for ever for this show of solidarity.

She sat down at his right-hand side and the woman on her right put a hand on her arm. Maggie looked around warily, to see the friendly face of a woman a bit older than her.

She said, 'Oh, my God—I felt so sorry for you. The exact same thing happened to me at a function after I had my first baby—in front of hundreds of people.' She stuck out her hand. 'I'm Melissa, and this is my husband Klaus—he's one of the chief parfumiers in the company.'

Maggie smiled with relief and shook her hand, confiding, 'I almost didn't come back down.'

Melissa said, *sotto voce*, 'I'm glad you did. Those women don't deserve a second thought—they're just insanely jealous that you've managed to tame one of the world's most notorious playboys.'

Maggie smiled weakly. *Had* she tamed Nikos? No… But maybe Daniel had. The problem was, she suspected Nikos was already chafing at the reality of being tamed.

Later that night, Maggie woke up with a start. She'd fallen asleep in the chair where she'd fed Daniel, who was now back in his cot, fast asleep. She'd come up to feed him after dinner.

She stood up and went to the window which overlooked the terrace. All was quiet now, the guests all departed. Her insides clenched when she saw the lone figure of Nikos, looking out over the view. It made her heart ache—especially now that she knew just how bleak his childhood had been.

She wanted to go down to him and slide her arms around his waist, offer him comfort. But she knew he wouldn't welcome it. That image belonged to a different scenario. One in which Nikos actually cared for her. Like she cared for him.

Loved him.

Her breath stopped as that cataclysmic realisation sank in. She loved him. Desperately. Futilely. And he couldn't have made it clearer that her affection wasn't welcome.

Monte Carlo was as tiny and picturesque as Maggie had always imagined. In her teens she'd been fascinated with Grace Kelly, and had read everything about her, so to be here now was overwhelming.

They'd taken a helicopter from Cannes, landing on a helipad near the Marchetti Group hotel where they had an exclusive suite. The hotel was part of the opulent casino where they were due to attend an event that night.

This last event of the tour was a charity auction in aid of all the charities that the Marchetti Group supported. Afterwards there was to be a high-stakes poker game with all the proceeds going to charity.

Once again a team had come up from the hotel salon and they'd transformed Maggie into a far sleeker version of herself. Her hair lay in waves over one bare shoulder. Her cocktail dress was black and asymmetrical, one-shouldered, down to the knee with a slit up one side.

Nikos walked into the living area of the suite, doing up his cufflinks. He looked up and that dark gaze swept her up and down. If there was a flare of interest in his eyes she didn't see it. She felt cold.

'How's Daniel?' he asked.

'Fine—fed and changed. Marianne has taken him out

for a stroll around the gardens. I've expressed some milk, so we shouldn't have a recurrence of—'

Nikos shook his head. 'Don't worry about that.'

She took a step towards him. 'Look, Nikos, is everything…okay between us?'

He put his hands in his pockets. 'Why wouldn't it be?'

Maggie bit her lip. 'It just feels like since London… Maybe you didn't want to tell me…' She trailed off.

'Everything is fine.'

Except it wasn't. There was a cold chasm between them. Even as her blood still hummed just at being near him. She hated the insidious feeling that he didn't want her any more.

He said, 'Ready?'

She nodded and walked towards him. As they left the suite she said, 'I presume once we're back in Paris things will calm down?'

The lift attendant greeted them and pressed the button for the ground floor.

Nikos looked at her. 'What do you mean?'

'Well, there won't be so much travelling…we can get settled.'

The lift doors opened and they got out.

Nikos said warningly. 'I do travel a lot. I can't say I don't. You won't always have to come with me, but your presence will be required.'

Maggie envisaged all those events with a stony Nikos by her side. 'I know that. But as Daniel grows into a toddler, and then older, he'll need a more regular routine.'

'That's what nannies are for.'

His easy response sent a spurt of anger up her spine. She faced him. 'After everything you told me the other day, you'd entrust our son's care to a *nanny*? Do you envisage sending him to boarding school too?'

Now his eyes flashed—but it gave Maggie no satisfaction.

Nikos took her hand. She tried to pull away but he wouldn't let her. 'We will not have this conversation here.'

Maggie dug her heels in. 'When, then?'

Nikos gritted his jaw. 'Later. After the event.'

Maggie noticed that people were waiting for them, so she let Nikos lead her towards them. They were swept into the ballroom—a magnificent baroque space, with open French doors and a terrace leading down to stunning gardens. A small orchestra played classical music on the terrace and Maggie accepted a small glass of champagne, feeling a little reckless from that rush of adrenalin just now.

But as she stood by Nikos's side and the auction got underway, the adrenalin faded and she'd never felt more alone. In the space of only two weeks, it was scary how used she'd got to him touching her, checking to see if she was okay.

But now it was as if he couldn't bring himself to look at her, never mind touch her. As if he wouldn't even notice if she left.

So she did.

CHAPTER ELEVEN

NIKOS KNEW THE moment Maggie walked away. He knew he was behaving like a boor. But he couldn't stop. When she'd asked him earlier if things were okay—when she'd mentioned London—he'd felt that awful sense again that he was toxic, and that with every moment spent in his company she was being tainted by him.

In truth, he was finding it hard even to look at Maggie, even though he burned for her more than ever. Looking at her…at those blue eyes…made him feel exposed down to his core.

Daniel was the only one who seemed to look at him and not expect anything.

That's because he's a baby.

Nikos scowled at himself. But the utter trust which with Daniel looked at him soothed something inside him. Something that Maggie rubbed up against. Making him remember…too much. Making him want things he couldn't have. Sweetness. Light.

Maggie hadn't returned by the time the auction was over. He sensed instinctively that she wouldn't. He'd pushed her away.

He told himself he was glad. She needed to know what he was like.

The ghost of his past whispered around him, beckoning to him. Reminding him of his worth. His true worth. Maggie had made him feel as if he might be worth something—something more—but it had been an illusion.

She saw too much. She wanted too much. He could feel it from her. A silent plea. One that he couldn't possibly fulfil.

It was far better that she remembered who he was and who he could never be. Before she got hurt.

When Maggie woke she had a crick in her neck. She realised that she'd fallen asleep in an awkward position on the bed after feeding Daniel—again. She padded out of the bedroom to find Marianne still awake, reading in the living area.

'Has Nikos come back?'

Marianne shook her head. 'Not yet.' Then she frowned. 'Are you okay?'

'Sure… Why?'

'I heard you…being sick.'

Maggie flushed with guilt. She'd been feeling nauseous all day. 'It was nothing.'

Marianne looked at her. 'Have you started your periods again?'

Maggie shook her head. 'No, so it can't possibly be—' She stopped talking, a clammy, panicky feeling washing through her. She looked at Marianne. 'It couldn't be…could it?'

Marianne stood up, her expression serious. 'I'm not sure, but I don't think a lack of periods or breastfeeding is foolproof protection.'

Maggie wanted to sit down. Was it possible? Could she be pregnant again? Already?

She remembered with Daniel that her morning sickness had been worst in the evenings. She felt sick again.

She forced a smile. 'I'm sure it's not… Would you watch Daniel if I go out for a minute?'

'Of course.'

It was only when the lift reached the ground floor that Maggie realised she'd forgotten to put on her shoes. But it was quiet down here. The ballroom was empty now, bathed in moonlight, staff were packing up chairs.

She spotted a person she recognised as being one of Nikos's assistants and asked him where Nikos was. He led her to another room, where a scary-looking bouncer opened the door.

Maggie gasped. It was a whole other world. It was like a scene from a James Bond movie. There was a bar and a raised dais, where men and women sat around an oval table. This must be the high-stakes poker game.

Nikos was there. Bowtie undone. Sleeves rolled up. There was something incredibly weary about him that caught at her before she could chase it away. Nikos didn't need her concern and he wouldn't welcome it.

He wasn't smoking, but a cloud of cigar smoke hung in the air. Maggie waved a hand in front of her face to clear it. Nikos looked up and saw her—and there it was. The flare. Before he blanked his expression again.

But it must have been her imagination. She knew something had been irrevocably broken between them.

He sat back in his chair. 'Ladies and gentlemen—my wife, Maggie.'

Everyone turned and looked at her. She blushed and glared at Nikos.

He stood up. 'Come join me. I need good luck.'

Against her better instincts Maggie went over and climbed the steps. Nikos reached for her and sat down again, pulling her into his lap. Her bones liquefied. His thighs were like steel. He hadn't touched her since Madrid and she could feel the ever-present need. Embarrassing.

She held herself rigid.

He wrapped his arms around her and said, 'Ladies and gentlemen, I can highly recommend getting married—I'm a transformed man.'

His mocking tone was too much. Maggie didn't like it—and she didn't like Nikos's volatile energy.

She stood up, but he pulled her down again. 'Don't go… I need you.'

She looked at him and said, for his ears only, 'You don't need me—that's the problem.'

She stood up again.

'I just wanted to make sure you were all right.'

She went back down the steps and he said from behind her, 'Don't wait up.'

She turned and looked at him. It was as if he'd morphed back into that louche playboy she'd first met.

'I won't,' she said. And left.

Dawn was rising outside when Nikos returned to the suite. It was quiet. He felt hollowed out. Like a husk. He threw down his coat and heard a sound. He looked up. Maggie was standing by the window.

She was wearing jeans and a long-sleeved top. Her hair was up in a messy knot. She looked tired. Pale. There was a jacket on the chair beside her. Daniel was in his baby seat, asleep.

'What's going on? Why are you up?'

Maggie lifted her chin and something about that tiny movement threatened to break something apart inside Nikos. But he clamped down on it. Hard.

'We're getting an early flight back to Ireland, via London. I'm just waiting for a taxi. Marianne is in bed asleep. She's going to go back to Paris later—she's taking a holiday until we figure out what we're doing.'

Nikos shook his head, a cold feeling spreading through him. 'What are you talking about?'

She said, 'You told me we'd talk about things after the event, but you stayed out all night.'

Even though Nikos knew he'd precipitated this very scenario, something that felt like desperation and panic curdled in his gut. 'So let's talk now.'

She shook her head. 'It's too late. This isn't working, Nikos. Daniel is my priority and he's starting to teethe. He needs to be in one place—not moving around. The apartment in Paris isn't suitable. We need a home, and clearly you're not ready to change your life to accommodate that if last night is anything to go by.'

Nikos felt a sense of futility wash over him. This was what he wanted. Maggie was too close. She saw too much. She needed to get away from him.

'What will you do?' Nikos asked.

Maggie fought to hold on to her composure even as she broke apart inside. He wasn't even putting up a fight.

'We'll go back to Kildare House, if that's okay?'

'That house is yours, Maggie. I gave it to you in the pre-nuptial agreement. It's yours no matter what happens.'

'You did?' She'd barely read the agreement. She was momentarily speechless but then it hit her—he cared so little about the house he was prepared to give it to her.

Stiffly, she said, 'I'll accept it on Daniel's behalf.'

'It's *yours*.'

Nikos sounded almost angry.

Maggie knew she should walk away now, but a rebellious part of her needed to push Nikos…push him all the way to articulating just how little hope there was. Because she knew if there was any doubt she would never rest easy.

She forced herself to ask. 'What else is mine, Nikos?'

His eyes narrowed on her. 'What do you want?'

This was it. A terrifying leap of faith. But she had no choice.

'It's not *what* I want—it's *who*. You, Nikos. I want *you*. All of you. I've fallen in love with you, in spite of all your warnings. Because you let me in to see someone that no one else knows. And I think you're pushing me away because of that…aren't you?'

She held her breath.

Nikos's face was pale. 'Don't be ridiculous.'

She walked over to him. There was stubble on his jaw. His weariness was palpable. She knew she was risking everything by doing this, but perhaps it was the only way to kill the flicker of hope that might destroy her.

'I know you want me, Nikos, and I think you feel something for me—maybe not love, but more than like.'

A harsh expression came over his face. '*Not* more than like! I told you I couldn't offer more than that. And as for wanting you? Desire always fades in the end.'

Maggie absorbed the cruel blow of his words and stepped closer. She put a hand to the back of his head, urging his head down.

Nikos was stiff. 'What are you doing?'

She pressed her mouth to his before she could lose her nerve, almost forgetting why she was doing it as his scent filled her nostrils and she felt those firm contours. She flicked out her tongue, tasting the seam of his lips. She could feel his tension.

Nikos jerked back and put his hands on her arms, pushed her back. 'Don't embarrass yourself, Maggie.'

He really didn't want her any more.

She faltered. Lost her nerve.

She'd just exposed herself spectacularly and Nikos hadn't crumbled.

She went on wooden legs to put on her jacket, picked up Daniel's baby seat.

She walked back to Nikos and forced herself to look into his impassive face. 'You know where we'll be. I need to do what's best for my son now.'

All the way to the door her treacherous heart hoped that he would try and stop her…tell her it had all been a huge mistake. But he didn't.

* * *

Nikos walked over to the window and looked down into the main courtyard. After a few minutes he saw Maggie emerge, and then the hotel manager, carrying Daniel in his car seat. Not even the image of another man carrying his son could break him out of the numb cold shell that was encasing his whole being.

Because the pain will kill you if you let it in.

He batted away the voice.

Nikos turned away from the window. And then he went straight back downstairs and into the casino. People looked up from the table, bleary-eyed.

'Ready for more, Marchetti?'

'Yes. Except this time I'm not playing for charity.'

One of the other men laughed. 'Does your wife know where you are?'

Nikos looked up, so cold and numb now that his voice felt as if it was coming from very far away. 'She doesn't matter. Let's get on with it.'

Maggie felt restless. She'd finished washing up the dishes in the sink and now she looked around the vast and gleaming kitchen which was situated in the basement of an even vaster house. A stunningly beautiful, period country house, to be exact. Set in some ten acres of lush green land about an hour's drive outside Dublin.

There were manicured gardens to the rear and a sizeable walled kitchen garden to the side. There was even a small lake and a forest.

And stables. But the stables were empty. Because the zillionaire heartless owner of the house couldn't even commit to a passing interest in racehorses, never mind an actual wife and baby—

Maggie put a hand to her belly, overcome with nausea for a moment. But then it passed and she drank some water.

She nursed her anger because it was the only thing that had got her through the last week and the headlines that screamed at her whenever she looked at anything online: *Honeymoon is over for Marchetti! Reformed Playboy no more! Is Marchetti back on the market?!*

It killed Maggie that she'd told him she loved him in a bid to try and get some reaction. A reaction he couldn't give because he was incapable. And the worst thing was he'd warned her all along.

At that moment she heard a sound from upstairs—the ground floor. A banging noise. The front door?

Maggie looked at the baby monitor on the table, Daniel was still asleep upstairs. She tucked the monitor into her back pocket and went upstairs.

The knocker went again, louder, and she muttered, 'Keep your hair on…' just as she switched on the outside light and swung the door open.

And promptly ceased breathing at the sight in front of her.

A tall dark man dominated the doorway, his hand lifted as if to slam the knocker down again. His other arm was raised and resting on the side of the doorframe. The late-summer sky was a dusky lavender behind him, making him seem even darker.

Maggie couldn't find her breath. Dressed in a classic black tuxedo, he was the most stupendously gorgeous man she'd ever seen. Thick, dark curly hair and dark brows framed a strong-boned face. Cheekbones to die for. Deep-set eyes, dark but not brown. Slightly golden. His skin was dark. There was stubble on his jaw.

His black bowtie hung rakishly undone under the open top button of his shirt. Those dark eyes flicked down from her face and moved over her body—

She shook her head violently. *Déjà-vu*. This had to be a particularly cruel and vivid form of *déjà-vu*.

She opened her eyes. He was still there. Nikos Marchetti. Her husband. Her ex-lover.

She'd known she'd have to see him again, but not like this. She wasn't ready.

She turned and walked away from the front door. 'You really should get a key cut to this house.'

'Ah, but would I be welcome?'

Maggie stopped and turned around. She hated it that she was even wearing almost exactly what she'd been wearing a year before. Cut-off denim shorts and a plaid shirt, tied at the waist. She'd spent the day cleaning the house, finding the monotonous work therapeutic.

Now she felt like a fool.

Once again Nikos was giving off an air of debauched hedonism, but she saw the way his sharp eyes moved over her. He was as sober as she was.

He frowned. 'Where's Mr Wilson?'

Maggie folded her arms. 'I gave him a few days off to visit his family.' And so she could lick her wounds in private.

She looked him up and down, trying to copy the way he looked at her—except she was probably failing dismally, because her gaze wanted to linger lovingly on every plane of his spectacular body.

'Were you at another function, shoring up the Marchetti brand?'

Or, worse, flirting with women? Her insides seized with pain.

'I was at a function in London, yes.'

Her heart thumped. He'd come all the way here straight from London?

'How's Daniel?'

Something inside her fell. She castigated herself. Of *course* this was about Daniel. He cared about his son. This was a *good* thing.

'He's fine—upstairs, asleep. If you want to talk about visitation rights I think it's best for all of us if we do it through intermediaries. This really isn't cool.'

He walked towards her, shucking off his jacket, letting it drop to the floor as he did so. He stopped in front of her. 'Oh, really? Intermediaries?'

Some of Maggie's bravado leached away. And some of the anger. Electricity crackled between them.

'Nikos…what's going on?'

For a second she thought he was going to kiss her, and then he stepped away and funnelled his hands through his hair. She could see the muscles in his back were taut. Of course he wasn't going to kiss her—he didn't want her. But then he turned around, eyes burning, and she was in his arms and his mouth was covering hers before she could form another thought.

Maggie's brain melted. And her bones. And her heart.

She clung to Nikos and he hauled her up against him. She wrapped her legs around him. His hands were under her bottom, holding her up.

She pulled back and sucked in air, heart hammering. He looked up at her. She pushed to get down and he released her.

She stepped back on trembling legs. 'What's going on? You said…you said desire faded…'

He emitted a bleak-sounding laugh. 'It was a lie. One of many.'

He reached for her hand with his. She looked at it warily.

He said, 'Please? Let me explain.'

She looked at him. Suddenly he didn't look so confident.

Against all her better instincts Maggie put her hand into his and let him lead her into the living room.

He let her go and walked over to the bookshelves. 'Your books are back.' He turned around. 'I missed them.'

'Nikos…'

She noticed then that he was unkempt. A bit wild. Dark circles under his eyes. Stubble. Actually, more than stubble. He looked as if he hadn't shaved in—

As if hearing her thoughts, he said, 'I don't think I've actually slept since you left last week. I went straight down to the casino and the whole week since has been a bit of a blur.'

Maggie felt anger rise again. 'I can show you the headlines if you want your memory refreshed. You fell out of the casino at lunchtime on—'

He held up a hand. 'I know.' He looked at her, deadly serious. 'But you see I was being an idiot. Because I love you. And when you said it to me I couldn't believe it. I already felt guilty for infecting you with my toxicity, and—'

Maggie interrupted him. 'What did you just say?'

Nikos frowned. 'Which bit?'

She went over and caught his shirt in her hands and glared at him. 'You know *which bit*.'

He looked intense. More intense than she'd ever seen him.

'You did say you loved me didn't you? It wasn't a dream?'

She shook her head. 'Not a dream—reality. I do love you, Nikos. I think I fell in love with you that first moment I saw you. Tonight…just now… I thought I was dreaming you up…' A dam was breaking inside her.

Nikos caught her hands in his. His hands were shaking. He tugged her to sit down on the couch.

He looked down. 'You're still wearing your rings.'

Maggie flushed. 'I meant to take them off.'

He looked at her. 'I wouldn't blame you… I'm an idiot.'

'You've said that.'

'I love you.'

'You—?' She stopped. 'You really mean it?'

'Of course I love you… I just didn't know what I was feeling because I've never felt it before. But I remembered what you said about your mother…about doing anything for Daniel…and that's how I feel about you. And Daniel. I couldn't breathe this week, Maggie. I need you. I need you both. *So* much.' Then he said, 'Do you know why this is the only house I've ever bought?

She shook her head, reeling. Afraid to move in case she broke the spell.

He said, 'The first time I saw this house it appealed to something in me. I think I must have seen you here in a dream. And then I came and here you were. I've never had a home. Not a real, proper home. But when you opened that door something inside me went quiet for the first time in my life. I was *home*.'

He went on.

'I used to have panic attacks when I was at boarding school. They were brought on by a sense of being totally isolated and alone. I used to be sent home for the holidays with whichever poor unfortunate kid's family had offered to take me in. I didn't ever get to spend time with my own brothers. Sharif was abroad by then, building up his stake in the business. Maks was being shuttled between our father and his mother.'

Nikos's mouth twisted.

'They were no better off—I can see that now—but I imagined they were happier than me. I would watch the families I was with and feel toxic. I thought they must be able to see all the way into me, to where I was so jealous of them and the happiness they took for granted, and I vowed never to let myself want that. Because it felt like weakness. My own family didn't want me, so I obviously didn't deserve to be loved.'

Maggie reached out and cupped his jaw. 'Oh, Nikos… of *course* you deserved it. You deserved it more than anyone. You lost your mum so young…'

He pressed a kiss to her palm. 'I believed for a long time that she left me because I wasn't worth living for.'

'I can understand that. Especially when no one was around to tell you otherwise.'

'I've never let myself feel anything for anyone until you. It took me a year to come back to you.'

'You're here now.' Suddenly Maggie felt insecure. 'Are you sure? You're not just saying this because it's better for the company—?'

He was shaking his head. 'I would sell all my shares tomorrow if that would help convince you. I want us to have a home. A proper home. In Paris…here…wherever you want. My life is with you now, and with Daniel.'

Maggie felt ridiculously shy all of a sudden. 'I don't mind living in Paris or wherever. I just want a home with you and a safe, secure place for Daniel to grow and feel rooted. For our *family* to feel rooted.'

Maggie took his hand and put it on her belly.

He looked at her. 'You said…family?'

She nodded. 'I'm pregnant. Again. I was feeling nauseous… I didn't think it was possible… But apparently even if you're breastfeeding and your periods haven't started again it's not impossible—'

Nikos pulled his hand away. 'Pregnant? Another baby?'

He stood up and left the room so abruptly that she felt dizzy. She stood up too, her insides turning to jelly. It was too much. Too soon. Even the strongest of relationships might not be able to cope with a second pregnancy so soon after the first…

She waited to hear the sound of the front door slamming but it didn't come.

Then Nikos reappeared in the doorway, with a sleepy Daniel in his arms, his face wreathed in smiles.

Maggie sat back down, her legs failing her. Nikos came and sat down too. He held Daniel in one arm and put his other hand on Maggie's belly.

'See here, *moro mou?* This is your little sister or brother—right now, growing in Mama's belly.'

Maggie was crying now…sobbing. Nikos reached for her and she wrapped her arms around her husband and her baby, a joy such as she'd never imagined possible filling every pore and cell of her body.

After a long moment she pulled back, wiping her eyes. 'I thought you…'

Nikos was shaking his head, and his eyes were suspiciously shiny too. 'This has been my dream all along too—I was just too scared to acknowledge it to myself. Too scared to believe I might deserve it.'

'You *do* deserve it, my love.'

They kissed. Daniel gurgled. Maggie laughed through emotional tears.

Nikos said, 'Marry me again? Here? I want to give you a proper wedding day—to show you and everyone how much I love you.'

Maggie wiped at her tears and nodded and smiled. 'Yes, I'd like that.'

Seven months later. Spring. Ireland

Nikos and Maggie emerged from the small country church near Kildare House. Cherry blossoms had turned the ground pink and white. Nikos held his son Daniel high in one arm and his other arm was around his pregnant wife, stunning in a lace white dress, flowers in her long wavy hair.

Everyone cheered and clapped—and then started groaning when they kissed for an indecently long time.

When Nikos pulled back he looked down at his wife and said, 'Any regrets, Mrs Marchetti?'

She grinned. 'Never. Someone once told me that regrets were for losers.'

* * *

Two months later, in Paris, they welcomed their daughter Olympia—named after Nikos's mother—into the world.

An emotional Nikos introduced his son to his little sister, and then he looked at Maggie on the bed, exhausted but happy. Never more beautiful.

She mouthed, *I love you*, and promptly fell asleep.

Nikos watched over his family as dawn broke outside on another beautiful day, and gave thanks for the woman who had opened his heart to love and shown him a world where not all sweetness was toxic.

* * * * *